PRAISE FOR *THE GOOD WAR*

"In *The Good War*, Costello captures post-war America with emotional depth and storytelling verve. Atmospheric and moving, the novel lays bare the inheritances of generational experience—the intensely intimate personal choices in love and also the familial wreckage of war—with characters who aim for forgiveness and understanding. Best of all, the two women at the center of this novel emerge, with subtle and surprising agency, at the helms of their own lives."

—Lucy Jane Bledsoe, author of *Tell the Rest* and *A Thin Bright Line*

"Elizabeth Costello's *The Good War* is the kind of once-a-decade work of fiction that compels you to reconsider everything you thought you knew about America. It's beautifully written, mischievous and crushing. The most self-assured debut novel I've encountered in many a year."

—John Wray, author of *Gone to the Wolves*

"*The Good War* is an impassioned, stylishly written story of two women—a mother and a daughter—set in mid-twentieth-century America. Elizabeth Costello's narrative mixes elements of literary expressionism à la Thomas Wolfe, film noir, and psychedelia, conducting the reader through a nightscape of thwarted or troublingly realized desires. Along the way, Costello offers a darkly brilliant study of women's autonomy and agency in a male-dominated and war-damaged world. The hand of a poet is visible in the composition of this stunning debut novel."

—Andrew Joron, author of *OO*

"To read Costello is to understand that our mothers and grandmothers lived as urgently, passionately, and desperately as we do today. She knows her achingly human characters from their grandest dreams to their most fleeting gestures and gets it all on the page with thrilling artistry. You'll think of Highsmith, Didion, Atwood, Jean Stafford, Zadie Smith, Sarah Waters, but Costello is a literary original. Read this novel with highlighter in hand—you'll surely be marking passages to savor again later—and join me in blasting it from the rooftops: Sentence by sentence, Elizabeth Costello is as good as anyone writing fiction today."

—K.M. Soehnlein, author of *Army of Lovers*

"Costello has created a captivating story with richly dimensional female characters who are intelligent, lusty, and burning down all of the rules. We need more female characters like these, who are not easily pigeon-holed. A rare novel that is surprising and haunting, all wrapped up in gorgeous prose."

—Nina Schuyler, author of *Afterword*

THE GOOD WAR

Elizabeth Costello

Regal House Publishing

Published by
Regal House Publishing, LLC
Raleigh, NC 27605
All rights reserved

ISBN -13 (paperback): 9781646035465
ISBN -13 (epub): 9781646035472
Library of Congress Control Number: 2024935073

Regal House Publishing, LLC
https://regalhousepublishing.com

For my beloved ghosts

David Maury Costello
1968–1988

Anne Garnett Maury Costello
1937–2014

THE RETURN

We who were once so bold
We who shall never grow old

I am we, beneath the sea
You are not done with me.

KISS OF DEATH

JUNE 1948

Louise arrived fifteen minutes late, intending to keep that hat-in-hander Kit Blunt waiting. She wasn't certain that she wanted to meet him at all. All week long she'd lived with a familiar sort of dread, a sense of being inexorably drawn toward a waterfall into which she would leap for the joy of one second of flight.

She scanned the bar but did not find him. Da Ronco's was one of those places that seemed to want to pass for European that had sprung up in Bethesda after the war. The walls were paneled in dark wood, the floors were covered in small octagonal tiles, the waiters wore ties, and the bartender was efficient, as long as you weren't a woman alone.

In the far end of the long, gilt-framed mirror that hung behind the rows of bottles, Louise saw several men from the Institute—chemists too, but syntheticists, not analysts like her. They were chatting with two women she didn't recognize. One of the men caught her eye, turned away, and looked back into their shared reflection, a smile just curling the edges of his mouth. Perhaps Harry Leopold had talked about her. He wouldn't have given the details—he wasn't that sort. Hinting would be his way, winking along, suggesting that Louise, with her Alpine beauty, her ethereal hair and slate-blue eyes, had drawn him to her. Over the years, even the most dedicated family man would find it hard to resist her lean and shapely figure, her cool and knowing ways.

Paranoia, then, was the price she would pay for having given in to Leopold's supposed charms. She was still baffled as to why she had done it—why she had allowed him to be the first man since Roland had shipped out for good. At least she had let her boss know that it was a one-time error. She would not be his secret piece. Then again, if she hadn't made the mistake of sleeping with him, hadn't had that drunken night, that late sneaking back into her own home, she wouldn't have made a mess in the lab and wouldn't have been told, discreetly, that she should take the rest of the day off. Then she would not have gone to see *The Kiss of Death* at the Capitol Theater and would not have met this Kit Blunt. Who seemed to be not just the average hat-in-hander, but someone who actually had known Roland. And who, for some wild reason she longed to discover, carried that photo of her at the helm of the boat on Long Island Sound. The very one she had pressed into her husband's hand before he left for good.

The bartender walked in her direction, and she attempted, unsuccessfully, to catch his eye. She sat on a stool and tried again, raising her index finger and lifting her chin, replicating the gesture of the men at the other end of the bar. But on her the move apparently didn't read, so she took to clearing her throat, and finally, when he was standing just across from her, vigorously drying a glass, she spoke.

"I'll have a martini. Replace one of the olives with a pearl onion," she said.

He kept his eyes downcast. Sicilian, she thought, looking at the bat's-wing fringe of his eyelashes.

"Aren't you waiting for someone?" he said.

"What's that to do with the price of peas? I gave you my order."

"I'll wait for your date."

Louise chose the trick that often worked for her, repeating her want as a matter of course.

"I'll have a martini, replace one of the olives with a pearl onion."

"No onion."

"But I see them right there."

"Not for a martini," he said, looking up at her with a narrow-eyed, obstinate expression.

"Fine. I'll have a martini with two olives."

"Every martini has two olives," he said, clearly enjoying himself. Louise said nothing. Having had the last word, he set about making her drink.

The glass he set down sweated beautifully in a beam of light reflected by the mirror behind the bar. She downed the drink in one small sip and two large gulps. She consumed each olive with a slow, deliberate relish, savoring the pickled pimento inside. Again, she made the ordering gesture, mistakenly believing the bartender would now see her. Again, he looked everywhere but at her.

"Excuse me," she said, more than once, each time more firmly. Finally, he looked at her.

"I'll have another."

"When your date arrives," he said, fatherly.

Louise stared at him. It would be so easy and gratifying to hurl the glass into the mirror. To slap his face, which no doubt he had shaved this morning, but which was host to a forest of incipient hairs bluing the surface of his chin. Instead, she reached into her alligator purse, extracting from the folds of its pink satin lining her cigarette case and an ivory holder—one of the many carved ivory things that Mother had brought when she sailed from Manila Bay in '41—that she sometimes used for effect. All things from the Philippines had strange creatures on them, not quite dogs or fish, not quite lizards. Two tiny animals crouched nose to nose on the holder—the South Pacific squirrel? Rat of the China Sea?

Louise screwed the cigarette in and asked the Sicilian ape for a light.

She leaned toward the flame when he held it out to her, drew, leaned back, and exhaled.

"Thank you. You are now my date. Please get me another martini."

"You heard the lady," said a voice. "Make it two."

Louise marveled that she hadn't seen him walk in. He was not a subtle presence, tall as he was, barrel chested, moving with that slight hitch to his hip. Must have been an above-the-knee. He slipped in beside her soundlessly, lightly grazing her elbow with his fingertips as he perched on the stool.

The bartender snatched Louise's empty glass from the counter like a dealer at a card table admitting that the house, this time, had lost.

"You're late," said Kit.

"Do you think that's funny?" Louise looked not at him, but into the mirror reflecting them both—that tricky strand of her hair had come loose from the bun and threatened to go into her mouth, but she kept herself from smoothing it back. In the mirror he seemed even more like Orson Welles than she remembered—that big forehead, that wry knowing smile, as if you could never surprise him. His eyes were darker than Welles's though. His coloring was not unlike the Sicilian ape's. Suddenly Louise wanted to unnerve him, to erase the grin. Yet there was, she thought, something kind in his large dark eyes, something noble in that mastiff-bulldog forehead. His fingers played invisible keys on the counter; perhaps he was warming up for his performance. Just then the man from the NIH group looked, once more, into the mirror, caught her eye, and winked.

"I'm sorry," he said, taking off his hat, wiping his brow with a kerchief, and replacing the hat.

"So am I. You've wasted my time."

"I've wasted much more than that," he said.

"That's profound, really. But I have a lot to do. I'm not sure I even want this now." She picked up the glass that had appeared and drank from it anyway. Then she sucked at the ivory cigarette holder, watching the little animals receive the cherry's glow.

"Lou—Mrs. Galle," said Kit, removing his hat once more. "I humbly apologize."

"Oh Christ, put that back on." The martinis were getting to her.

"You've read my letters, perhaps I don't need to begin at the beginning."

"I haven't, actually."

She felt him suck in his breath, an audible gasp. He lit a cigarette before responding.

"None of them?"

"Not a one. But my mother has."

"You must be the only human being in the world who could resist opening a letter addressed to them. Your mother! Christ, I wish I'd known."

Again, Louise finished her drink and again she held up her hand without effect. Kit did the same, and two new martinis arrived.

"Thank you so much," she said, but the ape didn't seem to notice her sarcasm. She tried her tone on Kit. "Oh dear, an elderly widow has caught you pitching woo."

"I wouldn't call it woo."

"Woe, then?" Did she imagine it, or was he beginning to beg her for mercy? His downcast eyes almost sorrowed her.

"Let's move to that corner booth. I'd like to talk privately."

"I thought I was going home," said Louise, gripping the glinting stem of the martini glass. But she took a small sip, put her purse in the crook of her elbow, then picked up both drinks and followed Kit to the corner booth. The seats had that smell—Naugahyde or whatever they called it, the fake leather that Louise had detected everywhere since '45, part of what the world called progress, these things taking the place of everything that was once real. This changeling world, she thought, settling in across from the hulking man she assumed wanted to love her.

He ducked into the seat and removed his hat once more, massaging his great bony forehead with muscular fingers. Like the ape at the bar, he had little patches of black hair between his knuckles. The hair on his head was jet black and thick, in need of a trim. Watching him massage his temples, Louise felt distinctly uncomfortable, as if she were receiving a low-grade electric shock from a great distance. At last he stopped rubbing his head and looked her in the eye.

"You didn't read a single one?"

"No. I assumed they were the same as the others," she said, stopping herself from saying that Mother had ruined everything with her prying, realizing how childish that would sound. But it was true, in the house in Shepherd's Glen, there was nothing that was truly hers anymore. Even the children belonged more to Mother.

He held her gaze just then, one beat, two. His eyes seemed larger, sadder; he caught her in them, and for a moment she was reduced to a child who had done something terrible.

"You mean Roland's?"

Louise winced. The sympathy that had been encroaching on her good sense evaporated. She had been comforted these last years by a blanket of formality. Major E. Roland Galle, Colonel Walter D. Diehl, PFC Bruce Diehl. All her men, wrapped in their titles like the flag folded triangle to triangle and saluted. Neat as a twenty-one-gun salute. (Oh, and Mother's brother, Peter. But she hadn't known him.) It struck her, as this Kit Blunt said the name she avoided saying aloud, that she wanted to see her husband's body. Her father's body, her brother's body. To touch the body of any of them, to be, for one moment, in possession of their bones.

"No, not his," she said, looking back toward the bar almost wistfully. She would have preferred the Sicilian ape's insolence to Kit Blunt's hungry, full-bore gaze. She hadn't said Roland's name aloud in years, not even to Mother. To say it was to lift a heavy stone and unearth a sticking moist world of grubs and worms. She could not say it above a whisper.

"I mean the others."

"What others?" he asked, lighting a fresh cigarette with an army-issue Zippo lighter.

"Do you think, Mr. Blunt, that no one else wants to pay their respects to the widows of Major E. Roland Galle and Colonel Walter D. Diehl? All the bastards of Bataan and Corregidor know their names."

It must be the martinis, Louise thought, but her words were like a talisman warding off his spell. He seemed to shrink, and just like that, her mood turned. Suddenly she found herself aching for a good time. A good game for them both. He shifted slightly, as if to reposition his false leg in preparation. Was it one of the aluminum ones, she wanted to ask—shiny as an airplane wing?

"You know what we call them?" she asked.

"Who?"

"The letter-writers, the gentleman callers. Not Mother, of course, she has no sense of humor. But the children and I, we call them the hat-in-handers."

He didn't laugh.

"Have there been so many?"

"Four or five. Six, maybe. Not since we came East, but when we lived in Los Angeles it was quite a regular Sunday ritual. They'd arrive and sit on the couch with their hats in their hands, talking with terrible reverence, using the word *honor* over and over again, to death," she said, regretting her casual toss of that word. His hands clenched to fists on the tabletop. "Flag that waiter, will you. I'm famished."

"I thought you were going home."

"Jesus Christ, Mr. Blunt, you started this. Here I am, all ears. I've surmised a bit about you from Mother. She steams open the letters, you see. We play a little cat-and-mouse. She thinks I ought to write you back so that you'll stop bothering me." She felt the swift vertiginous rush of the alcohol in her words, her lack of resistance to the truth serum.

"Forgive me, Mrs. Galle, but you came here of your own accord."

"Mother asked if I'd seen you by the NIH. Apparently, in one of your letters you said you linger there sometimes, gathering the courage to speak to me."

"It's true that I've looked for you for some time. To tell the truth, I went to Los Angeles when I was decommissioned in '47. Luckily enough, I missed you there. I wouldn't want to stand in line with my hat in my hand."

He was glowering now, stubbing his cigarette out with barely controlled violence. Now I have you, she thought, with the sort of assurance that martinis bring. She wanted to egg him on, to see if she could make him—do what, exactly?

"Oh, Mother would have welcomed you. You should try her meat-loaf sometime." He looked directly at her now, and there was no trace of a smile, wry or otherwise. She almost said, Does it hurt, Mr. Blunt, to be one among many? Instead, she told him she'd have the veal.

"What?"

"The veal. Wave that waiter over, order me the veal and get us a bot-tle of chianti. I'll be nicer when I come back from the ladies', I promise. When I come back, you can tell me your little story. I'm sure it's better than the ones I've heard."

She took her purse and got up, swaying slightly but righting herself. One of the dates for the men from the NIH was in the bathroom, arcing a bright red lipstick over her lips. She said hello to Louise, and hadn't they met somewhere?

"I don't think so."

"I know what it is. You work at the NIH, don't you?"

"Yes," said Louise, attempting finality and closing herself in the stall.

"So do I."

Louise hoped the sound of pee would silence the woman. It did not. When Louise emerged, the woman was still there, blotting her lips, removing some of the spackling, then unfurling the lipstick tube again, touching up, blotting, touching up, an endless loop of lipstick.

"Mrs. McKutcheon is quite a prig, don't you think?" asked the wom-an, folding the kerchief in half once more and placing the triangle into the corners of her mouth. "She's like a mother superior or something. As if we had no right to date a scientist!"

The words *I am a scientist* almost came from Louise's mouth. She wasn't the only woman to wear a lab coat at work, but the secretaries always seemed to take her for one of them. But she just nodded, found her own lipstick, and began to mimic the woman's movements, as if she had never before used this thing called lipstick. She extracted her own handkerchief and blotted her own lips, just like a woman.

"What is?" asked the woman.

"I didn't say anything," said Louise.

"You did, you said, 'just like a woman.'"

"Oh, well, perhaps I was quoting some poetry. Perhaps I was singing a commercial from the radio."

She dropped her lipstick in her purse and snapped it shut, stepping away from the woman without saying goodbye.

There was no one in the booth when she returned. In the middle of the table was a business card that read Kirstein Blunt, Managing Partner, Blunt Mills. On the back, these words: *It's not respect I want to pay. Next time.*

She stood for what seemed a long time, then sat again and lit another smoke, this time leaving the ivory holder buried in her bag. The waiter at least, had been summoned. Slowly and determinedly, she ate the veal and drank several glasses of chianti. She kept her gaze fixed on the door, on the table, on the octagonal tiles in the floor, avoiding the taunting gaze of the ape behind the bar, the snickering grins of the men and women from the Institute. She wiped the plate clean with a piece of bread, drank down one more glass, paid, and left.

Outside the sidewalk was lit. The sidewalk positively glowed. The moon was full, the moon was obscene. It shone on Louise without remorse. There was a policeman by her car, scratching in his ticket book.

"Ocifer," she said, half-falling off the curb and laughing, a little, at how drunk the word was. She corrected herself carefully and tried again, putting on her brightest voice. "Evening, officer."

"Ma'am, this your car?"

"Depends…is that ticket for it?" She smiled, but he did not return her look.

"Did you see the fire hydrant?"

"I suppose I didn't."

"Well, I'm sorry but this is for you," he said, tearing a ticket loose from the book and holding it out to her. Louise ignored his gesture, opened her purse, and took out her faux-gold cigarette case, which the unblinking moon turned a cinematic silver. She extracted a cigarette and asked the policeman for a light. He squinted at her.

"It's not a trick question," she said.

He seemed to want to tuck the ticket under the windshield wiper, but she stood between him and the car. He placed the loose ticket on top of the ticket book and stuck the book under one arm. With the other hand he patted the pocket of his uniform and extracted an army-issue Zippo lighter.

"Were you in the service?" she asked, accepting the flame.

"Yes."

"I thought so. Where were you?" She held her open cigarette case out to him, but he waved it away.

"Prefer cigars," he said. "I came in late. Germany, mostly. Eastern Europe. Would've been sent to the Pacific but the bomb saved me. I love the bomb. I was lucky."

"You were. My husband died over there."

"Lotta guys did," he said. There was something defensive in his tone, but he kept the ticket and book tucked under his arm.

"My husband lived through Bataan, then got torpedoed on a POW ship in the South China Sea."

"You don't say." He seemed a little suspicious now. "What was the name of the ship?"

"*Oryoku Maru.*" She could see that he was listening closely now. "My father was captured on Corregidor. Colonel Walter Diehl, died in a camp on Formosa. He was in MacArthur's class at West Point. And before all that there was my brother, killed in a test bomber explosion over Hawaii, six months before Pearl Harbor."

She changed the timing just a little bit; it seemed more poignant if Bruce had died in '41 instead of '39, when there was still some hope that somebody else would kill the fascists.

"Boy, that's plenty."

"Oh yeah, and my mother's brother, my uncle Peter. I never knew him. He was killed as a civilian in London during the Blitz. So, he's not part of our war story, which is the Pacific, really." She could see she was losing him a bit. She changed course, gave him her softest look. "I'm sorry, you must have had a time there too."

"Not as bad as that. I'm standing here now. Got a wife and a kid. I do all right. You got kids?"

"Four," she said, letting that hit before she landed the KO. "It's tough on a secretary's salary, but I get a lot of help from the other Gold Star widows in the neighborhood."

"Sounds like you better get home to those kids," he said. Was it a trick of the moonlight, or could she detect the beginning of a tear?

"Thank you, officer." She opened the car door and got in, then rolled down the window and held out her hand. "I'll take that ticket now."

"Consider it a warning," he said, giving her a straight-up American apple-pie smile. He lifted his cap and she flashed him a fine gleaming row of pearly whites.

She turned the radio on. It had been oddly staticky lately; sometimes it produced nothing but a strange metallic hum. This time it worked.

That apple-tree song came on again. She pulled out onto the road she knew so well and for a few blocks she sang along. "Don't sit under the apple tree with anyone else but me, anyone else but me!"

She felt gleeful about her small deception, about the perfect, tear-jerking detail of the secretary's salary. About slipping free of the rules that applied to other people. The foolishness she'd felt on discovering that Kit had left was altogether gone now. Whatever fun she'd thought she might have with Kit, the fun of a man who was alive, who was more than a memory overlaid with the dark water of the South China Sea, it was fun she didn't need. She had what she needed and everything she needed was hers.

But then the song was over, and that static returned, that sound of particles in motion, of magnetic fields. This is ridiculous, she thought, slapping the dashboard. I just bought you, car! She turned the dial, but the sound was all static, and the static, it seemed to her, was becoming increasingly mathematical. Rhythmical. The way a rush of wind in leaves can be a kind of rhythm, a sound that says everything is alive. Everything but you.

Stop it, Louise! She forced herself to stop moving the dial. To get back inside her feeling of glee. She had dispensed with Blunt almost as easily as she had dispensed with the cop. Yes, he hadn't left, she'd shooed him away! Had shown him how little she cared. That she was tired of caring. So many cared about her already. Her children adored her. They lined up to give her kisses! To show her their report cards! And every day she could leave them, leave Mother to the household drudgery. She was free! Let us take these days—who had said it? Someone had said, Let us take these days, these peaceful days, for peace. For prosperity. For pleasure! "For pleasure," she whispered, then said it aloud. "For pleasure, Roland!" She called his name out once, twice, three times! There was no magic in it, no curse. The static grew louder, its rhythms like a storm of applause.

She began to sing a children's song, the wheels on the bus go round and round, round and round, round and round, the wheels on the bus go round and round, early in the morning. All the way home she sang, and the wheels on her car turned round and round, and she was coming upon an idea. A marvelous idea. Roland, the idea has turned my wheels to wings! She flew home, out of Bethesda, across the river and over the hills. The moon was very bright, and it would aid her in everything. It was a summer night, and the children slept not knowing yet that she was flying home to swoop them up like Peter Pan.

She sailed over the hill just before the little house on Oxford Street, the one that she got a good mortgage for because she was a working woman, a chemist in fact. The neat house, modern and clean-lined but still made of brick. With its garage below the deck and its big picture window. With its azaleas and rhododendrons and silvery-barked magnolia. She had no need of hat-in-handers, she had no need of these worn and bedraggled survivors of dread circumstance. Of whatever they wanted to pay, respects or whatever it was. The children were hers, four of them for pleasure, for peace for prosperity! For pleasure most of all, on a summer night, for what was best, what was most important, was the sea, with the moon over it. The beach, children! We're going to the beach!

Breathlessly, she pulled the car into the driveway, a sea of small stones that made a satisfying crunching sound under her wheels. She leapt over the three steps to her front door, fished out her keys and opened it. The moon had only gotten bigger. The moon was ripe and laughing with her. "Wake up, wake up!" she called. Tunafish the spaniel came running from the kitchen, wagging her tail, barking. "Wake up and get your bathing suits!"

Mother's room was on the first floor at the foot of the stairs that led to the bedrooms—two small and one grand—above. Mother came out in her robe.

"Louise! What are you doing?"

"Hello, Mother! We're going to the beach! Get your suit!"

"Louise, you're drunk."

"On moonlight, Mother!" She ran up the stairs, ignoring Mother, who tried to hold her back, who clutched her arm but couldn't keep it.

"Get up! Get up and get your suits!" Louise flung open the door to the boys' room, where Ed lay facedown and shirtless, where Bruce snored with his mouth wide open. She grabbed Bruce's foot and tickled it. She grabbed Ed's shoulder.

"What what?" said Ed, turning up and then over again, showing his back to her afresh.

"Get up, get up! We're going to the beach."

Downstairs Tuna was barking and Mother was calling, "Let them sleep, Louise. It's nearly midnight!"

"Beach time! Beach time!" Louise sang and she threw open the door to the girls' room, where Helen slept diagonally, where Charlotte gripped her pillow for dear life. She kissed Charlotte's cheek, shook her by the shoulder.

"Help me, Charlotte! Mother wants to keep us from the moon, but the moon wants to see us to the sea!"

She turned on one of the pair of lights on the dresser between the girls' beds, admired the white fringe of the shades jiggling with joy. She opened their dressers, fished out their bathing suits and threw them at Charlotte, who was sitting up now, rubbing her eyes.

She roused them, as she knew she would. They were hers, and they wanted to play. Helen got up and Charlotte got up and together they got the boys up. It was a mutiny against Mother, and in her house, Louise thought proudly, the mutineers always win. Charlotte got towels and Helen took the big blanket that had just been waiting for them on the back of the couch. They got into the car. Tuna barked and tried to come with them, but Mother, having lost the fight, gripped the dog by the collar and held her back on the stoop. The headlights flashed on Mother's face, the withered planks of her cheeks and her small, tight mouth.

Louise let Ed light her cigarette. Let him take a little drag. He had resisted even more than Bruce, but they had won him to the mutiny, and he was her co-pilot now.

"It is a good night for a drive," he said.

"Oh, go ahead and keep that," she said, relishing another violation of the rules. He thought she didn't know he stole cigarettes from her sometimes. "And light me another." He shook one out of her pack as if they did this all the time.

She thought to ask her son something. Did he and Bruce catch anything in the river yesterday? What was he learning on his violin? But in everything she could think of to say there was some evidence that she didn't know him at all. She did not want that to be true. She turned to look at him. In profile he was much like Roland, fine-featured, with a long narrow nose. Angular, like a saint in a Byzantine mosaic. He drew the cigarette to his lips, exhaled two fine streams of smoke through his nostrils. The smoke from their cigarettes mingled with the milk breath of Charlotte, Helen, and Bruce who slept in the back seat, exhaling in time.

Louise and Ed settled into their silence. The land around them began to change from the dogwood and magnolia of Maryland to the piney woods of Delaware. Then the pine woods fell back and the dune grass rose up, and it seemed to Louise that the road was now white and the dune grass shiny black, as if they had traded their daylit roles. The air was heavy with cicada song and there was salt in it now.

This was her favorite part of going to the shore, how the scent of the sea teased and teased, how you could not see the sea for such a long time; you smelled and smelled it until you curved around a bend and suddenly it was there, a great shining silvery escape, the moon with her invitation on the water, her reflection that would gather you, carry you into her truest, most light and lovely heart. Remember, Roland, when we left the party and took the Chesters' rowboat out to the little island? How we stayed out all night and let Mother be worried, let Father be angry? Remember when I surprised you at camp in Virginia and we rode your spry bay into the woods until the skies opened up, until it rained like the mischief? Until it rained like God's laundry dropping sheets to wrap the faithful? Oh, you had a turn of phrase, my southern man!

The light was coming for her now, Louise felt. She went very slowly around the curving road, not driving as much as letting the moon pull her on and on. This moon was not the same as the war moon, it was the pleasure moon, it was the moon of lovemaking in the dunes. It was the moon of the beauty of the children before they were born, before they brought their troubles and their needs.

And then there were screams.

The children were screaming and the moon in the sea and the moon in the sky changed places and changed places again. The whole car was rolling, but it seemed to Louise to be rolling slowly, almost gently. As if they were all playing a game together. They went right off the road and into a ditch, all the way around and back up again.

"Jesus Christ, Mother!" Charlotte was the first to turn screams into words.

Louise was shaking violently now, every inch of her seemed to go in a separate direction, jiggling on jellied bones. She turned to Ed. He was there. He was all right. "Holy shit! Holy shit," he was saying. And then she heard them, heard Bruce too—"Holy shit!" And Charlotte's voice and Helen's voice and everyone saying, "Holy shit!"

"Are you all right, Ed? Is everyone all right?" Yes, yes, they said.

"I'm bruised like a peach," said Helen. And they all started laughing.

"It's okay. It's okay," said Louise. "We'll get some peaches tomorrow!" And she laughed more. Shaken to the core, they laughed and laughed.

"What a ride!" said Ed.

"We'll be safe now," said Louise. "Come, get the blankets and we'll sleep on the beach."

"But how will we get back on the road?" asked Bruce.

"That's a daylight question," said Louise.

"I'm going in the water," said Ed.

"Me too," said Charlotte.

"Me three," said Bruce.

"And me!" said Helen.

They were all awake now, shaking with fright and relief. They got out and stood on the bright sand. All of a piece, by some unspoken signal, they peeled off shirts and dresses and ran toward the waves. The tide was out. They ran what seemed a long time, hooting and hollering, their feet slapping the sand flat, the waves evading and evading them until they caught the water at last.

Louise ran with them, laughing and whooping. At last, the cold water shocked her sweaty feet, at last a swell to dive into. She dove and emerged. She counted her children's wet heads appearing in the foam like baby seals. One, two, three...was it only three, my God! No, there was Helen, there was Bruce picking Helen up and throwing her into the waves. There was Ed, there was Charlotte, sputtering up after being dashed in the foam. They were all there, together.

Above them the sky had changed its shape; it wasn't the vault of heaven, but it was itself a sphere fully contained. Heaven pressed in on them—there was no door to it. The stars, like souls of the departed, traveled in fixed orbits.

PURPLE HEART

JUNE 1964

When the other editors had gone, Charlotte placed the horseshoe carefully on top of the manuscript of *Hand G: Jan Van Eyck and the Turin-Milan Hours*. She was about to leave the office when her phone rang. She was so tired. Why did she pick it up?

It was Ed, pretending to speak French.

"Mademoiselle Charlotte, *je presume?*"

"You're drunk."

"*Tu es tres distingué*, such a critique."

"*Sans blague.* I can smell you from here. You've drunk something awful. Schnapps or something."

"Sleeve-o-vits but who's counting. Come over here."

"I'm going home, Ed. You should go to bed."

"Notchoo too. I told you I'm not a *homosexuel.* I don't go to bed with Billy."

"Drink some water and lie down on Billy's couch."

"Billy says hello. But he is a *homosexuel*, so all he means is hello."

"I'm going home now."

"You're *pas chez toi?*"

"You called me at work, Ed."

Billy or whoever was talking in the background. Then Ed must have covered the receiver. Charlotte almost hung up, but Ed swung back in, as he always did. Just when you were ready to kill him.

"Ah, but of course! At *le travail*, so near us now. Billy lives near. And the school. We're going to school tonight, and we want you to come." Billy's voice and another's gruff laughter mixed with Ed's giggles, which ratcheted up and up. "We want you to come to our little art school! We're going to teach it a lesson."

"I'm going home, Ed. Take two aspirin and call me in the morning."

"Charlotte! Come, come! We need you. You'll charm the police when we get caught."

"Ed! I'm hanging up now!"

"Come, come, swing your hips this way, hipsley Charlotte, that way, hips, the police will fall over."

"Ed, eat a whole goddamned bottle of aspirin and vomit blood. I'll call you tomorrow." Charlotte slammed the receiver into its cradle. It began ringing again immediately. She picked up the whole phone and went to drop it in the waste basket but thought the better of it. Through the open door that nosy secretary was covering her typewriter slowly, all ears.

Charlotte gathered her things and started out. The secretary whose name she had forgotten called out to her. Reminded her that they had her down for the index for *Art Through the Ages, Volume 22, Baroque and Rococo.* "It's a rush. Mr. Tisdale says they'll need it by Monday."

"Yes, of course," Charlotte said. She made her way to the elevator. Katie was coming back from Hawaii tonight. She could call her. Maybe they could have a drink or get some Swedish meatballs at Swenson's. But God, I'm tired, she thought. Down to the rot of me. Down to the stinking twisted black walnut of me, where nothing grows. Dr. Bedford had seemed to relish giving her the news. Had seemed inspired to poetry by it. Nothing will ever grow inside of you, he'd said. A regular Yeats. Some men might not mind adopting, he'd said.

She walked out through the lobby and onto the street. She went around the back of the building to buy cigarettes from the newsstand, passing the dwarf who roasted chestnuts. He stood on his stool with great dignity tonight, she thought. There was something noble in so big a forehead. Ed would have laughed at her. You and your jazz musicians, he'd said once. You always think people are noble. And you think no one is, she had shot back.

There was the entrance to the station, but she kept walking in spite of her shoes. Why did she insist on such torturous shoes? As punishment for her wide, unladylike feet, with toes that would fan out like fingers, given half a chance. And the girdle, the latest, so light, the woman at the shop had said, you'll hardly feel it while it holds you. It just caresses you into shape. Smooths your hips. The woman hadn't said child-bearing hips, but that was what she meant. Hips and rack, all this equipment, all this fanfare from the time Charlotte was twelve. This elaborate set for a play that would never begin. As if she'd been kidnapped and stuffed into a flesh costume that had swallowed her real body, which was small and light, like her soul. The sudden strange pains and blinding headaches and blood that no one had explained to her. You live near animals, Louise had said, you're an animal too. Clean that up or I'll tell the neighbors your secret, Louise had said, as if she would have gone knocking on doors telling people her daughter was a woman now. That was the sort of thing Louise said, the way she would blame you, Charlotte thought, for being alive. For not being Ed with his profound understanding of light and the beauty of a bowl of fruit. Or Bruce with his good, rough nature or Helen, so adept at tennis. What are we going to do with you, Louise had tsked. Louise, whose body had never given her a wink of trouble. Who had, apparently, borne four children without breaking a sweat.

When Charlotte was twelve, she took to walking the roads near her little Maryland town. When she felt reckless or lonely or both. She'd hear a car drive up, brace herself for the hoots and the honks. Once those farm boys had thrown a bottle full of milk at her from their truck. It had broken at her feet, splashing milk on her dirty brown loafers. They had said something—what was it? Hey, red! Give us a drink!

There was a soda fountain in Twombly's drugstore a few blocks down Fifth. An egg cream, no, a cherry phosphate. The air was cool in there, as if it came right off the chrome countertop. The cold shine, the summer light turned white, aimed directly into her head. She squinted, ordered, sat down. An egg cream appeared. The soda jerk turned away in his paper hat.

"But I ordered a cherry phosphate."

The paper hat pointed back at her, above a large Adam's apple that moved along the chord of his neck as he spoke. "You said egg cream."

"No, I didn't. I ordered a cherry phosphate."

"Look, miss, I got no dog in this fight. I'm just telling you what I heard."

"You heard wrong. Please take this back and give me a cherry phosphate."

"Okay, but I have to charge you for both."

"But I didn't take a sip of this egg cream. Give it to someone else!" The whole thing was a lie! Brimming there on the shining counter, faking cream with its foam, inviting one into depths full of false eggs like waves frothing over a fake sunken treasure. There was no egg, no cream! A young man plunked down on the stool next to Charlotte.

"I'm just in the mood for an egg cream," he said, placing some coins on the counter. "I'll take it off your hands. Please get the lady a cherry phosphate."

She noticed his hands. They were long and narrow and elegant. Soft and aristocratic, the nails slightly blue around their pale half-moons. He was clearly young, college age, like the soda jerk, but he seemed a different side of the same coin. Charlotte was certain he'd never worked a day in his life.

The soda jerk shoved the egg cream in front of the aristocrat and stalked off.

"My friend and I were just talking about you." The aristocrat gestured toward another young man, who walked over quickly. The other guy was husky, thick-thighed and broad. He sat down on the stool on the other side of her, setting his legs wide, so that one of his knees lightly grazed Charlotte's thigh, and the other blocked her escape from the back of the stool.

Charlotte didn't say anything, but she didn't leave. She reached into her purse, pulled out her cigarettes and lit one, carefully ignoring the light proffered by the newcomer.

"Yeah," said husky. "We were betting on what you do for a living."

"You don't say," said Charlotte, taking a sip of the cherry phosphate that had appeared.

"We do," said the aristocrat.

Charlotte took a long, cold slug of the cherry phosphate. It did her good, lightened her mood a little.

"Well?" said the aristocrat.

"Well yourself," said Charlotte.

"Don't you want to know what we guessed?" asked husky.

"Not in the least."

"Oh, come on, we bet on it!" He flashed a smile he clearly considered jaunty. "At least let us find out who won!"

Charlotte drank down the rest of the drink, smacked her lips, and to her own surprise and delight, belched without restraint. She dropped her cigarette in the empty glass, turned toward the aristocrat, then stood and pushed past him. He laughed and said:

"We never guessed you were with a traveling circus—Lady Belchley, a gassy gal!"

Charlotte made her way out the door while the two boys called out after her.

"Lingerie saleswoman!"

"Schoolteacher!"

"Undercover movie starlet!"

Let them pay for the cherry phosphate. They were so pleased with themselves. Their voices brimmed with it. Their summer pants and summer shirts and deck shoes. Their clean white undershirts, their light tans and muscled forearms. How she'd longed to trade bodies with Helen. Helen was lean and she tanned a little in the summer. She never missed a ball that was thrown at her. Stop it, Charlotte. She willed herself to stop the long whine, the list of complaints she tallied constantly. Let there be a new one today, just one. That all her equipment was good for nothing. A regular egg cream.

But a new thought came to her just then. That perhaps Dr. Bedford's news was not a curse. Perhaps it was a benediction.

She began walking more quickly. Leaping onto a curb, she collided with a blind man begging for change. His cup flew out of his hand and pennies and nickels and dimes flew all over the pavement.

"Hey!" he yelled. Charlotte apologized, picked up the cup, scrambled to gather the coins. She held the cup near the blind man's flickering lids and twitching lashes. Did she think that if she just brought them close enough, he could see them? He turned away from her, seeking some other signal. Even after Charlotte grabbed his rough hand and brought it to the cup, he kept calling, "Hey! Hey!"

She reached into her purse and added one dime and then another to his booty. Again he yelled, "Hey!" She shook the last penny out of her change purse, but she couldn't quiet him. "Hey!" He kept calling out as she hurried away. Then it struck her. The nature of the benediction. She had better keep her coins for herself since she would never marry. The thought was at once terrifying and delightful.

Nothing would thrive inside her. Some men might be willing to adopt, Dr. Bedford had said, as if granting her dispensation from her sin of false advertising. But what she and Katie declared on their drunken nights at the Fat Black Pussycat was true. Charlotte wasn't waiting for some man to catch her and knock her up. And she wasn't trying to rope one into marrying her. There had to be some other way to live. While Katie would, in the next breath, confess that she did want to have a family, Charlotte would remain silent. She wanted something else, something she could not see. Yet.

If there was no baby, there would be no man. What would be the point of one? There had never been one whose initial shine hadn't worn off quickly. She told herself she had no need for men, any more than they had need of her. She had a job. She could take care of herself. And furthermore, she wasn't going to help support Ed anymore. Let Louise and Granny pay for their golden boy's brilliant career. She was going to make a new kind of life.

Fueled by the treasonous thought, Charlotte walked all the way down Fifth Avenue, through Washington Square Park, where couples lounged on the grass pretending to be happy, and mothers pushed strollers, pretending to be awake. By the time she got to Houston Street and walked up her front steps, her feet were a ragged mess. She got inside and up the five flights to her apartment, the hard heel-rims chafing against new blisters. Her armpits had overfilled the sweat-stain pads, and puddles of salty sweat poured into her blouse like broth from the soup dumplings the landlady sold from the shop in the basement.

The key to her door was hot in her hand. She held it out in front of her like a talisman. Then the door at the top of the stairs opened and her neighbor Daisy was screaming. Daisy's baby was crying in the background. A man backed into the hall, then ducked to avoid a flying colander. He was unsuccessful.

"Jesus Christ! I'm bleeding, Daisy. C'mon!" Daisy slammed the door behind him. He touched his forehead and looked at the blood on his fingers. His close-cropped dark hair was speckled with gray. But he wasn't. Charlotte realized her way wasn't blocked by a man, but by one of Daisy's dykes.

"Can I get by?" Charlotte asked.

"Sorry," he-she said, backing against the wall to let her pass. "Hey, I'm sorry to bother you, but do you have a bandage? I hate to go out on the street already bleeding."

"Already?"

"I like to start fresh. You know, save the blood for the next time I get jumped."

Was this person joking? Charlotte couldn't exactly tell. She was about to say no, but just then the gash above this person's eye gushed a fresh rivulet of blood. Before she could think better of it, Charlotte took a handkerchief full of dried tears from her purse and pressed it to the wound. Then she grabbed the person's hand and replaced it where hers had been. She realized with some alarm that the dyke's eyes were big and dark blue, almost violet, and fringed with thick, dark lashes. The eyes of a beautiful baby set deep above a pair of leathery cheeks.

"Okay, come in. Pardon the mess." Charlotte pushed the door open, kicking a pile of newspapers out of their way, stepping around the coffee table and nearly toppling the very-full stand-alone ashtray, a sort of surrealist's joke on a pair of metal stork legs.

"Jesus, Daisy really winged me. I might need a stitch." The dyke was looking at the wound in the mirror by the door. Charlotte suddenly realized that this person had a name.

"I'm Charlotte," she said, taking the bloody kerchief away and offering a clean dish towel. "Hold that there while I get a Band-Aid."

"Make it two. Got any Mercurochrome?"

"No Mercurochrome, but I do have gin," said Charlotte, wondering at herself. Was she inviting this person for a drink? I need to rest, she thought. She remembered, distantly now, that she had cried after she left Dr. Bedford's office. Had at first been confused by the news that seemed now a special dispensation. But maybe drinking alone wasn't such a great idea.

"What's your name?"

"Gil."

"Short for Gillian?" asked Charlotte, coming back with two Band-Aids. She took the dish towel away, placed one Band-Aid and then the other. "X marks the spot."

"No, just Gil."

"Gil what?"

"What are you, a cop?"

"Sorry. You've quite a bit of blood on your face. Go in the bathroom and wash up. The sink's not clean but the washcloth is."

While Gil stepped into the bathroom, Charlotte took the gin out of her icebox, along with the ice tray. She took two empty jam jars from the shelf by the window that looked out on the airshaft. With a practiced tug she levered the cubes loose from the tray, her fingers sticking to the frosty metal. There was half a lime on the counter, its surface just barely dried. She sliced it in half again and squeezed the two quarters into the glasses, then added gin and a blast of soda from the soda canister Ed had given her for her birthday. It was the only thing in the whole apartment that smacked of urban sophistication.

When Gil came out of the bathroom, Charlotte held the drink out to her as if there were a habit between them. Gil took it the same way, guzzling it down all at once, smacking her lips, and wiping her chin with the back of her hand.

"Thanks, uh, what did you say your name was?"

"Charlotte."

"Thanks, Charlotte. I needed that as much as the Band-Aid. I should be going."

"Are you always in such a hurry?"

"Pretty much."

"Stay a minute, I'll make you another."

"Trying to get me drunk, eh?"

"So what if I am?" said Charlotte, downing the rest of her drink. Feeling suddenly like a heroine. Like she was doing something dangerous. Like no one knew what she might do. But flirting with this person was just like flirting with some man at the Pussycat, wasn't it? Gil smiled, but very slightly.

"Daisy wouldn't like it."

"I wouldn't think that makes much difference to you." The gin hit her when she stood. Must've been the walking. And the heat. The news. Ed's drunken idiocy. She lurched a bit, then righted herself, took Gil's glass out of her hand.

"Hey, there's still some in there."

Charlotte tilted the glass back, sucked on one of the cubes and then spit it back in the glass.

"Not anymore," she said, smiling.

"Are those the manners your mother taught you?" Gil was teasing her now. Charlotte watched Gil look her over, toe to head, the way a man would. Her curves and her volumes, her milky white skin. Red, red hair.

"Don't talk about my mother." It came out sharper than Charlotte intended. "I'm not drunk enough yet."

"Fair enough. But what the hell do you mean about Daisy and me?"

"You think I can't hear you fighting?"

The light in the airshaft was starting to turn from the dark that it was when it was the shadow it cast into itself to the dark that it was when the sky was going dark. Charlotte dropped fresh cubes in both drinks. She sliced a fresh lime. Then she looked in the fridge and got out what she found there: one pickle, two slices of ham, and a hard-boiled egg.

She added a box of saltines from the cupboard. What the hell are you doing, some part of her asked some other part. She ignored the question, put everything on the red-and-gold lacquer tea tray that had come, once upon a time, from the Philippines, and went back to the sofa. She put the tray on the coffee table.

"Are we that loud?"

Charlotte took a strong slug of her drink and rolled her eyes.

"Can you hear words or just sounds?"

"Depends on how close you are to the airshaft." Charlotte watched that sink in. "I know she wants you to get a better job and you want her to stop—"

Gil held her hand up, as if to keep Charlotte from saying what she was about to say. Charlotte changed it slightly. "Having boyfriends."

Gil gritted her teeth. A tremor passed along her jaw.

"Do you have a cigarette?" asked Gil, then seemed embarrassed. "Christ what a mooch! I'm sorry, here you are doing all this nice for me and I just ask for more—"

"Don't sweat it," said Charlotte. She picked up the ashtray by its stork legs—it was a sort of surrealist joke that Louise had brought back from a trip to New York and that Granny had banished to the basement—and went into the kitchen to empty it. Then she pulled her emergency pack from the drawer under the sink. It was too much trouble to locate her purse. She lit two smokes and passed one to Gil.

"Do you hear us…doing other things?"

"Whatever do you mean?" asked Charlotte coyly.

"All right, never mind. Tell me something about yourself."

"Like what?" That I'm free from the need of men? she thought. That no one knows what I might do?

"Like—" Gil looked around the room, her gaze landing in the kitchen area. She watched Gil's gaze take in the bare bulb over the sink and land on the table, on the lamp that had been at Charlotte's bedside when she was a child in Shepherd's Glen. It was ridiculous and girlish, an ivory silk shade with a little fringe, like a virgin's idea of boudoir furniture. Gil got up and moved toward it.

"What is this?" she asked, holding up a bit of wire and paper, one of Charlotte's creations. The one with four tiny feet and two paper-wrapped propellers, one as the head and the other as the tail.

"Oh, that's just a twittering machine."

"Of course! A twittering machine!" cried Gil. "Want another drink, while I'm up?"

"I'll get it."

"I got it, I got it. I'll make it as stiff as you would. Tell me about the machine." Charlotte held out her glass and Gil came to take it. Charlotte realized that she felt good. Very, very good. She relaxed into the couch and took off her shoes. Why had she waited so long to take them off? She spread her big wide toes as far as they would reach.

"I got a million of 'em. Just these useless things I make."

Gil came back with two drinks. Charlotte noticed that Gil hadn't freshened the lime or the ice, but she didn't say anything. She took a swig and leaned back, throwing her arm along the back of the couch. Her fingers curled very near the back of Gil's bare neck. Her hand filled with the heat emanating from Gil's skin.

"You mean you're an artist," said Gil.

Charlotte laughed and sat up.

"My brother Ed's the artist."

"I didn't know only one was allowed per family."

Charlotte looked at Gil sharply. She turned on the light next to the love seat—the match to the one near the sink—to get a better look. How old are you? she wanted to ask, but didn't. There was a small spray of wrinkles around each of Gil's violet blue eyes. The gray speckled through Gil's hair made Charlotte think of cobwebs in rafters; if you live long enough, she thought, your head will wipe the eaves.

Gil looked back at her, without a blink. A frank, open look. A question already answered.

"What do you do?" Charlotte asked.

"What I can. I've been a typesetter. Got mixed up in the union. Shot my mouth off. Everyone got fired, me first."

"That's rough."

"Yeah." Gil picked up another of Charlotte's wire machines, one of the many winged tricycles that she made and perched on top of books and shelves and window ledges. "Say, do you ever think about motorizing them?"

"What?"

"Your twittering machines."

"I don't know how."

"It's easy. It'd take about five minutes."

"Maybe you could show me sometime," said Charlotte, letting her eyes stay fixed on Gil's for an extra beat.

"Sure, I could show you. Hell, I could just do it for you," said Gil, looking back. "But I bet you get a lot of offers."

"What do you mean?" asked Charlotte, the coquette again.

"We've seen you too. With a visitor or two," said Gil. "You should be careful."

"About what?" Charlotte wanted her to say it. Tell me I'm a slut, she thought.

"You know what I mean. There are all kinds of creeps out there."

"It's my choice. It's not like I have to do it for money." Charlotte regretted her words. Gil stiffened. "I'm sorry, I didn't mean—"

"I know what you meant. I have to go now."

"Please, don't. Please stay, just one more drink." Charlotte hated the sound of her voice, the feeling that she was begging. But it worked.

"All right, one more. But no more holier-than-Daisy."

"I'm sorry," she called from behind the refrigerator door, where she was looking, unsuccessfully, for a fresh lime. "I know we all have to get by."

"How do you?"

"I work in publishing. I'm an editor. At Dunne and Crowne?"

"Of course."

"What d'you mean, of course?" She handed Gil another drink.

"You look the part."

Charlotte looked down at the faint chevron print of her blouse, her neat blue cinch-waisted skirt. She untucked the blouse and released the hook that held the waistband.

"Better?" She sat down and crossed her legs, letting her toe graze Gil's pant leg, looking into those violet-blue eyes. Found herself wondering what Gil and Daisy did together. What it would be like with a woman. With a sudden rush, she realized that it was not the first time she'd wondered that. Wanted that.

Then the phone rang. Charlotte ignored it, held Gil's eyes. Gil looked back, frank, open. Then came the banging on the door, Daisy's voice.

"Goddamn it, Gil, I know you're in there!"

"Stay, stay," Charlotte begged.

"Get the phone," said Gil, moving toward the door. "You'll see me again."

Charlotte watched Gil leave. The phone stopped ringing and then
started again. She picked it up.

"Charlotte?" She didn't recognize the voice. "Charlotte Galle?"

"Yes, yes! Who is this?"

"This Bolly. Billy."

"Who?"

"Billy. Ed's friend."

"What do you want this time of night?"

"It's nine o' clock."

"Who cares? What the hell do you want?"

"It's Ed. We're in jail."

The Chinatown jail had a distinctive smell. Part urine, part tobacco, part
chicken noodle soup—hot, sweet, disgusting. At least it was somewhat
quiet that Tuesday night. One handcuffed Chinese man stood near the
front desk, a wooden box next to his feet. Through the slats of the box,
Charlotte spied the tail of a creature, dark and thick. A possum? An
armadillo?

The cop at the desk was strange, an alien presence, tall and pale. Not
just bald, but hairless. Nothing but cold marble lumps where his eyebrows should be. He leaned down toward her, tented his fingers on the
desktop. His flesh seemed to Charlotte otherworldly; in the bright light
of the station there was something greenish about him. His skin had
an unhealthy—no, she would call it unnatural—glow, fed on the milk
of some unknown mammal. To Charlotte he was sort of beautiful, not
exactly menacing, but emanating an otherworldly cool, the ferryman on
the river Styx.

"No," he said, as if refusing her reverie.

"No? You're sure? Ed Galle? Edward Galle?"

"Nope, no one by that name."

"Can you check again?"

"I've checked," he said with finality, his pale bald forehead crinkling
like the courthouse steps. Charlotte waited a couple of beats, expecting
him to come up with another suggestion. Then it occurred to her—she
had come to the jail closest to her apartment, but of course there were
others.

"Maybe he's at another jail. He was picked up at the Art Students'
League in midtown."

"Could be over there," said the man, who was looking less beautiful to Charlotte by the second.

"Could you call them?"

He nodded, picked the phone up out of its cradle and dialed slowly with his long, languorous fingers. She waited while he spoke the codes of his position and profession, man and policeman. His words mixed with those of the Chinese man in handcuffs. No, yes, Edward Galle. No, no, follow the law, yes. Edward Galle, I'll wait. No, yes, permit! The keeper of the underworld put his hand on the receiver and asked Charlotte if her brother was a fairy. An arsonist, she explained with a mild laugh. No, no arsonists at midtown tonight, but they're full up with faggots, said the policeman, who had become downright ugly.

Charlotte thanked him and went to the phone booth to try Ed again. No answer. She thought to try Billy but didn't have his number. There was no book on the shelf in the booth. She stepped back out into the rain. The rain was dropping like lost laundry, sheets down from the line. She cursed herself again for her shoes, in which the rainwater cesspooled around the loose skin of popped blisters. But somehow the fact that she had run out of her place without having the good sense to change into pants and galoshes made her want to keep going. She told the cab driver to take her to Billy's place, which was above a pawn shop on West Fifty-Third Street.

He was walking out as she pulled up. She recognized the tight curl of his upper back, how he walked with his hands stuffed into the pockets of his slightly-too-small trench coat, his pork-pie hat squashed low over his forehead.

"Billy!"

"Bellevue," he said, as if they had already been talking.

They walked to an all-night diner and ordered eggs and toast and coffee. Billy talked and Charlotte ate and tried to listen.

"You know his girlfriend Brit, the Swedish one? Well, she ditched him again, and you know how he hates to be ditched…who doesn't, right?"

"I love it, personally," said Charlotte, just for the hell of it. He half-grinned, then pulled a small flask out of his pocket and poured a zotz of whiskey into his coffee cup. He reached across to pour some into Charlotte's, but she covered the cup with her hand.

"So, then she starts up with that Klaus Bruno, you know that guy?

No? I'm surprised; I thought you kept up. The one who uses the rabbit fur? He's the kind that Ed hates the most. You know how he is. We may be the only two left at the league who consider drawing from life as something more than a requirement you have to get through. We're probably the only two who think that saying a painting looks like a photo is not the greatest compliment."

"Billy, I've got nothing against abstraction, okay? Or photography. Get. On. With. It."

"Yeah, okay, okay, where was I? Right, we start drinking and he's getting madder and madder, talking about how the man lies to Brit and tells her she knows how to paint, when everyone knows that she's good at a lot of things. No, I know what you're thinking, Charlotte. I mean, she can sing, she's really good, but her painting is, you know, she doesn't have that thing—"

"You mean a penis?" said Charlotte.

"Yes, exactly. I'm joking, joking, come on. She doesn't have insight, you know, into the way of things, how the pitcher talks to the napkin." Billy leaned back in his chair and began looking around the room as if the greasy-windowed diner were a lecture hall full of freshmen he was going to enlighten. Charlotte snapped her fingers in front of his face. He tipped forward and crash-landed on four chair legs. "Okay, I'm getting back to what happened."

"Please."

"I mean Ed really is our Rembrandt. I'm serious, I would die to be half as good, but you know, it's, it's pearls before swine—"

"More coffee please?" Charlotte waved helplessly to the waitress, who stood stock-still behind the counter, her eyes slowly drifting shut.

"Tragic, Ed getting in trouble like this. After all your family's been through. My father, he was all set to go, he was on the train from fort wherever in Indiana, about to ship out and he gets malaria." Billy dragged on his cigarette twice in quick succession, forced smoke out of his nose in two fat streams. "He gets malaria stateside, and he doesn't go. But what happens is, his whole unit gets shipped out straight to the Battle of the Bulge and something like ninety percent of them die, bam, just like that."

"I've had an incredibly long day, Billy. Tell me the goddamn story of the fire."

"Okay. Yeah, our friend Brad comes over—you know Brad?"

Charlotte dropped her eyes. She did know Brad. She knew the smell of his breath in the morning, the dumb weight of his arm thrown across her chest on a morning of freezing rain during her first winter in New York.

"You've met him, right?" Billy went on. There was no suggestion in his voice, none of the smoldering disapproval that some men have for women who give them what they want. Of course, Billy didn't want that from her himself. Perhaps, Charlotte thought, Ed's friends really didn't care who slept with who, or perhaps they didn't talk about her at all. Billy went on.

"The one who does sets and things for plays? He's sort of an artist." Billy's eyes were beginning to wander again, so Charlotte reached over, took the cigarette from his fingers, and lit one of her own with it. For a moment he looked back at her. Over his shoulder she saw an old man opening and closing a newspaper. It's still Tuesday, June 16, 1964, thought Charlotte. It's still a Tuesday of far too much. Billy went on.

"Brad's like Leni Riefenstahl with his ideas, like his ideas make people forget about mercy and just want to suit up and kill. We all go goose-stepping after Brad. He quit the league ages ago, but he hates it still. Fascists of the fad, he calls the teachers. He starts saying let's burn it. Let's burn it and take pictures and call it art."

Charlotte stubbed her cigarette into the thick streak of dried egg on her plate.

"And?"

Billy took off his hat and scratched his forehead with tobacco-stained fingers. There in the smooth, pale dome left behind by dark hair receding like the tide was a thick little nub, a hatching horn. He pinched it with two fingers, then drew his fingers to his nose and sniffed.

"The next thing I know we're at our studio, and Ed starts pulling canvases off their frames, and then he starts breaking the frames, prying them apart. I'm just watching. I don't know why, but I don't even try to stop him. I'm just frozen. He puts the canvases in this big metal garbage can. And I'm sort of laughing because I can't really believe it and it's so horrible. He's putting the canvases in the can, and then he's pouring turpentine over them, and then he starts waving matches around." Billy's eyes filled with tears. "Excuse me but they really were beautiful, those paintings, and he just…lit them up…"

"All of them are gone?" Now Charlotte felt ill. The eggs and toast coagulated in her stomach, and a wave of guilt struck her. Her treasonous thoughts, her plan to say no to Louise suddenly seemed parts of this disaster. That she was planning to say his art is beautiful, yes, but that she couldn't afford to help him anymore. But after all, his work was beautiful. His work belonged to all of them, not just to her and Louise, not just to his patrons, but to Granny, to Helen, to Bruce. His work was their beauty in the world, their family's truth. Even now—especially now—that it was so unfashionable. She believed in it still, though she kept up as Billy said. Though she was interested in other kinds of art. She loved Ed for not giving in to the rabbit fur, for not making it new. For his own sort of rebellion. For that portrait of Granny that caught the sadness she worked so hard to hide. His work belonged to their father too. To their father, the words came to her, longing to be saved by beauty. Why would she think that of a set of barnacle-encrusted bones?

"That big curtain, you know, that we keep between us when we're working?" Billy continued, scratching his forehead again. "I'm thinking that's about to catch, so I start pulling it back and yanking it down to smother the fire. The fire is burning like crazy but everything else is in slow motion. Ed's just standing there, the room is filling up with smoke and I'm looking around trying to figure how I can put it out, then—bam! The fire alarm goes off and then there's the fire department bursting in and the police and everybody. And Ed and I get taken down to the station in midtown—"

"But I called over and he wasn't there." Charlotte took off her glasses and pinched the bridge of her nose to relieve the pressure in her head.

"Yeah, so he was there, we both were there. But, Lottie, that's when he really started scaring me. He was sort of—" He leaned toward her, whispering as if the waitress and the man with the newspaper were inquisitors and he a heretic. "Sort of possessed. I don't know what else to call it. The cops were trying to calm him down, but they let me have my phone call and that's when I called you. He's getting wild and yelling, then reciting something, some Shakespeare, I think, full fathom five my father lies. Over and over, he's saying that. So they send him to Bellevue. I'm worried and I want to follow him there. Somehow, I talk the cops into giving me another call, and I call Brad and I get him to come down and bail me out. And we go over to Bellevue but it's too late and they won't let us see him and that's the story as I know it."

Charlotte slumped down in her chair. She picked up her cigarette

case, then dropped it back on the table. The sound it made was strangely loud, and the other inhabitants of the café—the newspaper man
and another old man with wild white hair and a bulbous nose, and a
freckle-faced kid who looked too young to be alone in a café in midtown—started and turned toward her.

"Well?" said Billy.

"I don't know what to say."

"I know, it's horrible, horrible. I'm so sorry, Charlotte. I feel like it's
kind of my fault. I shouldn't have gone along with it. Even Brad said he
feels responsible."

"You are responsible," said Charlotte, but she could not stand Billy's
trembling lower lip. Could not stand this day. This moment on top of
the others. "No, I didn't mean that."

"Do you think he's gone bats? Did he have that in him, when you
were kids?"

Charlotte reached again for her cigarette case. It was the gold-plated one that used to belong to Louise, who had left it in Charlotte's
apartment on her last visit to New York. When Louise asked about
it, Charlotte had lied and kept it for herself. She managed to open it,
extract another smoke, light it. Her jaw was slack around what felt to
be the depth of some horrible hole, her bowels falling to the ends of
the earth. She might have said something when Billy asked her again.
She might have said, I don't know, I don't know. She recalled those
days of Ed, that summer when he was fourteen and she twelve. The
summer of Louise's man, of the car rolling into the ditch, that summer
of sleeping on the beach. How Ed would sometimes just disappear for
an afternoon or a day. How he stopped playing the violin so much and
started drawing more, how he began to treat her differently, how for
no reason that she could understand he suddenly seemed to loathe her.

"I mean when you were kids, did he ever…see things?"

"No," Charlotte said. But I did, she almost said. That summer I saw
things, real things. The one-legged man hitting Louise, Granny slumped
over the steering wheel. A blue ball of lightning rolling along the floorboards. Then she remembered how in high school every girl she tried
to make friends with proved more interested in Ed. She felt sick and
sicker as worry gave way to spite and spite boiled down to guilt. What
if Ed had gone crazy? If he were crazy, then she would have to support
him. In that case her entire fate had just been decided today, this very

Tuesday. And with the news that Dr. Bedford had given her today with such disdain. Well, who would marry these childbearing hips if they could not bear children? So, that was to be it then. She would throw herself over for Ed. But no, that couldn't be it, she thought. There must be another life for me. Just then Gil's face appeared in her mind like a moon over a sea. You'll see me again, Gil had said.

They sat for a while longer, puzzling it. Billy said Ed had been drinking for a few days, they both had. Maybe that's really all it was. Days of drinks instead of food. They decided that they would go to Bellevue the next day. Charlotte would go to Ed's place that night and get some clean clothes and things for him.

The waitress brought the check and Billy performed the standard poor artist's pantomime, pulling the insides of his empty pockets out. As she knew she would, as she always did, Charlotte paid.

She had gotten so tired that she was beginning to feel awake again. Billy went home and she walked the five blocks to Ed's basement apartment on Forty-Eighth Street. She slipped down the narrow steps and let herself in with the key she kept.

The place was tidy for the home of a maniac, she thought, remembering Katie asking, Are you ever not sarcastic? Ed had always been neat. When they were kids, it was his way of laying claim to the part of the room he shared with their brother Bruce, who was a colossal slob. Bruce, who had gone up to West Point like a dutiful Galle, was probably being forced to turn hospital corners and make sheets so tight you could bounce a coin. Ed the artist, on the other hand, chose neatness for himself. Even when he was drinking day after day, he kept his things in categorical piles; the dishes might be dirty, but he kept the plates on one side of the sink, the silverware collected in an empty bean can.

This was not the apartment of a crazy person, was it? If Ed were crazy, he would need her. She felt sick at the certainty that welled up within her, that if he were crazy, she would have to care for him forever. People wanted that—she thought, women wanted that, to be needed forever. To fill their hands with diapers and feverish foreheads so they always had something to do, some excuse for being. But she had an excuse, there were things she wanted to do, to make. And she wanted to be needed by no one. Or at any rate by someone who wasn't a child, who wasn't Ed. Was it so strange that among the feelings Dr. Bedford's news had given her was a touch of...relief?

She moved around the room, looking for what she didn't know. Ed's bed was a narrow mattress on a pallet, but it was neatly made, covered with a patchwork quilt Louise had found at an antique shop. At the other end of the narrow room, above a small dresser, hung the map of Nantucket that had been in the house in Shepherd's Glen for so many years, until Louise had tired of it and tucked it into the cellar. It had been made by one of the sea-faring Galles, that famous great-uncle who'd mapped the currents in the nineteenth century. Southern man. That he'd been a Confederate made Charlotte feel ill, but she loved the map. She'd asked Louise if she could take it with her to New York and Louise had refused. Then last Thanksgiving, after she retold the story of how the famous great-uncle mapped the ocean currents in spite of suffering from debilitating seasickness, Louise offered the map to Ed. She looked right at Charlotte when she said it. Winked at her, Charlotte thought. It was beautiful, as maps on yellowed paper always are, at once storied and withholding. Inked islands and peninsulas had always drawn Charlotte's child-eyes, which stared and stared at every Corregidor and Bataan she could find. If she could just memorize the places, if she could know every curve, she might understand what had happened to her father, her grandfather. "Full fathom five"...she had claimed that line from *The Tempest* as hers. No, she and Ed had claimed it together. Of his bones are coral made, they had whispered when they were young. As if it could draw their father back to them.

She went into the curtained corner Ed used as a closet and took down the leather doctor's bag he used as luggage. As she lifted the bag something slid inside. She sat on Ed's bed and opened it. It lay there like a hymnal, its title in fine gold letters. PURPLE HEART it declared, like a placard from a silent film. She lifted it out, feeling the weight of the flat leather box that her brother Bruce had been looking for since 1948. It was that summer she kept coming back to, or that seemed, lately, to be returning to her. Bruce had received the award in Father's name because, for a reason she could not recall, Ed wasn't there. She opened the box and lifted out the medal, turned it over in her hand, and read the inscription on the back: FOR MILITARY MERIT Edward Roland Galle. It was you, Ed, you had it all these years, she whispered.

Charlotte quickly put the medal back in its box and slid it into her purse. Then she put some fresh underwear and a clean shirt in Ed's bag, turned out the light, and left.

THE RETURN

Dark, rank, wet, and cold
We who were once so bold

Give me the lock that slips the key
You are not done with me.

Kiss of Death

July 1948

Two days after their meeting at Da Ronco's, Louise received another letter from Kit Blunt. She held it for a moment, considered destroying it and the others he'd sent, then placed it on the pile on the rolltop desk and walked away. It seemed to her that she could not act differently. That reading his letters would require her to re-read Roland's. And she did not want to do that. No, she could not.

After that, she began seeing that Blunt everywhere. When he actually appeared it wasn't a surprise, though it should have been. After imagining him in the parking lot of the Institute, after being certain that the person walking the widow Johnson's dog was not Victor Johnson Jr., limping with a football injury, but was rather this tall dark man who she had, apparently, so deeply offended. Who wanted to pay her something that was not respect. After nearly two weeks of seeing him where he wasn't, she was utterly unprepared when he appeared. And yet the whole scene seemed inevitable.

That day the air was thick and charged even in the first moments of the morning. Tunafish kept up a steady insistent whine, her delicate dog ears compressed by a drop in barometric pressure. The light was off too, clearly storm light. It darkened the darks in Mother's garden, infusing the greens with a sort of purple. But why had Louise called it Mother's garden, when it was hers too? They had planned it together, and Louise, of course, had paid for everything. She stood on their back porch smoking and watching Mother clip the rhododendron with quick, neat jabs. At her feet, Tuna raised and lowered herself, fussing and whining, going into the kitchen and coming out again. Mother really was skillful in the garden, and not bad in the kitchen. Louise should have known better than to think an appreciative thought. Mother looked up at her then, wiped the dirt off her nose with the back of a gloved hand, and passed judgment.

"You smoke too much."

"Good morning to you too." Louise perched on the porch railing, as the children often did.

"Couldn't you at least wait until after breakfast?"

"Are you making Saturday cakes? We have blueberries."

"Really, Louise, for someone who works on lung disease—"

"Please, Mother."

"Please what?" Mother took off her broad-brimmed hat, extracted her hands from the dirt-caked gloves, and ran her fingers through her shock of chin-length white-gold hair. It was thick and bright, radiant and alive above the long-lined plane of her forehead.

"Saturday cakes!" Louise made the appeal as a child would, Shirley Temple sweet.

Mother laughed in spite of herself.

"I wanted to get some weeding done before the storm, but all right. Make another pot of tea and wash the berries and I'll be right in."

Bruce appeared in the kitchen, hungry for bacon. He and Ed had been fighting again. Louise didn't know what it was about, but something had changed between them. Bruce suddenly seemed to have a sort of upper hand. He used it as Ed walked in, opened the refrigerator, and scanned its contents.

"Here he is," said Bruce. "The single-shot repeater!"

"Shut up!"

"Boy, Ed really showed the farm boys!"

"I said shut up!"

"Did you know, Mother, that Ed knows all about guns?"

"Oh, leave your brother alone, Bruce. Wait till after breakfast at least."

"See, Ed, your mama will protect you. You don't need to worry about being an ass."

"Watch your language, Bruce," said Louise.

"An ass is just a donkey," said Ed, sounding more like a grammar-school know-it-all than a teenager used to ruling the roost.

During breakfast they talked about the storm and wondered if there would be good lightning for them to watch from the screened porch, where they always waited out even the wildest of gully washers.

"When your grandfather and I were in the Philippines—" Mother began a story they all knew well. That particular morning, Louise wanted to hear it again herself.

"The first time or the second time?" asked Charlotte.

"The first time, before your uncle Bruce was born." Mother leaned back in her chair, as if to make room for the enormity of the story. "Your grandfather and I got a terrible case of the skeevies—"

"That's the scientific name," said Louise, right on cue.

"No, it isn't!" said Helen.

"We had a horrible case of the skeevies, one of the worst rashes you can ever imagine getting. Imagine if an ant colony has burrowed into your skin. It's like that. Nothing would get rid of it. Finally, when we were about to scratch ourselves into a bloody puddle, our maid spoke up with the local remedy."

"Dancing in the rain!" shouted Bruce. Ed punched him in the arm, just the way he used to when they were smaller and he pretended that the story they knew so well could possibly be ruined.

"Philomena told me, in all seriousness, that only way to get rid of the skeevies was to take off all your clothes and take a bath in the rain. And since our house was in one of the darker corners of the base, we decided that no one would be the wiser if we gave it a try."

Louise got up to take a cigarette from the sideboard, but Mother didn't even raise an eyebrow.

"It was the rainy season, so we didn't have to wait long. That very evening, after dinner, when the drops were falling thick and fast, your grandfather and I went up to the balcony, took off our clothes, and stepped out. At first we were embarrassed. Maybe Mena and her brothers were laughing at us. Maybe they were watching and giggling at our white bottoms flashing in the dark rain. But after the first moment of the water splashing on my bare ba-zooms"—Mother always said it that way, and the children always laughed, and this time Louise laughed too—"I started to feel better. And I looked at your grandfather, and he was smiling. Then he took my hand, and we began to dance the foxtrot. And your grandfather was a wonderful dancer. You felt yourself held in the most marvelous way when you danced with him. So there we were, dancing and laughing in the rain, absolutely starkers, and just as your grandfather was twirling me expertly, a pair of headlights flashed upon us, just as if we were center stage at the vaudeville. Your grandfather stopped mid-twirl, and we realized to our horror that a very important, many-starred and striped, visiting general had arrived at our house right on schedule. But what did Colonel Grandaddy do? Did he run inside in shame? Did he let me run inside in shame?"

"No!" the children yelled in unison, just as if they still cared about stories.

"He gripped my hand even tighter, twirled me three times more, and took a bow!"

Everyone laughed, Louise perhaps most of all. These were her pleasures, she reminded herself. Life could be simple—it could be just this, working and coming home to her family. Living. There were enough stories to live on, weren't there? She didn't need a new one, did she? She decided that she would simply forget about Kit Blunt. She would simply ignore him, and he would go away.

After breakfast the children drifted away, Mother went back to her gardening, and Louise did the Saturday cakes dishes, her weekly contribution to the household chores. Suddenly the day seemed long and empty; there was nothing for her to do but wait for the storm. Everyone else had something to do.

Bruce and his friends went down to the river. She knew they were teasing the poor old man who lived in a shack there with the chickens he'd been raising since the Depression, but what could she do? She knew they broke windows and climbed everything. Her love for Bruce was a sort of secret Louise kept from herself. Ed was the one she favored—the violin player, the artist, the moody one. Bruce was a boy like other boys, rough and hearty, slingshots and trespass, but generally good-natured. He loved her without bothering much about it and he loved himself so easily that he didn't realize it as love. He was on his own side but could be talked into doing the right thing, could be convinced of duty. At eleven years old, he talked of going to West Point like his father, his grandfather, his uncles.

Louise sat down in the overstuffed chair, *The Sun Also Rises* in her lap. Upstairs in his room, Ed practiced his violin. Charlotte and Helen played Tiddly Winks on the screened porch. They would fight as soon as Helen started winning; Louise could practically set her watch to it. Poor Charlotte! She cared too much about everything, sought meaning in everything. That was why she would never win; she thought her mind was the only tool, and it feasted upon her. Did any other twelve-year-old girl read *King Lear* for fun? Helen was more like Bruce—headstrong, simple, athletic.

Charlotte's body was surely from Roland's side; there was nothing so round and overflowing along the Diehl line. She was always an awkward child and now she was an awkward child in the body of full-grown woman, with breasts that proceeded her into a room and hips that couldn't fit through the door. Her growth spurt had made her clumsy, as if her hips and breasts were magnetized to the objects of the world.

Chink! The winks hit the bucket, hit the table, punctuated the sound of Ed's scales. Tuna's claws clicked across the floor, and the dog lay down at Louise's feet, lifting one eyebrow and then the other, in time with the sounds of the winks making or missing their target.

Louise didn't yet open the book. She looked at the map of Nantucket made by one of Roland's seafaring uncles, the one who had changed oceanography forever, but who hadn't gone far on any ship—the story went—because he suffered from a relentless, catastrophic seasickness. Roland had been all right on a boat, and he loved to ride horseback almost more than anything, but he believed himself to be a poet by nature. But he was a lousy poet because he had a tin ear. No sense of rhythm, no feel for image, and yet what he dreamed of, what he had always imagined he would be, was Yeats. Louise realized, with some alarm, that she was thinking about him. Something she had trained out of herself so long ago. Even before he was dead, before even she learned that he had been captured. Before she lost hope—if she had ever had hope—that he would return. In those early days, when the children were young and he was gone so long in training, on maneuvers, what have you, she willed her anger away, her mouth pinched around a diaper pin. He took his duties so seriously, seemed to think that if he did more today, the army would let him get back to his poems tomorrow. His letters full of excuses: *a junior officer's duties, dear heart...can't afford a plane and can't take the time away to travel home by train.*

His letters delighted her once, didn't they? There might not have been anything extraordinary in them, there might have been no art to them. But she was in love with him, and they were his adventures, and he did have some turns of phrase that seemed fresh to her, even exotic. Raining like the mischief! Like sheets down from the line! Mother tried to get her to write to him when he went off to war, especially in the Lockheed days when they were living in Los Angeles. Louise would come home, bone tired after working the lathe hour after hour, the smell of hot metal and soot in her mouth, sore of elbow and thumb and foot, and Mother would place the thin blue Victory Mail stationery in front of her and say, "Just a few lines. You miss him. You're thinking of him." And Louise would read his letters, would feel his longing for her, would feel the way he tried to reassure her from the prison camp. The way he would tell her who she was, a woman and the apple of his eye. His wife. And she would fill the pen with ink, and she would stare at the blank page and it would stare back at her. With the silence of the grave, she remembered thinking. And she would put the pen down and seek the dinner Mother kept warm for her so many of those swing-shift nights.

Just then Tuna whined, raised her head, and barked a brief accusatory bark. Louise put her hand on the dog's neck and shushed her. But Tuna barked again, pressed herself up, went halfway to the door, and barked again. Then, in accordance with the contradictory feeling in the air, the dropping barometric pressure, the storm that would not out, Tuna sat again on her haunches and whined at the door as if it were withholding from her the meatiest of bones.

Struck by a sudden assurance that someone was lurking there, that someone had come at last to pay her what was not in the least bit respect, Louise leapt up, flew to the door, and opened it. On first glance, there was nothing but the empty stoop, the three concrete steps that led down from the front door and into the rough crab grass that had taken over the front lawn. But as she squinted into the off-color daylight and felt the weight of greenish-purple sky that told her that the storm was coming, Louise saw him.

He stood in the road staring directly at her. A tall man, dark. Absolutely still.

She would take the upper hand. As if it were nothing, as if he were a member of the Gold Star widows come to invite her to join their sewing group, she invited him in.

"Well, Mr. Blunt, come in if you must." She could have been one of those brisk heroines. Rosalind Russell.

But the man was still. In the moment of quiet after her invitation, she realized that he was her neighbor, the Armenian. They all called him that, she and the children. Only Mother called him by his name, what was it? Gasparyan. Mr. Gasparyan. Doctor Gasparyan. He had apparently been a doctor in his own country.

"Can I help you, Mr. Gasparyan?" Louise changed her tone, sweetened it. Donna Reed. "Dr. Gasparyan?"

Again, he didn't answer. She had heard the children talk about him, how they caught him staring over the fence between their backyards. Screw loose, as Bruce said. When she looked at him then, Louise could see that he wasn't staring at her at all. Or even at her house, with its door wide open behind her, or Tuna creeping out tentatively, butting her head against Louise's legs. He was seeing some other place. A village burning, a sister raped by Turks. In a flash she understood that she had created a memory for him and that she was jealous of him. Because he had been in the place where the real thing happened. Blatant evil committed by a blatant enemy.

By the time he came to America, Doctor Gasparyan had already seen the worst that people could do to each other, Louise was sure of it. She didn't know his history, but she could see it in his face the few times they had passed on the street or in the post office. His hooded eyes had that lack of focus that comes when all is lost, a pair of charred circles where fear had burned away the will. When had he come to America? Maybe Mother had told her. Mother had a career once. Before she became an officer's wife and had her children, she had been something of a journalist. She had that story-telling sort of mind and remembered things about other people's histories. Mother had said he'd come not long after 1925, Louise thought it was, when that particular blood-dimmed tide was loosed upon that particular world. In those twenty years or so, perhaps nothing had happened to leaven this man. Or perhaps the leavening of peace was not enough to lighten his bones.

As if to revoke her poetic license, he screwed his face into a simulacrum of a smile and held a hand up in a sort of wave, his long fingers extending and then curling down into the palm. Then he turned and walked toward his porch, where the small, round woman who was his wife or housekeeper, Louise didn't know which, was whipping a rug with an old-fashioned rug beater.

When Louise went back inside, Charlotte and Helen were at it. Charlotte was declaring that Helen had nudged the little Tiddly Winks bucket with her elbow, as if cheating at such a stupid game were even possible. Louise could not bear the house a moment longer.

"Come on, girls, we're going to the pool."

"But there's a storm coming," said Charlotte.

"What storm? I don't see a storm, do you, Helen? Of course not. Because there isn't one."

"But you said yourself—"

"I said nothing of the kind. Get your suits."

She rapped on Ed's door while the girls gathered their things. He yelled the one word that succeeded in keeping her from entering—practicing! She did have hopes for him going to the conservatory. Bruce, who was probably still at the river despite the weather, would do the duty that made dead men proud, he'd go to West Point. But Ed was different. Special. He'd go to Julliard unless his habit of drawing took over. He could be that too. Rembrandt. At least one of her children was brilliant.

She and the girls walked to the Shepherd's Glen Pool under a darkening sky. They could do with a walk. Especially Charlotte, who had spent the summer so far reading poetry and movie magazines (she thought Louise didn't know that she was like other girls in that regard) and spending her babysitting money on ice cream. Hormones couldn't be blamed for all of that flesh. Helen at least roughed it up with the boys— she followed Bruce down to the river on the bicycle he'd outgrown and climbed trees. And she was beautiful, long-limbed and lightly tanned, her hair nearly blond, just holding the slightest tint of Roland's red. She wasn't an alarm bell like Charlotte, she was more of a penny whistle.

The Shepherd's Glen Pool was one of the reasons that she and Mother had chosen the house on Oxford Street. The pool was at the heart of the town, just off the village green as they called it, as if they could reinvent the pre-industrial world. Shepherd's Glen had grown as a railroad stop, but it had pretensions of substantiating some fantasy of bucolic perfection. As if a world full of cholera and smallpox had no dangers. Since '45, more and more people drove cars and didn't take the train at all to Bethesda or DC. The pool was outdoors and surrounded by a bungalow with locker rooms and a high hedge, but the high diving board was visible from the street.

The girl at the front desk didn't want to let them in.

"We're closing early," she said, curling a strand of hair around her finger and then looking at it as if it had come from somewhere far away from her. Louise insisted that they weren't yet closed and that they would leave the pool at the first sound of thunder. The girl rolled her eyes but agreed to let them in before Louise could take her to task for her sass.

Charlotte lingered in the locker room, telling Louise and Helen to go ahead, as she had been doing lately. As if Louise didn't know her body intimately already, hadn't seen her nipples through her nightgown or discovered before Charlotte herself did a blooming bloodstain. It annoyed her, this secrecy, especially when there was nothing subtle about Charlotte. Well, at least Charlotte was smart, though she behaved so often like a fool.

Helen ran straight to the diving board, climbed it, and dove in, jack-knife smooth. Louise walked toward the board to do her daughter one better. She put one foot on the ladder rung and the wind picked up. By the time she climbed to the top, the metallic taste of the storm in the air was unmistakable and the sky had noticeably darkened. She would remember that moment ever after as a kind of overture's end, the rising of a curtain on a drama that she had just begun to star in. Louise stood at the edge of the board in her white bikini and then everything happened at once.

From the women's locker room, Charlotte emerged with a towel wrapped around her waist, her breasts barely contained in last year's polka-dotted bathing suit. From the men's side Kit Blunt stepped out. Yes, it truly was Kit Blunt. He wore a red bathing suit and towel around his neck. His barrel chest was covered with a fine undergrowth of curly dark hair. The left leg, to the mid-thigh, was not a leg at all, but a shiny metal impostor. It was one of the better ones that Louise had seen when she had done some work at Walter Reed, the kind with an adjustable joint at the knee. In a gesture of expert smoothness, he unclamped the leg, took it off, and placed it on the deck chair. Then he hopped to the edge of the pool, looked her straight in the eye, and dove in. As if she were answering him or because she was stunned, or because she saw the cloud overhead darken and produce one distant arterial flash of lightning, she bent her knees, raised her arms, and dove.

She swam straight for him. She felt that she had no choice, if she felt anything at all. They were a pair of automatons, drawn together by an outside force, a pair of warships with no torpedoes left, no weapons to use but the carcass of themselves. In the center of the pool, they met. As her head came out of the water his hand arose, big enough to cover her face, and he pushed her head back under. It happened quickly. He shoved her head just under and kept it there for not more than a few seconds. By then the thunder was sounding, the lifeguards were yelling, the girls were calling her, and with a great wild rush of cool air, the rain came down in sheets like lost laundry. And they were tangled in it.

Purple Heart

June 1964

Charlotte had a Tuesday, June 16, 1964. An epic Tuesday, a Tuesday of beginnings that would slide into a Wednesday of endings. Or of the beginning of endings.

At some indeterminate hour she made it home from Ed's, back downtown and up the five flights to her apartment. As her Tuesday slipped into Wednesday and she tried to sleep, she felt that beginnings and endings were colliding. She did not sleep between those days, not exactly. The pitch-dark dream always felt like more than a dream. She could feel her brain transmitting the signal to move, but the signal was lost in a cold expanse of space between her head and her limbs. In the pitch her vision couldn't penetrate, in the silt-dark tomb of her body. She wasn't asleep, she was trapped. Her body, a heavy mantle. Were her eyes open? Did she see the dark of her own lids, two tons of sarcophagus stone? Her will was no match for this weight. But her eyes opened as if by some force outside; they opened into darkness, into the silt shadow. She became eyes then, two orbs rolling in ink.

That it had happened before was no comfort. That it had happened many times, that every time it was over she was delivered suddenly into daylight, and that when she tried to understand what had happened to her, to know it in the light of day, its meaning slipped away, was less comfort still. There was no comfort in learning it, in knowing what happened when she was caught there, fixed as prey to the web, because she never understood. She only knew it this way, her eyes finally fixing to a sliver of light, rolling to see the sliver of light widen as if by the slow opening of a door. Eyes straining to gather the shape of what then blocked the light, what announced itself as particular, as cut from the cloth of cold starless space. What crept, what scraped, nail by tooth, toward her. What took her, slowly, for its use.

That Wednesday morning came with a clap, the rattle of the trucks delivering flowers to the markets on Houston, as if it were a morning like any other that hot New York City June. The night tides of sweat ebbed across the salt flats of her skin, drawing away every wet from her tongue. I'm a mouth-open sleeper, a near-corpse just ready to lose its spirit. Hell of a thought, Charlotte, she said to herself, remembering suddenly two things—where Ed was, and that she had been under that tombstone weight again.

Later she would understand that she had woken up ready to falsify the index. To wriggle free from her career in publishing like a snake shedding its skin. Or maybe what came over her came over her as she walked up the steps to Bellevue, steeling herself to find Ed changed. To find that he had to pay for his brilliance with madness—wasn't that the true artist's bargain?—and that she would have to advance in her career so that she could pay for his care. Forever. There was no doubt in her mind that if he were crazy, she would be sacrificed for him.

What came over her was the slow-dawning confirmation of something she had begun to believe many years before. That things that other people said were good were the same as the things they experienced as misery. Things such as marriage and children and being an editor in the greatest city in the world, the burning center of the universe, had the same value as being a crazed pauper or a prostitute like her neighbor Daisy, with her male callers and her dykes. A marriage to a man or an affair with a woman. A nun in Des Moines or Bellevue's own best bed-pan changer. A Southern belle who pretended not to notice what Daddy did in the slave cabins or Dorothy Day changing the world. As she walked up the steps, pressed her weight against the great heavy door, and presented herself to the desk to ask where Bellevue might put a crazed drunken arsonist, she felt oddly relaxed, as if she were at ease in a new world of equivalencies.

And yet, she hoped, in some small way, to find Ed changed. Cured, even. Of what? Of his suffocating arrogance, she thought, nodding at the directions of the nurse who pointed her to the elevator that would take her to the visiting room of the psych ward. Of his habit of assuming the world's attentions, of throwing his presence around like royalty flipping coins to beggars.

And when Ed wasn't changed, when he was just…himself, well, that was further proof, wasn't it, that everything was equal to everything else. He sat in the psych ward the way he sat everywhere, with one leg looped over the other, his fine long fingers interlaced in his lap.

Ed was just himself. He had always been thin; that he looked slightly thinner than usual didn't seem surprising. The circles under his eyes were darker than when she had seen him last. His eyes seemed hungrier for the flesh of his face, and his chin and jaw had sprouted smatterings of gold-red stubble. The three of them—Charlotte, Billy, and Ed—sat in the tiled room, watching the sunlight pour through the smoke from their cigarettes.

"Was it Father?" Charlotte regretted asking this. She had not meant to invite that equivalency, of the dead to the living. She asked the next part anyway. "Did he tell you to burn your paintings?"

Ed and Billy looked at each other as if to say she, and not Ed, should be in the hospital.

"Billy said you were quoting that line from *The Tempest*. Never mind." She wanted to say, Don't you remember, Ed, how when we were kids we called out to Father to visit us, how we chanted full fathom five…how we were, briefly, the same together, supplicants together? How we told each other what he was telling us from the bottom of the sea? How we believed he was with us, how we could see the atoms of the air become electric in his shape, how we could feel the power of his invisible body?

"I'll be out of here tomorrow," Ed said, ignoring her. Righting the ship of their conversation. "It's no big deal, really. It really doesn't matter at all."

"That's good, Ed. You know you really had me going," said Billy, laughing. "Artists!"

Ed took off his wire-rimmed glasses and searched his pocket unsuccessfully for something to wipe them with. Charlotte took a kerchief from her purse and passed it to him. He breathed on the lenses and wiped each one vigorously.

"C'mon, Charlotte, *ma petite chou*." He reached across the table and squeezed her hand. "It's me. You know me. It was just the drinking, that's all. I hadn't eaten all day. Coming here kept me from a night in jail!"

"I would've bailed you out," she said.

"Of course you would have."

"Well, then, I should get to work. *Art Through the Ages, Volume 22* won't index itself."

Ed frowned and turned to Billy.

"Charlotte's angry."

"Yes, she is," said Billy.

"No, she's not, she just works for a living," said Charlotte, standing up.

"Look, I'll be all right, Lottie. They're just keeping me today to make sure it really was alcohol-induced psychosis. I'll get out and go about my business—"

Charlotte sat down again. She spoke softly to keep herself from speaking loudly.

"And what business is that? You think the league will keep you on after this?"

Ed and Billy exchanged a glance.

"I guess not," said Billy. "I guess we're done."

"You're not done with this. You might even go to jail."

"Not if I'm crazy," said Ed.

"You just said you're getting out of here. The league will probably press charges."

"My uncle's a lawyer; we'll figure it out," said Billy.

"We'll figure it out, Lottie," said Ed. Then his tone changed, became sharper. "But what will they charge me with anyway? I only destroyed my own property."

"Ed, if you think what you did is legal, you should stay here longer."

"We'll figure it out," Billy insisted.

"I guess so," said Charlotte. "I have to go now. Call me when you get out, Ed. Here are some fresh clothes."

She handed Ed the bag and walked away. She walked quickly, more and more quickly, half trotting down the long, sterile, terrifying hall, down the stone hard steps and out into the street. She felt absolutely terrible. Guilty. Of what she couldn't name, but she felt this feeling from the backs of her legs to her hips to the base of her skull. Though someone looking at her would see her moving, walking as any woman would walk along the streets of New York, she could feel, with each step, the tomb-weight of her bones. The presence that had fixed her in the dark stunned her still, continued its slow relentless progression.

The street was full of people who knew something about her. That was the effect that her body had on people. Or so she believed, because it often was the case, that it was true all the time. That her looks made people think certain things about her. This woman coming toward her, with the neat blond curls and the tight dress covered in tiny flowers, the tiny straw hat laid in place like the basket at the edge of the picnic, this woman looked Charlotte right in the eye. And her eyes said, Slut! The tall man in the light linen suit and the lilting gait and the arm upswung to hail the cab. This man looked her in the chest and thought, Milk bottles. Ed thought of her that way too, as food. As something to be used. He didn't worry about acting insane or getting kicked out of the league because he knew she would clean up his mess. He knew that she believed in him, in the vision of the world he painted. Of people in rooms, of qualities of light. She felt that she had this power to know what people thought, but that it wasn't the knowledge that she needed.

There was something she needed to know. It's June 17, 1964, she began telling herself. *Art Through the Ages* awaits. It's Wednesday, June 17, 1964, and I have an index to create. That was the seed of the thought, she would later realize, the seed of the thought that had led to her getting fired. All the way to Dunne and Crowne—as she held herself upright in the seat on the train, as she stood at the coffee counter, as she ate her bagel at the Chock full o'Nuts, looking across the street and up at the window she had been sitting behind for three years—she kept thinking, I, Charlotte Galle, have an index to create. But indexing isn't an act of creation at all, it is just an act of recording. Of matching a reference to a location. It is an act of believing that given the appropriate coordinates, you can find something. That someone looking for an explanation of the origin of egg tempera could look up "egg tempera" in the index and discover the number of the page that included that information. And she, Charlotte Galle, on that Wednesday morning, June 17, 1964, didn't believe that anything was ever where it should be, or that anyone really cared where things were. Or that things being in one place rather than another had any value. And though she was relieved that Ed was not crazy, she was terrified by the sudden thought that there was no need for her to advance in her career. With some alarm, she realized that she didn't really care about working in publishing. Even the possibility of her being promoted, something her boss and the whispers she'd overheard in the ladies' room had suggested recently, did not excite her. Not only that, she didn't really care about what Dr. Bedford had said, about what he had called the puzzle of her uterus. About his belief that all her equipment was useless. Children and a new title had equal weight, they balanced the scale at zero. And somehow around the edge of that vacuum of care, she felt guilty, as if she had been lying for years. She cared about other things, but she could not say what they were. If her name were listed in an index, she would want the reader to turn the page to find a description of a life she could not quite imagine. She only knew it did not say mother, it did not say associate editor.

Standing in the Chock full o'Nuts watching the people scurry toward her building, the illustrious Crowne 5, Fifty-Fifth and Fifth, she was struck with a sixteen-year-old memory.

That summer of '48, four of them had gone to the Hall of Heroes to receive the Purple Heart. She and Granny and Helen and Bruce had driven to Arlington without Mother and Ed. She could not remember where they were, or whether Granny herself knew. In her brisk and cheerful way, Granny had announced that since Ed wasn't there, Bruce would receive Father's medal. She kept referring to Bruce as the man of the house or the man of the hour. On the drive, Granny told them again the story of their grandfather's famous acrobatics. Just before she and the colonel—they always called their grandaddy the colonel—were sent to the Philippines in anticipation of the coming war in the Pacific, they had to attend a formal affair at the home of some wealthy people in Washington. The colonel was dressed in his full regalia and she was wearing an evening gown that, she said, made even an ugly little newt like herself look like a swan. Here the girls interrupted, as they always did, to say, You're not ugly, Granny! And Granny smiled and went on. An old West Point friend of the colonel's, a general who would later come to some renown, came up to them and introduced them to his second wife. The wife asked the colonel what he had learned at West Point. How to do a back handspring, he answered. I'd like to see that, declared the wife. So, he put the martini he was drinking in her hand and did two back handsprings in a row, right in the middle of the dance floor. Granny said she hoped to see that same general and his wife at the ceremony today. But when they got to the Hall of Heroes, no one that she knew was there. The list of Purple Heart recipients was long, and the name Galle was called between the names Frankel and Gibbons. Bruce had stepped up to receive the honor with great seriousness. Charlotte remembered that his usually merry freckled face seemed blank and shiny, a mirror reflecting the decorations on the uniforms all around them. Even Helen looked somber. And Charlotte had wanted to run after her brother as he made his way up the aisle, to grab him and drag him out of that stultifying place, out into the sunshine where he belonged. On the way back home, Granny had Bruce sit in the passenger seat, holding the precious medal in his lap. Charlotte, though the oldest was supposed to be in the front, sat next to Helen in the back, gritting her teeth against what she wanted to scream. It's not enough! It wasn't worth it!

She feared that Bruce was already following the Galle men and the Diehl men, that his training was leading him inexorably toward the current war. She had not slept but had been in that other place, in the tomb-light, where her specific gravity weighed more than her will. To where she waited, frozen, powerless, for what approached. For what she could hear scraping softly, steadily along the floor. That the paralysis had happened before was no comfort. That what was in that ink-black dark was more real than typewriters, than proofreader's marks, than the Wednesday she was now in, than *Art Through the Ages*, even than the counter she leaned against and the window she touched with her fingers—of that much she was certain. Later she would realize that before she sat down at her desk that Wednesday, she had already decided that the index she had been assigned did not matter at all, that she could pick any page number for any subject, because everything had the same value as everything else.

THE RETURN

This is the story never told
Dark, rank, wet, and cold

Unsaddled bones starved to free
Hungry spirit of you and me.

KISS OF DEATH

JULY 1948

There was the water above her and the water below. For one moment—
five seconds, ten?—there was his hand on her head and Louise could
not breathe. Then he pushed once more, harder, launching himself
away. She thrust her head through the surface, sputtering. A sound
came as if from a great distance, an air-raid siren—no, the teenaged
lifeguard's whistle. Along the pool these waving arms gesturing toward
her, but no one came to retrieve her and no one stopped that Blunt.
She could see his arms smoothly stroking, and she called to the guard
to get him, stop him! As if he were some cartoon villain. But the color
of the air had changed. The sky now was the enemy and the thunder
drowned her call. Louise's senses flashed full at once, the metallic taste
of the air, the pool brine in her nose, the clash of heat and cold as the
hard raindrops hit her forehead.

The box hedges at the edge of the pool were hurling their branches.
The lifeguard stood with her girls, his arm around Helen's waist, keeping her from jumping back in to bring her mother home. Charlotte knelt
by the metal ladder, her soft thighs flashed white against the dark crotch
of her bathing suit as thunder announced the lightning flash. Charlotte
reached out to her, but Louise found her strength, propelled herself to
the ladder, shooed Charlotte away.

Louise reached one arm out, then the other. She grasped the ladder
rung and began pulling herself out. She turned to look for Blunt's red
bathing suit, for his big, muscled arms, for the hands that could palm
her neck. Could drown her. There he was, at the other end of the pool,
pressing himself out easily, lightly. How lightly we travel without our
limbs, she thought, as Charlotte gripped one hand and Helen took the
other. They threw a towel around her shoulders and began dragging her
toward the dressing room. Before they reached the door, she cast one
look back across the pool.

The gawky lifeguard had picked up the metal leg. Kit Blunt snatched
it from him, then shooed him away. He reached into his shorts from the

bottom, for whatever it was that would fix the artful aluminum in place. He met her gaze with his own. There was no apology in it.

Louise let herself be drawn to the locker room. She and the girls threw their loose summer dresses on over their wet suits, slipped their feet into the damp, horse-smelling leather of their sandals, and made their way out through the entrance hall. There was no one at the desk. There were the sounds of the storm and the creak and scrape of chairs and umbrellas being brought in and doors being locked.

They stepped through the front doors and stood under the slope of the roof. The rain was really coming down now. Down and angling, slamming the steps, striking them despite the roof. The concrete hissed out the day's heat and the heavy water pooled in their clavicles and plastered their hair against their foreheads.

"What a glorious storm!" Charlotte yelled. She had poetic outbursts from time to time.

"We shoulda drove," said Helen.

"Should have driven," corrected Louise. "And that's not true. We'll be fine. We'll just wait for the worst of it to pass." Just then a birch across the green was hit by lightning and split to the root with a crack louder than the thunder.

"Oh wow!" screamed the girls.

The doors opened behind them, disgorging Kit Blunt.

"Hello, Mrs. Galle."

She would not be undone. Or outdone.

"Mr. Blunt, I was surprised to see you here. I didn't know you were a member of our community."

"I get around. These must be Charlotte and Helen."

"We are. Do we know you?" asked Helen. Her eyes crinkled with her wicked little grin. "Are you a hat-in-hander?"

"Helen!" Charlotte said. "You don't ask that."

"I am," he said, smug as Orson Welles.

Louise drew Helen close to her, farther away from that Blunt.

"There, it's letting up a bit," said Louise as the torrent increased and somewhere a loose door slammed in its frame. Everyone ignored her.

"How do you know our names?" Helen went on.

"Your father told me."

The girls turned to look at him, both at once. A pair of birds. If birds could act as if they'd seen a miracle.

The eye-rolling girl from the front desk appeared, telling them they had to leave now, she was locking the place up. Louise silently willed the girls not to say they were walking home. Of course, she couldn't really control them.

"We'll close the gate behind us. Can't we just wait under the awning for a bit?" Charlotte asked. "We walked here."

Of course, the Blunt offered immediately. Before Louise could say another word, her girls were following him to his car. The storm seemed to have washed away their brains and their respect. They heard none of her words of protest. She found herself following, and then wondering, as he politely opened his doors and they all got in his car, if what had happened in the pool had happened. Perhaps, she thought, it was an accident. She had just gotten caught in his stroke.

As he pulled out into the storm, the girls began asking him about the war. Later Louise would wonder why no one asked him how he knew the way to their house on Oxford Street. It was one thing to know an address, another to navigate the quick turns and odd hills of Shepherd's Glen so surely. Perhaps she hadn't been wrong these weeks, checking and checking again her rearview mirror.

"So you were captured?" said Helen.

"Yes."

"Did they make you pray to the emperor?" asked Charlotte.

"Sometimes."

"How'd you lose your leg?" Helen shouted over a great clap of thunder.

"Helen!" Louise could not hear that story, whatever it was. Not now. Not as they pulled up in front of the house and the girls' faces, chins perched on the seat back, shone in the light of dashboard like the faces of children in story time from forever, amen. "Go inside now, girls. I'll be right in."

They opened the back door and climbed out.

"Thank you for the ride, Mr. Blunt," said Charlotte.

"Well now, I couldn't have you walk in this mess." He could sound so terribly gentlemanly.

The girls slammed the back doors and ran toward the house. The rain sounded even harder and louder on the car's roof.

"Is that hail?" Kit asked, peering through the windshield.

Louise cleared her throat, tried to relieve herself of the feeling that her windpipe was closing. Her hand reached out to his chin and turned him to look at her as if he were one of her children in bad need of a corrective.

"So, is this the disrespect you threatened to pay me? You follow me around? Grab me in the pool?" She released his chin with a slight shove and moved to open the door. "Stay away from us."

He put his hand on her shoulder and she shrugged it off but turned to look him in the eye once more. Lightning flashed very close and in that sudden potent light, for one fleeting second, she saw not his face but Roland's.

"I will. But first you'll have to read the last letter I sent. Just that one. And then you must answer the question it poses."

They were still for a moment, and over the radio a crackling emerged, an announcer's voice, a flash flood warning. Had the radio been on this whole time? Suddenly it was that sound, goddamn it, that strange sound that plagued her own radio, the sound of magnetic fields overlapping, the sound of the march of metal filings colluding with the laws of physics. She looked at him again; he was Blunt again. He made her angry.

"Why should I?"

"Because it's not my question."

She didn't ask what he meant. Because she knew whose it was. And this package in her gut, this parcel of dread, like a lump of iron where her babies had grown, turned over inside her.

"And if I don't?"

"You'll dishonor him again."

She looked at him then, and his dark eyes seemed to grow darker and to fill great hollows in his skull. He drew her into that vast dark. The spell was not easy to break, but then it was. Just a drop of her eyes, a quick removal of herself from that car, a slamming of the door.

On the stoop his headlights beamed and flashed away. Everyone was on the screen porch, storm gazing as they called it. Mother had made popcorn. Tuna hid under the couch whimpering. Another clap, a flash, and the children counted between, trying to gauge if the storm was coming in or going out.

"Hey!" Ed shouted. "Wow!"

And bam! Like that, in a flash the lightning outside became the lightning inside, a bluish ball of light rolled along the floorboard. Tuna sat up and barked.

"It's Daddy!" shouted Charlotte, fanciful girl. Who always said she could feel Roland near, that he had given her this or that idea. That when she could not sleep he sat beside her and caressed her forehead. Who said that sometimes he could not caress her, because he was still under the water. Crawling back, inch by inch.

"I'm afraid it's just ions, dear," said Louise, settling into the old wicker couch that had never stopped smelling of warm hay. Petting the pointed fob of the dog's head. "Charged particles. It won't hurt you, Tuna."

"Charming particles?" said Ed, teasingly.

"Do you think Mr. Blunt is charming, Mother?" asked Helen.

"No," said Louise, a little too quickly.

"Who's Mr. Blunt?" asked Bruce, placing himself under Louise's outstretched arm, nuzzling close, the way he'd done when he was small.

"Another hat-in-hander," said Helen, eyeing her granny, who did not like the term. Louise too thought Mother would say something, but she did not. She sat closest to the screen, her fingertips grazing it lightly, feeling the suck and whoosh of storm air as it pulled at the mesh. For a moment it looked to Louise as if Mother was doing it all from where she sat, orchestrating the calamity of rain and wind. Mother, she thought, is this house. Without me it will go on. They will all go on.

"Was he just so honored to serve with Daddy?" said Bruce, getting in on the joke. But it was Louise who nipped it this time. She felt suddenly guilty, remembering the night in Los Angeles, when, after the third such visit in as many weeks, she had coined the term hat-in-hander. That the soldier that day seemed as kind and reverent as any of them, that he had come on a Sunday afternoon, to sit on the couch crushing and rolling his hat in his hands, and say over and over, what an honor it was to serve—was it with Major Roland Galle or was it under Colonel Walter Diehl, she could not remember—that he had refused to stay for dinner, but just wanted them to know how good her father or husband was, how real of a man, how full of a pure and silvery grit, all of it had made Louise suddenly furious. After he left, while Mother was in the kitchen finishing the croquettes that she had made so thriftily from last week's chicken, Louise had started the chant, and the children had joined in. "No more hat-in-handers! NO MORE HAT-IN-HANDERS!" And Mother had come from the kitchen carrying the platter of breaded chicken bits, saying, "Stop it, stop it! For shame!" But they had not, they had gone on and on, and finally Mother dropped the platter on the floor, right in front of Louise. Only then did they stop, the children transfixed, watching Mother chastise Louise, as if she and they were all of a piece. As if Mother was the only grown-up for miles and miles. Yet Mother had done this childish thing, breaking a plate for attention, making a mess of croquettes and crockery, now intermingled on the floor. Mother broke the quiet second, looked at Louise and hissed, "You clean it up. You feed them. I'm going to bed."

"Yes," Louise said to Bruce, without the slightest trace of sarcasm. "I expect he was quite honored."

She had wanted those men to tell her what it was really like over there, but they never would. They were themselves the censors, their stories full of black boxes where words should be. Just as Roland never would, in his endless letters, describe what it was actually like to starve in filth under a relentless Filipino sun. What it was like to be already dead. Goddamn it, all those years I wanted to know, she thought, I wanted to feel it. The real thing. The hot breath of the enemy that would consume me without the slightest hesitation.

The storm calmed. The children quieted and Mother shooed them off to bed. Charlotte lingered behind. Louise looked up at her from the couch. Her arm remained across the back of it. She could still feel the warmth of Bruce's body against her side.

"Mother?" Charlotte shifted her weight from foot to foot, her latest in a series of nervous tics.

"Yes, dear." Louise retracted her arm and stood up. Charlotte was almost as tall as she was now, how alarming.

"Did he do it on purpose?"

"Who, your father?"

Charlotte looked as alarmed as Louise felt, asking that odd and nonsensical question.

"No, Mr. Blunt."

Louise started slightly.

"What do you mean?" but she knew exactly what Charlotte meant.

"He pushed your head under the water."

"Oh, don't be silly, darling," said Louise. "Hat-in-handers don't do such things."

Louise offered a flicker of a smile. But Charlotte's big hazel eyes were full and solemn.

"I won't let him hurt you," Charlotte said.

It was a statement so utterly preposterous that Louise didn't know what to say.

"Hopefully I won't have to rely on you," she said, regretting the words the moment they escaped her. Charlotte dropped her eyes, revealed her smooth and longing forehead the way she did in the war days, when she bent her little head in sorrow. Goddamn! Was it the storm that had loosed these memories? Louise was again in the house in Los Angeles, having returned home from a double shift at Lockheed, so tired she did not know which end was up. There was eight-year-old Charlotte, bringing her a drink. Clumsy girl even then, before she was hammered by hormones into the woman-shape she walked in now. Clumsy girl, she tripped on the edge of the carpet and spilled the drink all over Louise. Who hit her daughter. Smacked her once and again. And Mother was saying, "Stop it!" And Charlotte was crying, and Louise then, crying too, and pulling Charlotte onto her lap, holding her and rocking with terrible tears.

Her daughter began to move past her toward the stairs, but Louise grabbed Charlotte and pulled her in for a brief, forceful hug. As if to force away the memory of hitting her, to believe that it never happened again. But Charlotte clung just a little bit longer than Louise could bear. Sometimes she wished that Charlotte would hate her, would slice whatever bond they had with cold, clean indifference. Outside, each drop of rain clung to its bit of leaf or roof and fell.

PURPLE HEART

JUNE 1964

Monday, June 22, 1964. Charlotte would later remember the date as a headline. As a beginning and an ending. Almost a week since Dr. Bedford and Ed. And Gil.

Stotsenberg, or Miss Schultz as she was actually known, looked stern as she waved her in. More stern than usual, which was a feat. Charlotte considered her Stotsensberg, after the fort where her father had been when the Japanese came. A place of last stands. A structure of impossible, useless rigidity.

"Close the door and sit down."

Charlotte had thought she was already sitting, but in fact she was standing by the door. Stotsenberg's office was small and free of decorations, as if she had only just arrived. As if she hadn't spent ten years at Dunne and Crowne, ushering in and pushing out. "Managing personnel," as they said. Charlotte didn't believe there was much to it.

Stotsenberg opened a file on her desk and pretended to read it. Charlotte knew that it was her file, and that whatever the fort had to say, she did not need a reference to say it. Stotsenberg closed the file, clasped her hands together on top of it and looked at them. They were thick, pudgy, porridgey hands. Stotsenberg's glasses were also thick, and through them Charlotte could make out the fine hairs on her left cheek.

"This meeting pains me, Charlotte. You have been a good employee. In fact, you were one of the brightest and most promising young women we've hired in some time. You came so highly recommended. And, truth be told, you were well on track for a promotion. Other than an occasional late morning—yes, we do notice what time you arrive, this is not a circus—you've been a fine editor, an eagle-eyed proofer. I was looking forward to adding to your responsibilities and to your pay."

Charlotte's stockinged feet began to itch in their tight little shoes. She should never have worn these ones, with their narrow, boxed-in toes and their hard, square, so-called sensible heels. Each toe swelled now, bulging and groaning into the next. Between each toe, a rash. A rash in every crack. As she looked up and back into Stotsenberg's face, she thought, with mild alarm, of the man she had left sleeping in her bed. Go ahead, she thought, then realized she had said it aloud. Stotsenberg's cheek, and the little hairs on it, twitched.

"Well, you're making it less difficult. Did you know that we could see to it that you never work in publishing again? Misnumbering an index is a serious thing. Do you understand that?"

For a moment Charlotte considered denying the crime. But what possible excuse could she have? She had been given the wrong proofs. Her eyeglass prescription had run out. She was worried about the civil rights workers gone missing in Mississippi. No, no, the timing wasn't quite right for that. Better to say she was still reeling over the death of the president. How could anyone work or pay attention to anything while they were mourning as a nation? Many nations, many cultures, I can assure you, Miss Schultz, take a full year of mourning. And it had been only six months. And it was only six days since Tuesday. Tuesday, June 16, when everything had happened. Dr. Bedford, Ed, Gil. Why was Gil in the list, when she hadn't seen her since? And after that it had been Wednesday, when she had understood.

She almost said aloud, today is Monday, June 22nd, as if that would explain everything. As if Stotsenberg could care. She held her tongue and just nodded, looking back down at her big feet pinched into little boxes, little coffins. In her armpits, the expanding pads soaked in her sweat.

"I'm asking you for a response, Charlotte."

"Yes, Stots—Miss Schultz."

"Whatever possessed you? We consider you one of our strongest lines of defense against inaccuracy, and here you, you perpetuated it. You chose it. Over Dunne and Crowne and over your own career."

As Stotsenberg spoke, Charlotte recalled again, with increasing alarm, that she had left a strange man sleeping in her bed. She had met him at the Pussycat and had taken him home. She and Katie had met at their spot. She had tried to explain to her friend that Ed was fine and that she did not care about the news from Dr. Bedford, but Katie had taken her explanation as a performance of stiff upper lip. When Katie left, Charlotte had stayed, had kept drinking.

"I don't know." But she did know. She knew that the only answer to why was, always and forever, why not.

"I'm offering you this chance, right here and now, to explain this to me. I don't usually involve Mr. Dunne in such matters, but he did get wind of this. His recommendation is that we let you go today, without pay. Do you think that's fair?"

"I suppose so." On Wednesday, when she arrived in the office after seeing Ed in Bellevue, she had for a moment been meticulous, had felt sheltered by the careful act of locating, of noting the page numbers, of aligning the text. But the shelter soon dissolved, and one number had begun to look exactly like another.

"You suppose so? Well, my dear, I'm going to pretend I didn't hear that. I'm going to pretend that you gave me something approximating a reasonable excuse. I'm doing this because you have been such a strong employee, and I have to confess that I considered you something of a kindred spirit."

Charlotte started slightly at these words. She looked up from her shoes to Stotsenberg's neat white blouse with its faint chevron pattern, at Stotsenberg's rosy cheek sprouting fine white hairs behind the thick magnifying lens of her glasses. She thought again of the man, Luigi or whoever, of letting the ash fall from her cigarette onto his hairy back. When's the last time you brought a man home, Stotsenberg?

"So many of your peers are, well, silly girls, Charlotte. You, I considered a woman of some sensibility. You don't seem to gossip and talk with the others about face powders or come to me with complaints I can't solve, petty squabbles that should have been left behind with our school days. I understood you as a woman of substance—thoughtful, intelligent. Interested in publishing because you are interested in books. Not cocktail conversations about books, but books themselves. Ideas for their own sake."

"Yes. Well, thank you, I mean I am interested—"

"You'll have a lot of time to read now. And I am sorry that I can't recommend you. You understand, I'm sure, why Dunne and Crowne cannot praise someone who has behaved so erratically. I will, however, do my best to plead the fifth to any potential future employers. And, I have made a successful case for two weeks of severance pay. You may stop by payroll on your way out. Please get your things now. I don't have to tell you to avoid speaking with anyone. And please, hold back any tears until you have left the building."

Charlotte left Stotsenberg's office as quickly as she could. At her desk she collected her jacket, purse, the stupid horseshoe, and the carved ivory box filled with news clippings, most of which were about Mississippi. She left the sickly schefflera and the postcard Katie had sent from Oahu. She took the long way around, avoiding even Katie. She wanted to talk to her friend, but not here, not now. There was far too much to say, all a-twist in her gut. Sympathy would undo her, but not to tears. Maybe to violence.

If she could get to the elevator…but there was Katie, there were the others. With a neat turn she dodged them, struck the sticky door with her shoulder and found herself in the stairwell—the musty edge of Crowne 5, Fifty-Fifth and Fifth. People talked about the building as if it had character itself, "Crowne 5" as if it meant something to work there, as if just walking in the doors was some sort of laurel or passport or proof. She'd thought so herself once, just as she'd thought her college education was something. Philosophy, quite a something.

"Aren't we here, New York?" she said to the dim damp brick walls the elevator hid from important people. The back halls smelled of library paste. But not just any paste, intentional library paste. Paste created in a laboratory to assume the smell of paste, to give to people who might investigate, who might have a doubt that Dunne and Crowne actually created books or anything more tangible than contracts and sales plans.

The back stair had served its purpose when Charlotte began working at Dunne and Crowne three years before. She'd slipped out here for a smoke more than once.

She got down five flights of stairs before the idea of intentional paste finally got to her. Took her by the scruff of the neck and bent her over. The laugh spasm struck deep in her gut, then wrapped her around it until she fell to her knees. The reality of paste! The sticky, sticky realness! It was the kind of laughter that relieved nothing, the way a pneumonia cough only generates more coughing. Her skirt, a pale-yellow linen thing that was as too small around her waist as the shoes were around her toes, had been straining since the morning. Now she heard the unmistakable sound of the soft cloth along the zipper tearing. The spasm that had almost subsided returned in full.

When she finally stopped heaving and gasping, she used the wall to press herself up. The bricks' rough surface chafed her soft, sticky palms. Her purse fell open and the contents tumbled out. Lipstick and compact and wallet and box of clippings and empty pack of Camel straights and the stupid horseshoe, which fell down the next flight of stairs and crashed into a gun-metal-gray door that must lead to the boiler room.

She and Katie had long joked about the boiler room that connected all the buildings in midtown. That in it they would find a mute, grease-covered giant who walked round and round, turning the wrench around the axis that turned the gears that heated the steam that made the electricity that made everything possible. That made books and people talking about books and contracts and typists and editors and proofreaders and lawyers and whoever else believed that they were doing something and that that something was important.

She ought to go back up and out through the lobby. If she were a reasonable sort of a person she would. But instead, after she gathered up her other things, she followed the horseshoe, bent to pick it up. If she could get to the loading docks, she might find a man there who would give her a cigarette. She had finished her last that very morning, watching what's-his-face snore. She elbowed the door open.

The door was heavy, but propped ajar by a slice of wood, so that it was not so difficult for her to open it. She must have kicked the slice away, because behind her it fell back and crashed closed.

She found herself in a dimly lit hallway. To the left there were more and brighter bulbs hanging from the ceiling, so she took that route. Turning a corner, she heard a flurry of female voices—tones distinctly Brooklyn and Queens. Jewish-Italian-Greek. She thought she knew something about the other boroughs, though she rarely left Manhattan. WASP was her lingo, but the men she picked up at the Pussycat were never members of her own tribe. Still, she couldn't help the restrained ironic tones of her people that came through her, the view of life that defined all who were not like her as "ethnic." A roiling sea of female voices in varying degrees of ethnicity spilled out of the opened door ahead.

"Crowne 5, hold the line, yes, hold the line please, Dunne and Crowne, ringing you through, hold the line please, Dunne and Crowne, Crowne 5, hold the line please…"

Before the wall of winking lights, hands reaching, pressing, plucking, each voice oblivious to the one next to it, catching and finishing and rolling over the same words. Pigeons, thought Charlotte, scratching after the spray of seed. Cooing in calamitous arrhythmia, some piss-poor jazz attempt. Then at once, as a flock takes a turn, they turned and looked at her, then all but one—a densely built dark-haired woman in a tight blue dress—turned back to plucking, plugging, and announcing. That one stood up, took off her headset, flipped a switch, and strode toward Charlotte. "You the new girl?"

"No, I'm—"

"What are you, lost? How'd you get in here?"

"Well, I just got fired."

"Fired! What did you come here for, sympathy? We've got work to do. Go talk to Miss Brown. You want a job…you might just be in luck. This new girl never showed up today. Who knows, maybe she got lost trying to take the subway. I heard she comes from Pennsylvania or something. One of those farm towns, Pennsylvania Dutch. Apple butter. You like apple butter? I never touch the stuff myself. Miss Brown's in the break room. Come on, I'll take you."

She walked at a quick, low-flying clip. Charlotte trotted after her, not trying anymore to explain herself, just hoping that the break room might be a place where she could bum a cigarette. The woman in the blue dress kept talking. By the time they got around two more corners, Charlotte had learned that the woman grew up in Jersey but lived in Bay Ridge now, that her father was a mailman with ideas that, taken out of context, out of context mind you, might make you think he was a red.

"He just wants a break for the working man. Is that so bad? Working woman too, and I'm with him. Here's Miss Brown, she's all right if you get a drink in her."

"I'm on my break, Sue. Don't bother me." The woman at the table put down her newspaper and looked, not unkindly, at Charlotte. She was dressed in a dark gray suit that seemed too heavy for a New York City June and included pants, which Charlotte had been told never to wear to the office. She and Sue might have been sisters, Miss Brown the leaner and taller of the two. "This Pennsylvania?"

"No, she says she got fired. I didn't ask where from."

"I'm from Maryland, originally," said Charlotte stupidly.

"Go back to your post, Sue." The two women exchanged a loaded look, Charlotte thought. She wanted to know what was in it. But more than that she wanted a cigarette. Miss Brown had left one smoldering on the lip of an ashtray full of plump butts.

"Sue was very nice to bring me to you. But I should be going. I just don't know my way around down here. Where's the door to the street?"

Charlotte's voice was clipped and feathery. She was struck, suddenly, by how she must have looked—eyeliner pooled in half-moons, lipstick smudged on her chin, a handprint of kohl and cherries in the snow on a face clutched in laughter. Mark of an attempt to contain the chaos wrought by Ed and Dr. Bedford. No, it had begun years ago. It wasn't just her impostor of a body, it wasn't just Ed, if she were to tell the truth. If she could summon the truth.

"You sure you don't need a job? I've just about given up on Pennsylvania, and we were already short staffed." Miss Brown took up the cigarette and dragged slowly, as if to taunt Charlotte.

"I could use one of those."

"Oh yeah?" said Miss Brown, holding her cigarette out in front of her as if she were examining its value in a new light. "What's in it for me?"

"I'll give you my lucky horseshoe." She extracted it from her purse, held it out like a schoolgirl showing before telling. At that, Miss Brown snorted softly.

"You don't seem so lucky to me. Here, I'm just having you on." She picked the pack up off the table and shook it in Charlotte's direction. One cigarette appeared in the pack's soft mouth. "Ah, but you are lucky, it's not every day I give up my last."

"Thanks." Charlotte's hand shook as she took the cigarette and accepted Miss Brown's match. She cupped her hand around the flame, as if the two of them were standing in a gale or a foxhole. As if there were wild winds and dropping bombs and this tiny flickering light was the only hope.

"Well, I really should be getting back. Short staffed as I said."

"But wait, how do I get to the street?"

"Try going out the way you came in." Miss Brown got up, snubbed out her cigarette, and maneuvered around Charlotte and into the hall.

"But the door slammed behind me."

Miss Brown stopped and cocked an eyebrow. She didn't look that much like Sue after all. Her face was long and fine-featured, and her dark eyes were very big and set in deep hollows.

"You didn't kick out a doorstop, did you?"

Charlotte nodded. Miss Brown sighed.

"You just browned off the cafeteria staff. That's their shortcut. You better go out through the laundry. They won't even notice you if you make a beeline for the back exit."

"There's laundry here?" Charlotte blushed as the words came out, realizing her stupidity too late. All sympathy left Miss Brown's face.

"Do you think those tablecloths in the cafeteria wash themselves? What about your boss's shirts? Or were you doing those for him? That why you got fired, left too much lipstick on his collar?"

"I'm an editor. Was an editor."

"Right, right. Not that kind of girl. You probably get that sort of thing all the time, looking like you do." Miss Brown gave Charlotte the toe-to-head, the kind of appraising look men usually gave her. The kind Gil had given her.

"You don't know about me." Charlotte was angry now, but the words came out low and soft. Miss Brown's eyebrows unpinched.

"I suppose I don't. Go out here and take your first left. Follow that corridor to the end, just past the breaker switches and the punch clock. You'll see the laundry machines and the ironing tables. There are stairs at the back of the room, they lead to a street-level door. You can't miss it."

"Thank you."

"You're welcome. Oh, and what did you get fired for?"

"Faked an index."

"Attagirl!"

"I had my reasons."

"Everyone does."

Charlotte stepped out into the corridor and took a left. Just as Miss Brown said she would, she passed the circuit breakers and the punch clock and found herself in the laundry. Three women dressed in white aprons and hairnets were gliding irons over tablecloths and spraying starch onto collars. Behind them, two other women were loading a row of gape-mouthed washing machines.

Above the machines there was a window onto the street. Charlotte stood for a moment, watching the parade of shoes: pumps and sandals, deck shoes and wing tips. One of the ironers looked up from her work.

"No smoking in here."

Charlotte walked in and moved quickly toward the stairs, pretending she hadn't heard.

"Hey, no smoking in here!" the woman said louder. Charlotte reached the stairs and climbed them. She got to the door, opened it, then leaned back in and flicked a bit of ash off of her cigarette.

"Sorry!" she yelled down the stairs. Then let the door close behind her. She took another drag, then dropped the cigarette and ground the butt under her foot.

She was free. She was New York's again, as she had been when she arrived three years ago, with two hundred bucks saved from working the front desk at a home for unwed mothers while sleeping in her narrow childhood bed. She had been so excited to be in the city, the great burning center of life! To have coffee in a café with Ed instead of seeing Louise over breakfast, listening to her and Granny trade jabs they thought were subtle. Why she had thought that her brother would be any better than her mother escaped her now. He'd been at the Art Students' League for a month when she got to the city. Louise had suggested that Ed would marry her off to one of his friends. As if that was what she should want, to be the door prize.

But Louise was wrong. Goddamn it, thought Charlotte, giving the dead cigarette butt an extra grind with her foot, Louise was wrong about a hell of a lot. Her gut clutched at the thought, but she pursued it, yes, Louise was wrong. Sure, Charlotte had gone to bed with one or two of Ed's friends—dared them to take what they claimed to want—but she wasn't interested in marrying one of those artists. In being the midwife to their drinking habits or having the children they would promptly ignore. In fact, in her time in New York, and especially since Tuesday, June 16—she kept thinking of it that way, as a headline—Charlotte had become less interested in Ed's friends and even less interested in her brother himself. In being his sidekick or his "best girl" or whatever the hell he called her when he introduced her to them. As if he were giving her away like a father at a wedding or an appliance salesman. My sister, my best girl, my topnotch-oven-and-fridge-in-one. That was what everyone always thought she was for—to be used for the comfort of others. She hadn't told Louise what had happened to Ed. Let him tell her himself. And she would tell neither of them about Dr. Bedford. Well! Ed wasn't crazy and she wasn't a mother-in-waiting. And now she was free!

The door from the laundry had let Charlotte out on Forty-Ninth Street, where that dwarf sold chestnuts from a stand. He stood on a step stool, opening the metal lid that covered the nuts and adding charcoal to the brazier. She always wondered how he managed to drag that cart to the corner every morning. Such things were the mysteries of New York. What did people do in the early hours, setting the stage that she and all the other WASP stuffed shirts walked through on their way to their important jobs?

Where did the carts come from, anyway? And how did a person get one? Since her career in publishing was over, she should probably learn a little bit more about how things were done. Maybe she could drive a flower delivery truck. The sound of them rolling down Houston Street often woke her at four in the morning, after she'd stayed up reading until she could see the nerves of her eyes, strained fibers like jellyfish glowing at night in Long Island Sound. She got those ocular headaches more frequently lately, often before she had the paralysis dream.

Charlotte approached the dwarf, intending to ask him where he got the cart and how he had gotten started in the business. But he gave her such a sorrowful look, his wide-set eyes drooping, his mouth grimly set, that she bought a large bag of chestnuts and determined to walk up to the park and eat them there.

She walked two blocks north, then stood on the corner to watch a mounted policeman clop by. She had always feared and even hated horses. Their big eyes and knowing nostrils. She felt that they understood something about her. She had kept the horseshoe not just as a token of her country childhood, but as a kind of inoculation against—what? Her fear of horses? A life of too much...publishing? Well, that had worked, hadn't it? A whiff of her earlier laughing fit returned.

It occurred to her that she had forgotten to stop in at payroll. Well, maybe they would send the check...and she had that jar she kept under the sink and maybe a little something in the bank. She would be all right for a month or so at least. She could ask Katie. Katie would pick up her check. Yes, it would be all right, she thought. But when she reached into the bag of chestnuts and found that nearly all of them were badly charred, she lost her nerve. Jesus Christ, she thought, what the hell am I going to do? She began crossing Fifth Avenue. As she came near, the horse dropped its nose down and nuzzled the bag of chestnuts. The policeman chose to blame Charlotte for this.

"Keep your goods away from the service animal!"

Flush with a sudden rage, Charlotte stopped and flung the bag of chestnuts straight at the policeman. The light was changing. She ran across the street, narrowly escaping an oncoming taxi. She could hear the policeman calling after her and half expected him to chase her into the park. Was that his whistle? She ran.

But what was she doing? She'd left what's-his-name sleeping in her apartment, something she had vowed never to do again. So she turned around and walked to the train, with every step vowing to end her sluttish nights altogether. Two trains and a five-story walk-up later, she opened the door to her apartment on Houston Street. Things were indeed missing.

First there was the radio, gone. The invisible radio in its place hummed with nothingness. And there, under the bathroom sink, the little curtain was bunched up and the lid of the cracked casserole sat on one side like the sideways cap of a newspaper boy calling out, "*New York Herald Tribune!* Monday, June 22nd! YOU'VE BEEN ROBBED!"

She'd picked up the man at the club, where she and Katie had gone to see a trumpeter who once played with Art Blakey. But Katie had claimed exhaustion and left before the music even started. Luigi was her type, dark and swarthy, black hair on his knuckles. He hadn't had much of a line, and he'd let her buy the drinks. But she'd taken him home anyway, with the hope of an obliterating fuck. A fuck to live and lose six days at once. He'd come too soon and left her in the worst of all waking states, not drunk enough to pass out and not sober enough to read.

She'd lain there in the tight square of her bedroom, which was only slightly larger than the bed itself, and ringed all the way round with planks she'd dragged in from the street and nailed up to the wall to hold her books. The plank was barely wide enough for the Chaucer and Shakespeare that Louise had had rebound in green leather—some sort of deal that included adding the owner's name to the binding. You'd think Louise Galle had created *King Lear* and the Wife of Bath. The heavier books were all dragging the plank down toward the window, while *Meditations in an Emergency* and *O to Be a Dragon* practically leapt off the end near the door. Neither O'Hara nor Moore could save her in that moment.

She'd just begun to doze when the roar of the flower delivery trucks woke her. The jerking axles rattling tender carnation petals, which somehow never fell. In the markets the flowers appeared whole. She'd lain there wondering where things come from, the way a child would. Then she got up, dug her last cigarette out of the pile of clothes, the late-night snakeskins shed on the floor, and smoked it, tipping bits of ash onto Luigi or whatever-the-hell-was-his-name's hairy back. He'd slept on and on, the sleep of the just, the sleep of the thief, the sleep of those who always live by the game of getting by. How simple.

And then she did that damn fool thing in the string of damn fool things, she left a stranger sleeping in her bed. The cherry on the parfait of disaster that had started layering with a vengeance that Tuesday. Truth be told the disaster had deeper roots, if she had someone to tell the truth to. She'd left Luigi or whoever sleeping in her bed. And lo! He had stolen her radio and her rainy-day fund. And she'd been fired and would have to ask Katie to pick up her check. And she'd have to ask Granny for money. Or worse, she'd have to ask Louise.

Still, Charlotte didn't cry. She ran to her drawer to see if what's-his-face had found her truer treasure in its leather box. The prize she'd claimed from Ed. If Luigi or whoever had taken it, she would need to do something drastic.

She wished she had someone to tell the truth to, the whole of it. That is, if truth was something she could summon. Not the drunken declarations that she and Katie made, that they would be the ones. That all of it is bullshit except art and jazz and the struggle for civil rights that they would one day join in earnest. There was something else she wanted to tell. Something terrifying, something that was coming for her in the night when she lay fixed under her own weight. She didn't have the words for it, but she knew that it was after Ed too. It was what approached her when she slipped into that place in the dark and could not move. Giving Ed that piece of her paycheck every month wouldn't help him. Nothing would help them. Well, nothing would help her, she corrected. The world of women would always help Ed.

There, at least, the treasure. In its cozy velvet cove beneath the sea of pantyhose and garter clips. She held the box in her hand, felt its weight and knew what was inside, but didn't open it, fearing her talisman had no power after all. Of course, the army had given out hundreds, probably thousands of them, but Luigi or whoever might not have known that. He might have thought a Purple Heart was worth money.

Here I am, she thought, exactly where I'd feared being. Jobless in the city, plagued by paralyzing nightmares. Free flying in the void where barren women fall. Where there are no rules to hold me, no niche to rest in. But I have this at least, Father. I have your Purple Heart. And that, at least, is real.

THE RETURN

Hungry spirit of my life
When did you replace my wife?

Dank, stark, hard, and thin
Are these the bones you kept me in?

KISS OF DEATH

JULY 1948

For several days Louise went about her life as if she had never met Kit Blunt. She went to work, she donned the rubber apron, the rubber gloves, the goggles. She poured pulverized penicillin into a tall glass column, she boiled more silicate solution and made the medium through which to pour the pulverized penicillin and poured it through again. She released a sample from the bottom of the column at the appropriate time, she weighed it and noted its weight. Compared one weight to the next.

There had always been something soothing to her in this work, its careful repetition. If she had been the woman she ought to have been, if she had done what her father, Colonel Walter Diehl, had wanted her to do, she would have gotten her PhD in chemistry. She would have been running the people running the experiment, like Alice O'Day, who was in charge of Louise's particular group at the Department of Infectious Diseases. Rather than grinding and pouring and measuring, she would have spent time the way Alice did, talking and writing. Louise would have had many more conversations about what to do with the information gathered by the grinders and pourers. She, not Alice, might have told everyone that this was the right strain of penicillin to do battle with *Mycobacterium tuberculosis*, might have said, with some hint of humor, that ten thousand mice could now report for duty.

Her father, the colonel, had always said she was the next Marie Curie. He'd whispered in her ear, from the beginning of her time on earth, that she was someone special. She had disappointed him by falling in love with Roland. Yet if she could muster a truth for herself, it was this: she liked the grinding and the pouring. At Lockheed during the war, she had been proud to advance from working the line to drafting designs for airplane parts, but to this day she missed the metalwork, the spark of the torch, the thwack of nut on bolt. She had been among the women who had thought Lockheed would keep them after the war.

After several days of leaning back into the rhythms of rubber gloves and apron, of goggles and grinding and pouring, one day she looked up from her log and realized that she had let Roland use her to make his children for that very reason: that she liked to work with things that she could touch, that she liked objects more than ideas. Another thought followed and she banished it nearly as quickly as she removed Roland's image from her mind: that the children had been a kind of shield against the colonel. Her own children, who belonged to her and her husband, who could not and would not follow his orders, made her home into a fort that the colonel couldn't enter without a pass.

That night at dinner there was something mild and peaceful in the air. Bruce and Ed succeeded in making Helen laugh so hard that milk came through her nose. Louise even saw fit to tuck Helen in, and then to sit for a moment on the edge of Charlotte's bed, ask her what she was reading and what she liked about it.

Mother was in the living room when Louise came downstairs. She had her reading glasses on, and through the tight metal circles of their rims she examined the heel of a sock she was darning.

"It's too hot for socks," said Louise, sitting on the couch and extracting a cigarette from the black lacquer box on the coffee table and a kitchen match from a smaller lacquer box. She had begun her own collection of boxes, not to be outdone by Mother. There were boxes of all sizes tucked in corners and shelves around the house. Ivory and lacquer boxes Mother had brought back when she and the other officers' wives sailed from Manila Bay in '41. Also painted wood boxes and brightly colored glass boxes full of cardamom pods or aspirins or paper clips or what-have-yous.

"You can't help yourself," said Mother, laying her needles in her lap and pushing the enamel ashtray toward Louise's end of the coffee table. "You're always on the attack."

"Well, you're always darning the boys' socks when they won't wear them for another month or two."

"Someone around here has to prepare." She said *prepare* as if it had three syllables, two in the second half, as if she were asking God something.

Louise didn't ask what Mother expected her to ask. Didn't say prepare for what, didn't play that game they played. She sat still for a moment, blew a smoke ring. Let her eye fall on the rolltop desk beneath the map of Nantucket.

"You ought to go ahead and read them," Mother said, picking the sock back up, whisking one needle across the other.

"What?"

"That man's letters."

She ought not to be surprised anymore when Mother read her mind. "I was just thinking I should destroy them."

Mother's response was sharp, swift: "Don't you do that, Louise."

"Why don't you just tell me what's in them." She sat up and threw her left leg over her right, shifting forward as if she were preparing to take dictation.

But Mother would not take the bait either. She spoke very calmly, slowly. "They are addressed to you. From a man who gave a lot for the country that employs, feeds, and entertains you."

Louise pulled slowly on her cigarette and leaned back against the cool, pale linen of the high-backed couch.

"Read them, know something about him, tell him you're sorry for what he has suffered, and then ask him to go away."

"But why not just burn them in a pit in the yard?"

"I've already said why. It is a very small sacrifice on your part."

Louise lifted her head off the back of the couch, sat forward, and ashed her cigarette. Sacrifice. They'd used that word so often in the war years. But it was true, wasn't it? Roland and the others had done that. Thrown their bodies into the sacred pit, injected themselves into the body of the world, attacked the fascist bacteria with the penicillin of democracy. God, she thought, I'm a worse poet than Roland was.

"All right," she said, very softly. More to herself than Mother.

"Good," said Mother, holding up the sock to examine her work, then putting it in a basket by her feet and standing up. "I'm going to bed."

"Good night."

"Good night, dear."

Mother made it all the way across the red and black rug she had brought back from the Philippines and was almost in the door of her room, which was at the foot of the stairs, before she turned back with a final instruction.

"You're not to fall in love with him, Louise, not even for a moment."

"Don't be ridiculous!"

"I couldn't be more serious," said Mother, touching her fingers to her lips and blowing a good-night kiss.

Louise waited until Mother closed the door. Then she went to the rolltop desk, rolled it open, and took the thickest envelope from the top of the pile. She went to the sideboard, poured herself a stiff whiskey, and sat down to read.

From the desk of Kirstein Blunt
Managing Partner
Blunt Mills
Wilmington, Delaware
June 24, 1948

Dear Mrs. Galle,

I suspect you have your reasons for not responding to my letters. Let me be dishonest and pretend here that I understand.

I truly do not want to cause you any pain or difficulty. Yet the story I am about to tell you is one of pain and difficulty.

They tell us we now live in happier times. Truman says so, so it must be true. I feel it in the air we breathe, the suffocating stench of optimism. We want to forget, to pretend that the sun of today obliterates the years-long night. When people see me, they remember the living cost. They give a moment of pity, then they turn away. If I had burns across my face or were missing half my jaw, they might turn away more quickly. Yet it does me no good to feel that it could have been worse for me, as it was worse for so many others.

Everyone wants to know, when they see a man like me, who has paid with a portion of themselves—an eighth, let's say—a portion of the story. They wonder, for at least a fleeting moment, how I lost my leg. Well, if there hadn't been a war, or if somehow we had nipped the fascist cancer in the bud instead of letting it metastasize—well. I suspect in peace times people linger a little longer over a man with a missing leg. More people these days know at least someone with a horrible scar, someone who is living with the great sucking emptiness where someone they loved once was. There are many widows, I don't have to tell you.

But you, Mrs. Galle, are unusual.

I have an uncle who survived the *Titanic* disaster. He would never speak of it to me, until one night, when he was in his cups, he described trying to climb onto an overturned lifeboat. He kept saying he was the last possible person to get on. There was room for no other! He repeated that phrase several times. I knew then what he'd done. As I fell asleep that night, I saw the man he had to push away, the clenched fingers he uncurled, the face he pushed under the water. It was a practical matter, of course. When my uncle returned to his small town in Pennsylvania, no one would speak to him. Not because they knew what happened, but because he'd returned, but his wife had not. Women and children should be first, shouldn't they? You are our lives, what we do without you is what we must to return to the hearth.

The war is what we did for you. E. Roland Galle did it for you and for your children. He offered up his body so you could work at the National Institutes of Health, and not as some foot-bound geisha or hausfrau cleaning the kitchen and making schnitzel.

Most women seem to know that much. But you are not most women, are you, Louise Diehl Galle? As I said, I know who your father was. And you're even more than Colonel Diehl's daughter. You're a scientist these days. Perhaps you can quantify something for me.

Why did you never write your husband?

Oh, forgive me, you did write once. I was with Roland then, in Cabanatuan. You sent him two decks of cards and a set of tiddlywinks. The cards were a good thought, we used them. Being a prisoner of war is so boring you get willing to bet your boodle—that's what civilians might call loot, but translates in war time to canned pineapple and cigarettes—just for something to take your mind off your Guam blisters. But for the love of Roosevelt, Mrs. Galle, tiddlywinks are an insult! Every chip you aim that hits the mark is a day you've given over to the emperor, every one that misses is a friend who died in the march from Camp O'Donnell. Who fell into the latrine pit and suffocated.

I met Roland stateside. He made junior officer before I did, but for a time we were the same rank. I do not wax poetic when I tell you he was a finer man than I. The genuine article.

I think it was in Santa Monica when I got a load of just how genuine. We had some free time and were let loose from the base. A bunch of soldiers strutting around the pier, soon to ship out for parts unknown, you can imagine what we were looking for. We succeeded in finding some female companionship, but your husband wouldn't play. There was only one bucket for his tiddlywinks, Mrs. Galle, if you'll forgive the pun. You were it for him. He went back to the hotel to write you a letter. I think you and the children were up at Fort Lewis then.

We teased him for it. But when he showed us your picture we were all jealous. Blondes aren't usually my type, but you had that certain something. I said he ought to get you an agent. He smiled and said his Louise wasn't one for the limelight.

We got to know each other best in the worst of times, Roland and I. If that sounds Dickensenian it was, but multiply the woes of a nineteenth-century English orphan by twenty thousand and you'll start to get the point.

If all the little boys in the world dreaming of being soldiers knew that they would one day kill for a ham sandwich or a piece of pie, we'd barely ever get anything done, would we? We were already on half-rations when MacArthur decided not to come back for us. At Camp O'Donnell, our fantasies had already shifted, well before the Japs landed, from the likes of you, Louise Diehl Galle, to the likes of ham on rye. I dreamed of my mama's chicken fricassee for days on end before I lost the energy to dream at all.

Listen. I don't expect you to have any idea what it's like to starve slowly over the course of years. There may be a sort of grace to it, if a guy were a saint. But I never met a saint, though E. Roland Galle was close. I mean that in all sincerity.

You were his reason and his light for so very long. When the Japs landed, we were hardly ready, though we got in a few good licks. Major E. Roland Galle himself and I tied dynamite to ropes, swung them in the air like little Davies aiming for Goliath (not to imply here that the underdog had a chance). The Japs were hiding in caves waiting for the arrival of their full contingent. We stood on top of a hill, lit the sticks, swung them up and around a long arc and down over and into the mouth of the cave. We relished that explosion and those screams, but not for long.

When we discovered that that feeling of dread was not just our bile eating us from the inside out but was our fear becoming real—there would be no backup—we went about smashing windshields and sugaring gas tanks. We destroyed the radio equipment last, after sending our final message. I wanted to hide it, keep some hope of contact, but there was no time. To tell the truth (my aim on this page) we took some sick pleasure in smashing and destroying the crap equipment we'd been given. We were aiming at Jap planes with Howitzers that hadn't seen combat since 1918. You don't get that story in the newsreels.

It became pretty clear pretty quick that Hirohito hadn't had the

Geneva conventions translated into Japanese. They kept us outside in the blazing sun for days before we even began to move. Complainers received a response from a bayonet.

Here's the part of the story you want to hear. E. Roland Galle saved more than one life on that scenic march through the Bataan peninsula. He did it partly with your picture. Yes, he kept it clean against remarkable odds. I touched your face like it was my talisman too.

But he truly saved me with a piece of candy. When I was at my weakest, when I was ready to fall down from exhaustion, the little bit of hoarhound he had and shared kept me from my death. Because those who fell did not get up. One soldier, Hobson I think was his name, fell into the latrine pit and got stuck. Major E. Roland Galle went in after him and pulled him out. As it happened the guard was busy beheading another soldier and did not notice your husband's foolhardy bravery.

I had almost fainted when he split the candy with me. Imagine the boy dreaming of war eating twice as much candy in half as much time. I can see him now, singing pow pow. Mowing down Comanches in his backyard. Roland told me about your children too. For the first time in my life, I was jealous of a settled man.

There are too many stories to tell here. Suffice it to say we survived, made it to Cabanatuan. That was where a different hell began. I had my own but I'm telling you about his.

Because, Mrs. Galle, when you did not write you fell. You were no longer an angel, and when you fell you took him with you.

The enemy saw his value. They made him the prisoners' liaison. They thought he was trustworthy to distribute supplies. They even thought he'd rat out those who participated in the black market. But he wouldn't even give up the Navy prisoners and their secret store of canned pineapple. He did get first dibs on tobacco. I was lucky enough, he shared that with me too.

One night, after we had been two years or so at Cabanatuan, living with our hearts and souls carefully billeted away, your husband wept like a baby. They don't tell you about that in the newsreels either. I tell you because there is no shame in it. I tell you because you should be ashamed.

For months on end, when I visited him in the small dark office the prison guards had given him, Roland would talk about you. He'd tell me stories of your early days. How he roomed with your brother Bruce

(God rest his soul) at West Point. How he knew, the moment you walked in the room, that you would be his wife. He shared news of you—that you were working at Lockheed and had been on the radio, being interviewed about your designs for airplane parts. He would talk about how healthy the children were, though the baby he'd barely met was colicky. In all the months we'd nearly died together, he had pretended he was getting this news from you.

But that night, when the word coming our way was that we were to be shipped out, and even he didn't know where to, he took me deeper into his confidence. He had managed to get his hands on a fifth of whiskey and invited me to share a snort. I kept my pants tied on with string at that point, so you can imagine it didn't take much to get tight.

He had managed actual Lucky Strikes, fresh smokes. So much better than the stale damp schwag we bastards of Bataan got used to. I was savoring the taste of home when I saw the first teardrop fall onto the desk. I didn't ask him what was wrong. I didn't want to embarrass him.

I asked him to tell me again the story of how you met. The one about you hiding the spider in your brother's drinking glass and enlisting Roland in the joke. But that cued him to break down completely.

I tried to let him have some privacy, but he told me stay, stay. Then he told me that anything he learned about you since Camp O'Donnell he had learned from his mother, who in turn had learned things from your mother. His mother wrote him all the time. He wrote you every day, though he didn't send them all.

I just want, he cried, one whole letter from her. Telling me today Helen walked, telling me today we had meatloaf. I just want to see the pretty scene, the children around the table, my beautiful wife wiping her hands on her apron.

But you would not give that, Mrs. Galle. And then he gave me the photo of you. He wouldn't take no for an answer. He was a monk who'd lost the holy spirit.

Here's the thing, he might have lived if you had written. Say what you like about fate or calamity or acts of God. A man like Roland could have lived if he'd had hope. When we were packed onto the *Oryoku Maru* and set adrift, I lost sight of Roland for a while.

When the ship was hit and it was clear we were going down, I saw Roland again. He stood by a rift in the hold. He helped three men out into the water before he helped me. I told him he had to jump and jump now! I tried to take him with me, but he slipped my grasp. Black smoke and orange flame, but I could see his face, Mrs. Galle. Again, I gestured to him to jump. He looked right at me. His eyes had lost their light. He shook his head and went down with the ship.

In the name of Major E. Roland Galle, I want to know why you took his hope. I want to know why you made a lie of your pretty face. What could you possibly have to do that was more important than writing to the man who put you above all creatures in the world?

When I came back here to run my family's business, I could not stop thinking of how cold beauties like you can blind us foolish men, who would lay down our lives just to make you smile. You made America seem false to me, and it has not been the same to me since.

Yours most sincerely,
Kit Blunt

Purple Heart

July 1964

Charlotte woke too close to luncheon time to really plan out what she was going to say to Louise. Louise always called lunch *luncheon* when she came to New York. They always met at Mitchell's, a place in midtown that had been around since the twenties. They sat in red leather booths with dark wood paneling and chose from a long and weighty menu listing things like squab and shad roe, along with pastrami on rye and matzoh ball soup. The Dunnes and the Crownes themselves met there with artists and writers. Charlotte had seen Jean Stafford there once, alone in a corner booth, smoking and frowning, and Shirley Jackson shaking hands with the older Dunne, then sitting down and tucking into a piece of key lime pie.

Charlotte woke far too close to luncheon time to rehearse. To sit with her coffee and cigarette and write out her list, craft her approach to Louise. Her defense, as she thought of it. She had barely enough time to shower and dress—number one, appear washed and composed—before she had to leave. She tried to list mentally as she brushed her hair. She wore it simply these days, chin length and curling lightly around her ears. Not bothering to straighten it and shape it as she had in her early days at Dunne and Crowne.

Number two, pace yourself. Don't offer information, let her ask. Number three, be brisk! Tell her you're fine! Show her that getting fired is really not a big deal. You didn't want to work there anyway. It was such a stuffy place. Don't tell her they were going to promote you, much as you would like her to know, don't play that little good report card game, you are done with that! And anyway, you want to help people. The way you did at the Montgomery County Home for Unwed Mothers. Yes, that was a filing job, but you were learning case management. You got to talk to the young women, Negro and white, who were in trouble. It meant a lot to you to help. Funny that those young women had your opposite problem—having been used by love or nature, overtaken by its bounty, rather than cut off from it like you. Rather than placed in the void you are navigating now. Number four, do not, under any circumstances, tell Louise what Dr. Bedford said. Number four, no, number five, under no circumstances mention that you have spent most of the last week constructing mobiles and winged bicycles from the pile of wire coat hangers you found in front of your building. Six, under even fewer circumstances are you to tell her that your current job prospects include transporting, on the subway, rough diamonds from a wholesaler in Morningside Heights to a jeweler on West Thirty-Seventh. Though actually it seemed that Katie's uncle couldn't use you anyway. Number seven, under no possible circumstances are you to say that you have absolutely no job prospects whatsoever.

"Okay, okay, okay," Charlotte muttered softly. I'll wear pants. Louise will see and right away know that I'm not working at Dunne and Crowne. So, she won't be surprised when I tell her. And I'll be comfortable at the very least. She buttoned a lime-green sleeveless blouse and zipped up her cream-colored capris. Then she wasted precious minutes tying and untying a silk color-block scarf around her head. Jesus Christ! She threw the scarf across the room, then picked it up and tied it as fetchingly as she could. She stepped into the hall. There was Gil.

"Hello," said Daisy's dyke. With her deep blue eyes and the cobweb dust of silver in her short-cropped hair.

"Hi," said Charlotte, locking her door.

"How's the artist?"

Charlotte realized with a start that her mental list didn't include a word about Ed. He was supposed to tell Louise what had happened to him, but he had called Charlotte last night to say he wouldn't make it to luncheon.

"In bed with a cold."

"She looks all right to me," said Gil, giving Charlotte the once over. Why did she like the way Gil took her in? So frankly, as if lust were nothing to fear.

"Oh, you mean me."

"Yes, you." Just then Daisy's door opened. She was wearing a flowered kimono, eyebrow pencil, and a scowl. Charlotte nodded at her neighbor, then made her way down the narrow stairs to the street.

After two nights at Bellevue, Ed had gotten out with the approved diagnosis of alcohol-induced psychosis. It was recommended that he stop drinking altogether, a proscription he had celebrated with Char-

lotte and Billy at an Irish tavern two blocks from the hospital. In the
course of a week, he was off the hook with the League. Billy's uncle
the lawyer was, apparently, very effective. It seemed there would be no
charges brought, but Ed could not return, though Billy was still in.

As she walked to the train Charlotte began again. Eight? Nine? Under no circumstances, no circumstances! Are you to blurt out Ed's story.
Let Louise ask. Act like you thought she knew already, like you believed
that Ed was going to tell her himself. Ten. Tell her, firmly, that you will
no longer give money to Ed. That you are resigning your role as Louise's
partner in supporting Ed's career. And not just because you're running
out of funds.

In Mitchell's shiny window she caught a glimpse of herself. Her hair
tousling around the scarf and her cat's-eye glasses. The artist. You. For
a moment, she believed it.

But then she saw Louise. Her mother was sitting in the booth, reading the newspaper the way a man would, arms wide to contain its full
width, her white-gold hair swept back from her forehead. She looked
as beautiful and as absorbed as she had in the famous photo of her
in the *Saturday Evening Post* back in '43. Helen, Bruce, and Ed all had
framed copies of the picture of their mother, dressed in gloves and
goggles, working a lathe at Lockheed. The perfect Rosie the Riveter.
But even better—she hadn't just worked the line, she had become a sort
of industrial designer, figuring out the best way to break an airplane
into its component parts. She had gotten some sort of commendation
and even been interviewed on the radio. Charlotte remembered Helen
sitting on her lap in the overstuffed chair, the boys and Granny piled
on the couch, all of them crowded around the radio in their rented
house in Los Angeles. What magic Louise was to them then, her voice
humming through the wires!

Louise lowered the paper, folded it, and placed it on the table, then
turned up her cheek to receive Charlotte's kiss. Before Charlotte sat all
the way down in the booth, she began spilling the story of faking the
index, as if it were a joke. And then she was telling several stories, all at
once. And looking down at the menu, and then back up at Louise.

"Well, I hadn't slept well you see. Or I guess I just...I didn't think of
the consequences," said Charlotte. "I wasn't thinking."

"Clearly not," Louise said. "Let's have a drink. What time do you
have to go back?"

"That's just the point, Mother, I don't have to go back at all. They don't want me."

"Of course, you've seen to that." Louise looked at her watch. "Where is Ed?"

"I told you, he's not coming."

"You didn't say that."

"I did, Mother. I said Ed called last night to tell me he has a horrible cold."

"You didn't say that."

"But I did, just a moment ago."

"Well, I suppose I didn't hear you."

"That's because you don't listen," said Charlotte, picking up the menu with shaking hands. She kept her eyes on the list of sandwiches. Louise didn't miss a beat.

"Is this about money?"

"Is what?"

"Are you going to ask me for money?"

"Well, I wouldn't mind some, truthfully."

"I don't have a lot to spare at the moment, Charlotte. But if things are really dire—"

The waiter appeared. Louise ordered cream of asparagus soup, Charlotte ordered a Reuben. When the waiter left Charlotte waited for Louise to make a comment about her weight, but the comment didn't come. Charlotte should know by now that Louise never took a shot when she was ready for it.

"No, not dire," said Charlotte, struck suddenly by a vision of Luigi (or whatever his name was) ordering a Reuben. His pockets stuffed with the loose bills and change of her rainy-day fund. In the weeks since she'd been fired, she'd seen him twice at the Pussycat, smirking at her from across the bar. Daring her to ask for anything he'd taken from her.

"But there's Ed now!" Louise was waving at the entrance.

It was Ed indeed, waving and walking toward them eagerly. His eyes were puffy and red, Charlotte gave him that much, he could actually have a cold. Almost as much as a hangover.

"Well, look at you! You look well enough," said Louise.

"Why shouldn't I be?" asked Ed, squeezing in next to Charlotte.

"Charlotte said you called to tell her you have a cold and weren't coming."

"Lottie doesn't listen," said Ed. "I didn't say I wouldn't be here. I do have a bit of a chill though."

"So, it's not so rotten after all," said Charlotte.

"What?" Ed pulled the ashtray toward him and lit a cigarette.

"You said, and I quote, 'I have a rotten cold and won't make it out of bed today or tomorrow.'"

Louise put the back of her hand to Ed's forehead.

"No fever. A bit rheumy-eyed, but I think our boy is all right," she said.

"In spite of getting kicked out of the League for almost burning the place down," said Charlotte. If she was going to spill one part, she would spill them all. Louise didn't miss a beat.

"Don't try to shock me, Charlotte. I know all about it. Ed told me what happened."

"All right enough for Paris," said Ed.

"Paris?"

"Mother's got connections."

Charlotte's Reuben arrived. She stared at it. She did not say, What the hell are you talking about?

"Yes," said Louise. "Do you remember my boss from the early days at the NIH, Harry Leopold?"

Charlotte picked up her sandwich and took a big, unladylike bite. She nodded.

"His son is a professor at the Sorbonne, an archaeologist, and he's going off to Iceland for a year," said Louise, stirring her soup. "He's well enough off that he just wants someone to stay in his apartment, rather than let it to a stranger."

Someday, Charlotte thought, she would find a way to mock Louise for her Britishisms—to let, indeed. Her Frenchisms too. What American called mayonnaise "my-o-naze"?

"Mother thinks a change of scene will do me good, and I couldn't agree more," said Ed.

"Let's have a drink to that!" Louise waved over the waiter and ordered martinis for everyone, without asking. She asked the waiter to replace one of the olives with a pearl onion, the way she always did. Ed ordered a pastrami on rye.

"I'll read Proust and start painting again."

"Yes, we'll find you a studio, won't we, Charlotte?"

Charlotte pointed to her mouth, which was full of Reuben.

"Lottie picks perfect moments not to talk with her mouth full," said Ed, elbowing her as if they were children.

Charlotte swallowed hard. She would say it, she would. Number nine.

"You mean we'll pay for a studio for Ed." Her voice sounded distant to her, flat. She wanted to say Ed's not crazy, and he doesn't need us. He could get a job. Her mouth was suddenly dry. "I told you, I lost my job."

"Well, you'll get another, dear. You're very smart."

The martinis arrived. Louise raised her glass. Charlotte and Ed raised theirs.

"To new beginnings!" said Louise, grinning a glorious Hollywood grin.

THE RETURN

Metal burns upon the sea
You are not done with me

My bones dispersed across the floor
Black water blots my soldier's lore.

KISS OF DEATH

JULY 1948

She did not read it twice. She did not destroy it.

Louise folded Kit's letter and placed it back in its envelope, which she folded in half and in half again, and placed it in the far-left drawer of the rolltop desk. Then she took hold of the little latch and began pulling the rolled top, which had been open for years, down. It got stuck about a third of the way.

She controlled herself at first. Jiggling it. Cursing softly. Then loudly, stupidly, she slapped it as if it were the face of someone smug. The metal latch tore a little at the skin of her palm. "Damn me!" she yelled. But no one woke.

The house was quiet around her. That was what Louise had wanted, a house in a quiet place to raise her children. Or for Mother to raise them. She had found that for them, had found herself a job at this big, important place. First she had made herself important at Lockheed, had risen up from working the line. Had shown them how her mind—Father always said your big, glorious mind—how her big, glorious mind could envision every aspect of a plane's wing, break it down, and reassemble it more efficiently. And because she had done that, because she had re-made the wings of bombers, made them better and faster, she'd earned her reputation as smart, direct. Her reputation for handling herself, for handling whatever came to her. And then she had known people who had known people at the new National Institutes of Health. She knew her way around a chemical column, around weights and measures, and she could show them what she knew without any hesitation.

I have done this for them, Roland. Once she began addressing him, she knew she would not stop. She carried the empty tumbler to the sideboard. The cut glass was heavy in her hand. She had bought it herself. This is mine, Roland. She took the stopper out of the decanter, poured a second stiff drink. She gulped and spoke to Roland, let him emerge from where she kept him—from that small, tight box in her chest. But she kept the actual box in the bottom drawer of the rolltop desk. It was filled with neat bundles of his letters and the three telegrams that announced his death—first to regret to inform her, the second to regret that the first was sent in error, the third to regret that the second was sent in error—the actual box she kept locked.

Just then, in equal measure, she wanted and did not want to open that box. She gulped again. Then froze. Began to whisper. To let the rolltop desk be her witness.

They are not yours anymore, Roland. The children are mine. Mother cares for them by rote, the way she does for Tuna, the way she did for me and Bruce and Father. She cares for them, but they're not hers. I wasn't hers. I was his. I belonged to Father until I belonged to you. He believed in me, in my mind. He wanted me to keep going, to get advanced degrees, to be his very own Marie Curie.

Her voice was getting louder. Well, we shut that door, didn't we, Roland? We littered my path with nappies, didn't we?

That Blunt. He was the one making her angry. As if she didn't write! She must have. More than once. As if she could have written more than she did. When she knew so well that Roland would not survive.

She felt wildly certain that she had had a reason. Or that her reason was as simple as her own survival. The tumbler felt too heavy in her hand. She put it down. Reached into the pigeonhole that held the key to the locked box in the bottom drawer. Pulled out the drawer, opened the box, and took out the last of Roland's letters. She resisted the urge to take the letter to her room, to prop herself with pillows as she read it, to nurse the wound it would give. No, she would turn on the light in the dining room that she paid for and read it at the dark wood table that Mother had brought back when she sailed from Manila Bay in '41. She knew that she would want to stop reading, that every word would make her want to turn away, to refill her tumbler. To step away. But she would read it again, right now, every word. As she had done just once before.

Letter to the Wife of Major E. Roland Galle
Extracted from official records maintained by him and con-
tained therein
Cabanatuan, P.I.
March 1943

Sweetest Love,
    My heart aches. I understand now that we may never again see one another on Earth. I have to write that, in the hope

that in writing it, I can somehow relieve this terrible
dread. I want you to feel what I do, and to understand this:
we are together, always. God brought us together, and in Him
we are eternal. I know that you try on faith and prefer science, but whether or not you bring the children to church,
I pray that you believe we are one, forever.

Next to being without you, living so closely with others
is the hardest thing for me in this prison. When we were on
the road, I thought nothing of stepping away from the officers' mess to join the men. I liked to remember my earlier
days, elbow to elbow. No possibility of giving orders, only
of obeying them. Now I cling to what small privilege I have,
typing in this storeroom where I am told to keep records and
to report to the XXX emperor's children, who jab me with
their guns, for no reason at all. But I did not intend to
complain. Because I do have faith, and that sustains me. I
know our cause is just, and that if I die, I die proudly,
for the place I call home is His under the canopy of heaven.

It's nearly a year since my capture, and since '41 I have
had nothing from XXX you but one telegram and that package
that came six months ago. I know that letters don't always
get through. But from my mother I have had six letters in
that time. Once she included a letter you had written to
her, telling her about your Christmas of '42, with the
children. I felt so privileged, darling, to catch a glimpse
of the shining tree and the pudding you and Martha made.
Oh, darling, I try not to feel this bitterness, but it is a
sore medicine, hearing second hand about the joy that was
once mine. You were smart enough to include in your package
those beautiful pictures. But your note was so brief, and
contained nothing of you, of your days. It could have been
written to anyone. The men were grateful for the game set,
you made yourself quite popular among them. And of course,
any who come to see me, if they are lucky, are allowed a
glimpse of the pictures. I only show them the ones with the
children. I keep the one of you on the boat in Long Island
Sound to myself.

Do you remember, darling, the first time we spent the
night? At the Astor, you sighed in my arms. You said, "Oh
God, you have done me good!" I was so honored to be your
first, to join with you and make a real woman of you. I
think of that so often, sometimes as I fall asleep I swear
I can smell you, a ghost scent in my pillow. I have written
you so often of my dreams of you, you with a baby in each
arm, you with the bald eagle on your shoulder. Do you dream
of me, darling? I know, I am childish, begging and crying

for your attention. I shall stop now and leave it to God. I
don't know when I forgot how to write. I keep thinking that
if I could put together the right sentence you would answer
me. More than a sentence, perhaps. Perhaps a poem, if I
could just write the poem that I know is in me. I will bring
it to you, hear me, dearest! Not even death can stop me.

(Between these lines, another year has passed. It is now April, 1944.)

I keep trying to write and finding my words so weak.
Months go by, and I take comfort in the pictures, and in the
hope that you are happy, darling. I believe that you can and
should be happy, with or without me. And then I wonder, has
there been a mistake? Do you think that I am already dead?
Perhaps none of my letters to you in the last year and half
have gotten through.

I write this believing it will get to you. I don't mail
it, but leave it in the cupboard here, in the tiny storeroom they have given me for an office. We are leaving soon.
Though I am the adjutant and sometimes privy to the plans
made by our overseers, I don't know where to. But I can
tell that the letters will not go out as they normally do.
I pray that this letter will be found when our troops are
triumphant at last.

In case we don't meet again on this Earth, I have written
this for Edward. Please share it with him. The others are
so young, but I thought our Eddie might understand. I trust
that you will choose rightly for him and all the children
and so have no particular request regarding their education.

To Edward: you are the oldest, and you must behave as
such. First and foremost, listen to your mother, obey her
laws. The laws we choose to obey define us, son. If someone
tells you that there are no laws worth adhering to, they
are inviting you to a life of hopeless wandering. More than
that, they are inviting you to follow a lie. Because in
wandering, we follow the laws of wandering. You must protect
the others. You must watch over Charlotte especially, keep
a place for her in the home you build in the future. She
is a sensitive child and will be a vulnerable woman. And
today, help her to help your mother and grandmother, so that
she and you can be examples to all. And here is something
very important, son: as you grow you will be attracted to
women, and they to you. Always respect them, always consider
their feelings. Don't run around, son; don't flatter when
you don't mean it, and don't revel in false attention. Aim
toward a good marriage, a real marriage, of mind and spirit
first, and then of body. And when the others are old enough,

please pass these messages to them. Be honor bound, be dedicated to truth (which is beauty as the poet said).

There is more I would like to say to them all, darling. And so much more I want to say to you. If only you knew how much I crave a word from you, more even than a lock of your hair. I feel you would send me a real letter if you knew how I could live on it, how it would be better than food. Or if I could write like Yeats, even from beyond the grave, you would write to me! Oh, but I am peevish! And possibly mad. Forgive me. I am grateful for the glimpses of you my mother shares. I am so proud of you and how wonderful that you were on the radio. Though I confess I don't understand why a worker from Lockheed would be on the radio. Industrial designer, I should say, that is the title they've given you. I confess I don't understand what that is.

What is hardest to bear now is not even the elbow to elbow, the cheek and jowl with other men. Our sickly bodies have become a joke to us. We must laugh or we cannot live. But when we are closest to giving up, to feeling our spirits depart from us, it is because we fear we shall never tell our stories to you, to all of you, dear. I mean you and all like you, all our wives, all our pretty ones. There is hope among us. We feel we are now likely to live through. We have survived the Bataan, when about sixty percent of our personnel did not. That must mean luck, mustn't it? Please ignore me, darling, I am working my peevishness out on you.

I have enclosed a poem. I have put all that I could muster into it. I have tried to serve what moves me, my faith in God and country. And you, darling. You. There is no one in the world like you. As I wrote this, I heard you reading it back to me, tried to imagine the places where you would shake your head and say, "No, dear, that line has no music." It's true, and it has no proper form either. But I have hope, darling, that if I keep tapping away at this typewriter, something true will come out.

As Yeats says, one man loved the pilgrim soul in you. I am that one who loves you now and forever, though my face may soon be hid amid a crowd of stars. For you I will try, again and again, to write a decent line. I will try and try and try, even if I first must die. You belittle me now, laugh at my foolish rhyme. My pearl, am I the oyster you discard? You made a shell of me.

But I do mean it, when I beg of you, darling Blondie, be happy.

Your own,
Roland

```
The Test
For you, here, near, and always, if waiting is
    required
I will wait. If God has spoken, forever tired
And never, I shall wait. No more to see
The sky arcing free, I beg it carry me
Home. The word I cannot say.

No more shall we together breathe
The sap-scent pines, sharp and clean.
Death, thou cheat-hound, I seethe
Forgetting you and I are seen.

For we have truly loved, and having loved truly,
Our love infinite cannot be divided, as infinity
Cannot be approached, but recedes unduly
So as two we remain one, in our affinity.
```

At the sound of Tuna's nails on the floor, Louise started and looked up from the worn pages. The dog came into the room and butted her head against Louise's leg. She pushed herself away from the table and reached down to scratch the pointy fob of dog skull. Held the pitched bone in her fingers and squeezed. Then she sat down on the carpet and took Tuna's two ears and held them together underneath the dog's chin.

"Tuna, you're the woman of my dreams. You are the perfect picture of a dog."

Tuna whimpered, then licked Louise's nose with a long slice-of-ham tongue.

"You need to go out?" She got up and followed the dog into the kitchen, letting her out the back door. She reached for a cigarette from the box on the windowsill but stopped herself. There was something else she wanted. The colonel's pipe was what this moment required.

Louise opened the door to the narrow closet and took out a step stool. She stepped on it, opened the cupboard above the refrigerator, and took down the smooth wooden box with its neat geometric inlay of brown and blond wood. Inside, couched in red velvet, was Father's meerschaum pipe, the bowl shaped like a dragon's wild-whiskered head. She opened the red velvet pouch and took out the fragrant tobacco, tamped it into the bowl and lit it with a kitchen match. Then she stepped out onto the back porch.

A light, fine rain had cooled the air, and the leaves of the magnolia tree dripped onto the porch railing. There was enough moonlight that she could see the dog sniffing and picking her way through the yard. She blew the smoke through her nose in two fine streams that seemed to cool her mood, the quality of which she could not name. There was frustration in it. A measure of heat along with the dark weight that she felt on rereading that lonely thing. For a moment she thought she should burn that letter, all his letters. Let them be a quick bright flame in the dark, like her poor husband's life. But the itch of frustration returned.

"It was you, Roland, whose letters could have been written by any-one. To anyone," she said aloud. "Don't you know I am not good?"

She dragged a bit too hard on the pipe, as if to quell the itch of frus-tration with an actual itch in her throat. Then she let the thoughts come.

Roland, everyone who looks at our family sees the perfect picture of a family—a war family, that is. Your fatherless children beam, and Mother and I are the picture of widows who carry on. During the war I was exactly what I ought to have been. Except what you wanted me to be. Because I never really was that.

There was so much to tell you, Roland. Yet I had nothing to say. I was living, not talking about it. And you were not going to live, I knew that. And Mother was always hovering, giving me the paper, telling me what to write. Telling me what was right. But long before you were captured, from the earliest moments of the war, even before we were in it, I had already lost a portion of hope.

Even after Bruce died in '39, we had hope. It seemed that he had died for something, even then. You believed in the army and in duty, how you laid claim to soldiering. You, the poet in training, told us that Bruce hadn't wasted himself. You comforted us. Someone had to test the bombs. I worked hard not to think about my brother, not to let his sudden absence distract me from caring for the children, who were my only job then. Mother and Father were in California then, and we were at Fort Lewis. Every time Mother called or wrote, she told the story again—that Bruce had radioed in from his flight above Honolulu to say, Tell my wife I'll be home for dinner. Two minutes later the bomb went off in the hold. My brother, handsome and dutiful, hot cinders falling through the clouds.

Working at Lockheed was the cure for my grief. Everyone was full

of purpose and muscle. But then we were hit again when Corregidor
fell and Father was taken. I could not think, it didn't bear thinking that
Father, taller, stronger, smarter Father, that he should be captured, that
he should be sick. That he should live through so much only to die
of moist beriberi. To starve to death in a prison camp full of officers
so sick and weak they fought over a spring onion. Mother told me he
had discovered that the snails that crawled the yard were edible. His
letters to her had something real in them. I couldn't write to him either,
Roland. The blank page was like a door I needed to keep shut.

My own thoughts felt like an infection. I couldn't afford to be sick.
In my head this drumbeat, this rhythm, that said you were lost forever
too. I knew it from the minute I learned you were captured. But I kept
making better wings. In the mornings Mother and I would not let our
eyes meet over the children's heads, even for a few extra seconds. We
kept in our worry, spoke in short sentences about swing shifts and gro-
ceries.

Father didn't want me to marry you or anyone, Roland. Oh, he gave
you a glad hand and a welcome. But I knew he was disappointed. It was
the end of his dream of me, the end of our secret. I never told you,
Roland, of Father and me, of our secret hours. You freed me from him.
I planted your seed in me and crowded Father out. In the early days I
thought of you all the time, but then I had to stop. There was not room
in me to think about you as I drove to the plant, as I punched the clock,
as I raised and lowered the lathe. I was tired all the time. Don't you
see? I joined the other women in coveralls, fought with them. And as
Father had always told me, I was better than them, and so I rose out of
the line and became a designer. I did that for our country, Roland. Our
country needed me too. You thought that only you needed me, that I
only mattered to our little home.

You left me, Roland, again and again. On your glorious maneuvers!
You, Bruce, Father, you all left me. Not only that, you didn't see that I
was a soldier too.

Standing on her own porch in 1948, Louise leaned against the rail
and tried to go back in time. She used her will to make it real, to feel
the thin paper of the victory mail, to feel herself pulling the lever of
pen, drawing the ink from the inkwell, writing his name. *Dearest Roland...* She willed his vision of her into being, the image of a woman
who, after a long day at the plant, drove home and unfolded the blue

paper and scratched the surface with the nib. Who wrote to her prisoner husband about bread and children. Her mind was full of the soot of the plant, the sound of the torch being lit, the hum of the soldering iron, the clamor of metal on metal. But she should have written about Charlotte's good grades and Ed's violin recital, about Bruce and Helen climbing a tree and getting stuck like a pair of cats. Instead of what was more real to her—what happened at the plant, like the time a wing she had designed slipped its rigging and killed a young woman who had that morning punched in for the first time.

If Louise tried hard enough, she might convince herself of this delusion, that she had been the woman Roland wanted her to be, not the woman she was. The woman he had enchanted away from the realms of molecules and into a world of tiny hands and sucking mouths. But the war had turned her away from those mother-realms, just as it had taken him. Because she was a woman who worked like a man, and after work, drank like a man. Who held her silence and paid the rent, and when Mother came back from Manila, Louise left the nose wiping and vegetable chopping to her. For a moment Louise could hold the images together in her mind, believe them both, that she was Roland's sweetheart, his counterweight, and an industrial designer. Just as she had believed as a girl of sixteen that she was both a perfect student, virginal and correct, and a young woman who had tasted her father's tongue. That she was a dynamo on the tennis court and fixed as a statue in their secret temple.

"Dearest Roland," said Louise to the wet air, as if she were finally ready to tell him of her days.

As if in response there was a rustling along the edge of the fence. Tuna was all the way down at the base of the hill, snuffling through the ivy. A cloud passed over the moon and the light became fuller. Near the fence a tall figure, the glowing cherry of a cigarette. Louise's stomach lurched.

"What rolled?" asked the figure, who was, after all, her neighbor Dr. Gasparyan.

"Oh! You startled me." They had been neighbors for nearly three years, but she still didn't know his first name, this man who had barely escaped the rape of Armenia.

"Nice night," he said. He had rarely spoken more than two words to her at a time.

"Yes."

"Good for smoking."

"Yes," said Louise, feeling suddenly giddy that her strange silent neighbor would speak to her in his heavy accent that smacked of barren fields and rusted gates.

"My wife says smoking is good for forgetting."

"She might be right." Louise tried to think of something else to say to keep him talking, to keep herself from asking for excuses from the dead.

"Good night," he said, before she could. He turned and walked away.

Just then Tuna scrambled up on the porch and dropped a headless, pregnant squirrel at her feet. Through the gash in its side, she could make out four baby heads, blue pollywogs in the moonlight. "Drop it," she yelled, reaching for the dog's neck. But Tuna had shown her prize, and now would claim it. The dog ran back down the steps to bury it in the yard.

Louise did not try to chase her but lit the pipe once more.

Later, when she met Kit Blunt to answer his question, she would remember that squirrel body, so full of potential. She would remember and tell so many things about the war days. All sorts of things she had not spoken of before but had kept so carefully locked away.

Purple Heart

July 1964

Charlotte was struggling with her only clean brassiere when Katie buzzed. She left it on backward, with the clasp in front, straps hanging, and opened the door wearing only it and a half-slip.

"Vogue-ready, as always," said Katie, who wore a turquoise shift and gold sandals. She was almost Charlotte's opposite in looks—petite and olive skinned, with light brown hair and dark eyes. "I brought wine. Should we drink it here or wait for Ed's?"

"Please. You know where the opener is."

Katie stepped toward the kitchen, but stopped in front of the coffee table, which was entirely covered by a mass of twisted coat hanger wire.

"Geez, Lottie, you've been busy."

"Good garbage luck. Huge pile of coat hangers just asking to be turned into—something. I think I need tools. I also need tools to get these volumes into their bindings." They had a running joke about Charlotte's rack as a set of encyclopedias.

Katie passed Charlotte a jam jar of wine and sat on the love seat. Charlotte gulped a gulp, then turned the brassiere buckets to the front, bent at the waist and attempted to tuck herself in. She levered her arms through the straps and stood up.

"That's some serious hardware," said Katie, admiring the torpedoed tips.

"The shop girl made it look easy, but I can't quite get it so it doesn't pinch." Once more she freed her shoulders and turned the clasp around and changed the hook and eye. Once more she adjusted the straps. Again she turned the cups back to the front. Her breasts were hard and tender and full. With the flat of one palm and then the other, she lifted each mound of flesh over the wire. She felt the bite of the contraption's scalloped edge as she levered the straps into place once more.

"Isn't it supposed to pinch?" asked Katie, lunging into the kitchen area to light two cigarettes on the stove. "You didn't buy that thing for comfort, did you?"

"The shop girl called it modern."

"Modern? Like a horseless carriage?"

"Exactly," said Charlotte, taking a drag from the cigarette that Katie held out to her, blowing smoke out with her pronouncement. "Straight out of the industrial revolution. Ready to torture tender bodies like a threshing machine raping the earth, bringing tits from their small farms to the cities to beg for art as a reprieve from the relentless machinations of progress."

"Geez," Katie said, watching Charlotte struggle. "Your volumes sure are voluminous."

"Christ," said Charlotte, admiring her substantial and now torpe-do-shaped rack in the mirror. "Get a load of those dangling modifiers!"

Katie laughed so hard that red wine came streaming out her nose and spilled on her dress.

"Shit!"

"Don't worry, that's just about brooch-size," said Charlotte, pulling out a dresser drawer. "I'll find you something. I don't know why we're fussing, it's just Ed's."

"Yeah, who'll be there anyway?"

"The usuals, I imagine." Charlotte handed Katie a rhinestone brooch that looked like it belonged on top of a Christmas tree. Katie shrugged and pinned it over the stain.

"When does he go off to Paris?"

"We're not sure—has to do with Louise's friend's son and his plans or something."

"And how are you, Charlotte?" Katie asked, in that way she had, her sudden, disarming seriousness. They both knew that Charlotte had been avoiding Katie. They had hardly seen each other in the weeks since Charlotte was fired.

"I'm fine, other than the fact that I'm running out of money and—" She was going to say having nightmares but stopped herself. They weren't nightmares, exactly, were they? They were something else. Experiences.

"It must be so hard."

"What, relying on you for job leads?" teased Charlotte. She slipped her reliable black cocktail dress on over her head, then turned to let Katie zip her up.

"I mean about your—"

"My useless uterus?"

"I just think you might want to talk about it."

"What's there to say? Plenty of women don't have children." She felt a dull pain in her belly as if on cue.

"Well, maybe the doctor's wrong. You should really get a second opinion."

"Look, it's all right, Katie."

"But—"

"Really, you go ahead and get married and move to the suburbs. I'll stick around here and learn to motorize my mobiles. And every so often we'll trade places. I'll make your kids' lunches and you can do low-wage work and cut your fingers on wires and try to get men to look you in the face when they tell you women can't make art."

She had gone too far. Katie was laughing a little, but her eyes were sad.

"Come on, that doesn't mean you won't find a husband."

"I thought we didn't care about that anyway. Weren't we going to be independent? Weren't we going down to Mississippi? Go find Chaney, Goodman, and Schwerner and set things to rights?"

"We could still," said Katie. There was a touch of pity in her voice. "Anyway, your life's not over because I have a boyfriend. You're too wonderful not to find love."

"Oh, shut up and drink!"

Charlotte couldn't bear pity. Or too much kindness. Or too much fantasy, or at any rate, only a certain kind of fantasy, the mobiles she was making, and the bigger sculptures she was beginning to imagine, the interlocking wires that were starting to make sense. But she hadn't told Katie how she spent her days bending coat hangers, how she had filled her sketch book with what the wires would become. She drank down the wine and shuffled her friend out the door.

Sounds of smoke-choked laughter and high drunken seriousness spilled out onto Forty-Eighth Street from Ed's window. Charlotte and Katie stepped inside, into the party air, that particular heat where whiskey meets cigarette.

Brad was there, of course. He should have forgotten their one night together, but he never seemed to. When he caught her gaze he always held it too long, raised just one corner of an eyebrow like some dapper English actor. Their night was one of a string of nights she had wasted soon after she moved to New York. She thought of it as a kind of experiment, to see what would happen if she said yes to all of Ed's friends. She'd had some misguided idea that if she gave them what they wanted they would stop pursuing her. Instead, the word had spread like news of a new soup kitchen on skid row, and they all lined up like hungry beggars. And every drunken, squalid night led her to the next. It never occurred to Charlotte that she would actually care for any of them. And, so far, she hadn't. Brad's hair was somewhere between a mousy blond and a muddy ginger, not her type at all. He wasn't even a true redhead, like a Galle, or a Nordic blond like a Diehl. He stood by the door, waving his hands around emphatically, his pursed lips wet and red in his pale English face.

"The worst one yet," he was saying. "Hello, Charlotte. I was just going to go for cigarettes, would you like to take a walk? I'd like to be alone with my thoughts."

Billy and eight other young men and two women—all familiar to Charlotte by face at least—had crammed into Ed's studio apartment. Three sat on Ed's narrow bed, two perched on the arms of the one stuffed chair, and the rest hovered and slouched where they could. Charlotte didn't point out the error in Brad's invitation.

"But she's the best one," said Ed, grabbing Charlotte around the waist and pulling her against him. He kissed her cheek and offered her a mint julep, but without the sugar and the mint.

"Thanks, I'll get it myself," she said, taking the bottle from Ed's hand like a drowning swimmer grabbing a buoy. "Here's Katie."

Brad raised a toast to Katie. And then to Katie's brooch. Christmas in July!

"Aw, get out," Katie said, taking the glass of whiskey that Charlotte offered. "Worst what, Brad?"

"Model."

"We're talking art again," said Billy.

"Screw art!" said a woman sandwiched between two men on Ed's narrow bed.

"We'll screw you first," said Ed.

"She doesn't screw. The worst kind of model."

"Shut up, Brad!" said the woman, whose spanking white pants seemed to glow in the light from a candle stuck in a bean can. Above the dresser, the map of Nantucket reflected the small white flame.

"I'm taking that map when you go to France," said Charlotte, who had a knack for stopping conversation.

"Lottie only loves me for my things," said Ed.

"It's not yours," Charlotte said, elbowing Ed away with a vehemence that surprised her. The room was suddenly quiet.

Ed reestablished his grip on her waist. Charlotte pushed him away again. He made an exaggerated gesture of begging for mercy, then gave up and put his arm around Katie, who didn't shrug him off, despite the look Charlotte shot her friend.

"As I was saying, Charlotte was the best model. Maybe she can take it up again, now that she's lost her job."

"I'd pay for that," said one of the men on Ed's bed.

"We know you do," said Billy. "But it's better not to admit it."

Everyone laughed. The whiskey burned in Charlotte's gut. They were all so knowing. As if they'd been with whores in every port. She felt ill. The burn opened in her gut like a fat hot peony. Thick sweat drops sprouted at the roots of her hair.

Charlotte had stared at that map for years and years. All through her childhood she had willed herself into it, imagined herself as a whale-widow watching the water for the husband who would never return. Or an orphan who dressed as a boy to slip aboard a ship, to see firsthand the killing of a great, wild, innocent creature so that lamps could be filled and waists cinched. By the right of her knowing its every line, by the right of her seeing it when she closed her eyes in her childhood bed, by the right of her putting herself in it when the house on Oxford Street became dangerous. By all rights it was hers.

Billy was talking to her, offering her a cigarette. She took it and moved next to him, perching herself on the dresser's edge.

"What will you do when Ed's in Paris?"

"What I always do. Get a job, pay the rent. Why would anything be different for me?" To herself she sounded cross, almost shrill. Billy didn't seem to notice.

"We'll have to visit him together."

"Yes." Ed lurched toward them. Only then did Charlotte realize how drunk he was. How deep in the repetitive stage of drunkenness. "When I run out of French girls, Lottie will have to model. She was always the best one."

Just then someone put on a Beach Boys record and Katie grabbed her hand. Charlotte wanted to say, for all to hear, that she'd never modeled for Ed, but Katie wouldn't let her be serious.

Ed stumbled toward the record player.

"Who brought this garbage? Turn it off!" Ed shouted. Before he could get to the milk crate the record player was on, the woman in white pants shimmied an interference, twisting high and low. Then Brad joined in as if he and white-pants were working together to keep Ed from stopping their fun. They must have heard his diatribes before, his declaration that art need not be cheap and easy, that he was not afraid to make something beautiful, to reflect the actual beauty that the world had in it. Not afraid to let art have a human face. Billy usually supported Ed, but not this time. He grabbed one of Charlotte's hands and Katie grabbed the other and they threw their bodies between Ed and the Beach Boys.

"Shake it off, Ed!" Billy yelled, bumping his hip into Ed, so that Ed bumped against the white-panted woman.

"Yeah, Ed!" Katie yelled. "Be one of us for once!"

Charlotte drank down her whiskey and poured and slurped one more snort, and then she gave in. They danced on top of the bed, they danced on the coffee table. They danced until they fell onto the ash-strewn carpet, and then they got up and danced some more.

Katie made her laugh. Katie was twisting and Charlotte was twisting and the sweat poured down her face but Katie wouldn't let her stop. Charlotte fell, laughing, onto the one padded chair in the apartment, an overstuffed thing covered in heavy red wool punctuated with yellow fleur de lis. Another thing from the Oxford Street house. Katie fell on top of her, kissed her playfully on the cheek, and begged her for a story.

Just then Charlotte began to bleed. She cursed herself for once again not adding up the signs. Perhaps it was part of the curse itself, part of the magic of it, that she felt the gut wrench and the billowing clouds of a vicious mood as unrelated events. In the years since her first terror, at the age of eleven, of discovering that she was an animal, really and truly an animal, with an animal's fate, she had been surprised so many times. No matter how often she felt her flesh swell and turn dense as marble, a moon with a pomegranate core, even as her breasts got hard and hurtful, no matter how many times she could smell individually every ingredient in a Chinatown garbage can, she kept being caught unprepared.

"I've got a flower in my knickers," she said into Katie's ear, using their code.

"Well, shit," said Katie, who had nothing in her purse that would help. "Do what you can with toilet paper, and I'll take you home."

Charlotte didn't argue that she wasn't an invalid, not when Katie took that motherly tone. Kindness like that—simple, direct, knowing, was almost too much for Charlotte. She was parched for that drink of milk, had to keep herself from wanting more. From begging Katie to take her home and bathe her, as she had done once after a particularly disastrous night at the Pussycat. Katie did such things naturally, combing Charlotte's hair, deftly popping a zit between her thumbnails, shouting, "Let me get it!"

Ed was caught up in conversation with the blond on his bed, and barely seemed to notice Charlotte's departure. Katie hailed the cab and got in with her. Suddenly Charlotte didn't want the help.

"You know, I'll be all right. You go back to the party."

"No, dear, I'll see you home."

They argued for a moment while the driver cleared his throat. Finally, Katie admitted she didn't want to go back to the party, but she agreed to let Charlotte take care of herself. Charlotte gave the driver Katie's address on Twenty-Third Street, which was closer, so they would stop there first.

"All right, all right, I guess you're not dying," said Katie. "You never told me you modeled nude for Ed. Wasn't that a little weird?"

"That's because I never did." As she spoke, Charlotte realized that she was lying. That she was telling a lie she wanted to believe.

"Why did he keep saying you were the best?"

"He's just trying to embarrass me," said Charlotte. Her gut contracted just then, her belly closed like a fist. They were almost to Katie's or she would have changed the directions to the driver. She would soon bleed through her clothes and onto the seat. At least she was wearing black. She crouched forward and tied her jacket around her waist.

"Oh dear," said Katie. "That bad?"

"I'm afraid so."

"Let's go to you first then."

"Nonsense, we're a block away."

They said goodnight, and Charlotte watched Katie walk up the steps of her brownstone, the blue of her dress suddenly bright in the porch light. Charlotte saw her friend as at once distant and particular, as if she were watching her through a telescope that reduced everything to its essence. Katie became a blue rectangular note moving along the stairs of her brownstone, which aligned with the stairs of other brownstones in a long musical staff. Charlotte's head rang with the note that seemed to have come from Katie, from the tap of her shoes on the steps or from the air around her, the swoosh of air on skin. Was this vibration, this indescribable sound, really always there, just outside the range of her hearing? Her belly clutched again, she felt it as molten iron.

She got up the five flights to her apartment and through the doors outside and in. She managed pajamas and the pads and belts, swathed herself to prepare for sleep. But as she closed her eyes, she knew that something was wrong. The blood was coming too fast and too thick. Her body clenched and unclenched, a rhythmic throb and release.

She knew that she should do something, but she could not think what it was. There, a surge and a clench. She was it and was carried by it, something just beyond her knowing. A great emptying and then a great filling. As if the whole ocean had gathered itself into a fist, left the sea floor flopping full of gape-mouthed fish and sailors' bones, then pummeled the reefs from a terrible height.

In the darkness of her room on Houston Street, in her grown-up bed, she felt herself again as a child, lying in the darkness of the room she shared with her sister Helen in the house on Oxford Street. Helen was there, Charlotte could hear her breathing. Someone was there in the dark. Maybe it wasn't Helen, but Charlotte could hear the breath, steady, undisturbed. Then, in the pure dark, just one bright sliver of light, the slow steady creak of the door. Her gut clenched, released, clenched. Then she was in Louise's room. Ed was there, and, yes, Louise was there too. Why were they there, looking at her? Was she sick? Sometimes, when she was sick, she was allowed to rest in Louise's bed. But, no, that wasn't it. She was naked, lying diagonally across the bed, propped with pillows behind her head. Her right knee was bent, her left leg straight, an enforced posture of ease. Her arm was thrown back behind her head, revealing the red down in her arm-pit. She had volumes even then. Had slipped into this woman's body seemingly overnight. And Ed was there, and he was drawing her. She felt it there, in the house on Oxford Street, that summer when she was twelve and Ed fourteen, and she felt it now, the summer when she was twenty-eight and he was thirty, that the blood was pouring and pouring out onto the coverlet, onto the sheets.

She had tried to tell them, but they said, Be still. Like a specimen. She was still and the blood was pouring, pooling. Then Louise saw the blood on the coverlet and she was angry. She threw Charlotte's dress at her and yelled, "Clean yourself up! Clean it up!" And she shuffled Ed out of the room, shielding him from her, from the contamination she was.

Suddenly Charlotte understood. A laugh came through her, feathery and anemic. The laugh did not belong to her. She was back on Houston Street now on her grown bed, but she was young Charlotte too, who bled everywhere. Who dropped a trail of blood from the schoolhouse steps to the living room couch. She was shame and what caused shame. When she bled the first time, when she was just eleven, and she was sad or complaining, Louise had said, "Be quiet or I'll tell the neighbors your secret."

Now Charlotte understood, she was the white whale herself! The enemy of the sailor. The widow's nightmare. The orphaned creature, longing to be. The laugh came through her again, a rushing river. Sent her marble white flesh down the surging blood river, out toward the horizon on the blood ocean's tide. And yet, she was the widow too, pacing and watching the horizon, hoping for her own return.

THE RETURN

Your bone my bone toe bone thigh
Where are you and where am I

Walking walking the ocean floor
Ever opening your weighted door.

KISS OF DEATH

JULY 1948

This time it was Louise who sent the note. They would try again, meet at Da Ronco's on a Thursday after work.

Louise got up quickly and easily that morning, did not wait for Charlotte to bring her a cup of tea. Of course, Mother was on to her. She placed Louise's oatmeal down gently, poured Louise's tea smoothly, then sat back down at the foot of the table and unfolded the *Post* as she always did, laying her daily snare, hiding her face behind the headlines. Louise spooned oatmeal in silence, waited for the pounce. She was taking the last bite when Mother folded the paper in half and began.

"We'll have a nice roast pork tonight."

"I won't be home for dinner."

"Oh no?"

"Yes."

"Yes, you will?"

"Yes, I won't be home for dinner."

"Working late?"

"Yes." Louise pushed the bowl away and leaned back in her chair, tipping the front legs off the floor.

"Stop that! You'll break the chair or your neck. You're as bad as Bruce."

Louise came down with a thud, then reached into the pocket of her robe for her cigarettes and a matchbook that said Da Ronco's in gold letters. She lit the cigarette, and then tossed the matchbook onto the table, daring Mother to notice the clue in front of her. Mother kept talking. "I'll save you a plate."

"No need." Louise stood up, tipped a bit of ash into the oatmeal bowl, and tied the sash of her robe more tightly. She turned to go, but then stood still to deliver the punch, fixing Mother with a cold, even stare. "I may be out all night."

Mother looked right back at her, not blinking. But Louise could see the spasm beneath the thinning skin of Mother's cheek, the ripple of flesh around the clench of her jaw. "I see."

Mother unfolded the *Post* once more, and that was all. Louise stepped away. She wanted to be called back, to hear Mother's final jab. But Mother did not oblige.

Mother's silence irritated her, planted a wriggling little maggot of doubt in Louise's mind, so that she began to wonder if she should meet Kit after all. All day she felt uncomfortable, as if her clothes belonged to someone else. Or as if she had stacked the deck against herself—if she didn't see him, Mother would win, but if she spent time with Kit Blunt, if she tried to explain herself to him, she would lose. But at the end of the day, as she reweighed the residual solution for the third time, she knew that she would meet him. This time he was waiting for her in the booth in the back corner.

She saw him right away. He was hard to miss, tall as he was. His great glowering forehead, his tie-less white broadcloth shirt with the sleeves rolled up, as if he'd been working hard for hours and hours. He weighted the room. The white octagonal tiles on the floor pointed to him with all their corners. He made as if to stand to greet her, but she waved him back into his seat. The waiter brought martinis, though she hadn't had a chance to order. That was the sort of thing that usually annoyed Louise, but in this case, he was right. She wanted a martini. Or four.

"Nice to see you, Mrs. Galle," he said.

"Is it?"

"I don't just say things, you might have noticed."

"I suppose so. You're full of intentions." The waiter approached. Kit ordered them a dozen oysters. Louise ordered a steak and Kit ordered the sole almondine.

"I'd say curiosity," said Kit. He drew the ashtray to him, lit two smokes, and passed her one, as if they had done this a thousand times. As if they were soldiers in a foxhole, clinging to hope with their Lucky Strikes and army-issue Zippos.

"Yes, you're clearly a curious man. Is that why you run a mill? Is it interesting?"

"Mrs. Galle, I believe you are the most sarcastic woman I ever met. Quite different from how Major Roland Galle described you." But Kit grinned ever so slightly as he spoke, raised an eyebrow like Orson Welles as Mr. Rochester. Like a survivor of the madness of women.

Louise crossed legs under the table, leaned forward, tipped her ash into the tray. Blew smoke out of her nose with a protracted sigh.

"And how did he describe me?"

"He truly thought you were a saint. At least at first."

"That's funny."

"But he made it clear that you were as smart as you were pretty. He said you could hold your own in any conversation, about any subject."

"Did he now?" Now she was irritated. Why hadn't Roland said that his Louise was working at Lockheed, designing airplane parts, that she had a degree in chemistry? That she had gone to MIT? Hadn't he ever thought about what she had given up, having his babies?

"But come on, you finally read one of my letters. It's your turn to talk."

"Yes." Louise paused as the waiter put the oysters on the table. She squeezed lemon and one acid drop landed in her eye. She blinked, grabbed the hard-horny shell and tipped the smooth flesh into her mouth.

"Well, are you going to answer the question?"

"You want to know why I didn't write. How do you know I didn't? Not all letters got through to those camps."

"Don't toy with me, Mrs. Galle."

"You played with the cards I sent."

"Are you trying to tell me that in two years, only one letter got through?"

"All right, all right. Another martini and I'll tell you what you want to know." The drinks came, she gulped. Swallowed another oyster. He kept pace with her. She said she wanted something in exchange.

"Anything," he said.

"I want to know more about what happened over there. And I want to know how you lost your leg." He dropped his eyes, ran his fingers across his temple.

"All right. Your turn."

"Do you have any idea what it's like to raise four children and be the breadwinner?"

"That's your answer? You were too busy? I thought your mother takes care of the kids?"

"It's not easy, that's all."

"War isn't supposed to be easy."

They finished the oysters and ordered a bottle of wine for their entrees. Louise was beginning to feel loose. Sort of good. With the drinks she began to warm to Kit Blunt, began to notice that there was something sad and kind in his deep-set mastiff's eyes. And she began to like the sound of her own voice, telling the story of herself.

"I wasn't going to marry. I thought I'd have a career. My father thought so too. He always believed in me. It made Mother angry. She was jealous. My brother Bruce was clever, and he was physical like Father. They were both big men. All American footballers at West Point. Father played tennis with me, he trained me a bit in that way, but mostly he cared about my mind. Bruce was clever, but I was brilliant. I wanted to know the secrets of the universe, so I studied chemistry."

"At one point I wanted to be a mechanical engineer," said Kit, leaning back to let the waiter put the plates down. "Ended up taking over the family business."

"Roland was Bruce's roommate at West Point," said Louise, sawing into her slab of steak.

"I remember."

"I had no intention of falling in love."

"Isn't that how it happens?"

"What are you, a Hollywood producer?"

"In my spare time," said Kit, laughing a little. Making a frame for her face with his fingers. "Go on, we're ready for your close-up."

"Well, this will sound Hollywood enough. I knew when I saw him. The very first time I laid eyes on him I knew I was in trouble. It was as if the world stopped spinning on its axis, then began to turn the other way. As if for the first time, I could see myself from the outside, as a woman like other women."

"Well, he was a good-looking fellow."

"It wasn't just that. He was funny and at the same time utterly sincere. He made fun of West Point, all of its high-mindedness, and yet he was dutiful, dedicated. Right away I saw that he would never lie to me, never cheat."

"He wasn't the cheating kind."

"We played a joke on Bruce, put a spider under his drinking glass. It was funny to see my big brother jump like a girl."

"I bet. Roland told me he knew you'd be his wife right away too."

"Yes. When I left, he said so to Bruce, who said, 'It'll never happen!'"

"Famous last words!"

"Indeed." Louise paused, chewed steak, let Kit refill her glass. "It happened very quickly. Father was disappointed. But after a time, Roland won him over too. Well, not completely, I suppose. Father thought I might still be some sort of scientist. He always said I should wait to have children, do my master's first at least."

"Funny, I'd have thought the celebrated colonel would want women in the house."

"Father was unusual in many ways." Louise paused for a moment, feeling exposed. Feeling as if this near-stranger could see what she kept so carefully locked away. She took another bite and chewed and swallowed. Looked down at the white tablecloth, as if to make her mind as blank. As if by her choice of where to look, she could censor the past like a piece of victory mail. "He even told Mother she could be his wife and be the journalist she wanted to be. But that didn't happen. She was an officer's wife. And when Ed was born in '33, it seemed that's what I would be too."

"So, you were a woman after all, not really a scientist," said Kit. She looked up quickly, narrowed her gaze. He was egging her on, she could see it in the little smirk he wore. She wouldn't give him the satisfaction. She shrugged.

"At first, I was too in love. And I thought that Roland's love for me was like Father's—that it included the whole of me. Have you ever noticed the way a small child will wave with the back of their hand? They see the palms of those who wave at them, so they sit grinning at their own palms, thinking they're communicating with someone else."

"How does that play in Peoria?"

"I mean love is like that. You get confused between yourself and the other person. You think they know you better than you do, or that they care about what you care about. Haven't you ever been in love, Mr. Blunt?"

"That's the Hollywoodest thing you've ever said to me." He finished his glass of wine and poured another.

"Well?" I can poke at you too, thought Louise.

"I plead the Fifth. Anyway, you're on the stand."

"All right. Here it is, my glorious story."

"I've been waiting for it for years," he said, without the slightest hint of sarcasm.

"I had always been rebellious in school. I argued and talked back to my teachers. I fought with boys when I was young. I climbed trees. Mostly I didn't like other girls. They were simpering fools, as far as I was concerned. And then suddenly I got what they wanted. I fell wildly in love with this beautiful man who was in the army but could quote Yeats and Wordsworth. Hell, he wanted to be Yeats! I knew he wasn't good enough as a poet, but I loved him anyway. I thought maybe he would get better, maybe he would grow into it."

"You were his muse."

Louise snorted but admitted it.

"Yes. I wanted that, I wanted to be that for him. It was as if I could see myself from the outside for the first time. I got caught in that lie that women believe, that they are only as good as their smiles and their asses and the hearths they can tend."

"And here I was admiring asses and smiles all over the world." He shifted in his chair and folded his arms over his chest.

"Suddenly it seemed that winning didn't matter, but what mattered was loving. Was bringing other lives into the world. I started baking goddamned pound cakes!"

"He said yours were the best." Kit was grinning. They were both glassy-eyed now, seeing each other through lenses smeared with Vaseline. He waved the waiter over, ordered another bottle.

"Pound cakes are easy. But now, when I remember how completely I was taken over, I can't believe it. One baby and the next. We were in Fort Lewis then, in Washington state. I even pretended to like the other officers' wives. To be interested in exchanging recipes, that sort of thing. I wrote sweet notes to my in-laws. I sent holiday cards. I darned socks. I had Ed in '33, Charlotte in '35, Bruce in '37, and Helen in '39." Louise paused.

"'39," said Kit, seeming to know that the story was about to shift.

"Yes. Did you believe we wouldn't join the war? To me it always seemed clear. Father went back to Manila, then Corregidor. He had been there in the Great War, you know. Everyone knew it was just a matter of time before the new war would break out in the Pacific. And then, out of nowhere, when it hadn't even begun, we lost my brother."

"Roland told me the story. That he was test flying a B-17 over Hawaii."

"Yes." Louise pushed her plate forward, leaned back in her chair, and lit a smoke. "He radioed in to tell his wife he'd be home for dinner and—"

"The bomb went off in the hold."

"I hardly need to tell you anything."

"Except that you haven't answered the question."

The waiter came over with another bottle of chianti and they ordered floating islands for dessert.

"But you see, that was the beginning of it. I had these small children, and Roland was gone all the time. Roland was always in training or training others or being at camp on maneuvers. I began to feel that I had been tricked."

"Tricked how?"

"That I'd fallen into the trap Father had warned me about. That I'd traded my mind for my uterus. And Roland wasn't even around to help with the kids or to love me. Mother was with Father in Manila until '41, so I was on my own mostly those early years. And suddenly Bruce was dead. And then the war started in earnest, and I had a new baby and three toddlers. Roland wasn't even home for Helen's birth and now he was going away even farther."

"But didn't you still love Roland?"

"I suppose I was angry. Even before he shipped out overseas, he never came home on leave. There was always a reason. We can't afford a flight, not enough time for the train, and so on."

"So, you were too angry at him to write?" Kit's voice was tight.

"And too busy." She said it quietly. They were quiet for a moment. The desserts came. They poked at the sugar mountains with their forks. Kit's expression changed. He looked as if she had struck him.

"That doesn't seem like much of a reason, Louise." He straightened his back, drew his false leg under the table. "Didn't you know what it meant to him? Didn't you believe him when he begged you to write? There must be more to the story."

"Mrs. Galle. Could be."

"Let's go for a drive, Mrs. Galle."

"I really shouldn't."

"Come on." He called the waiter over and paid the bill. "You owe me a little more story."

"I don't owe you a thing, Mr. Blunt."

"But you owe Roland, don't you? And I haven't lived up to my half of our bargain. Come, we'll drive to the beach." He spoke with absolute authority.

She ought to go home. Her children waited for her. She ought to tell him no in just the right way. To insist the way Father insisted, without having to insist at all, by brooking no other possibilities. Instead, she found herself flustered, like some sort of schoolgirl. Chattering like a fool.

"Mr. Blunt, I really can't. Ed, that's my oldest, he's going to show me his sketchbook tonight. He's doing the most beautiful work these days."

"He can show you tomorrow."

He stood up from the booth, held his hand out to her. She might not have agreed, but for the minor adjustment he made to steady himself around his false leg. Surely it was the wine as well, and the martinis and the sudden outpouring of herself, the enchantment of hearing herself speak of the war days. Something she never wanted to do, even when they were happening. She didn't take comfort in the Gold Star Widows groups, the gatherings to celebrate suffering or to make do with cheer and a thrifty recipe. She was a Lockheed woman in those days—that was the war she loved, the collision of metal and pliers, the spark of the flint to the torch, the whoosh of the flame, the thwack of the bolt in the wing. But now she wanted to tell him more, this one man who out of thousands had survived, who had known Roland. Who had returned, yes, but had traded bone and veins and gristle for something shiny and aluminum. For the rust-free promise of a different world. Oh, she was caught in it!

Louise went with him. They got in his car and drove toward the beach. He rolled down the windows and without warning began to recite that John Masefield poem, the one she and Roland had loved. Kit knew it too, and just as well. They recited the poem together, sipping whiskey from Kit's flask:

> I must go down to the seas again, for the call of the running tide
> Is a wild call and a clear call that may not be denied;
> And all I ask is a windy day with the white clouds flying,
> And the flung spray and the blown spume, and the sea-
> gulls crying.
>
> I must go down to the seas again, to the vagrant gypsy life,

To the gull's way and the whale's way where the wind's like
    a whetted knife;
And all I ask is a merry yarn from a laughing fellow-rover,
And quiet sleep and a sweet dream when the long trick's
    over.

When the poem left them, they slipped for a moment into silence. As they came around a familiar bend, Louise recalled rolling the car over in this very spot earlier in the summer. She didn't tell Kit about that.

He pulled up and parked in the dune grass. She opened the door and ran down to the shore, expecting him to chase her. She chased the wave's edge and laughed like a fool. But when she looked up at last, he was standing on the firmer sand at the top of the dune, watching her, absolutely still, as a cat watches a sparrow.

She wanted to say what came to her mind in a flood of sympathy, a great washing away of doubt and principle and memory. To say that perhaps it was hard for him to walk on the sand.

Instead, she stood still in his line of sight, and one by one she unbuttoned the buttons on her blouse. And with a practiced hand she unzipped her skirt. Then she walked toward him, unhooking and removing, and stood before him like a mermaid on land-legs. And together, without a word, they removed his clothes, and they unhooked his leg. She was surprised by how soft the skin of his stump was, pressed against her thigh, and by the sudden close of her throat, the quick well in her eye. What was this tender feeling as he leaned against her? As this big man who had lived while thousands around him died used her leg for his as they moved over the shifting sand and into the waves. Not love, but maybe mercy.

Perhaps it was mercy that moved Louise's hand, when they lay on the blanket on a clear summer night with a waning moon, and she touched the place where his leg had been. The silken scar was not, as she had thought, a place of dulled nerves. He flinched at first, when she ran her fingers across the strange smooth surface, but then he softened, expanded under her touch. He whimpered softly as she moved her hand away from the stump and drew her fingers through the air, as if she could shape an electric field that was his absent leg. He whimpered and begged her to touch his body that was and that wasn't. When she drew him into her there were tears in his eyes.

And later, when he pinched her nipple and bit her neck with great soft bites, Louise thought this is how it shall be. She laughed and screamed and cried out with the gulls and gave no thought at all to Mother brooding away on Oxford Street.

Purple Heart

July 1964

Charlotte could feel and she could smell, but she could not move. This time, at least, she knew her own name, and she knew that she was in her room above Houston Street. She knew she was a vessel pouring out, and she knew that something was very, very wrong.

The scent was sweet and metallic. Her eyelids were made of lodestone. Her eyelids were pinned to the center of the earth. Her shoulders were curved closed like the vessel bottom, her pelvis was open like its mouth. She was pouring through it the whole of the bloody sea. She would go with it into the place of the widest expanse. There was no need of holding, there was no need of trying, only the surge. In the great flood she was the faintest glimmer.

The tiniest spark of light. Yes, that was her will, floating out with the tide, but then returning. But in that great sea there was a voice: Charlotte, Charlotte, wake up! She heard it outside of her, in the room she lay in, all around and outside of her this voice, willing her, lift your eyes with all your might, lift the lids and look around the room, all is not lost. It seemed to her that the voice belonged to her father and that it came from where he lay, from where the coral had made itself of his bones.

The door creaked. She felt for leverage in the vessel, the smooth stone surface of her body. With the muscles of her head, with the sound of the voice in her ears, she pulled and she pressed and she heaved her eyes open.

The thick dark was sliced with a slit of light. The door creaked, the light slice grew wider. There was again the sound of something moving across the floor. The sound she knew from the times before, the creature coming for her. The creature who might or might not mean her ill. Who might or might not be him, full fathom five. Who might, after all, be jealous of the living, who might manifest a rotting body while trying to be again.

The sounds fell away, there was a shadow at the door. A narrow nose, the long lines of Byzantine profile. The dark brightened to gray light. A voice, a face she could feel more than see. Something familiar in it, something at once young and old.

Call for help, Charlotte! Get up, wake up!

Then a crash! As of the collision of a colander against the wall. A rumble as of the flower trucks coming down Houston. It was morning and she was awake in a pool of her blood. This was not ordinary bleeding. Somehow there was laughter again, the laughter that came through her, though she was not laughing. It was the feathery anemic laughter of something demonic, something that wanted to take her from the world. Such an imagination, Charlotte, the laughter seemed to say.

Then above the laughter, the voice of the night before, the familiar voice, young and old at once. The voice that she had heard her first day on earth. Get to the phone, Charlotte!

The phone, so far away in the living room. The phone sleeping in its cradle, waiting to give itself to her. The phone! Her savior.

Rolling to her side, she pressed herself up. Her head was thin and dry and pinched, she was dizzy with its emptiness. As if her flesh were exiting through her bottom, leaving her head and chest and bones as light as desiccated snakeskin. She pried herself up from the bed, tried not to look at the pool she left behind. There was a hand towel on the floor. She took off her blood-soaked pajama bottoms, folded the towel, placed it between her legs. She found pants—why were they all light material, so easily soaked? So insubstantial. And they fit her too well, there was barely room for the towel. But she couldn't dig through drawers. She put them on, these ridiculous gingham capris. A picnic massacre, laughed the demon in her head. She left the pants unhooked and unzipped at the top. Left her pajama top on, her great tender breasts falling loose. Her knees too were loose. She walked as on a ship, the ground careened beneath her.

She reached the phone. Lifted the beacon for her life from its cradle. Held it to her ear. She started at the sound she heard, what she realized was the suck and surge of her own blood echoing back to her. The phone was as useful as a conch shell. She remembered them now, the pile of unpaid bills that lay beneath the twisted wires of the half-made sculpture on the coffee table.

She knew that it was hot outside, but she felt cold. The desiccated snakeskin where her head once was congealed into cool hard marble.

I carry the weight of my own tomb, she thought, but this time did not erupt into light, feathery demonic laughter. There was a sound in the hallway; her neighbor was opening the door.

There was a voice then, the voice that had come in the night. Call for help! Help! She slammed her door with her fist, then the voice said, Unlatch the chain, turn the bolt, turn the knob. She did these things and when the door was open, her legs buckled beneath her and she fell into the hall.

Gil caught her. Gil of the silver-streaked hair and the violet-blue eyes.

"I didn't know you cared, Charlotte!" she joked in her low, smoky voice.

Gil knew just what to do. Carried her into the apartment next door, put Charlotte on a couch covered in strange material, some plastic that was like the skin under the desiccated snakeskin that was once Charlotte's head. The strange smoothness of the material made Charlotte feel hopeful. Gil called an ambulance and they waited. On the coffee table was a great big black dildo.

"Don't look at that, you'll pass out again," Gil said, throwing the thing in the direction of the bed. The apartment was in disarray. A wardrobe door was open, hangers hung empty in it. Gil watched her look.

"Yes, Daisy left."

"When will she be back?"

"I don't know. I don't even know where she went. I think back to Indiana."

"I'm cold," said Charlotte. Gil brought her a shirt. It was heavy and solid, almost canvas. A work shirt. "It's good."

"Yes, probably good that she left, took the baby."

"I mean the shirt."

"Oh." Gil laughed a little.

The door buzzer buzzed, and Gil let them in. Charlotte grabbed Gil's hand.

"Will you come to the hospital?"

"Oh, I shouldn't. I mean, you should call some family."

"I don't have any family."

"What about your brother, the famous artist?"

"Not him. I don't want him."

"What about a friend?"

"Aren't you my friend?"

There was a knock at the door and the men came in with the stretcher. "I can walk," said Charlotte.

"Yeah, and you can fall down the stairs," said Gil, who went with her after all. Who waited with her after she was checked in. Who stayed after Charlotte called Katie and got no answer. Who told the nurse that she was Charlotte's brother. The nurse clearly did not believe this, but let Gil stay, even as she explained to Charlotte that they couldn't reach Dr. Bedford, but that they were going to stop the bleeding with dilation and curettage. Gil stayed while they waited Charlotte's turn to have her uterus scraped clean.

And after the procedure, Gil was there again, sitting by her bed in the sterile room.

"My mother bled to death," said Gil suddenly. "I think she tried to have an abortion. There were seven of us already."

"Jesus, that's terrible."

"It was. She wasn't a nice person, but I wouldn't wish her life on anyone."

"My mother is not nice either."

"That's too bad. I think it's a rumor maybe, that there are nice mothers out there. Nice grandmothers maybe."

"My grandmother isn't terribly nice either," said Charlotte, then felt guilty for betraying Granny. Who was once Martha Diehl, aspiring journalist. "Well, I guess she's kind in her way."

"I guess I wouldn't call my grandma nice either. But she was tough."

"My granny too. But if we start talking about our families, you'll be here all day and into the night."

"Oh hell, I'm still unemployed," said Gil, cupping her head with her hands and leaning back, as if she were putting herself to sleep.

"All right, you first. Tell me a story about your tough grandmother."

"Naw, I'd rather listen to you," said Gil, sitting comically upright and miming taking dictation. Charlotte laughed.

A nurse came in and set a tray with cups of juice and clear broth on the nightstand. Her fingers were light and practiced, pressing into Charlotte's wrist, one finger then the other as if she was playing an instrument. She took Charlotte's pulse, but she was looking at Gil, who slouched in her chair, her legs spread wide, the three top buttons of her plaid collared shirt open to reveal a white T-shirt underneath. There was a clear expression of disdain in the nurse's florid face, and Charlotte watched Gil receive it and slouch more, let her knees go ever so slightly wider.

"I could use some coffee," said Charlotte. "And a cigarette."

The nurse pulled a thermometer from her pocket, shook it, and pointed it at Charlotte's mouth, opening her own as if Charlotte needed mimed directions.

"Just have the juice and broth for now. We'll keep you overnight. You should wait until tomorrow for heavier food and stimulating things like that. No smoking in the rooms anyway," said the nurse, looking at her watch while Charlotte held the thermometer in her mouth and breathed audibly through her nose. Then, looking at Gil out of the corner of her eye, "Visiting hours are over at eight. Your boyfriend will have to leave then."

The nurse left and they laughed.

"She reminds me of the woman who fired me. Same chin hairs," said Charlotte, drinking the broth and frowning. "Nothing like dishwater to get your strength back."

Gil brought a second chair over from the corner and put her feet up on it. She leaned her salt and pepper head against the wall, which was painted a shade of green that Charlotte had only ever seen in hospitals.

"You were about to tell me about your grandmother," she said.

"I can't talk about Granny without talking about Louise," said Charlotte.

"Who's Louise?"

"My mother."

"You call your mother by her first name?"

"Apparently." The broth and juice did make Charlotte feel better. "Do you really want to know about my family?"

"Yeah, really. I told you, I'll find a job tomorrow. I'm all ears."

Charlotte adjusted herself against the pillows, finished the juice, and began.

"Louise lives with Granny now still."

"What about your dad?"

"Died in the war."

"Oh, too bad. Do you remember him?"

"Thought you were all ears?" Charlotte teased.

Gil took her fingers to her lips and made a locking gesture, threw an invisible key over her shoulder. Charlotte began again.

"I do remember him, to answer your question." Charlotte paused, wondered if she should admit what she was about to admit. Gil was watching her intently with that frank open face of hers. There was something so solid about Gil, so all-of-a-piece. "You'll think I'm crazy."

"Not so far," said Gil, smiling her easy smile, her leathery cheeks crinkling up around her eyes.

"I know him now, better than when he was alive."

Gil slouched a little bit in her seat, but she kept her eyes on Charlotte's and didn't miss a beat.

"You talk to him?" She asked this as if Charlotte could pick up the phone and get a direct line to the bottom of the South China Sea.

"Well, not exactly. But I think he talks to me."

"I wish I could have a touch of your crazy. I talk to my grandma all the time, but she never talks back," said Gil. "But I guess she didn't say much. Knew how to deal with a violent drunk. And how to treat a scalp wound."

"If you keep interrupting, visiting hours'll be over and you'll have to come back tomorrow." Charlotte hoped Gil didn't mind her teasing tone. The begging she heard in her own voice unnerved her. Why did she suddenly feel she needed Gil?

"I'll come back tomorrow if you need me," said Gil.

Charlotte pressed her hand over Gil's. Gil's skin felt dry to the touch, her knuckles big and hard as bolts. She let herself look into those violet eyes and take in the silver slivers cobwebbed through her savior's hair. Then she gave an extra squeeze and withdrew her hand to break the looking spell.

"I guess I have a wild imagination. But I swear to you that my father helped me, saved me from bleeding to death."

"Aw, damn, I thought I was your savior!"

"No, you were. I mean, he wouldn't let me slip away. I just wanted to float away in the blood. But I heard his voice, felt him willing me to get up, get to the door."

"Well then, I'm grateful to him. Thank you—what's his name?"

"Roland. Edward Roland Galle. The third."

"The third, you say?" Gil slapped her thigh. "I must be moving up in the world, talking to the daughter of Roland the third."

"His family was a bit—ever so. We don't really talk to them anymore."

"Wealthy people are like that."

"Oh, they were more like shabby genteel. You know, like maybe they had some money once, but then they just had social position."

Gil seemed to take that in. She leaned back in the chair again, picked up her right leg in her hands, then folded the leg so that her right ankle was just above her left knee, and leaned forward.

"Sorry—typesetting cricked my back. Have to stretch it. Well, you had a roof over your head growing up, so to me that's wealthy."

"What, you grew up in a tent? Joined the circus?" Charlotte laughed, but Gil did not.

"We were talking about you," she said, but the merriness had left her eyes.

Charlotte suddenly felt that Gil's life was something she would never understand. Even if. Even if what she wanted from Gil was what Gil wanted from her. "We were but I don't want to keep you—"

Gil waved the air impatiently as if to say, Enough of this polite dance.

"I guess to tell the truth I've always felt that Father is with me. Sounds like a greeting card I know but—"

Gil waved the air again, mimed pulling a thread from Charlotte's mouth. Charlotte laughed and kept talking.

"I mean, Ed used to say it too. Father hears us." The memory rushed in as Charlotte spoke, the words tumbled out of her as if she couldn't think of them fast enough. "We used to hide in a crawl space and light matches. We'd say the words—"

"What words?"

But Charlotte didn't want to say them. Not just because the words were Shakespeare's and it would seem precocious and pretentious that she and Ed had known that song of *The Tempest* but because it felt wrong to her to say them here, with Gil. Without Ed.

"I can't remember now. We had a thing we would chant and if we could chant it before the match went out, we said he is here." Charlotte could feel herself blushing.

She was relieved just then that the nurse came in and announced to Charlotte that visiting hours were over. Without looking at Gil, the nurse said, in an excessively loud voice, that all gentleman callers must vacate the premises.

Charlotte and Gil shared another laugh. A pressing of hands.

"I'll come back tomorrow and see you home," said Gil. "As any good gentleman caller would."

When the door had closed and Charlotte was alone in the antiseptic room with its sheets as starched as cardboard and the faint tinge of green on its walls that reminded her of the psych ward at Bellevue, a flood of memory overtook her. Vivid images of that summer when she was twelve and Ed fourteen arose in her mind. She felt as if all the blood she had lost had been covering up these memories, which were now as clear to her as razor clams in the low-tide floor of Long Island Sound.

She recalled that Ed would no longer go with her into the crawl space to call out to Father. That she went alone through the closet into the space behind and whispered the words—full fathom five, my father lies. That it was the summer of Ed drawing her naked, that it was the summer of her bleeding so much that she fainted, that it was the time that Granny had tried to die. That it was the time of Louise and her one-legged man. That Charlotte had seen, that very summer, the one-legged man and Louise through the picture window of the living room in the house on Oxford Street. They had appeared before her like characters in a film, Louise stepping hurriedly into the frame, and the man, with his awkward gait, galumphing after her and slapping her, hard, across the face.

THE RETURN

A light is light compared to dark.
My skin was chuffed and shed as bark.

As false is not as is true
I am not done with you.

Kiss of Death

July 1948

They woke under Kit's scratchy wool blanket, the cold damp seeping up from the wet sand and down from the layer of morning fog. They moved their outlaw idyll to a seaside motel in Rehoboth, one of those new places that had sprung up for the more and more people who owned cars. Louise could tell he wanted to care for his stump in a warm, dry place. He brought a doctor's bag from the trunk of his car. She watched him open it and extract a cream and rub it on the soft neatened end of his leg, which looked to her like the pinched end of a loaf of unbaked bread. Through the cracked-open door of the bathroom, she watched him rubbing his flesh motheringly. Watching him work the flesh as a baker would a loaf or a mother would a baby's bottom, she felt again the tender feeling. She wouldn't call it love, exactly. It was a kind of humility. When he caught her looking, he closed the door firmly.

In the bleach-smelling sheets of the motel bed Louise couldn't sleep. What made the damp sand and scratchy wool blanket of the beach better? Was it just that their lust had made them roll in the sand like Hollywood lovers? Naked in the crisp sheets under the pilly coverlet, she lay listening to him breathe, hearing the rattle of his chest and the whistle of his nose. She watched the headlights of a passing car come in through the thin curtains and roll across the ceiling. Through the thin walls she could hear a couple arguing. Not the words, just the tones of their voices, the woman's rapid, high pitched, jabbing; the man's low and lumbering and thick. Behind their voices was another sound, one she could just barely make out. She sat up and strained to hear it—that susurrus of overlapping magnetic fields that had come from her car radio. For what seemed a long time, she turned her head slowly like an antenna seeking a signal, but the sound was too even, it was present but indistinct, just out of the range of her sense-making.

Just before the light came up fully, she reached across Kit to drink from the water glass on the nightstand. Her nipple must have brushed his face. He woke to it, took her breast in his mouth like a hungry baby, drew her against him. Again she felt the strangeness of his absent limb, pressed her right leg against the stump of his left, as if to say, Use this.

It was already ten when they went into the motel dining room, if you could call it that. It was two tables and a counter, a view of the gas pumps outside through a lacy-curtained window. There was a phone box by the pumps. She went out to it to call the Department of Infectious Diseases. Marjorie or whoever answered and seemed not at all interested in the news that Louise would not be coming in that day. It was almost too easy. She wondered for a moment why, in the years since she had brought the children east in '45, she had so rarely called in sick. In fact, the only other time she could recall not working was when Harry Leopold had told her to go home after their disastrous night together.

As she opened the door to go back to the dining room, she caught a glimpse, just over the grease-filmed counter, of the humpbacked cook. She was about half as tall as Mother, but she turned the bacon with sharp, efficient Martha-Diehl-like movements. One, two, three, she cracked eggs on the griddle, and one, two, three, she turned them over.

Perhaps feeling herself looked at, the cook turned and looked back for half a beat. Three more eggs appeared as if they had fallen from her sleeve. This time she sliced them with the spatula's edge, folded them over, sliced them again, even the scrambles were mathematical. Mother was wondering where she was; Mother could claim terrible worry. Louise had told Mother she might not come home. Wouldn't Mother assume Louise would go to work, even if she had been out all night?

A kind of battle of wills rose up in her. She should call Mother because Mother would call the lab. Would find a reason. What do you mean? Louise could hear Mother saying, What do you mean, she's at home sick? But she shouldn't have to call her mother. She was a grown woman, a woman of science, a woman of satisfied lust. She was alarmed, suddenly, by how good she felt, by the fact that she hadn't felt so good with a man since, well, since Roland. Since their early days.

Kit loomed large over the small café table. He was a dark shadow in the light coming through the glass window with its painted sign FULL BREAKFAST 45 CENTS. As her eyes adjusted to the indoor light, she admired his broad shoulders and his hair, jet black and thick. For the first time she noted the shape of his eyebrows, how they peaked, ever so slightly, in the middle. His hands, the hands that had cupped her bottom just an hour before, looked huge holding the menu. He looked up at her and smiled, and she felt a clutch of something, a feeling of admiration for a creature so different from herself. But that was how they got you, the lovers. The menfolk you thought you wanted. The ones who make you think that what you want is possible and has a particular shape that is them. That what they want is what you want, that all the angels of heaven and demons of hell are singing along with you in unison, when in fact you're hearing the hum between your own two ears, a spiritual tinnitus. I screamed in ecstasy, Louise thought, as this man with one leg opened me, and my inner ear is still adjusting.

"Eggs and bacon?" he called out, grinning wildly now.

"There in a minute," she called back, returning his grin, just as if the corners of his mouth were magnetic poles that drew her own flesh into the same pattern.

She stepped quickly back outside and into the booth and picked up the phone. But her hands were shaking now. Why? Her palms were sweating, her hand stuck to the phone, but she couldn't seem to lift it out of its cradle.

Mother would assume she had gone to work that day. I don't really need to call, Louise thought again. But she could never trust Mother to do what she wanted her to do. Mother always found out what Louise wanted and then did the other thing. She could see Mother planning, deciding what to say. Oh, she just needed to tell Louise something about the children, to remind her to pick up some castor oil. Goddamn it, Louise heard herself say, I'm too old to be afraid of my mother.

She dialed. It rang. Once, twice, five times, ten. She was about to hang up when Oxford Street answered.

"Galle residence," said Charlotte.

So polite, thought Louise. "Charlotte, why aren't you in school?"

"Oh, hello, Mother. It's, you know, summer now."

"There's no need for sarcasm."

"I wasn't being—"

"Can you put your granny on?"

"She's not here," said Charlotte, clearly yawning.

"Well, where is she?" Louise felt her fear froth over into irritation.

"Don't know. No one's here. I'm just getting up."

"You really shouldn't waste all your days on earth, Charlotte. It's nearly eleven."

"It's not all my days—"

"Listen, tell your granny—" Louise paused, turned in the booth and looked through the window at the broad shoulders, the wild dark hair of the man who had made her cry out with joy. Had made her forget herself and Mother and everything. She was struck suddenly by a glorious idea.

"Yes?"

"Tell her I've gone to a training for work. I'll be back on Sunday night."

"You have a training on the weekend?" asked Charlotte, yawning all over the phone with a big, soft, wet breath.

"Yes. Starting Friday, starting today. It's very important," said Louise, then adding, stupidly. "It's in Virginia."

"Virginia?"

"That's what I said. You're too young to be losing your hearing."

"Okay, goodbye, Mother."

"Goodbye, Charlotte. Be good."

Kit was talking to the frumpy little brown-haired waitress when Louise returned to the table. They were laughing together, as if they'd known each other for years.

"This is Mrs. Galle," said Kit. "I'm sure she'd like the breakfast special as well."

"But, Mr. Blunt, I haven't even looked at the menu," said Louise, sounding to herself like Scarlett O'Hara.

"The special is the menu," said the frump, taking a pencil from behind her ear and a pad from the pocket of her apron.

"With or without hash browns, that is," said Kit, and they both laughed. His good mood was getting the better of him; he seemed to have an excess to share with anyone.

"I'll take it with," said Louise.

"Just as I thought," said Kit. "Two of those and two coffees."

"I prefer tea," said Louise.

"Tea's not part of the special," said the frump.

"I'd like a pot of tea," said Louise again.

"She means they don't have tea," said Kit, placing his hand on the back of her chair as if to steady her for the disappointment.

"You got it all figured out," said the frump, winking at Kit. She wrote the order down, stuck the pencil back behind her ear, and walked away.

"She has to write down the one thing on the menu?" said Louise.

"Oh, she's all right. Reminds me of my niece."

"I see," said Louise, fishing the gold-plated cigarette case out of her purse, only to find it empty.

"Here," said Kit, lighting two of his own and handing her one. "I thought we were in a good mood?"

"Oh, we are," she said. Soften yourself, she thought, you're a lover now. She made a smile.

"That's more like it. You're a fine-looking woman, Mrs. Galle."

"Well, thank you kindly, sir. I'm also free of obligations until Sunday."

"Thought you had to get back to those kids?"

"Mother's taking them to Virginia for the weekend."

"Virginia?"

"You're too young to be losing your hearing, Mr. Blunt," Louise said, feeling suddenly vulnerable. She had offered too much.

"Too bad I can't join you," he said, Orson Wellesing her again.

"Oh?" Louise stumbled to recover from a quick stab of shame. "Have to see your niece, do you?"

"I have obligations too, Louise."

"I see," she said, peering through the window at a battered truck that had pulled up to one of the pumps. An old Negro man in overalls and a battered straw hat got out. She watched the gas station attendant, a white boy about Ed's age, approach. The old man held out money and the young one snatched it from his hand.

"My father's not well," said Kit.

"Ah," was all Louise could answer. But when he covered her light thin hand with his big dense one, she didn't move hers away.

Purple Heart

July 1964

The first night back in her apartment, Charlotte woke to the sound of hard equipment slamming into hard ground—a sound she imagined that oil wells made. She opened her eyes, alarmed to find herself alone in the dark. Her window over Houston Street was open. The old white sheet she had refashioned as a curtain had become soft and gray with city soot. It moved in the air, but only half a breath. There was quiet outside—the one precious moment of quiet on Houston. She felt she was a tennis ball thrown in the air, hovering for a millisecond before the fall.

Then she did feel the drop, heard the sound again, and realized with a start that the oil well was in fact her heart laboring mightily to refill her with blood. No one at the hospital had told her it would be so painful. She had been hollowed out, and now every part of her was trying to grow itself out of nothing. In the quiet before the flower trucks began their roll down the uneven half-cobblestoned street, she felt the whole of her as a pause, her whole existence a mirror to a half-breath's steam.

When she woke again, she was surprised to discover herself face down on the couch, her cheek pressed against the damp powder-blue eyelet of her robe, for which she felt a sudden, nauseating hatred. Louise had given it to her for her birthday, but it was the robe of a girl, not a woman of twenty-eight. Not a woman of experience. Her right arm had twisted itself into an unusual position, and her neck and chin had followed suit. As she pressed herself up, her eye fell on the dismembered coat hanger that she had been attempting to transform into a bicycle with a set of dragonfly wings. A pair of needle-nose pliers lay like a casualty next to the wreckage on the coffee table. In the daylight her apartment seemed completely alien to her, not because anything was different from how she had left it two days before, but because it was exactly the same. Next to the mangled wire, the pile of unpaid bills was pitched at exactly the same height, with the one on top precariously frozen at half-off.

The front door buzzer buzzed, but she could not make herself answer it. Someone must have been downstairs, because she heard the footsteps closing in, the creak and sigh of the stairs, the steady thuds on the two landings between. She heard their voices before they knocked, and she was relieved that they were there, even as she wished she was alone.

"Open up, dear. I've brought steaks," called Katie through the keyhole.

"It's true, she has!" said Ed's voice.

She got to her feet to let them in, trying to shrug off a dim feeling of betrayal. When she had called Katie, just before she was let go from the hospital, she had asked her not to tell her brother what had happened just yet. Standing up, she felt as feeble as a woman of ninety. The nurse had told her they would have transfused her if she had lost half a thimbleful more blood.

With shaky steps Charlotte progressed to the door and opened it. Katie held out the brown paper parcel of meat almost defensively. At the scent of raw beef Charlotte's stomach let out an audible roar.

"I knew you'd be hongry!" Katie walked in and made straight for the kitchen.

"I thought you were dead, myself," said Ed, throwing himself into a chair.

"He called me just as I was on my way here," said Katie. Her back was turned toward the sink, but Charlotte could hear the apology.

"Did you know your phone's been disconnected?"

"Yes, Ed. Thank you, and don't worry, I'll be fine." Charlotte tightened the belt of the detestable robe and sat back down on the love seat.

"I'm sorry, Lottie. My goodness, you do look even paler than usual. Katie, we better get something else to eat. Charlotte needs all the steak. Here." He held his wrist out to her. "Suck on this."

"She's a woman, Ed, not a vampire," called Katie. She took down the bottle of Chianti that Charlotte always replaced, opened it, and poured three glasses, but Charlotte waved hers away.

"Not wanting wine is the first sign of vampirism," said Ed, taking a long slug from his glass and then crossing his thin, elegant legs. Charlotte had a word for it this time, the collusion of envy with admiration for his beauty, for the way he threw one leg over the other and settled against the chairback as if he awaited a soft-footed waiter at a gentleman's club.

Contemptible, that was it, a contemptible ease. A hard, clean line drawn from him directly to the world that wanted him, so that he did not have to think about it or be at odds with it at all. He was never wrong-sized or in pain or bloody. She announced she was getting dressed, took some things from the dresser that did not fit in her door-less bedroom. She stepped into the bathroom to get dressed over the toilet so that she would not feel his gaze on her as she changed into pants and a loose sleeveless gingham blouse.

"Louise is coming next week," said Ed. When she stepped out of the bathroom, he looked her over, as he always did, from toe to head, as any man would. "Well, now you're ready for a picnic! We'll luncheon. Does she know what happened to you, poor thing? And what did happen exactly?"

"She bled gallons!" called Katie, over the smell of steak and onions. Charlotte thought Katie sounded almost gleeful. She was hungry, and there was no food in the house so she told herself to be grateful, but she wished they would go away now. The magic moment of quiet, the pause in the night, she wanted to stay in that wordless rest.

"But what caused it?"

"They don't really know," said Charlotte. "A wrinkle in the system."

"You mean that just can happen, to any woman, that she can start bleeding and just not stop?" Ed asked, rubbing his face with his hands. "But no, don't tell me. I don't think I can stand to know that much about the mystery. Save it up for when Brad or somebody puts a bun in your oven."

Katie had drained one glass of wine and was pouring herself another. Ed held his glass out and Katie filled it. She'd brought mushrooms too. Charlotte could smell them cooking along with the onions and the meat. Her mouth filled with saliva.

"Charlotte's oven can't hold any buns." Katie looked up just then, realized her mistake, and flushed a deep red. Charlotte shot her a flinty look.

"What do you mean?" asked Ed, clearly taking in Charlotte's expression.

"She doesn't mean anything," said Charlotte firmly, willing Katie not to make it worse, but finding that once again, her will had no purchase in the world. She was on the verge of telling them to leave but felt too weak to say it.

"It was just what one doctor said," said Katie, as if trying to make amends. She took the cracked porcelain platter, one of the many things Charlotte had pilfered from the house in Shepherd's Glen, down from on top of the refrigerator, and put steak and mushrooms and onions on it. Then she pulled up a step stool for a third seat and gestured at the tiny kitchen table. "Come, come."

"What did the doctor say?" asked Ed, perching on the stool.

"Katie is not going to tell you that, and neither am I," said Charlotte, feeling her hands shake and begin to sweat. "I love you both but please shut the hell up about my health now."

"Oh dear, I'm sorry, I really didn't mean to—" Katie was clearly uncomfortable. She had a way of digging herself in deeper once she started to offend someone. That it was a habit Charlotte shared did not make her feel better.

Charlotte interrupted Katie. "Ed, tell us something about yourself. You're so good at that."

"Touchy Lottie!" Ed sawed into his steak. "I've got a commission. Billy's uncle wants a portrait, so I'm staying in New York a bit longer."

"I thought Louise's friend was so anxious to give you the keys to the flat in Montmartre," said Charlotte. She fixed her gaze on her plate so that she didn't have to look at Katie. If she looked at her friend, she might have to tell her to leave.

"The flat can wait, and it's good money," said Ed, and then almost accusingly, "Someone around here has to make some."

"Oh, are you going to have my phone turned back on?" asked Charlotte. "Maybe you can help with my rent for once." Her mood was softening as she chewed the meat, felt the roaring approval of her anemic cells.

Ed batted the comment away with the flick of a wrist. They talked of other things—of Chaney, Goodman, and Schwerner, the civil rights workers who had gone missing; Katie held out hope that they would reappear but Ed and Charlotte were certain they would not; of Katie's boyfriend Alexander, who had himself been jailed with the freedom riders in Mississippi, and whose parents were both "experimental psychiatrists," whatever that meant; of the oddness of Billy's uncle; of the war drums beating in Vietnam, and Charlotte's fear that Bruce would be sent there and Ed's gladness he was not a soldier and never would be one. They left the subject of Charlotte's body behind, but even as she teased Ed for being a coward and decided to forgive Katie, she felt the presence of her weak and forlorn animal self. A dream-like doubleness overcame her, the sense that she was at once inside and outside of this creature of clotted cream and blood, this thing whose softness had consumed its bones.

"Oh, Charlotte, you look tired." Katie squeezed her hand, then got up to do the dishes.

"I am."

"We'll go," said Ed with finality. "But listen, Lottie, get your phone back on and call Louise. She's worried about you."

Charlotte didn't answer. She started at the sound of a knock on the door. Ed leapt up and opened it. There was Gil, wearing a fresh plaid shirt and white T-shirt and a pair of jeans that looked stiff enough to be brand new. From where she sat, Charlotte could see their two bodies stiffen, like a wolf and a fox with a chicken between them.

"I'll come back later," Gil said, starting to back away.

"We were just leaving," said Ed, as if delivering orders.

"Please come in, Gil," said Charlotte, rising slowly from the table. "That's my brother Ed."

"I guessed," said Gil.

"And you are?"

"Charlotte's neighbor."

"My savior," said Charlotte. Ed and Gil stood facing each other, not moving an inch.

"Right place, right time," said Gil. "I can come back."

"No, it's all right, really. Ed was just leaving."

"Well, no doubt there's a story here, but I really do have to go," said Ed. "Katie, I'll walk you to the train."

"Okay, just after the dishes," said Katie.

"I'll finish them," said Charlotte.

"No, I will," said Gil.

"Jack of all trades, are you?" Clearly Ed thought this funny, and he laughed even more heartily at the next words out of his mouth. "Well, Lottie. Get better. I love you when you're happy. When you're sad you just bore me."

Katie swatted Ed with a kitchen rag, kissed Charlotte on the cheek, and promised to come by again the next day. The door closed behind them and Charlotte and Gil were alone.

When Charlotte spoke, she sounded nervous.

"How are you?"

"You stole my line," said Gil in her low voice. Charlotte loved Gil's voice. Just then she wanted to hear more and more of it. Gil's voice is like a stone baked in the sun, thought Charlotte, feeling suddenly virginal and shy. "Why don't you sit down?"

"Sit with me." Charlotte patted the cushion next to her.

"I'll finish the dishes."

"Hang the dishes!"

"They'll break."

"Do you ever stop joking, Gil?"

"Not if I can help it." She sat down next to Charlotte and pulled an odd little book out of a brown paper bag. "I got a job in the stock room at The Strand. Brought you this."

The book had a red velvet cover and no apparent author. The pages were filled with sketches in fine black ink of useless machines and small animals. On one page was a pigeon wearing a crown of hands that appeared to be plucking its feathers, on another a pair of cabbages with hands were tearing each other's leaves off. Charlotte paged through, laughing with delight.

"This is hilarious! But are you sure it's not just someone's notebook? There's no information…"

"It must be magic," said Gil.

"Yes," said Charlotte.

"There are all kinds of weird things at that store. Queer ones too. They keep us in the back, but they want beautiful women to work the register."

"Is that what they told you?"

"Everyone wants beautiful women to work for them," Gil said, leaning against the back of the dusty love seat, opening her arm across it. "You should apply for a job there."

"That's not a bad idea." Charlotte leaned back, placing herself under the shelter of Gil's arm, testing…something, feeling the warmth of Gil's arm against the back of her neck. "Do you want to know something strange?"

"Yes," said Gil, turning to look at her.

"When I was bleeding that day, it really was my father who told me to get up." Charlotte returned Gil's gaze. "He wouldn't let me slip away.

Do you think I'm crazy, receiving messages from a pile of bones at the bottom of the South China Sea?"

"Naw," said Gil, cupping Charlotte's shoulder with her warm big hand. "I told you, you're an artist."

Charlotte could see the question in Gil's eyes. She smiled, and Gil smiled and kissed her, just once, on the lips. And the question was answered, Not just yet. And though it would be weeks before Gil undressed her, Charlotte would remember that night, so different from her nights with others, as the beginning.

Gil took a throw pillow and put it on her lap, gesturing for Charlotte to place her head there. Charlotte complied, felt Gil's fingertips graze her forehead, let herself fall asleep to that soft rhythmic touch as she inhaled Gil's scent, a mixture of pipe tobacco and fresh-turned earth.

THE RETURN

I am not done with you
What love is love is true

A boy is once and then a man
From the blue I will do what I can.

Kiss of Death

July 1948

She almost refused his offer to drive her back to her car. Once Kit showed Louise up for wanting more time with him, she wanted desperately to leave the café of the motel with its one special and its overly friendly waitress. She was watching him chew as the thought arose, watching the bones of his jaw work under the thick and stubbled flesh of his cheeks. She had been a fool to let him take her, she thought. But as she watched his jaw, the flick of his tongue along the pink rim of his lips, she felt the traces of his touch and lick across her body, and behind her good sense grew a familiar haze, a version of the soft confusion she had known with only one other man. And so, when he finished his last bite, took a great slug of coffee, and put the mug on the table with an emphatic slap, she nodded her assent. Anyway, she told herself, it wasn't as if there was a taxi available.

He seemed to read her softness, to know that there was no sentry on duty. Your drawbridge is down, Louise, she heard herself say to herself, stop smiling like that.

"I'd like to take one more walk on the shore, but I really should get back to Wilmington."

"Wilmington?"

"For a scientist you're not very thorough." She looked at him quizically. "You didn't even read the return address on the one letter you bothered to read."

"Oh, of course, Wilmington. That's a lot of driving, isn't it? Why don't you just take me to a bus station, or better yet, I'll stand by the gas pumps and stick out my thumb." She meant for her tone to be light, but her voice betrayed her.

"Come now," he said, and put his hand on her knee. His big palm was warm and cupped the whole of her little cap and all around it.

She smiled with excessive brightness and stood up, feeling suddenly like an actress playing the role all wrong. You're not a jilted lover, she told herself, and now that he got what he wanted he'll leave you alone.

Be done with it. "Well, Mr. Blunt, it seems you're the one who can't take a joke. Thank you for the offer."

It wasn't until they were well on their way that she realized that he hadn't really told her anything about himself. But then again, she hadn't asked much. He was turning the dial on the radio, going right past Glen Miller.

"I don't like him either," she said, rolling down the window and sticking her arm out, diving her hand through waves of air the way the children did, a move that Helen called "dolphining."

"Who?" Kit turned off the radio altogether.

"Glen Miller."

"Oh, come on, everyone likes him!" He was teasing her a bit, so she played the straight man.

"His music is so obvious and boring."

"Give a dead guy a break."

"We have to move on now, don't we?" To herself, Louise sounded like a secretary parroting the meaning of the day. She squinted into the sun. "Talk about other things than the war, listen to new music."

"What a relief. I thought you were going to ask me for more war stories, and to tell you how I lost my leg."

"And I thought you were going to tell me."

"I will sometime." He kept his left hand on the wheel as he stretched his right arm across the seat back. He didn't touch her, but she could feel the warmth from his palm on her bare neck. She had lost one of her favorite hairpins but had speared her chignon with a pencil begged from the bratty waitress.

"We have nothing but time right now. Tell me a war story." Louise stopped her dolphining and turned to look at him. His eyes were on the road, but she could see a tremor in the lids, as if he were blinking something away.

"To everything a season."

"Summer is as good a time as any."

"Not every season is seasonable." He pressed the dashboard lighter in a bit too forcefully.

Louise felt the prick of memory, a jab that made her realize she was dangerously close to falling asleep at the wheel of her own life. The wheel she had wrested from her father's hands, and then from Roland's, like the wheel of the boat they had piloted across Long Island Sound, disappearing from the Diehl family gathering to rut in a bed of moss on an island too tiny to be named. In her ecstasy with Roland, Louise had later understood, there was more than a touch of revenge against her father, the satisfaction of locking him out. Leaving him at the table with the guests, leaving him to what was approved of, what was spoken of in polite company. Now I am free of you, she remembered thinking, only to realize that the very thought was proof that she was not.

"Not every season is seasonable," repeated Kit, elbowing her to draw her attention away from the window and passing her a lit cigarette. He spoke as if they were both actors and he was cueing her.

"Roland used to say that," she said. "Not every season is seasonable, he'd say, not every reason is reasonable."

"He did? And here I thought I had an original thought for once."

"I'd like to hear about your original life."

"What would you like to know? My log cabin days?"

He was grinning now and so was she. All right, all right, she told herself, just play.

"Yes, exactly."

"We'd just got the sucker built, and Ma had just popped me out when the Injuns attacked." He gave her that curled eyebrow grin, straight out of the Orson Welles playbook.

"Very funny. But really, you could tell me something."

"Born in Indiana, raised in Wilmington. Played football. Never went to college, preferred reading on my own. I've always read poetry, though I kept that quiet on the gridiron. Meant to do something different from my dad but never got around to it. I figured we would join the effort eventually, and that I would be drafted, so I signed up in '40. I couldn't think what else to do."

"That's the only reason?"

"Well, the war was just brewing. I was working at Dad's business—"

"The one who's sick now?"

"Yes, I only have one father."

"Now you sound like my daughter."

"No one's ever said that to me before."

"Sarcastic, I mean. Of course, yes, I too had one father."

"I heard about him. A big man."

"He was." Louise slipped her shoes off and put her feet on the dashboard the way Helen often did. The boys also flung their bodies around thoughtlessly. But not Charlotte, she was never at ease. Louise thought suddenly of the lie she had told, of how she could take a trip since they weren't expecting her at home. She could go to New York if she wanted to. "But we were talking about you."

"Colonel Walter P. Diehl was a legend. I used to hear of him and MacArthur in the same breath. Once I thought of West Point. Your father must have made a lot of guys want to go there and go all-American. I might've done it myself but—"

"You didn't get around to it?" asked Louise.

"Fate sort of interfered."

"What kind of fate?"

"Injury." He said it with finality. "I couldn't play ball for a while, and so I never applied. And then, well, I just started working at Blunt Mills. And then the war—"

"Yes," Louise said. The heat of the day was getting to her. The air was thick. They had driven away from the shore and into the pine bottoms, along a marshy wood. She began to drift off, let her feet slide off the dashboard, let her head and shoulders slide down the seat back. As she fell into the well of sleep, she could feel the rearrangements of the last day and night, a feeling of his hands on her, of her body met, of her head emptied of questions. A rapid descent in a deep well, down, down to a moss bed on a little island, a rowboat pulled just over its rocky lip. Mother was there saying, "My, you were gone a good long while."

Louise's tongue was thick in her mouth when she woke. Kit was pulling up to her car, which was parked across the street from Da Ronco's.

"Here you are, Miss Diehl," said Kit.

"What?" Louise sat up rod straight.

"I said we're here."

"You called me Miss Diehl."

"Did I? Must have been the long night." He was smiling at her again, in that bemused way, the way a father might smile at a daughter to tell her that what worried her was only an illusion.

"Don't call me that again." Once more she tried, unsuccessfully, to change her tone. She hadn't meant to sound so severe, to be so bothered. Roland had called her that at their beginning and sometimes later, invoking the springtime of courtship when she was a young mother. He would return to the house some evenings, find her sweaty and covered with baby's milk-puke. For you, Miss Diehl, he would say, holding a daisy or a slim volume of Wordsworth. The world is too much with us.

"Come now." He cupped her bare neck in his warm palm. "Can't a guy make a mistake?"

In spite of herself, she relaxed at his touch. Of its own accord her head turned toward him, and her whole body followed, so that she was slumped against him, inhaling his sour-salt scent, wrapping her arm around his dense warm belly. And he held her close, kissed her on the forehead like a father kissing a daughter.

As she gathered her things and opened her door, he made as if to help her to her car. But she waved him away. They did not say they would see each other again, but she knew that they would. She drove home slowly. There was something, she knew, that she was not seeing. Something terribly familiar in how strange she felt, as if she had put on a secondhand coat that fit her perfectly. Her thought of staying away from home evaporated.

Mother was in the kitchen cooking fish when she arrived. The scent struck Louise as she walked in the door. For a moment she took it as the smell of herself, a creature hooked and plucked out of her element. The salty smell of a woman served. Mother had on her green apron, and she was chopping carrots in her quick efficient way, her sharp elbow following the knife like a bellows. She looked up as Louise walked in and wiped her hands on her apron.

"Char—" Mother started. "Oh, it's you. I thought you were off fishing in Virginia."

"Fishing?"

"Or at your conference or whatever you called it. Charlotte told us not to expect you." Mother opened the refrigerator, pulled out a bottle of milk. "Pour some for your growing children. I'm afraid I didn't buy enough sole—"

"Yes, Mother. It's all right."

"Well, no, it's not. You can share mine. I've got extra potatoes at least, and some really bright, fresh green onions."

"All right, thank you."

"Are you?" Mother put down her knife and turned to look at Louise.

"What?"

"All right?"

"Just a little tired, I suppose."

"Well then, pour the milk and set the table. Those girls of yours aren't helping." Mother stepped past Louise and went to yell up the stairs for the children to come for dinner.

Louise poured the milk and began to take down the dishes. She was placing each napkin in its place when she felt the memory. It was not in her mind, but in her body. The way that Kit touched her, the way he stroked her thigh with his warm hand, let his fingers touch her lightly, once, twice, three times. The way he cupped her until she pressed against his hand. Teasing and holding her until she cried for him to enter her. It was exactly Roland's way. Just exactly the way that made her wet as she stood in dining room thinking of it, holding a napkin by its ring.

PURPLE HEART

AUGUST 1964

Tiny stones in the sidewalk concrete seemed to Charlotte to vibrate with the bass's thrum. She and Katie were not familiar with the opening act, but seeing them suddenly seemed of the utmost importance. They had taken too much time getting ready, waiting at Charlotte's place for the drug to take hold before stepping out into the night for the short walk to the Pussycat. She had changed her clothes three times, finally following Katie's lead, keeping it simple, black capris and a sleeveless blouse with a pattern of gray, white, and black diamonds, that pattern the first of many that would come alive before her eyes as the LSD had its way with her. Her hair had grown unruly in the weeks of her rest and recovery, and she pulled it back from her pale forehead with a white headband that seemed to her to have a special relationship with her cat-eyed glasses. Katie wore one of the shifts that were her summer uniform, this one an orange-on-red floral that offset the beauty of her lean, tan arms, which Charlotte was admiring when they realized how late it had gotten, and made their way into an August night that was no cooler than the day had been.

With a look they agreed, Charlotte thought, that there was a buzzing in their heads, that a wire had tripped their nerves, that their jaws were suddenly as tight as their limbs were loose. The sidewalk above the stairs that led down to the cave where they spent so much of their free time held a small tight throng of people.

"Two kinds," Charlotte whispered to Katie. "The hopeful and the bored."

"We're the latter," said Katie, lighting two cigarettes and passing one to Charlotte as they positioned themselves on the periphery, but within view of the doorman, a friend of theirs.

"Of course, dahling," said Charlotte, streaming smoke through flared nostrils.

The hopeful couldn't help themselves, of course, freshly arrived from across the rivers and through the tunnels, from some amber field of grain where they'd dreamed of eating or being eaten, to taste the banquet or to be cursed and spat out by something less dumbly accepting than a threshing machine or a small-town high school. Of gathering what crumbs they could to tell the ones who never left what it is they are missing—oh yes, the Village; oh yes, Italians; oh yes, Negroes; oh yes, even jazz musicians. There was a hopeful now, a strapping dark-blond field hand, a guitar strapped to his back like some weapon New York City was going to beg him to use, telling the short plump female version of himself, who squeezed his elbow with her fingertips and buttoned and unbuttoned the top button of her blouse to be cool, be cool.

The bored were too bored to say hello, thought Charlotte, though she and Katie also did not say hello to the wax-faced poet they stood behind, the organizer of an open-mic night that was really an excuse to read his own abstractions to a crowd that talked over him. Drainpipe Allegory, they called him, or sometimes just The Drip.

Of course, Charlotte and Katie and The Drip and the other regulars were all too bored to laugh openly at the hopefuls, who were far too easy a target, being so obviously impressed by this fabled place, New York City, lower Manhattan. The field hands and their girls, so clearly trying to get their passports stamped or burned a hole in by the cigarette of a genuine beatnik gathering in this natural beat habitat, a little café that was hosting jazz men who through some twist of fate or problem with licenses or plumbing were playing here instead of the Vanguard. On jazz nights the crowd was always more mixed, more Negroes than the usual few among the Jews and Italians and know-it-all WASPS who spent their pennies on cheap whiskey and Gauloise, which for some reason the Pussycat kept in the vending machine. Would it kill you to sell Camels? Charlotte had once asked Danny the doorman, who had forgiven her their disastrous one-night stand during her first days in New York but shrugged off her question, declaring himself a Luckies man, as if that war-time brand were still somehow indicative of victory.

In their haste to hear the music Charlotte and Katie dropped their cigarettes and nearly fell down the steep stairs, leaping at the chance to skip the line that Danny promised them with a wink and a flick of the wrist. Inside people were packed elbow to elbow, and the air was thick with tobacco and marijuana—or tea as Katie's boyfriend Alexander called it with great authority. What a know-it-all, Charlotte thought, then wondered if she had said it out loud, imagining his tone as he quoted

The New Yorker without crediting it for his view on a film or a play. He had given her his ticket, she reminded herself. He had given her and Katie the drug that—even as she thought disdainfully of Alexander's puffy lips and straw-blond hair, so carefully tousled to look laissez-faire, his smug flair with a tennis racket—was beginning to light her up from the inside. The risk Charlotte had chosen to take to celebrate being strong enough, after three weeks of mostly rest, to go out into the world rearranged by the chemicals that Alexander had access to because both of his parents were psychiatrists.

Oliver Nelson's group hadn't set up yet and Charlotte didn't recognize the opening act on stage now, a trio of bass, trumpet, and piano. Sound came from behind and beneath, from all around her, though seemingly not from the musicians themselves, who as far as she could tell were working on a different time signature than the rest of the world. They seemed to her to be playing at a different rate than that of the sound that was being produced, as if their instruments had been dubbed in later, like English over some Italian actors' voices. The thought of "later" led her to question the meaning of "now" and following her own line of reasoning, she began to laugh and then laugh at her own laughing. And then laugh at knowing that she was beginning to feel very, very high. She was transfixed by the bass player, his long fingers plucking the strings, striking the spine of the instrument; she was certain she could feel his fingers on her own spine. She took hold of Katie's arm and squeezed it. When their eyes met, they both began to laugh. Somewhere in front of them a man shot them a look, slid his stubby finger across his throat as if to slice his Adam's apple in two. The woman he was with, a gamine beauty with cropped hair and a neck as long as Audrey Hepburn's, turned back to look at them and shrugged. Another man turned and told them to hush, his face a rat's face with a pointed, quivering nose and long front teeth. They could hold back their laughter, Charlotte thought, as long as they didn't look at each other. She turned her eyes to the stage, but her sight was confused by the thickening of the clouds of smoke that became opaque things. Katie handed her another lit cigarette, her hand emerging into Charlotte's field of vision as a disembodied thing, the reach of an angel from the depths of a sweet, brown-leafed paradise. Charlotte wanted to go there, tobacco heaven. She drank in the smoke like a sacrament, let it fill her throat and lungs with holiness, let her breathe holiness out into the holiness of the room filled with supplicants genuflecting to the jazz men.

The bass line was a transmission of a heart beating; the sounds were warm and dark. The room, Charlotte thought, was full of hearts and lungs. If she closed her eyes, she could see them beating, the division of colors into squares of themselves. Blue is as blue does, she thought, alarmed by the clarity of the thought, how full of meaning it was. Meaning that could be extracted from everything and painted onto everything else.

"Whoever they are, they're really, really, really good," Katie was saying. She was squeezing Charlotte's arm now, so hard that Charlotte thought that it should hurt, but it didn't hurt, because hurt was just something on the list of possible feelings.

"Yes." The word was the only one that came out of Charlotte's mouth, but there were others, thoughts embodied in these packages known as words. They were like children running for the front door, trying to escape some parental tyranny. They fell into the door and collapsed, blocking their own way out.

Katie had somehow maneuvered them to a table, and they were sitting down, Irish coffees in front of them. In a flash Charlotte missed the end of the opening act. The stage now held no one but the bass player removing his instrument. She believed for a moment that the stage was framed by her eyes only, that its clearing and filling was a matter of the opening and closing of her eyelids. What else could explain the disappearance of that beautiful trio? I shall call them Shadrach, Meshach, and Abednego, Charlotte said into the room. The clouds of smoke had dissipated; some people must have stepped outside between sets.

"Do you feel as funny as I do?" Katie was asking.

"Funnier. LSD, what does it mean, even?" said Charlotte.

"Let Sue Decide!" said Katie, her mouth twisting around a laugh she was trying to withhold for no good reason.

"Who's Sue?"

"Must be that bull dyke over there," said Katie, pointing to the bar.

"Where?" She followed Katie's finger, but could see only the Pussycat's lone waitress, scowling and sallow-faced in her beatnik uniform of French sailor's shirt and black tights. "That's not a bull dyke, that's a French poodle!"

That set them off laughing again. Charlotte was breathless with laughter that overtook her from the inside, that stretched her guts thin as a wire, spooled them around spools and recombined them and tied them together in a very complicated knot just below her rib cage. Her jaw was tight and her stomach was starting to hurt, but these feelings arose as distant signals and passed away quickly as taps in Morse code.

"I love a dyke," she said. "Oh, did I say that out loud?"

"You did. You've always been queer, Charlotte, but not like that. You just think you love her." Katie sounded very clear, full of absolute authority.

"Who, Sue?"

"Yeah, Sue," said Katie, waving wildly at the waitress who was leaning against the bar, smoking a cigarette, her thousand-yard stare skimming the tops of her customers' heads.

"What do you want?" asked Charlotte.

"From life?"

"No, from the French poodle."

"I want poodle snacks!"

This set them off again, into the laughter that was sickening, hollow, the merry-mad dance of chemicals firing in their brains. Charlotte fell forward in her chair, grasping her gut, then stayed in that position admiring a spill on the floor, the shimmer along its surface. The different ways of light on liquid revealed to Charlotte the simple truth that she, "Charlotte," was actually nine personalities, at least three of which were male. Three threes, holy, multiple, evolving ever after. After what may or may not have been a long time, she pressed herself back up and planted her elbows on the table, prepared to explain this to Katie. But Katie wasn't there.

The close, dark room had gotten closer, darker. Charlotte felt, more than saw, the presence of other bodies streaming in from the world outside this place, this classroom or cell or club like a club foot. Like some appendage to the body of the city, thick and limping to its own rhythm, yet, yes, real, integral to the whole body of Manhattan. A place like this was where people came to be with others, to be aligned with the heat and rhythm of each other, to give themselves over to the heat and rhythm of the next jazz men, Oliver Nelson's group that they had come to see. Charlotte could see them now stepping onto the small stage as if they had come from separate planets but arrived here all at once with perfect, easeful timing. The declaration of the trumpet, the clarification of the saxophone, the conversation of these instruments transfixed the presences that filled the room, Charlotte among them, her jaw dropping open, staying open. The other sounds coming from the other instruments she might distantly name, the profound disordered order of the sonic interchange that played as colors across her tainted vision. The piano making bright prints across the throbbing living carpet of the bass, the brass receding, threading through the weave to explode along the fringe and then return to center, to seed the new arrangement, to bloom and burst forth.

When they paused their playing a fraction of a silent second came, and then the hollers, the listeners laying claim to what was good, what was great, what was needed. Charlotte was silent, her mouth open, tears pouring down her face.

That was when she saw Gil. Yes, it was Gil, she was sure of it, sitting just two tables over, her arm casually draped across the shoulders of a slender blond, a woman Charlotte didn't recognize. It could not be Gil, but then she thought it must be, didn't she know the shape of that head, the shape of her savior. The one who had kissed and held her—only that at first. Who had waited, but then so gently, just last week, in the late afternoon light, had removed her clothes like a husk, had made her cry with joy. But Gil was out of town, wasn't she? Didn't she say she was going back to Ohio, a friend in trouble, a relative dying...

"Poodle snacks!" Katie was there again suddenly at Charlotte's elbow, holding two more Irish coffees, though the first two remained on the table, half drunk.

Charlotte didn't laugh then but sat transfixed, staring at Gil's head, trying to confirm the arrangement of silver hairs, the cobwebs her hair drew from the rafters of the longhouse of human experience. Gil was tall, physically and in life, she had a real view of this and all places. That was what Charlotte wanted from Gil, she realized with the alarming clarity she kept forgetting was a function of the drug. The one-way telegram from herself to herself, from the everlasting to the momentary that supplanted the next in urgency, in spine-tingling clarity. The news was this: I, Charlotte, we, the nine Charlottes, we want Gil's vision, we want her understanding. For her to see and know me, that is how I will know myself. My selves.

"That was fucking in-cred-i-bull," Katie was saying.

Charlotte turned to look at her friend, at the great black basketballs of her eyes, eyes that filled with everything but reflected nothing. She looked over Katie's shoulder, which obstructed her view now of the strong shoulders of her savior, of the dyke she was now more than ever certain that she loved. But that was Gil, wasn't it? Wasn't she there with a slender blond, pretty as some young Louise? She was wrapping her arm around her, whispering something in her ear.

And then the lights were dimmed, and again the music came and took her over. The jazz men bent Charlotte to them, they brought the whole Pussycat to its knees, begging for more and more and more of the deeper, truer mirror it held to them, one phrase and then another, it played with their expectations. Some old familiar melody—don't sit under the apple tree, was that it? The brass said yes, then upended the formula, turned short pretty parts long, pulled and exaggerated and then trimmed off, brushed with the silver brush across the drumhead, the trail of little stars in water like phosphorescence in the ocean, the flute that flew like a hummingbird—no, a butterfly; no, a flutterby! The laughter boiling up again inside her, the thoughts that flew like fast-moving clouds that rode away on the smoke clouds that were in this basement room and were as thick and real as her own hand, her own mouth. Like the cigarette she found now in her fingers that she remembered now to bring to her lips. There was Gil. Gil and Louise, each on a cloud, each that hung in the air, that blocked her view of the jazz men. No! It was them! They were truly her saviors, these men, these masters, they who were right here and now remaking America, who could, Charlotte was certain, save America from itself.

People were snapping, people were calling *yes* and *right on!* Charlotte and Katie among them, all together as one swelling presence the crowd was begging the jazz men to keep on and on and on. But they would have to stop sometime. And then they stopped. The clouds of smoke that contained the music the way outside clouds contained the rain, the clouds sealed up and the droplets would not fall. The colors returned to their origins. Charlotte wanted more, wanted to go back into the thrilling living weaving carpet of colors they had made, but as they had arrived at once from other planets, so now the jazz men disappeared.

Charlotte looked over Katie's shoulder once more, but Gil was gone. The table was empty. The crowd was shifting, the presences lessening. People, Charlotte informed herself, were leaving now. They were climbing up the stairs and back out onto the sidewalk, into the city night, with all its false lights and fake colors, blinking and winking and destroying the jazz men's truth. Now that she could not see Gil, Charlotte was overtaken by the need to see her. She must see her before they left this place, of that she was deadly certain.

"Did you see Gil?" she asked Katie, but Katie was just shaking her head, saying, Wow, that was beautiful. Wow. "I have to find her."

As she stood up, Charlotte could hear Katie saying, "Wait, wait for me." But Charlotte was already standing, moving into the crowd, the thick crowd of presences. A man spoke to her. "Hey, doll, what's the rush?" She was stepping over legs, around the people still at the tables, into the flow of the crowd, the crush of arms and legs and lungs and hearts. She tripped, fell into the lap of a strange man, fell against him, chafed her cheek against the rough stubble of his chin. She tried to get up, but he held her to him; the laughter coming now was not Charlotte's own but came from around the table, the faces of the men, their dusky chins long and short, their gray teeth chattering in their heads.

But the sight of you is what saves me, thought Charlotte, seeing Gil again, the back of that head, the strong and noble neck. Somehow, she pressed herself free from the men, shoved herself into the stream. And then she was pushing, elbowing her way, trying to get to Gil, who was just up ahead, maybe three people away, maybe two. She could see the blond now, the young Louise tucked under Gil's arm, the young Louise who had come to steal Charlotte's own true love. She was having these thoughts and they were real, though some tiny voice, one of the nine personalities who lived inside her, one that was a scientist or otherwise rational, that one was whispering in Charlotte's ear, It's okay, it's okay, it's only the drug.

Charlotte felt more than heard Katie calling after her as she shoved her way through the crowd, as she placed her foot on the bottom step, squeezed and pushed her way up the stairs toward the sidewalk where the young Louise stood carefully tucked under the arm of Charlotte's own savior. Stealing away her love, as Louise always did. Had Charlotte said that out loud? She had nearly reached the top when Katie grabbed her arm, but Charlotte twisted and yanked her arm away. Her flailing arm struck the person in front of her. But Charlotte pushed past, stumbled onto the sidewalk and she was upon them. She grabbed the young Louise's arm and pulled, because she knew she had to get her away from Gil, had to keep Gil for herself.

Three things happened at once. The young Louise showed her face to be not Louise's face; Katie arrived breathless and calling her name; and the Gil was not her Gil, was not any Gil at all, but a man with Gil's hair and shoulders not even as broad.

"What gives?" snarled the man.

"She's sorry! Sorry!" Katie was apologizing for her, threading her arm through Charlotte's, turning her away from the angry couple. "C'mon, let's get an ice cream, wouldn't you like that?"

"What am I, fudge ripple?" said Charlotte. "There's no ice cream this time of night!"

They laughed again, but the drug was beginning to wear off. One laugh did not beget so many more. They were walking on the sidewalk, moving away from the throng and toward Charlotte's place.

"I thought it was Gil," said Charlotte as if an explanation were needed.

"You're always talking about her."

"Because I love her!" exclaimed Charlotte, though some part of her said to some other part of her that it was the drug talking.

"No, you don't."

"I kissed her."

"You told me. You made love like you never made with a man. You were fragile and sick, but you're better now."

"But you don't understand."

"But I do." Katie stopped, turned Charlotte to look at her, one hand on each of Charlotte's arms. "I do understand. You think you love her because she saved you. Just like a patient falls in love with a nurse. But you're not—" Katie paused, looked around as if she feared saying the word aloud.

"What? What am I not, Katie?" Charlotte followed Katie's gaze, repeated the question.

"You're not an invert, Charlotte." That was Alexander's word, Charlotte was certain of it, the word of a child of psychiatrists, of a person studying to be a psychiatrist.

"You don't know that."

"But I do." Katie said it firmly, as firmly as she said c'mon, and relocked her arm in Charlotte's and quickened their steps on the sidewalk.

THE RETURN

I traded bones with other men
You'll miss me when I've come again

I am not done with you
My wife of black and blue.

KISS OF DEATH

AUGUST 1948

Louise no longer liked Alice O'Day. This freckle-faced, auburn-haired woman of good cheer, of heart-shaped face and neat little chin, who had been a WAAC officer stationed in France and had, it was said, done something heroic wiring messages for the Resistance while managing a corps of nurses in a field hospital in the Dordogne. This woman who was not much older than Louise, but whose accomplishments were so much finer. Who had never married, who had been at the front, who had finished her advanced degree in chemistry. Jealousy was not something Louise admitted in herself. The bitter bone of it was something she tried not to choke on, but Alice, who had once managed Louise's team, and had reported to Harry Leopold, was now stepping into Leopold's role. Suddenly Alice was Dr. O'Day, someone who led big meetings, someone who received phone calls from reporters, who stood before them all now in the auditorium, welcoming them all to her reign of utter excellence. Louise squirmed in the uncomfortable seat as if she could get away from herself, from her relentless inner sarcasm.

Dr. Leopold had retired quietly, without celebration. Apparently, he had been sleeping with Marjorie or whoever, whatever her name was. This was a bitter little joke Louise had with herself, pretending not to know the names of the women she had worked hard not to be, the little creatures who answered phones. The secretary who had been fool enough to think that Dr. Leopold would leave his wife for her. Apparently, while Louise was arching her back and pressing her pelvis against Kit Blunt's stump in that seaside motel, on the very day Louise had begun to feel, against all possible better judgment, the glorious presence of the animal she was, this Marjorie had made a scene. Had argued publicly with Leopold and his wife. Had let all who would listen know that she was as natural as Hawthorne's Hester Prynne, and was going to bring up Leopold's baby alone if she had to.

Louise had learned of the affair in the ladies' room, her only venue for hearing the gossip that she assumed streamed steadily out of other women's mouths over open compacts and pedicures. She was the only woman in the group of chemists she worked with, and after she carefully deflected a couple of flirtations, her fellow scientists for the most part treated her like one of them. She felt at ease with them, talking politics and sports in the cafeteria, and sometimes echoed the things they said about their wives and girls, about women's ways of scolding and cooing, placing Mother in the role of nag. Even as a girl she had not been interested in the intrigues of girls, had excelled in school but had been roundly disliked, called Mother Superior and Her Holiness. Smarty smarty had a party, the girls in her class would say, and nobody came but smarty.

She had first learned of Dr. Leopold's fall by reverting to one of the tricks of her high school years, stepping gingerly onto the toilet seat in a bathroom stall and crouching there, still as a gargoyle. Among the three voices she heard discussing Marjorie's dramatic moment with Mrs. Leopold was a staff writer, someone Louise had previously respected.

"Right there, right out in the open, she said to Mrs. Leopold—"

"Wait, you mean right there in the lobby?"

"Yes, as I've said, right there she says—"

"He won't be your husband much longer!" The interrupter was the writer, as full of vicious glee as the other two.

"Well, you know she's not the only one," said the first voice who had spoken.

Louise held her breath, pressed her fingertips to the stall wall to steady herself.

"Priscilla, you didn't!" exclaimed the second voice.

"Oh, but I'm afraid I did. What a night it was! What can I say, dipsomania runs in the family."

"Don't blame it on the booze. He's as charming as Jimmy Stewart," said the writer, in a tone of absolute authority.

"Sure enough. Least I never figured he'd give up the savings and loan for me."

For a couple of minutes after they left Louise stayed crouched, waiting for the bilious feeling in her stomach to pass. Why should it matter, that she had given up what others had given up to a man like that? It wasn't as if she truly believed him, when he said that it was her unique beauty that had driven him from the path of rectitude.

Is that what he had said to Marjorie, I am a good man, but I can't help myself? And now Marjorie had lost her job, but Dr. Leopold got to keep his wife and his laurels and his respectability. What will Marjorie do now, she had found herself thinking, alarmed by her concern for the pretty, silly creature.

That a woman took Leopold's place, this Alice O'Day, standing before them all now in the auditorium, talking in a brisk, bright, authoritative voice about the Division of Infectious Diseases, about tuberculosis and polio as if she knew them personally, as if she had the measure of every disease, that such a woman should now direct her division made Louise decidedly uncomfortable. She shifted in her seat and re-crossed her legs. What could she call this feeling overtaking her in the stuffy auditorium where the air conditioning had quit again, the back-up generator power was reserved for the labs and rightly so, said Dr. Alice O'Day, apologizing for the building and everything in it, as if it were all an extension of her ferocious and unyielding competence.

The windows had been opened to let in the edge of breeze that ran like a seam along the thick wet sheet of August air. Louise let her attention wander to the little bird that had landed on the sill outside the window nearest her seat. A tufted titmouse, she reckoned, wearing its neat blue-gray suit, its tuft like a jaunty Rosalind Russell cap. Silently she begged the creature to fly in, to distract them all from Dr. O'Day, or perhaps even better, to fly right at the dear doctor and disrupt the smooth coif of her auburn hair. Peck an eye out, even. Louise re-crossed her legs as if to banish the bile in her gut, the threat that the burning there would consume her completely.

It was two weeks since Kit had left her at her car, since she had let pass between them what she felt was a wordless agreement to see each other again. She had tried to keep herself from thinking of him as she drifted off to sleep, tried not to think about the way he had touched her. But she thought of it then, sitting in the uncomfortable chair, and she uncrossed and re-crossed her legs once more.

How could Kit have known just exactly how she liked to be touched?

Roland wouldn't share such intimate details, would he? She had always wondered what was happening to the prisoners, what their days were really like. It was bad, Mother said, wasn't that enough to know? Louise knew the letters that went out were censored, but couldn't Roland tell her something about what really happened in Cabanatuan? Couldn't he find a way to share with her the truth of it? In his letters he begged for details from her, cried out for descriptions of the smell of baking bread, as if Louise had ever been a baker. He wouldn't want the letters she had thought about writing, about the soot and spark of the factory, the particular smell of metal on metal as the drill bit the plate. He didn't want to know about the young woman, newly arrived in Burbank, who had been killed when a wing Louise had helped to design fell from a crane and crushed her. He didn't want to know how glad Louise had been to leave the house, to leave Mother to the children's relentless needs and intrigues, to break at last the spell that had kept them attached to her, sucking her dry. How she loved to come home to dinner cooked and children bathed, how she loved the nights she worked late and found the food Mother had kept aside for her with a cheery note, then climbed into the bed the girls shared then, warming herself with their clean little bodies. How she relished, she longed to write to him, being the man of the house! Once she almost wrote that fate was funny, freeing her from imprisonment while it locked him in. But because that was what she wanted to write, she wrote nothing.

Surely there was more to being a prisoner than genuflecting to the emperor and proving yourself worthy in the eyes of the enemy, so that they gave you the privilege of keeping accounts. What did it feel like, Roland, what did you see and smell? Surely you could have given me more than assurances that God was with you. Or maybe I knew your god would not see you home.

In their early days together, Louise had tried to make and see and smell what she was told to. She welcomed Roland home with pie; she followed the instructions in *Ladies' Home Journal*. Having given up her father's dream for her, the dream she had taken as her own, the dream of living a life of revealing the secrets of the universe, the deepest magic of molecules, she had fallen under the spell of woman-magic as it was described in magazines and books that proclaimed that domesticity was its own kind of science, that tried to pretend that women should accept the door prize as if it were a trophy. Those magazines that fueled the flames of a different kind of jealousy, competition among women for the crumbs of attention from men, those roving saviors, those knights of the possible who would populate their wombs and give them meaning.

Yet here was Louise, whose life had taken her back to the road of science, the road to the Institute, to a place where she could work among the columns, where she could wear an apron closer in weight and shape to a blacksmith's than to a housewife's, and here she was, dreaming of the attentions of a one-legged man. Dreaming of the strange softness of the place where his wound had closed, the oddly smooth scar tissue on the stump of his leg, dreaming of pressing herself against him, of giving her flesh to him, of being, for a moment, what he was missing. Of taking his other great protuberance, his thick and marvelous stalk, into her mouth.

The bird hopped in. Louise watched it drop from the gray sill to the gray-industrial-carpeted floor, watched it hop down one step and then another along the graded seats of the auditorium. She learned the pattern of the motion of its little head, to the left to the right and up and down, a peck at the carpet, a look up and to the side and then another peck, as if the carpet held some invisible seed that birds could not peck without a dance.

Should it really be so easy to discover a creature's habit, she thought. Shouldn't there be more mystery to life, shouldn't the bird be able to choose something different, to tuck its head into its breast and somersault? No one else seemed to notice the bird until it let out its call, its pee-oop, pee-oop! Then the murmur of laughter, that sound of joyous awe dutifully made, as when a baby is passed around among adults. Louise saw the chance, took off her lab coat, and leapt up and draped it over the bird.

"I've got it!" she called, abashed by the sudden round of light applause.

"Galle for the win!" someone called.

"I'll take it outside," she said, and walked hurriedly up the aisle, away from the window that could easily have been the titmouse's portal. She could feel its rapid, tiny heart through the cloth, thought she could feel the way its terror kept it from singing.

Perhaps she was as silly as the bird, a chickadee herself, just like that Marjorie, like some fool in a movie, dreaming of the man who made her a character, who made her someone real. After all, it wasn't Kit she was dreaming of, but of what he made her into, a lover and nothing else. One of two on a stage set for a duet.

She walked out of the auditorium, down the long, smooth hall and all the way down the front steps before she peeled open the coat and let the bird fly off, calling out to the world the joy of its return. That Kit

Blunt was perched on the low brick wall, watching her, somehow did not surprise her at all.

"Hello, Mrs. Galle."

"Well, Mr. Blunt, fancy seeing you again."

"Don't say you have work to do."

"But I do."

"Take me for a ride instead." He smiled at her with his noble mastiff forehead and his deep dark eyes, and the curl of his lips was a shape that drew her own lips to mirror his. He didn't even have to point out that it was Friday, nearly the end of the day, didn't have to show her the silver flask of whiskey he carried in his pocket. Before she could think she had gone inside to get her things, moving quickly to escape before the others left the auditorium. Before she could think she had wrapped her arm around his, letting him lean slightly into her with his aluminum leg, so that they could almost run as a three-and-a-third-legged thing to her car.

They got in and she started it up and they drove out of the parking lot before it occurred to her to have a destination.

"Where to?" she said, resting her hands on the wheel.

"I'm sorry it's been so long." She didn't look at him but felt the tone of his voice as genuine chagrin.

"Has it?" She kept her eyes on the road, sped up as she came to the end of the driveway and out onto the road that led toward the river.

"For me, it has. Thinking of you, as I have been."

"How deep," said Louise. "Did anyone ever tell you you're a poet?"

"Roland did." He said it so simply. "But we both knew what he meant."

"What was that?"

"A poet of life." He held up the silver flask, took a long slow drink, bared his teeth as if to wipe the liquor from his gums.

"I see."

"Well, lately I have been writing some lines down. But they're not mine." He handed her the flask and she took a drink.

"Oh yeah? Is Yeats speaking through you?"

"No, Roland is." He spoke with utter gravity, and his voice was soft and low. She felt the hot bile that had risen in her gut earlier turn cold, metallic. She would not let this man be insane.

"Oh, shut up. You're ruining my good time."

"All right." He leaned back against the seat and unbuttoned the top button of his shirt as if to show her the silky dark hair of his chest. "I'm in your hands."

She took the flask from him, pulled a man-sized slug of whiskey down her throat.

"I know just where to go."

She took him to a wooded place she knew of along the banks of the Potomac, a secluded spot where the road went from asphalt to gravel and then ground down into dirt. It was a place that seemed to have been part of an idea about building the town up or out, but then had been forgotten by progress, left to the dogwood and birch who witnessed themselves there. Who witnessed lovers like Louise and Kit, drinking whiskey and running fingers along the soft skin beneath waistbands, along the cream of inner thighs. They drank and opened the car doors and climbed into the back seat. He removed her blouse and she removed her brassiere, he unbuckled his belt. They both laughed to relieve the seriousness of their struggle with his pants and stopped laughing when they succeeded.

She climbed on top of him while his aluminum leg extended from the open door, the false foot pressed into the ground among the mosses and the roots, his real leg pressed against the back of the front seat. She rode him, pressed herself against him to find the sweet seam that would open her, and he began to whisper and then to call out the name her true beloved had called her in their first days, when they too had found hidden places to be together—"My pearl," Kit called. "Oh, my pearl."

Then, just as she opened to that shining place, just as she felt herself as one in a chain of human bodies connected by their rooted rutting parts, these flowers opening unto flowers, he reached his hands around her neck and squeezed.

Purple Heart

August 1964

Charlotte saw Gil next the way they had seen each other when they met, out in the hall in front of their apartments. Gil had a duffel bag on her shoulder, and she placed it down, then patted her pockets in search of her keys.

"You look good," said Gil, but it seemed to Charlotte that the appraisal was distant and sisterly, and she shrugged it off, feeling suddenly embarrassed by the bright greens and reds of her Marimekko dress.

"I feel almost like my old self," she answered, trying not to look too long into Gil's eyes, trying not to search them for some confirmation of what they had shared. Trying not to show how grateful she was, not just, she told herself, for the feeling of their legs entwined, but just for the fact of Gil. "So, you're back from Ohio."

"Yep," said Gil, holding her key out.

"Well, I'm off to luncheon with Louise and Ed."

"Your favorite thing," said Gil, a sarcastic little note of familiarity that stirred Charlotte's hope—of what? she asked herself, as if she could be coy even inside her own head. She knew exactly what she wanted from Gil, and how soon she wanted it.

"Second favorite," said Charlotte. "Root canal's got it beat, just by a hair."

Gil smiled, let her eyes stay with Charlotte's for a moment long enough to let her believe that what had happened was real enough to happen again. To give her some courage, Charlotte thought, but also to let her see the dark circles under Gil's eyes, the tiny red road maps the capillaries made in the whites.

"Well," said Gil, unlocking her door. "I'll see you."

"You must be tired."

"Exhausted," said Gil, opening her door and throwing the duffel bag in.

"Well, could I feed you?" Charlotte blurted out, and then kept blurting, words begetting words. "I mean not now, not even tonight but tomorrow, maybe, would you come for dinner then? I mean I'd love to cook a nice dinner for you, to thank you for—"

"For nothing," said Gil, with a wave of her hand as if to chase off a gnat. "And, yes, thank you, I will. Tomorrow night?"

"Six sharp," said Charlotte.

"Six it is." Gil smiled.

Charlotte kept the grin she'd caught from Gil, the lover's grin, all the way to Mitchell's in midtown, where she found Louise and Ed already ensconced in a red leather booth, martinis and salads covered in blue-cheese boulders in front of them.

"Don't get up," said Charlotte, as if they had intimated for a second that they would disturb themselves to greet her.

"Funny girl, someone get her a martini," said Ed, waving the waiter over.

"I'll have a Tom Collins," Charlotte told him. "And the steak and frites, rare."

"You're looking well," said Louise. "Ed tells me you were in a dire way. Anemic. I suppose that's why you're having steak on a hot day in the middle of summer."

"We're having lobster rolls," said Ed, as if by way of correction.

"I wish you'd told me, dear," Louise went on, extending her hand across the table to cover Charlotte's. "I could have come up to help you."

"I know you would have. Thank you, Mother," said Charlotte, who had not called her mother "Mother" in years. When exactly did I stop using that word? she wondered. When did I take hold of the name Louise as a shield? Was it that summer of the car in the ditch? Another memory of that summer struck her—a time when she and Louise had been driving together near their house in Shepherd's Glen. A doe and a fawn had stepped out of the woods, almost into the road, and Charlotte had said, "Look at the mother and daughter deer!" With absolute authority Louise had said, "No, there's nothing there."

There was a pause. Charlotte realized that they were both looking at her, surprised perhaps by her use of the word. Or maybe they really did care, maybe there was real concern in their eyes.

"But there was nothing anyone could do. I just had to rest for a while."

"Yes, Lottie's got good friends," said Ed, leaning back slightly to allow the waiter to place Charlotte's drink in front of her. "Katie was looking in on her, and what was that new friend's name, Christopher?"

"Oh, is there a Christopher now?" said Louise, biting the olive and the pearl onion that she always requested off the toothpick. "What sort of man is he?"

"No, there isn't," said Charlotte, knowing very well who Ed meant. "I don't know who Ed's talking about."

"Sorry, I must have been thinking of the street where the queers go," said Ed.

"Ah, so this Christopher is a queer, and I don't need to worry about Charlotte's virtue," said Louise, patting Charlotte's hand.

"I told you there's no Christopher," Charlotte said, taking respite in a swallow of cold, citrusy alcohol.

"Sorry, I was trying to be funny," said Ed. "I suppose I should know better!"

"Yes, you should," said Charlotte.

Ed pushed his half-empty salad plate toward the table's edge. "Listen, I was just trying to tell Louise about your new friend, the one I met. The queer, the she-he."

"Well, is it a she or a he?" asked Louise, gesturing to the waiter for another drink.

"Ask Ed, he seems to know everything."

"Lottie, you're impossible! It is a bull-dyke. A dyed-in-denim Sapphite. Seemed quite cozy with our dear girl."

Charlotte gritted her teeth and said nothing. She vowed she would not utter Gil's name, which hung in her throat like an amulet. She pretended to seek a cigarette in her purse, though she knew she had run out. Louise passed her one, and a lighter, and oddly, a reprieve from the line of conversation.

"Charlotte's a grown woman. I'm sure she can manage her own affairs," Louise said. Did she wink at her, Charlotte wondered, or was there something in her eye?

"Yes, let's talk about something else. Ed, whenever are you off to Paris?" The Tom Collins was loosening her. But maybe the drink didn't relax her, really. Maybe it just made her believe the lines she spoke when she spoke to her family, that slightly theatrical way they had of speaking to each other, their precious club. Their extra syllables. Whenever are you off to Paris? As if Paris were a place they all knew so well. Suddenly they seemed to Charlotte as not people at all, not flesh and blood and contradiction and hidden impulses, but three characters drawn with as much depth as a cartoon in *The New Yorker.*

"We were just talking about that. We think end of September, but of course I need to finish the portrait of Billy's uncle first." Ed finished his drink and put his glass in front of Louise, so that she could eat the vegetables. It was a little ritual of theirs. "Speaking of queers. I guess Billy had to get it from somewhere. That man's wrists are so limp it's a miracle he can feed himself. He thinks I don't get his references to Roman emperors and such."

"If you hate it so much, why don't you just quit?" asked Charlotte, with a bit too much force. "I'm sure Louise will find a way to help you with the money."

"No, no, of course I'll finish it," said Ed, spearing a piece of blue cheese with his fork.

"And speaking of money, Charlotte," said Louise. "When are you going back to work?"

"As soon as I get a job."

"Well, I hope it's soon, but here's a little something." Louise slid an envelope across the table. Ed watched it eagerly, narrowing his eyes when the gesture was not repeated in his direction.

Now Charlotte was really taken aback. Louise was giving her money! Maybe it was the beginning of something new and easy between them, something generous.

"It's from your granny," said Louise, reading Charlotte's softened look.

"I'll write to her."

"You should do more than that," said Ed. "Under the circumstances."

"What circumstances?" The waiter placed the steak in front of her, and Charlotte's mouth flooded, but she held her knife and fork aloft for what seemed a long pause, watching Ed and Louise exchange a look.

"She fell and broke her hip," said Louise matter-of-factly.

"What? When? How?"

"I told you I was trying to get in touch with you, Lottie." Ed's voice had an accusatory tone. "But you were nowhere to be found. And you still haven't turned your phone back on. And when I did come over you didn't seem to want to talk much. And you were sort of delicate,

I didn't want to hinder your recovery. You were too busy with your friends."

"That was weeks ago, Ed."

"Yes, that's what I mean, you could have called."

"But my phone's turned off!"

"As I said, you need to get it turned back on. Anyway, ever heard of a pay phone?"

"It was about three weeks ago. She slipped and fell down the stairs." Louise was always calm when she delivered bad news. "I'm sorry, I thought you knew. She'll be all right. They're good at Walter Reed at rehabilitating people. They've been impressed by how quickly she's learning to walk again."

Charlotte pressed her lips together to hold back her anger. Ed could have told her. He could have come over and told her, he could have told her something useful for once, for once! Instead of saying what was on her mind, she called the waiter over and ordered another drink.

"Listen, Charlotte, why don't you come home for a visit and see your granny," said Louise. "I'll stay in town tonight, and you can come back with me tomorrow."

Charlotte thought of Gil, of the dinner she was planning.

"Well—"

"It's not as if you have work to do here," said Louise with finality. "Ed has his painting to finish, and he already visited. Your granny would love to see you and you can help with her recovery. Bruce can't get leave right now, and we can't expect Helen to just up and leave the Peace Corps. Though I wish she'd never gone to that part of Brazil—it sounds horrible. People eating dry dirt."

Charlotte wanted so much to say no, to say, I have plans. But she couldn't bear the thought of their questions—who with? As she had done so many times before, Charlotte gave in.

THE RETURN

Scrape along the ocean floor
Being dead is such a bore

These are pearls my eyes my pearl
Your life my love shall not unfurl.

KISS OF DEATH

AUGUST 1948

The sound of magnetic fields overlapping, the sound of static, little pebbles of sound, fine grains of sonic sand filled Louise's ears. Her eyes met Kit's in the gathering dark in the back seat of her car. He clutched her throat, their two sets of eyes opened to each other, and she could see that his eyes were not his. Like billiard balls in cleaning fluid they rolled away and a new pair floated to the wet surface. They were not the brown-black eyes of the one-legged man she rutted against, but the green-brown eyes of the man she had married.

She felt her own eyes widen, felt her lips part to let a sound escape. A whimper, a plea, air escaping a narrowed passage. As abruptly as he had clutched her, he released her throat, and to her shame she came just then, released a shattered moan. But instead of falling against him in joyful satisfaction, she slapped him squarely across the face.

"That was for your pleasure," he said gruffly.

She shifted to one side, extracted herself from him.

"You strangle me for my pleasure?"

"It seemed to work." He smiled. "I wasn't going to kill you." His eyes were his again, dark brown, almost black.

Louise pressed herself out of the car and stood on wobbly legs in the darkening glen they were parked in. The dust and gravel road they had driven in on reflected the last putsch of daylight. For a moment she didn't rebutton her blouse or draw her hiked-up skirt back down over her thighs. She stood there like...like what? Sacajawea, some native girl, the thought came to her, some native girl raped by a colonist. The thought was utterly absurd. She was herself and this man was himself, and if one of them was insane, it wasn't she. And yet. Yet she'd seen Roland's eyes, and Kit her lover had called her what Roland her husband called her only in those sweetest moments of their connection, Pearl. His pearl. The name, she only just then realized, of Hester Prynne's love child in *The Scarlet Letter*. Something beautiful born of sin. He had been a virgin when they met, but she was a woman of experience, though of a kind that couldn't be named. That she never named to Roland or anyone. That she would never tell anyone. Her times in the garden shed, her times in Father's study, the hours she spent as a statue being acted upon.

"How did you know? Did he tell you he called me that?" she asked, watching without sympathy as he held his cock, as he finished himself off with two hands and rubbed his cum on his own hairy belly.

He lay there without answering for a moment. Then he pressed himself up.

"Called you what?"

"Pearl. You called me your pearl."

"I did?"

"You did."

"I don't remember," he said, reaching for the pants that they had forced down around his ankles. He buckled his belt and pulled his undershirt down over the expanse of chest. Despite herself, Louise felt that animal thrill that made a fool of her as she watched him. She hated to lose sight of the dark hair that spread so silkily there, the thickness of his pectoral muscles, even the soft layer of fat on his belly. Civilian fat, she thought. "But you know, in the throes of passion, things are said—"

Louise didn't want to tell him what she had seen. The change of his eyes could be, after all, a trick of the light. And perhaps she had misheard the pearl. And perhaps...perhaps he'd really wanted her to have her pleasure. Well clearly, he wanted that. Perhaps he hadn't meant it either, that day that seemed so long ago, in the Shepherd's Glen Community Pool, when he had pressed her head under the water for a few seconds. Barely a moment. Or perhaps, perhaps, those were really Roland's eyes she'd seen just now. And Roland was angry. She laughed a sticky, nervous laughter.

"Let me not be mad," she said aloud, meaning only to think it. She turned away from Kit, looking out into the forest scrub where the unfinished road was swallowed by the brambles. In the thicket she could make out nettle and yellow dock, the stinger and the easer of the sting. Nature's lovers. She straightened and buttoned her clothing.

"I never said you were," said Kit, levering himself out of the back seat. "I'm the one writing a dead man's poems."

"I always thought that was the saddest line in all of Shakespeare. I've always had the utmost sympathy for Lear, feeling his madness come on, being unable to stop himself from ruining everything. Everyone."

She couldn't stand another moment without a cigarette. She dug two out of the glove compartment, lit both, and passed him one, as had become their custom. A flurry of gnats rose out of the thicket; she leaned against the hood of the car, watching their frenzy in the last of the daylight.

"Until I read *Lear*, and then went to see a production with my parents, I thought of madness as a sort of vacation. An enchantment, like being in some kind of Disney spectacle," she said, forcing the smoke from her mouth into the cluster of dancing gnats. "I used to think that my problem was that I am not crazy in the least. That I see everything too clearly."

"And now?" asked Kit, as he moved next to her.

"I know that madness is not a joke. And you shouldn't treat it like one."

"You think I'm joking about the poetry? About Roland? 'Cause I sure as hell don't know the punch line."

"So, you expect me to believe—what, that my husband is possessing you?" She flicked the ash from her cigarette and blew smoke in his face as she turned to look at him. He blinked his dark mastiff's eyes. He was nothing like Roland, nothing at all. He was from a different tribe altogether.

"Look, call it whatever you want to call it. But as I told you before, I never wrote poetry until the war—"

"I'm sure you're not the only one moved by the glories of battle—"

"Louise, please, just listen for a goddamned minute." His voice had genuine anger in it; his usual playful quality was gone. "If you had read all of my letters, I wouldn't have to tell you this. And I am tired, see? I am still tired from what happened over there, and what happened since. Don't interrupt. I'm not going to repeat all of what I wrote, just one part of it."

"I'm all ears." She shifted up to sit on the hood of the car, letting her feet dangle off the ground as if she were a child.

"You broke his heart, Louise, even more than the enemy broke his spirit. Do. Not. Interrupt. He wrote to you all the time, every day, every minute that he had the energy. Once he traded canned pineapple for a fountain pen. There we were at Cabanatuan, we had every fucking ailment known to man and probably a few brand-new ones. We were starving. I saw the most dignified officers get in fights over a spring onion. He was an adjutant and had just a little bit of privilege, just the slightest bit more, and so he got things sometimes. Usually the navy prisoners, not we, the army, got treats, but that's another story. Anyway, he got his hands on some canned pineapple, which was even better than the fresh because we were so weak and didn't want the trouble of slicing it open, plus there was the juice you just wanted to swim in, so sweet and delicious. No one who has been well fed their whole life knows what it is to starve. Roland knew. But when he got his hands on that pineapple, he traded it for a fountain pen, because he told me, in one of his moments of weakness, he told me he thought you might answer if he wrote you in his own hand, instead of on the typewriter the Japs had him using to keep accounts."

He paused for a moment, as if to give her a chance to react, as if to let the weight of this dramatic description sink in. If Louise felt something she did not show it. She knew she was good at that, at keeping her face a hard blank, a skill she had developed over many years of rejecting what people told her she was supposed to feel. Kit dropped his cigarette, ground it into the dirt with his foot, and continued.

"The day came for us to leave the camp. No one seemed to know where they were taking us, but we figured Japan. They packed us into trains, so many of us in one car that my feet didn't even touch the ground; I was held up against the other bodies. I lost sight of Roland for a time. From the train they took us to the ship. I didn't learn the name of it until after the war was won. The *Oryoku Maru*. It wasn't until near the end, after I don't know how long of living in a dark, rank pit below decks full of dysentery sick and vomit, no fresh air, like being a piece of meat in a horrible stew. We heard the explosions, the only thing loud enough to eclipse the groaning, and there was suddenly a blast of air and light. The ship was peeled open like a can of pineapple. I saw Roland then, helping soldiers up a ladder that they could jump from, to leap out through the hole that was torn in the side of the ship. I went toward him, and he helped me too, held out his hand and helped me get to where I could see the water and the smoke and burning metal. Through the smoke I could still see the shore, and I realized that we had been drifting but we weren't that far from land. Go! he told me. Swim! The ship was groaning, listing. I yelled at him. Jump, jump, jump now! But he would not. He shook his head. He pushed me. I fell into the water. Oil burned on its surface and metal objects fell from the sky. I swam hard to get away from the ship going down, from being pulled under. All my life was in my mouth. I swam hard as I could—I still had two legs then. I was swimming to live, and the tide against me was horrible. As I got closer to the shore, the bullets came. Later I learned the Japs were firing on the men swimming back, keeping us in straight lines. Making sure we were orderly in our fight to live. But through all the rush and commotion I began to hear Roland's voice, the voice that I have heard now for years. For years it has come and gone, for years it has kept me awake, kept me looking for you. I hear it without warning, it startles me out of sleep, and it keeps me awake. My love, my God, my love, my God. Where are you in the whole of the aching sea?"

Louise's throat contracted, her mouth went dry. She squinted into the last bit of summer sun, keeping her head carefully turned away from him, silently begging him not to touch her. Because if he'd embraced her just then, she would have wept, and she felt that if she cried, well. She would never recover. So, she waited until she was certain he would not touch her in that one inviolate moment, waited until the moment passed and the first of the crickets began to chirp.

"I'll take you to your car," she said.

Purple Heart

August 1964

Louise picked Charlotte up at noon. The smell of pastrami emanated from a white paper bag on the passenger seat. Charlotte moved it to the floor as she got in.

"Don't you like sandwiches from Katz's?" Louise asked.

"Of course!"

"So why are you stepping on them?"

"I'm not stepping on them. I just moved them out of the way."

"Well, put them on the back seat, for heaven's sake. It's dirty down there."

Rather than arguing, Charlotte made an exaggerated reach for the door handle, as if to get out of the car she had just gotten into. Louise responded to her theater by pulling sharply away from the curb, barely missing a bicyclist riding behind a portable ice cream icebox. The tinny bells on the ice creamist's handlebars rang out in dismay. Charlotte tossed the bag of sandwiches into the back seat.

"Do you want everything to spill out?"

"Nothing spilled."

"It easily might have," said Louise, moving deftly into the stream of traffic on Houston Street. Charlotte clamped her mouth shut. Silence was her best, no, her only defense against Louise. Eventually her mouth would open and she'd give Louise an excuse to attack. But for a moment she just watched the stream of city people—the brisk walkers and the saunterers, the hat lifters and neck rubbers and lemonade sippers, the elbow scratchers exiting doors, the vacant-faced perchers on stoops, the peerers into flower shops and the watch checkers at newsstands, the gawkers lasciviously eyeing the barbecued ducks hung by their necks in the window of Li Po's.

She had waited until the last possible moment to leave a note on Gil's door. Somehow she could not bring herself to knock, but had listened carefully all morning, poking her head out the window onto the airshaft with the hope of hearing Gil move around in her apartment.

When there was no sound at eleven, she had written:

Dearest Gil,

My granny broke her hip and so now I am drawn home. I guess we both have families who need us. I won't be gone too long, maybe a week at most. Can't wait to cook for you when I return.

Love,

Charlotte

Now sitting in the car, watching New York through the window, Charlotte regretted every word. What a stupid note! Dearest! Who said that? Some nineteenth-century fool? Love? How desperate, how presumptuous she sounded.

"How about a little music?" Louise's tone shifted to brisk. "You haven't said a thing about my new car. They call it a Barracuda, isn't that rich? The radio is far better than in the Buick."

"Nice car," said Charlotte, though in that moment she could not have said what it looked like from the outside, except that the hood was dark green, and the upholstery was a reddish brown that radiated heat like a brick in an oven.

Charlotte scanned the stations, moving through some dizzy pop and advertising to find some Bach Louise would like. She leaned back against the seat as they merged into the traffic feeding through the Holland tunnel. She let her eyes begin to close, not so much because she was tired, but because she did not want to watch the city she loved go away. The tunnel suddenly seemed to her to shrink around the car like some steel and tile intestine working them out of its system.

"Light me a cigarette, will you?" asked Louise, who could easily have done it for herself. "Take one for yourself if you like. I've taken up Camels, following your lead, darling. They do taste better."

Charlotte recognized a peace offering when she heard one. That was Louise's way, her dance. Condemnation and disdain followed by these little offerings see, we're just the same. We're friends, darling. She lit one and passed it to Louise.

"Thanks, I'll have one in a minute."

"Go ahead and sleep if you want to. I know you've been through a terrible ordeal. I do wish you had told me. I would have liked to come up and take care of you a bit."

"I didn't want to worry you." Charlotte didn't say what she knew to be true, that she would have ended up taking care of Louise.

"But isn't that what children do, worry their parents?"

"Don't know, don't have any."

"But you will."

Charlotte didn't answer. She let her neck get soft and her head get heavy against the leathery headrest. Perhaps Katie was right, that some other doctor would find her a way to have children. Katie was so insistent sometimes, wanting Charlotte to join her in that exalted realm of motherhood. But the truth was that Charlotte felt that Dr. Bedford's pronouncement was more benediction than curse. What do you want? Gil had asked before licking her vulva. I want to know this body as my own, she thought, looking down at her white-panted thighs on the red-brown car seat. The blood loss had thinned her; her body had worked so hard to heal. Gil had so many scars, but she refused to say how she had gotten them. Charlotte thought they were beautiful, hard-won marks that stopped time. Character marks. Gil seemed like a miracle to her, perseverance and strength incarnate. I want to be that, I want to live a different life, she thought. An uncharted life. She let her eyelids slide down over the orbs of her eyes. But then it came, the jab she should have been expecting. The poison dart to the neck. She sat right up when Louise said it. If Louise hadn't had her eyes on the road, she would have seen in her daughter's eyes something akin to hatred.

"I think you should get a second opinion about your infertility." Louise tapped ash out the window with a deft flick as she landed the blow.

"I don't know what you're talking about," Charlotte said quickly. With a swell of pride, she thought, yes, that's my strategy. Denial, good as a politician.

"Ed and I talk about you because we care."

"Well," said Charlotte, giving up on sleeping and reaching for a cigarette, for the smokescreen of actual smoke. Something to mask the horrible feeling that she had absolutely no control over her own life as she sped away from her place, from Gil, and toward the house on Oxford Street that would stuff her into her old self, some scratchy childhood pinafore. "I don't know what Ed told you, but he doesn't have a clue."

"Oh," said Louise. "I guess it's a bit of the telephone game that we're playing."

"Telephone game?"

"Yes, we do it at work—did I tell you we have a little theater group?

We play the game to warm up sometimes. You know, sit in a circle, say a phrase in someone's ear, they repeat to the next person and by the time it goes all the way around, the phrase has become something altogether different."

"Yes, must be something like that."

"What was the original phrase?"

"The original phrase?"

"What did Ed hear that made him think that you can't have children?"

"I guess he just leapt to a conclusion."

"Well," said Louise, letting the cigarette hang from her lip like a tough guy in some noir film while she yanked the ashtray open from the dashboard. She smashed the cigarette and sent two cool smoke streams through her nostrils. "I'm relieved to hear that. You'll be a wonderful mother. It's what I've always wanted for you. Helen will do fine, once she gets over the Peace Corps. I'm sure she'll find someone, I hope here and not in Brazil, of course. But you, I think you have a gift for it. You've always cared more about others than about yourself."

The feeling Charlotte was having as Louise spoke was of her intestines being rearranged. Some complicated interlacing was occurring in the plump pit of her belly, a wet, cold pathway of dread subsumed in a burning spiral of anger. It struck her that her mother—even more than the men who assumed she'd grown her breasts for them—was utterly blind to who Charlotte was, to what she wanted, to what she cared about. She expected that from the men, hungry as they were to feast on the body she wore, to enlist her in their care. The whole world seemed to collude with them, to make them uninterested in whatever else she might be than in their service. She was almost grateful to Louise for placing her in that hallowed cathedral niche where women were supposed to revel. It made her see more clearly where she did not want to be. But it was the thought of Gil that stirred her to answer more truthfully.

"Actually, I care about quite a few things." She stubbed her cigarette out in the dashboard ashtray and shut it. "Many have to do with me."

"Yes, of course, but you're a giver, Charlotte. It's not an insult." Louise spoke with the finality that was one of the strongest assets in her armory. Case closed.

Charlotte settled in, and they drove on in silence, the radio losing the

New York City station to static. She was dimly aware of Louise keeping the dial in a staticky zone for what seemed like a long time.

She must have dozed off, because a DC station was the next thing she heard, an announcement of breaking news: the bodies of Chaney, Goodman, and Schwerner had been found.

"Not a surprise ending to that story," said Louise.

"No. But it's still outrageous."

"Yes. Your father's family were confederates, you know."

Charlotte rubbed her eyes and sat up. She'd never really known the Galles growing up. Somewhere in Tennessee there were cousins, but she'd never met them.

"I know. Is that why you stopped talking to them?"

"They cut me off after Roland died. Before that, really. They weren't in the Klan or anything as far as I know. But they had certain ideas."

"Such as?"

"Things that weren't scientific. They didn't like it much when I spoke of Negroes as people," said Louise, turning off the radio. "It was something my father didn't like about your father, his people's beliefs. Father's own prejudices were different."

"What were they?" Charlotte was fascinated now.

"He had a rigid belief in essential character and that character is fate. People are what they are from the start and everything they do only proves it. The excellent can do nothing wrong, the weak can rarely do anything right."

"And was my father weak in his eyes?"

"I'm afraid so, or at any rate, he was not fully excellent."

"And then they both died prisoners."

"War is a leveler."

Just then, Charlotte saw a big-antlered buck step out of the woods.

"Look there's a buck!"

"No, there's not," said Louise, with a wicked little grin.

"Yes, there was. You always do that, why do you always—"

"Science, Charlotte. You don't know, it could be a freemartin, they grow antlers."

"What in the hell is a freemartin?" Charlotte wished she did not sound so irritated.

"A mostly female-appearing animal lacking the female goods on the inside. Lacking the female function. You know, like a lesbian," said

Louise, her grin growing to epic proportions. Charlotte folded her arms and clamped her lips shut.

They drove the rest of the way to Shepherd's Glen, through its quaint town square with its post office and shops for baked goods and hardware and sundries, past the community pool, past the houses of different styles—some Victorian dripping gingerbread decorations and wrapped around by porches, some, like theirs, more modern and clean-lined and built half into hills—they drove all that way in silence. The sound of the tires crunching the loose paving stones of the driveway, the sound of the return to Oxford Street, filled Charlotte with a fear so familiar it felt like resignation. Here she was again, a foolish child.

Louise brought bottles of beer and they sat by the table on the screen porch, making an early dinner of the sandwiches from Katz's. Warmed by the car ride, the pastrami felt almost too slick in Charlotte's mouth, but she ate quickly, in big bites, as if she could chomp her way through the house on Oxford Street and the states of Maryland, Pennsylvania, and New Jersey, and arrive in her own little apartment by sandwich's end.

"Slow down, dear, you'll choke," said Louise.

THE RETURN

What once was shining clear as light
Has turned to bracken in my sight

What dies within me was not born
A hopeful soul forever mourned.

KISS OF DEATH

AUGUST 1948

The boys were playing catch in the front yard when Louise pulled up. As the Packard's tires crunched over the loose stones of the driveway, she caught her own scent—her sweat and Kit's, whiskey and tobacco. They smiled at her as she got out of the car. She couldn't help but wonder what had led to the apparent détente between them. Ed and Bruce hadn't played anything together in years, and lately Ed's interests seemed limited to the violin and the neighbor girl he thought she didn't know about.

"Well, well, if it isn't the United Nations," she teased.

"I'm teaching Ed to play ball," said Bruce, a big grin cracking his freckled face.

"Shut up, Bruce," said Ed, lobbing the ball at him with excessive force.

"You shut up," said Bruce, catching it with ease.

"Oh, good, you're still the boys I know," said Louise. "Try not to kill each other."

When she opened the door, Tuna whined with delight and ran toward her, bobbing her silky brown and white head. Mother greeted her with a somber expression. Helen and Charlotte were clearing the dishes.

"You missed dinner," said Mother.

"Sorry about that. Is there anything left over?"

"Not much, but I can make you a turkey sandwich."

"I'll make it, but thanks." Louise took as light a tone as she could, trying to balance what she read as Mother's black mood.

As she passed, Mother grabbed her arm and hissed into her ear: "There's a bruise on your neck and you reek of whiskey. Go clean yourself up first. And I need to talk to you tonight."

"All right, Mother," she said in a normal voice. "No need to whisper."

"Yes, there is a need. We'll talk when they go to bed." Mother's lazy eye, which she worked so hard to train, was veering wildly toward her left ear, as if it were trying to escape her head altogether.

Louise went to the bathroom to examine her neck. The mark was faint but it was there, not a full-blown bruise exactly, but a redness where Kit's hands had been. Mother would have thought it was made by his mouth and not his hands, a more acceptable kind of love mark, like the one that Roland had put on her that day so long ago, when they had slipped away from the Diehl family gathering and taken the boat out into Long Island Sound. Roland, she thought, you surprised me when you sucked my neck like that, as our babies would later suck, for dear life. And, Father, I'd never seen such a look from you before, your rank disapproval. That flash of puritanical loathing when you saw us walk in together, tousled, trying not to grin.

When the children had gone to bed, Louise showered and put on the thin blue eyelet robe Mother had given her, hoping it might inspire mercy in her judge. She sat on the couch sipping whiskey, waiting for her punishment. The small boxes of curiosities they kept in a row on the top level of the rolltop desk, above the pigeonholes full of letters and bills, seemed to call out to her. Her eyes roved in search of distraction. She knew her mother was about to take her by the scruff and force her to smell the mess, as if she were Tuna soiling the carpet. So, she put her drink down and stood before the row of beautiful boxes. There was the soft green and cream Victorian wallpaper box full of cardamom pods; the three-tiered tiny wedding cake box, each section containing a different color of embroidery thread; the baroque egg decorated with gold filigree and containing an alarmingly precise scene of skaters on a frozen pond that could be viewed through the magnifying lens of the peephole. But since her childhood, Louise had loved best the container made from a smooth seed of some tropical fruit. She never learned what the fruit was exactly, but the seed had come from the Philippines, perhaps from Father's first tour there, during the First World War. What was inside it was made by hands there, hands clever enough to hollow a seed and fill it again with works of art small enough to be lost in a spoonful of soup. Every time Louise pried open the tiny lid, which was the seed's own natural attachment to a long-lost branch, and tapped its contents onto the dark wood surface of the desk, it seemed at once a true miracle and a biblical joke. She opened it with her pinkie nail, placing the lid carefully to one side, and tapped the elephants made from ivory shavings onto the desktop. Each one was precise, exactly an elephant and nothing else, and each one was slightly different from the next—a trunk raised high or low, a front foot or back foot up, a tail straight or curled. The shavings were so thin that a strong breath or a passing body could send them flying, as Mother moving behind her with a quick, clipped step toward the couch proved. Louise captured the flying shavings in her moist palm. This was the irritating part of the visit to the infinitesimal elephants, the way they stuck in the folds of her hand, the way, once free of the seed, they resisted being funneled back in.

At the sight of her own hands struggling, Louise suddenly recalled Kit's hands on her neck. That he had been choking her struck her forcefully, as if this were the first time she'd known it. Why that thought should arouse her was something she could not fathom.

She tied the sash of the thin eyelet robe more tightly around her waist, as if she could squeeze out some discomfort that way. With her back to Mother, Louise stood very still, waiting for the ferocious ache in her loins to pass. She wanted him terribly, wanted him for a year of rutting. She placed the seed-box back in the row of tiny wonders, took a breath, and turned around.

Mother sat in her usual chair, holding her own glass of whiskey, a rare appendage. She drank a long, smooth slug and then placed the highball glass next to Louise's on the coffee table.

"Come and sit down, dear," said Mother.

Louise obeyed, settled herself back on the couch, and stroked Tuna's head when the dog came and leaned against her leg, presenting herself for love.

"What is it that's so important, Mother? I'm awfully tired."

"I suspect you are."

"Say what you mean for once, can't you?" Louise felt the fool for blurting this out, for showing her hand too soon. The game they played could not be won outside its rules, which including pretending there was no game.

"Maybe it's best if I just show you this," Mother said, as if she too were putting some rules aside. She handed Louise two pieces of yellowed newsprint, carefully folded along a single crease.

Louise opened the paper to discover what appeared to be a wedding announcement in the *Wilmington Post Intelligencer* dated March 16, 1946.

Alice Maeve Combs and Geoffrey Kirstein Blunt, said the headline. The photo revealed the happy couple grinning wildly, a pair you could almost take for siblings, both dark haired and big-eyed, though the shape of her face was longer and narrower. She didn't have the same mass in the forehead, and there was nothing knowing or duplicitous or Orson Welles-like in her smile. Louise could not read the announcement without reading it, yet she could not exactly take it in. Alice… daughter of…a fairy tale romance…Geoffrey, "Kit" to his friends…a survivor of Bataan…a hero of the Pacific. Goddamned boy next door!

Louise could not, would not look up at Mother. The hot bloom of lust that had overcome her earlier returned in force, turned outside in and expelled itself, becoming something different. She dropped the clipping onto the table as if it had infected her, as if it had tied her throat to itself. She picked up the second clipping. It was also from the *Wilmington Post Intelligencer*, dated September 12, 1946. This time Louise read each word clearly.

HERO OF BATAAN LOSES LEG IN MILL ACCIDENT

Geoffrey Kirstein "Kit" Blunt, a future inheritor of the Blunt Mills fortune, who is expected to helm the company when his father retires next month, lost most of his left leg yesterday in an accident at the Blunt Mills processing plant. A decorated veteran who survived the Bataan Death March and the sinking of the Japanese prison ship Oryoku Maru, Blunt's life story has been marked by extraordinary luck. That is, until now.

Blunt Mills issued a statement noting that the injury does not reflect a lack of commitment to safety standards at Blunt Mills and does not besmirch the company's exemplary twenty-five-year history. When contacted by this paper for a statement, a spokesman called the accident "a tragic act of God," and asked the press to respect the Blunt family's privacy during this difficult moment.

Louise put the second clipping down on top of the first. She leaned back into the couch and dropped her hands into her lap. The house seemed extraordinarily quiet. She wished it could stay that way, that the only sound could be that of the owl they often heard lately, calling from the trees by the creek, *who who, whoooo.*

"Listen, Louise. I didn't want to tell you," Mother was saying.

"But you did." Louise thought to reach for a cigarette, there were some in the lacquer box on the coffee table right in front of her. Instead she sat still and willed herself to look Mother in the eye.

"I wanted you to know—I don't know what he's told you."

"Nothing," she said softly.

"What, dear?"

"I said nothing," Louise said. "He told me absolutely nothing."

"Well, maybe you're relieved—"

"Relieved?"

"Now that it's over. It has to be over now, Louise."

"Oh?" said Louise, reaching at last for the lacquer box, for the cigarettes and the book of matches emblazoned with the Da Ronco's logo.

"Louise, I'm serious. This is a married man—"

"I'm not looking for a husband."

As Mother became more agitated, Louise found it easier to remain calm. This had always been a strength of hers; she could hold herself hard and still and cool as a stone on the moon. It had been a strength of hers since the first of their men died, a strength she'd developed as she found herself in the company of other widows who seemed to relish their displays of grief. Their theater was not her theater. She had always wept in secret.

"Louise, please! Listen to me. Do not make another woman miserable. Do not be a homewrecker! They have a child!"

"Do you have a clipping for that too, Mother? The birth announcement? Where did you get these clippings anyway? You must have gone to a great deal of trouble."

"Hold your sarcastic tongue!" Mother kept her voice low when she was angry. She kept it low now, but her words came more and more quickly. Little flecks of spit struck Louise in the face as Mother put her elbows on her thighs and leaned forward in her chair as if she were about to launch herself out of it. "You and your father both, you both treated me as if I hadn't two brain cells to rub together. I may be nothing but a drudge now, but I was a reporter once, and a damn good one. I won't let you ruin two families just because some deceitful man has stoked the eternal embers of your vanity!"

"I've told you before. And I'll say it again. I earn the money around here. That means I make the decisions." Louise mashed her cigarette out in the ashtray, finished her whiskey, and stood up. Mother stood up too.

"And I told you what I'll do if you don't stop this affair," said Mother, blocking the path to the stairs. She looked right into Louise's eyes with pupils that seemed to deepen and darken. "You'll see how it is around here without me."

Louise stepped around her without a word and walked slowly and steadily up the stairs to her room. As she lay on the bed, one silly thought arose out of the cloud of her confusion. Alice. Why did Kit's wife have to be an Alice like that efficient accomplished woman who had become her boss? It's a joke, she thought. This is a cruel joke on me, thinking I'm different from the Alices of the world, whether they are girls next door or heroines of the Dordogne. I'm just the same as anyone else, just as likely to be played. Just as likely to see only what I want to see.

As she rolled to her side, her gaze landed on one of the objects she loved most—a stone stamp of her name in Chinese characters that Father had given her when she was just a girl. She reached over and picked it up, felt the weight of the smooth cool stone, admired the lion's maned head that topped it. The bottom was stained with red ink, from the many times she had stamped notes and cards and drawings with it. The stamp of character, she thought, as Father had called it, with which to make my mark on the world. These raised red lines are like a labyrinth, the lines like walls that keep out the grief and fear that gnash at me still. I long to walk those halls that lead back to that place where I was admired, where my shining character was ready to receive my fated power and righteous, endless love.

Purple Heart

August 1964

Out of the thick dark of Charlotte's immobilizing dream, Louise's face appeared at first as the only lit thing, a full moon in an otherwise ink-black sky. The dream began the way it always did, as a message from her extremities to her brain—the distant outposts of big toe and pinkie telegraphing distress, an unheeded request that they be allowed to move. Her eyes the only thing that seemed to heed the command for motion, she could feel them rolling in the ink-black dark beneath their lids. Without an image to steady on, her eyes were orbs rolling in all directions, and while the lodestone of her flesh was hard-magnetized and rock-still, seasickness sloshed in the pit of her gut. As usual in the dream, the sound of the creaking door came next, then the thin sliver of light that at last gave her eyes something to aim for. This time there was no sound of the creature's feet, no scraping claws on floorboards. Only the clap of daylight, the sudden presence of Louise, of her breath on Charlotte's face.

Here she was again, tucked in her narrow childhood bed in the house on Oxford Street, the place where nothing, not even her own body, belonged to her. The light in her head and in the room began to equalize, the intricate floral-patterned wallpaper becoming clear. Here was Louise, faintly smiling, gripping the sheet that Charlotte also gripped, clamped at her collarbone, her hands in the rictus of terror that was the dream's residue. For a moment Louise held it as if she were going to pull it back and get in, a habit of hers that Charlotte hadn't minded in her youngest days but had hated as a teenager. Louise seemed to find it very funny, to come into the room that Charlotte shared with Helen and climb into bed with one of them rather than getting them up. Charlotte snatched the sheet closer to her chin.

"Time to get up, dear," said Louise, releasing her hold on the sheet as if to say, All right, I'll let you be this time. "Your granny will be so glad to see you."

Charlotte nodded, let her eyes close again as Louise moved toward the door, her tone brisk as she announced oatmeal and grapefruit for breakfast.

By the time they got to Walter Reed, Granny had already taken her rehabilitation and was sitting in a large, sunny visiting room. The tile on the walls was fully institutional, a kind of off-white that seemed to have been chosen because it repelled the tobacco smoke that had stained the wall above an acrid yellow-brown.

On the way over to the hospital Louise told Charlotte that after Granny's fall, while they waited for the ambulance, Granny had insisted that Louise bring the dragon-head Meerschaum pipe that had belonged to the colonel. Lying at the foot of the stairs in what she would later admit was horrific pain, Granny announced that she was going to smoke the good tobacco in the best pipe every one of her last days on earth.

When they were small, Charlotte and the others used to vie for the chance to get up onto the stepladder and open the doors of the cupboard above the refrigerator. There the pipe sat in its box, the smooth geometries of blond and chestnut wood that meant special days—Thanksgiving and Christmas and Colonel Walter Diehl's birthday in March. Of all the objects that Granny had managed to load into the hold of the ship that had sailed from Manila Bay in '41, bringing officers' wives and their belongings stateside, the pipe was the most precious, the most mysterious and powerful to the children. The great Colonel Grandaddy, who had, they were told, laid eyes on Ed and Charlotte (but not the others) when they were babies, had been given the pipe by the family of a faithful servant he'd once had, a Filipino gardener whose talents the colonel had graciously recognized and celebrated. When the gardener died, the story went, the colonel continued to pay a part of his salary to help his family and the family had given him the pipe in thanks. Granny said that the colonel preferred his simple rosewood bowl for everyday, but when he was working on a very tough problem—calculating the azimuth of a new type of projectile, for example—he "consulted the dragon-head." Perhaps, she would tell their star-eyed grandchildren, if he had kept the pipe instead of sending it back with her for safekeeping, he would not have been captured by the Japanese. Smoke from the dragonhead, the children concluded, could cast a spell that confuses the enemy.

On holidays, when they remembered their father and grandfather and uncle with prayers and stories, whoever was tall enough and got to it first would bring the box to the dining room table and offer it to Granny with great solemnity. In her child-mind Charlotte saw the smoke from the pipe curl to heaven to caress Colonel Grandaddy's chin, which was covered in the long white beard he'd grown when he became an angel.

In the bright visitors' lounge Charlotte found Granny immediately. Her unruly white hair caught the light from the tall metal-rimmed windows, making clouds with the smoke streaming from her nostrils, so that her head seemed to float above the drab gray back of the wheelchair. Walking toward her, Charlotte read the ivory dragon-head as a tiny skull, and Granny in her frailty, her body clearly bonier and scalier than Charlotte remembered, could have been an exhausted dragon mother, kissing her baby's tail.

"Charlotte, can it be you?" Granny called out from the depths of the chair, gripping the wheels to turn herself in Charlotte's direction with surprising vigor. An orderly moved toward her as if to help, but Granny waved him away.

"It is she," said Louise, bending to kiss her mother on the forehead, a gesture that Charlotte could not recall having seen before. "I'm going to talk to your doctor and get the real story about you. You two get reacquainted."

"Isn't she Mrs. Full-charge," said Granny teasingly as Louise turned and marched off. Charlotte perched on a beaten-down brown corduroy couch and looked at her grandmother more carefully. There were dark blooms under the paper-thin skin of Granny's hands, the fingers were gnarled but nonetheless nimble as she pulled the tobacco pouch out of the pocket of her thin cotton robe and tamped a fresh plug into the dragonhead. Before she could finish the operation and dig out the matches that were no doubt buried deep in her pocket, Charlotte presented the fast flame of her lighter, and Granny aimed the pipe and drew.

"Well," Charlotte said, feeling unnerved by the unavoidable fact of Granny's frailty. "You look—"

"Old? Yes, I am that."

"I was going to say well, considering—"

"That I took a tumble down the basement stairs?" said Granny, shifting slightly in her wheelchair. "I always knew those stairs would get me. Remember how Tuna tumbled down them, that time you almost killed yourself?"

Charlotte felt a sharp, steep dizziness, as if her head and pelvis had suddenly changed places.

"What do you mean?"

"That summer when you were twelve or thirteen or so and you thought that turning on the car without opening the garage door was a good idea."

Perhaps unintentionally, Granny blew a cloud of smoke into Charlotte's eyes. For a moment she wondered if Granny was right. Perhaps she had tried that in her misery. But no, no, that wasn't quite right.

"I can understand, I don't think you were too happy in those days." Granny patted her hand, and her dry touch seemed to shake Charlotte out of her confusion. Because there was something wrong in Granny's telling. Depressed as Charlotte had been that summer, she had never thought to end her own life, only that she wished to trade it—or at least the body she was so uncomfortable in—for another's. She hadn't wanted to die; she had wanted company. Sympathy. It was the summer of Louise rolling the car into a ditch, of Ed's sudden contempt for Charlotte, which she now realized, began around the same time as her bouts of wild bleeding. It was the summer that she and Ed had stopped chanting for their father's return. It was the summer that she had seen Louise slapped, right in the picture window of the house on Oxford Street. And there was something else. Something she had papered over in her mind.

"But, Granny, that was you! I found you. You were passed out over the steering wheel."

Granny blinked and her old wandering eye wandered and wavered to the left edge of her face as if it wanted to leave altogether. She let the pipe lower to her lap and ran her fingertips along her forehead, as if she could find the memory there.

"Ah dear, I suspect you're right. Isn't that a hoot! Here I made that whole story up. And I thought I was doing so well, surprising the doctors with how I'm learning to walk again like a regular soldier."

"Why did you do it, Granny?"

"I'd like to walk again, even though I'm eighty-four, so I'm doing the exercises religiously—"

"No, I mean why did you gas yourself?"

Granny looked around, as if she were just remembering that they were not in a private place. But it was almost private. In the farthest corner of the big sunny room, a one-legged man crutched toward a pale-faced woman standing by the open window. Closer to the entryway that Charlotte and Louise had walked in through, two men in hospital pajamas played a grim-looking game of chess.

"Hmm, that story might require whiskey."

"As it happens, I brought you some," said Charlotte, removing a silver flask from her purse. "Found this in the dressing table in my old room. Helen must have been having a secret nip when she was home before going off to Brazil. Filled it up for you."

Granny winked the same sweet quick smack of her eyelids that she used to give Charlotte when passing her the batter-licking spoon behind Louise's back. When Louise called her fat, Granny would say, You're just a healthy growing girl.

"Aren't you a sneak!" Granny took a quick drink, pressed her lips together, and folded them back against her teeth, grinning the grin of a whiskey-drinking skull. "Thank you, that's good. Let's see. I think it was an accident. I must have just been preoccupied."

"Whiskey deserves the real story!"

"All right, all right. Truth-telling might just be the province of the old."

"You're not old. Not in spirit anyway," said Charlotte, lighting a cigarette and moving the heavy institutional glass ashtray on the little table by the side of the miserable brown couch toward her. She looked up at Granny. Would Granny tell her something true, something Louise wouldn't? The skull-smile, the wink of Granny's wandering eye said yes.

"No, you're right about that time. If I weren't close to my end now—you don't have to pretend it's not true, Charlotte—if I weren't close to the end, I probably wouldn't tell you that I wanted to die that summer."

"It had something to do with that man, didn't it? The one I saw slap Louise."

Granny clamped her lips around the pipe and leaned forward for Charlotte to light it again, drew on it, and then lowered it to her lap with her blood-pocketed paper-covered hand. The smoke seemed to come as much from her ears as her nose and mouth.

"Yes. Your mother was getting drawn into something dark. But the worst was that another woman was involved. And a child. Kit Blunt was his name, and he was a liar and a cheat, and not just on his wife." She paused for a moment. Charlotte followed her gaze, which landed on the one-legged man who was shrugging off an attempted embrace from the woman standing by the window.

"What do you mean?"

"It was the lie about his injury that was worse than the lie about his marriage, his fatherhood. He had written your mother some letters that said he lost his leg in the war. He went about receiving the kind of sympathy and respect that a war loss garners, but it was a lie. His injury was a peacetime injury, happened in the mill his father owned, the family business he inherited. From what I found out, he had been drinking when he got caught in the machinery."

"And that was enough to make you want to die?"

"I suspect there might have been other things at play. You know, in those days most people didn't go poking around in their minds the way they do now. People didn't talk about the unconscious or anything like that."

Granny paused again, straightened herself up in the wheelchair, smoothed the blanket over her knees, then looked around the room furtively as if spies could be hidden in its corners.

"What other things?" Charlotte looked at the entryway, watched a stream of white-shod nurses ushering limp-backed patients attached to rolling IV units, a doctor checking a wristwatch and then a clipboard. Louise would be back any moment, and Charlotte sensed that Granny was about to tell her something important.

"That man was going to destroy us. He didn't love Louise. He wanted her for dark reasons. But she couldn't see that. I thought she was going to invite him into our home, thought she was going to break up his marriage. And suddenly there would be this new man in the house, telling you kids what to do, telling me how he liked his eggs. I was a reporter once," said Granny, as if to lay claim to truth-seeking by profession.

"I know." In the entryway, a doctor interrupted two nurses having a conversation. When he walked on, one of them took her thumb to her nose and wiggled her fingers in his direction. The other laughed.

"We'd lost so much. All our men gone. There had been so much that was wrong that I'd seen and ignored, even before the war. We struggled. The army barely provided a pension, and your mother's work at Lockheed had dried up. Finally she got this great job at the National Institutes of Health, and we were settling in. You kids were getting old enough that I thought I might even start writing again. And suddenly Louise was going to wreck us and another family for the sake of what? Some cheap passion based on a lie. Death seemed like the right escape, as absurd as it seems now. But you saved me, Charlotte. It was you!"

"What do you mean, so much that was wrong?" asked Charlotte.

Just then Louise walked in through the entryway, practically arm in arm with the doctor, a slight man with a face that pinched around his round wire glasses. He was short, his nearly bald head lined up with Louise's shoulder, but he moved like someone much taller, like the right dance partner for Louise. There was a way that Louise entered a room, a way that her elegance seemed to accord authority to a space. A way that Charlotte could not help but admire, even as the moment of admiration soured into a feeling of lack. Mother, you always were the conductor, the instructor passing out the test that I had already failed, thought Charlotte. Some creeping shame and fear—a feeling as pervasive and subtle as the tiniest gradient shift of daylight toward twilight—this feeling that Louise's presence aroused in her began, then stopped. There you are, Louise, in your mandarin blouse and seersucker capris, at home anywhere in the world. But there were things that were wrong, Granny had said. Things about Louise.

Charlotte recalled the paralysis of the night before, the experience that was more and less than a dream. Then Louise's face above hers. She felt the fear she had felt as a child, nameless and pervasive. She remembered Louise waking them all and taking them to the beach in the middle of the night. The sudden electric presence of Louise, for good or ill. She changed the rules of gravity, Charlotte thought, because none of the rules applied to her. But maybe they did, and Louise was not the interpreter of the law, but subject to it.

"Well, Mother," Louise was saying. "Dr. Schatz says you can come home tomorrow. You can do your exercises there."

"Wonderful," said Granny.

"Yes, isn't it wonderful, Charlotte?" said Louise. "Dr. Schatz, this is my daughter Charlotte."

"Of course—makes sense that the two most beautiful women I've seen all year would be related," said Dr. Schatz, flashing Charlotte a wink and a smile.

Charlotte smiled and nodded, murmured a thank you or a wonderful news or some other words, but she was looking at Louise, wondering how long she had made love with a married man, wondering what else Granny would tell her. Wondering if she could ever tell Louise and Granny about Gil. She would make them terribly uncomfortable, she realized, but perhaps that could be a strength. What would they say, if they knew how she longed for the strong arms of a mannish woman? If they knew how little she cared for men's compliments, for the attention she received as a result of the accident of her birth into a body so many of them wanted to claim? What would they say if they knew she didn't care about the things this body was supposed to do—the harbor, the food it was supposed to be?

She felt a strange surge of pride, a thought that she had beaten Louise at this game anyway, of taboo love. Lesbianism was surely better—or worse, depending on your view—than being with a married man. It was beginning to feel like her own way in the world, like something real and right. Gil's strong, scarred body is my port, she thought. She is the rock I will live on. Louise broke her reverie.

"Well, Charlotte, shall we go home?"

THE RETURN

Enemy mine you cannot hide
A cave, a home, a box inside

For I am in my longing lost
For that is what my body cost.

Kiss of Death

August 1948

This was not jealousy. Not of that Alice Maeve Combs. Jealousy was not what kept Louise awake that night. I do not long to hold your briefcase and slippers, she said to the ceiling. I do not aim to rub your temples and take the stresses of running the mill away from you, or to take you from your little Alice and her rag rugs and batter spoons. I do not want what Mother fears I want, to ride in and steal you from her and smash your homespun idyll.

She felt the presence of the judge, whoever that was, the judge who perhaps only lived inside her mind but who she felt all around her, who held the lens through which she lived her life as if she were any other character. I don't believe in God, she thought, but I feel you watching me. This watcher, this reader of me, assumes I'm writhing here in jealousy of that simple Alice; my jealousy is what makes you laugh as you turn me sick with bile. But my envy is my own and it is of me, of the woman I was supposed to be, the woman that you promised me, Father.

She felt herself falling into the labyrinth of her own character. She walked along the tight corridors, heard from behind the high walls the outbreaths of the dead. Around one corner her brother Bruce extinguished in a blast of flame; around another, Father, the colonel, clung to corners with his withered hands, moist beriberi sucking him into the blank smooth wall. Around the next Roland pressed his face through the plaster as he tried to force the floor of the sea to move his way, the weight of water to do his bidding. His loneliness, she could see it now, was one prick of light in the vast dark, one life in the book of death, one white period on a black page.

At the center of the labyrinth was the gift that Father-the-Colonel had tried to give her, of herself, her great and glorious mind aching after formulas and visions of molecules bonding to arise and make it all.

I am not jealous of what I had, of what took me away from you, Father. Oh, I did love those babies that were mine and no one else's and I was good at it—four easy pregnancies, four mostly smooth births.

I don't care about other people's babies and I don't long for the days when I was their food. I don't care that Kit goes home to her, but why would he think I need to be lied to like any other woman? My fury isn't the fury of a woman scorned, but of a woman lost to herself. There is no room in the world for a woman like me. If a woman like me really wants to be what she ought to be, there is no room for the furry realms where babies lurk.

At the center of the labyrinth was Father's study, where he had drawn the white lace across her hard teenaged nipples. Where he had birthed her from his own head. Where she should have stayed and sharpened her sword. That this barrel-chested one-legged man should have what all men feel they are owed, the hearth that holds them, that Kit should have that and still have her to slam into…that he should treat her like a fool who could not know he had it all. No. She should have sliced his desire to pieces, should have sliced them all to pieces.

From her shallow sleep Louise was awoken by the maddening susurrus, the sound the car radio transmitted between stations. It was the static trying to be a signal, the sphere aching to form from the plain, to rise up from the sea and sail into the air. In the gray dawn she bolted up in her bed yelling, "Stop it!"

The radio was not on. She was sweating and shaking with the rage left in the vacuum of love. She would get even with Kit. The susurrus of the radio was the signal searching for its definition, the muscle defining the pearl that she, Louise, was not. She was something else—a molecule of carbon, a hard blocked thing, a dark and nasty thing. She was not going to make a scene at Kit's workplace or tell his little Alice about their affair. She would do something more subtle.

She considered silence, a smooth block. It would be easy enough, she told herself, to warn the receptionist at her work about him, to file a restraining order with the Montgomery County sheriff's office and the Bethesda police. But that was too passive. Silence was her weapon against Mother; Kit should get something different. Something more directly painful for his sins of omission, for the lies she had discovered were so neatly turned out in the early letters he had sent and that she read at last, trying to make sense of the clippings. Mostly they were polite messages and entreaties to see her, but they said, more than once, that he had left a limb on the battlefield. In one he'd even written that Roland had saved him from creeping gangrene by insisting that the leg be removed. More than sins of omission then, the letters contained downright—what had Father called them?—bafflewalls. Structures intended to confuse, to encourage the enemy to drop his guard.

She entertained the idea of going to Blunt Mills, of somehow embarrassing him at his workplace. She envisioned walking into an important meeting, declaring in front of a panel of disapproving businessmen that she was pregnant with his child, inventing a perfect little melodrama based on a lie. That was, after all, what they had been engaging in together. But, she thought, there has to be a way to shame him without shaming myself.

On the Monday after she had learned the truth, she made up her mind. She went into work as usual, but left before lunchtime, claiming a migraine. By early afternoon she was in Wilmington, poring through the pages of the phone book in a booth at a gas station. It wasn't hard for her to find the house—a big cliché of rectitude, a white colonial with green shutters that sat in the middle of a long, elm-lined block in a pleasant residential neighborhood.

She pulled the Packard up across the street and watched. She allowed herself to listen to that static sound between the radio stations, seeking the susurrus that had come at the end of that tormented night. It was a sound, she realized, that she had been hearing for some time and that had come to her like a warning that Kit was coming into her life. The sound she found was not exactly right, but it was comforting, somehow emboldening.

There was no porch on the house that she could see, though there was probably one in the back, a screened-in thing that let the Blunt family enjoy the breeze across their backyard without paying in mosquito bites. The front was all of a piece, a white clapboard wall that admitted no errors, as correct as Protestantism claiming its members of the elect. The door opened before Louise could finish rehearsing the lines she intended to say. Three figures emerged—a woman, a small girl, a dog. The dog was a sloppy golden retriever grinning with its whole body. The girl must have been about two. Even from across the street Louise could see Kit in the child's shiny black hair and deep-set dark eyes. The woman was petite with short-cropped light brown hair. She wore a polka-dotted sundress and was clearly pregnant, Louise guessed about five months in. She looked different from the photo in the paper; her hair and eyes were lighter than they had seemed, but the round little face with a perky chin was unmistakably that of Alice Combs, the girl next door. Very pretty, she thought, if you like that kind of thing, petite and soft, ready and waiting to be used by a man like that child bride in the film *Kiss of Death*.

Before she could think another thought about it, Louise got out of the car and approached the trio. She crossed the street briskly, her purse swaying in the crook of her elbow.

"Excuse me, Mrs. Blunt?"

"Yes?"

The woman slowed, let the girl walk in front of her a few steps, but then pulled her back, lifted her onto the shelf of her belly, at once shielding her and using her as a shield. The sloppy grinning dog came straight at Louise, wagging its tail and presenting its head for a scratch.

"Are you Alice Blunt?"

"I'm Mrs. Kirstein Blunt," she answered in a chilly formal tone.

"Of course, pardon me, I don't mean to be overly familiar. I've just heard so much about you."

"That's all right," Alice said, smiling now. "If you tell me your name and how you know me, I'll let you call me Alice."

"I'm Mrs. Roland Galle," said Louise, searching Alice's eyes, which were not brown as Louise had thought they would be, but cornflower blue. Altogether too trusting, Louise thought, searching for the slightest reaction to her name. The eyes remained empty and docile, eyes of a cow, she thought, no reaction at all. She extended her hand. "But you may call me Louise."

"How do you do?" said Alice, taking Louise's hand with an exaggerated formal flourish. "This is my daughter Loretta, and this is Goldy." The dog licked Louise's hand. The girl looked at Louise doubtfully, then pressed her face into her mother's neck.

"I thought you might know my name, or my husband's at any rate," said Louise, brushing away the thought that the child should not hear what she had to say.

"No, I'm afraid I've never heard of you."

"Well, I know your husband. He knew my Roland in the war. They were prisoners together."

"I see. He's never spoken of you or your husband, but then, he never talks about the war."

"He doesn't?"

"Not to me. Will you walk a bit? I'm afraid Loretta is getting rest-less." As if on cue, Loretta struggled against her mother's arms and demanded to be put down.

"Of course."

"Does your husband talk about it?"

"He didn't come back," Louise said, delivering the euphemism with a slight quaver in her voice. She watched for and enjoyed the tremor of discomfort in Alice's pleasant, open face.

"Oh, I'm so sorry," said Alice, touching Louise's arm lightly as she dropped her eyes. "Do you have children?"

"I'm afraid so. Four, in fact."

"Four! We're just getting ready for our second," said Alice, smiling more broadly, almost sheepishly as she grazed her belly with her fin-gertips. "I'm one of five myself. I might be back in the will now we've almost got more than one."

"Congratulations in advance. Do you have a feeling, girl or boy?"

"Kit thinks it's a boy, but he's wrong. I can just tell, you know what I mean?"

"No. I'm afraid I don't. I didn't have any such premonitions."

"Really?"

"Not a one."

Alice seemed to take that in and decide that Louise must not be looking for a friend. Or at any rate, for one of those conversations about the blessings and curses of childrearing.

"So, what can I do for you, Mrs.—Louise?"

"I don't suppose your husband is home?" she asked, knowing full well that Kit would be at work.

"No, he's not. In fact, he's been working late quite a bit lately. Going on business trips. I suppose he doesn't like seeing me fatten up!" Alice was clearly only half joking, her lips fluttered in that nervous way of a woman sabotaging herself.

"Well, I was in the neighborhood, and I thought to bring him some-thing. You see, he had kindly written to me with some recollections of my Roland. I came across some interesting news about another soldier, so I thought I would share it with him."

"Oh, do you live in Wilmington?"

Louise pretended not to hear the question as she opened her purse and extracted an envelope with Kit's name and address on it.

"Everything but the stamp," said Louise, smiling. "Will you give this to him?"

"Of course. Looks like you forgot the return address?"

"He knows it. Oh, and can I ask one more small favor?"

"Yes?"

"I'd like for him to be the one to open it."

"I don't read mail that's not addressed to me," said Alice in a wounded tone.

"No. Of course not," said Louise.

They were almost at the corner, where Loretta was pulling Goldy's tail, and Goldy was turning toward her with a large slice of ham tongue, ready to lick away any trouble.

"Loretta! Leave Goldy be!" shouted Alice. "As you can see, Louise, I've got my hands full. Is there anything else you'd like me to tell my husband?"

Louise's effort to control herself, which she had enlisted and exercised so well, almost failed in that moment. She had so carefully folded the clips Mother had given her, Alice and Kit's wedding announcement, the piece about his accident at Blunt Mills. Very carefully, she had controlled her shaking hand as she wrote the address on the envelope. And as violently as she had written the letter she did not include, as violently as she had torn it up, stuffed it in a coffee can and burned it in her backyard, she had cooled herself with the sheer force of her will. Had channeled all her anger into this one gesture, giving him not her words, but those of the newspaper. Letting him know that she knew, letting the fates decide whether or not he would have some explaining to do to his wife. But at that moment, when the sweet compliant Alice offered to give him a message, she came very close to asking his wife to tell him to go fuck himself. Tell him, she almost said, that I'm not his fucking pearl. Instead, she summoned something different.

"Tell him: I must go down to the seas again, to the vagrant gypsy life." She was smiling wildly as she backed away from Mrs. Blunt and her offspring, and with every word Masefield's poem came out louder and more like the way she and Kit had sung it as they cruised toward the beach. "To the gull's way and the whale's way where the wind's like a whetted knife; and all I ask is a merry yarn from a laughing fellow-rover, and quiet sleep and a sweet dream when the long trick's over."

Purple Heart

August 1964

Charlotte peeled back the rough skin of the sunchokes or Jerusalem artichokes or whatever the man in the Chinatown market had called them. Like a potato, he'd said, only delicious. She sliced them thin and dropped them in the heated oil, then began deboning the cod. Gil would be there in half an hour. She wanted to tell her everything that had happened in Shepherd's Glen, but that kind of report, she realized, was for Katie. For Gil, she had bathed and shaved, put the lightest touch of Shalimar perfume on her wrists. It was Louise's scent. Charlotte had wasted money buying a small bottle of it when she returned to New York. She had always loved the smell of it, and now, with what she had learned about Louise, it seemed the scent of women of experience, women with hidden lovers. After what Granny had told her and what she had found in the house on Oxford Street, she felt that she had earned the scent of secret things. She told herself it wasn't that she wanted to smell like Louise, but to lay claim to the mystery that the perfume had always suggested to her.

She had slept in her childhood bed longer than she'd intended to. More than a week passed before she boarded the train to New York. Every night, to varying degrees, she had the experience, the more-than-dream, the feeling of her consciousness pricked awake inside the dark and immobile mass of her body. She was tired every day and every day she felt the pain of Louise's derogatory remarks, her little jabs. Yet she had gotten a taste of something that seemed truthful and deeper and more important than proper rest, and the stings did not sting the way they once did. A light had come on in the dark, illuminating a crawl space where she could sit and overhear the young Louise being slapped around by circumstance.

The day after the conversation in the visitors' lounge, they brought Granny home and set her up in her downstairs room with a walker, wheelchair, and pulley system that Louise rigged up—a sort of trapeze that hung over the bed, so that Granny could pull herself up and get strong. The days took on a rhythm—breakfast, Granny's exercises, lunch, Charlotte taking Granny on a wheelchair ride around the neighborhood, more exercises for Granny, reading or errands for Charlotte, Granny napping while Charlotte cooked dinner. Louise came home from work and they ate together on the screen porch.

After dinner they sat in the backyard in the wicker chairs on the flagstones that bordered the garden, smoking together as if that was their music, exhaling plume after plume, making melody with the smoke from the coil of punk that didn't do quite enough to dispel the mosquitoes. There was a kind of penitential beauty to the days. A relief from the anxious hum of the city and her feeling that, three years in, she hadn't quite found her place in it. This must be what makes monks and nuns, she thought, the certain rhythms. Every day, a cup of coffee, set the oatmeal bubbling, bring Louise her tea, see her off to work, then into Granny's room to wake her gently, encourage her to use the trapeze to pull herself up, tell her that she was getting stronger, that today was better than yesterday.

One day, while Charlotte was pushing her around the neighborhood in her wheelchair, Granny revealed something about Louise that was far more troubling than an affair with a married man. Something that made Charlotte feel nauseous, something that made her want to forgive Louise for all the shame she dispensed, for her countless belittling remarks, even for her clear favoritism of Ed, even for the confusing cruelty of her hands—the years of slaps that were followed by tears. For the many times that Charlotte had comforted Louise after Louise had hurt her.

She had just pushed Granny to the top of the small hill near the house and paused, panting, under the huge magnolia tree that was so pungent it practically made her eyes water. As a girl she had often stood under that tree, which she had always understood to be the parent to the one in their yard. Its enormous white flowers, which were now bruised and yellowing in their late summer way, had always exerted a certain power over her. Their scent drew her to them, made her climb into that one low branch and sit soaking in the liquid they made of the air, feeling repelled and aroused in equal measure.

"Because I am near the end, I feel I need to tell you something, Charlotte," said Granny, reaching up to touch Charlotte's hand, inviting her to come around to where they could look at each other's faces. "But I need you to promise me that you won't tell anyone else until I'm gone."

"Of course, Granny."

"This is hard for me to say out loud." Granny closed her eyes, then opened them again.

"Please tell me."

Granny sighed, placed her hand over her eyes, then let it drop to her lap.

"Your grandfather—he was—interested in your mother." Granny was looking up into the tree. Then, as if by supreme effort, she leveled her eyes with Charlotte's. "The way a man is interested in a woman. I didn't want to know, but I knew."

Charlotte felt her head and stomach change places. Her eyelids dropped down over her eyes like heavy metal gates protecting a closed storefront on Houston Street. The colonel—she had always thought of him that way—her granddaddy, not so much as a human being but as a position. As alive as an Ionic column, fixed as a brooding bust, one eye squinting to take aim at the target. He was a player in the great game, taking down the American flag when the Japanese invaded Corregidor, hoisting the flag of surrender. He had cut out a piece of the flag and sewn it on the inside of the shirt he would wear for almost a year as his body and the clothes on it turned to rags. His war diary and a piece of the flag had survived his death on Formosa and sat in a glass case at West Point. He was an all-American footballer with a big Germanic body; he was the one her uncle Bruce and her brother Bruce ran for when they ran, the very same they caught the ball for, the one they aimed to top. It was the marble memory of the colonel, even more than the dream of their father, that had enticed her brother Bruce to go to West Point, to make a career in the military that was burning villages in Vietnam, as she and Granny stood underneath a magnolia tree on a suburban hill.

"I knew and I was jealous," said Granny, drawing shaking fingers from her temples into the center of her forehead as if to remove the memory. "I'm telling you now while I still have my faculties—I don't want to die without this being known. I could see the way he looked at her, the way he just assumed her as belonging to him in every way. I had always been told it was good I had wit and brains since I didn't have looks. Your grandfather was this glorious catch for me, in the eyes of the girls I grew up with. Many others had their sights on him, but I was smart and well-read and I had a sense of humor he shared, a certain irreverence despite his being a military man, or maybe in part because of it. I was considered old to start a family; people thought I'd be some old blue-stocking reporter. I was twenty-eight when I had your uncle Bruce. But then came your mother, smarter and more beautiful than I. And your grandfather had an almost obsessive interest in her, even before her body began to develop. When she began to fill out, I would catch him looking at her—" Granny paused and held her breath. She looked up into the branches of the tree and swallowed and blinked. "It happens all the time. It is something too common and too horrible to acknowledge. I knew and I didn't try to stop it. Partly because she reveled in his attention, because from early on they seemed to have private jokes and understandings. I was not invited to the world they made. Mostly I felt the fool. I had given up reporting. I had believed in your grandfather, in what he stood for, and I just let myself be what I was supposed to be. I gave everything to them and they betrayed me."

Charlotte looked into Granny's eyes, felt Granny's effort to keep the left one from wandering. They held each other's gaze for what seemed a long time before Charlotte spoke.

"I see," she said, squatting so that she was no longer towering over Granny, but bent-knee, childlike, at her side. "I don't know what to say. Have you ever talked to her about it?"

"Not exactly. I did once, but it didn't go so well. If I recall correctly, we seemed to agree to bury the subject. I don't think we could keep living together if we really talked about it. I don't know how much better it makes things, talking about them."

"We're talking about it now," said Charlotte.

"I suppose so. The times have certainly changed. I know that more people now go to a shrink or whatever you call it. Maybe it is helpful for them. But your mother and I, over the years, have learned to live pretty well together. Every few weeks she stays away for a couple of days. You remember when you were kids, she would go away on her little sojourns. Her supposed workshops. I don't ask her anymore where she goes, and that allows us to live in peace."

"How long did it go on with her and the colonel?"

"I can't say exactly. I think it started when she was about fifteen and went on until she met your father when she was twenty."

Charlotte thought of Katie's boyfriend Alexander, and all his talk about his parents, the analysts who used LSD and uncomfortable conversations to—shake people loose. That's what he said, that it was all about shaking people loose so they could be free. Maybe Louise could use that kind of help. Granny spoke again just then as if she had read Charlotte's mind.

"Your mother is not a proponent of what they call talk therapy. I think she considers it beneath her somehow. That it is something for the weak. She's always been someone who deals with what's in front of her. Even when we had all the dead to mourn, she wasn't one for mourning. Get on with it, that was her saying about life."

Charlotte got back behind the wheelchair, turned it around, and began taking Granny toward lunch. She gripped the handles of the wheelchair more firmly as they went tilting down the slope, drawn back to the house like ball bearings to a magnet. She asked the question that made her hands sprout sweat. "Should I talk to her about it while I'm here?"

"Heavens no! Please wait until I'm dead."

The way that she exclaimed these words made Charlotte feel foolish for asking. But what was she to do with this ugly truth? The image that arose in her mind was of a labyrinth, of halls and doors, of turns around one blank corner to another, on and on, until without warning, without a way of tracing the path that she had traveled, she had arrived in the center. There, in an airless room, Louise and the colonel were engaged in—what? A rape, a seduction? Along the way there were doors that led to other windowless rooms which held other scenes she had lately stumbled upon—of herself lying naked on Louise's bed while Ed drew her, of Granny's head slumping over the steering wheel in the exhaust-filled garage, of Kit Blunt slapping Louise's face. There were things happening in those rooms, and it seemed to her that they were happening forever.

She started seeing Louise differently. Her beauty, her self-assurance, the lift of her chin and her long, straight back, all of her seemed to Charlotte as counterfeit as a movie set. One morning while Granny was still sleeping and Louise was at work, Charlotte stepped into Louise's room, looking for what she didn't know. Some confirmation of what Granny had said? Something to prove what she now knew about Louise?

Louise's bed was still that island fortress—a four poster mahogany antique, another piece of colonial furniture that had been found in the mythic Philippines of Granny and the colonel's day. Each of the four posts was topped by a carved wooden pineapple crowned with batches of sharp leaves that nearly scraped the room's white ceiling. This was the place where Louise, their queen, had awaited the nighttime kisses of Charlotte and the others. It seemed only right that her bed be so grand and big that the children had to climb onto it from its running boards or launch themselves onto it from chairs. She trailed her fingers along the crocheted coverlet, then lifted the four sturdy pillows one by one. She got down on her hands and knees and looked under the bed, but there was nothing there but a hearty space that had always been too big and clear to hide in.

Then Charlotte dug into the chest of drawers—slowly at first, carefully lifting every folded thing and replacing it carefully, keeping the shape and fold. Then more rapidly, pawing the cottons and thin wools and silks. She found something that seemed almost illicit enough, a full set of black lace underwear, including garters and a scalloped, breastless sort of corset, straight out of a brothel. Quite something for a woman of fifty-two, she thought, even if she was Louise.

Having gone this far, Charlotte felt she had to go a little farther. She spread the garments on the bed, took off her nightgown, and picked up the breast-less bustier of dense scratchy black lace and wire. But when she tried to stick the tiny wire hooks to their corresponding eyes, she couldn't make them meet across the expanse of her rib cage.

Whose body is that? she whispered, catching sight of her reflection in the square mirror above the dressing table that was so neatly built into the wall. From her vantage point, her head was cut out of the reflection, so that she could only see her midsection, the voluminous breasts that magnetized eyes, the hips on which so many assumptions rested. This flesh the tight little garment meant to truss, to ready it to be served. The flesh so pale it looked almost luminous in this light, like some marble at the Met that if examined closely revealed faintly colored veins. Was she grotesque? Was she incorrectly costumed, not just in the bit of Louise's black lace, but in the body that wore it? Was hers the body of a lesbian?

All the ways her body had been constrained seemed to come for her at once. The garters and clips, the sweat pads in her armpits that kept her clothes almost unstained but made her sweat the more. The stockings washed the day before the event and laid to dry, the "tummy tuckers" and "figure smoothers" to keep the swells along the wanted lines, the pointed cones she jammed her volumes into.

The four posts of Louise's bed were that too, a restraining frame. It must have been that same summer, Charlotte realized with the feeling of alarm that accompanies the revelation of a pattern. It was that same summer of Granny's suicide attempt and Louise's affair with the married man, that she, at twelve, had been stuffed into the frame of Louise's bed so that Ed could draw her, so that he could tell her that she had the hips of a New Orleans madam. She and Ed had once had a kind of friendship, hadn't they? They had chanted the lines from *The Tempest*, tried to bring Father back. But before that, she could almost see it now, could almost hear their very young voices, could almost feel the ball and the jacks in their hands, the dolls they danced together under Louise's big bed. She remembered it now, there was a time when there was no difference between them. Before her body had betrayed her.

The creature that she was, the one so many hunted, was not, she was certain, she. What she was, what was true, was instead the flickering consciousness, or no, the light beneath even that.

Why should I be trapped in this? she thought, as the light shifted slightly, so that again she could make out the body, the crucible she lived in. This material she acted in was prized and loathed, wanted not for what it was but for what it could take, the thick swath of oily pubic hair a place men wanted to slam themselves into, the hips a great breadbasket they wanted to fill with yeasty replicas of themselves.

Katie had said she should get another opinion. I want our kids to play together by the pool, she had said. Katie's invitation to joy in the prescribed way, to the place of their future happiness, the home they'd all been taught to dream of. Their version of it had the other things along the far corners, in the blurry, distant, undescribed areas around the perimeter of the family fence there lived some vague ideas of art and activism. But right at the center the image was always the same, a place in the world that they should want. Because it was the way the world wanted them. Except, of course, the world that they knew, or that Charlotte knew anyway, was not actually that tidy technicolor suburban dream. Shepherd's Glen had no sheep, and the house on Oxford Street had almost swallowed her whole.

You're not really an invert, Katie had said. At what point will I become that, Charlotte thought, really an invert? She couldn't explain to Katie or anyone the joy she felt when she thought of Gil. A woman absolutely unafraid of being a man—but, no, that wasn't it either. Gil was just herself, completely and unapologetically. And if she had been beaten for it, and Charlotte knew that she had, the beatings had persuaded Gil to hold fast to her way of dressing, talking, being. To insist upon it. The world had marked her, had tried to cross her out; the white and purple scars she bore were proof and she bore them without shame. Charlotte loved Gil's voice almost more than her eyes, it was low and sonorous, not a man's voice exactly, but not exactly a woman's. Or not what a woman's voice was supposed to be, or what women's voices were so often. Chipper or cajoling. High pitched and rapid fire or cooing and infantile. It was a voice tempered by real reckoning, a voice that spoke Charlotte's name in her ear, as one hand held her hand and the other cupped her vulva.

Her breasts dolloped over the edge of the unclaspable corset like cream over the edge of a parfait glass. Dr. Bedford had acted as though she had cheated him by having, as he called it, a black walnut for a uterus, by having all this equipment that could never be used. But here you are, she thought, holding her gaze on the being that had always troubled her, always been too white and too red. But oh, you're beautiful, Gil had said, good girl. Sweet cream. Charlotte lifted her breasts in her hands. "Are these the breasts of an invert?" she whispered. "Who do you belong to?" she asked aloud. When the phone rang, Charlotte jumped. It was Louise.

"What are you doing?"

"Nothing," said Charlotte, grinning a secret grin.

"Good. Go down to Johnson's and pick up some tea for me, and coffee if you need it. You could stop at the fish market too, get some sole or snapper, whatever looks good."

"Okay."

"I left you some money on the kitchen counter."

"All right."

"How's your granny?"

"Sleeping."

"Are you listening?"

"What do you mean?"

"You sound—distant."

"I'm right here."

"Are you in my room?"

"No," said Charlotte, frowning. How could she always know?

"Okay, dear, see you tonight."

Charlotte hung up and took off the whore's corset and carefully placed it back in the drawer with the matching black lace panties and garters. Just then, Granny began to call out to her from her bedroom downstairs.

The voice from below startled her. Jumpily, she pulled the drawer all the way out of the dresser and dropped it, face down, on the floor. There, taped into the back, was a smooth, cream-colored envelope. Before she could think about it, she unsealed the tape around its edges and tucked it under her arm.

Later that night, after everyone had gone to bed, she stood by her narrow childhood bed and opened the envelope to find three smaller envelopes, all addressed to Louise, each in its own distinctive handwriting. She read the three pieces furtively, as if Louise or Granny would pounce on her at any moment. Then, in a movement that didn't seem like a decision at all, but just natural, a forearm gliding through an elbow joint, she put the smaller envelopes back inside the large one and slipped it into the slim zippered back pocket of her suitcase.

Her last day in Shepherd's Glen was a Sunday. The three of them sat on the flagstones after brunch. To celebrate Charlotte's visit and Granny's slow but steady recovery, Louise had made gin and tonics. They sat drinking and smoking and reading the *Washington Post*, emitting grunts or groans of dismay about what Granny called that Indochine mess.

"That's not what I want Bruce to fight for," Granny said.

"I expect he'll go where he's told," Louise said.

"Well, that's grim, Mother," said Charlotte.

"I'm a realist." Louise refolded her section of the paper and tossed it onto the table.

"It's not our business," Granny persisted. "If they want to go red. I wouldn't put anyone's grandson in the line of fire for an argument over an idea floating above some rice fields half the world away."

"The army was good enough for your husband and mine," said Louise, as if that explained anything.

"I think Bruce should quit the army," said Charlotte, in a sudden rush of anger. "I can't believe you even let him go to West Point."

She looked from one to the other, but they didn't return her gaze. There were things she couldn't say, but she could say this.

"Bruce made his own choice," said Granny.

"You encouraged him! Both of you!" Charlotte felt her face turning red with the combination of alcohol and eggs benedict and coffee and the sudden desire to crack open all the closed spaces her family hoarded.

"We did no such thing," said Granny with finality.

"Why do you think I'm sending Ed to France?" Louise said suddenly.

It hadn't occurred to Charlotte that Louise was trying to protect Ed from the great machine of war by arranging for him to go live in Paris. She'd never thought he could be drafted, not after his stay in Bellevue. Brief though it was, surely it could be trotted out as evidence of his unfitness for service. She was certain that Ed would find a way out if need be. Suddenly she felt a surge of love for Bruce, her dutiful brother, the believer. Then she felt an equal measure of disgust with Louise, for her constant, clear favoritism. Bruce could play football anywhere; why had she let him try to fill the bloody shoes of his father, his uncle, his grandfather?

"I'm tired," said Granny.

"I'll help you in," said Louise.

And with that, they got up and left Charlotte to her glass of half-melted ice and sad puckered husk of lime. They said no more about Bruce, or West Point, or the current war, or the wars before.

Now she was back in New York, putting fish in the oven, waiting for her secret lover. She wore Louise's scent, and in the cigar box where she kept her other stolen family treasure, Roland Galle's Purple Heart, she had placed Louise's secret letters. At first, she'd thought to show them to Katie, tell her everything that she had learned in Shepherd's Glen. But she realized it was Ed who should see them, or at least one of them. When he least expected it, she would show him the evidence of all he didn't know about the world he thought was his.

Gil knocked. Charlotte took off her apron, smoothed the skirt of the red dress that fastened at the neck and revealed her white shoulders to good effect, and opened the door to her lover.

"Oh, hi," said Gil, holding out a bunch of lilacs. "I'm here to fix the plumbing."

Charlotte laughed and let herself be lifted in Gil's arms, kissed her and let herself be kissed and thrown onto her bed, and barely managed to keep the fish from burning. They went at each other for hours, Gil sucking and teasing her until she screamed and flooded the bed with her warm sweet juice. Charlotte woke from the doze they fell into afterward to find Gil's face very near to hers, calling her just exactly what her father had called her mother in one of the three letters she had stolen.

"My pearl," Gil said. "Oh, my pearl."

THE RETURN

I the master of the soldier's art
Watching souls of men depart

You the woman God had given
To falseness and to baseness driven.

KISS OF DEATH

AUGUST 1948

He sent a note the very next day. Louise had expected him to wait a week or two. Maybe she wanted a year to go by, so that she could accustom herself to being without him. Without his intrigues and his large and shapely cock. She did think of his member fondly, did enjoy his body, the heaviness of it, the density of his arm muscles that remained well formed, despite what he claimed were dissolute days. Despite the layer of civilian fat on his belly, the architecture of his muscles was sound and always present, even when he lay on his back. His very bones had an unfamiliar density, as if he and Roland had different specific gravities. I let other people do the heavy lifting, or all the lifting, he said once of his job at the mill. Those who do the least make the most money, didn't she know that. She expected him to show up just when she had returned to some workaday rhythm and no longer believed in herself as a lover, but only as a widow, mother, woman of science. And that last category seemed questionable the day after her visit to Wilmington, as she found the weight of the residual material so wildly different on different assays that the entire morning's work had to be trashed. She removed her gloves and goggles and apron and decided to take an early lunch.

She was on her way to the cafeteria when the woman at the front desk, whatever her name was, who had replaced Marjorie, called her over. Grinning from ear to ear, the receptionist presented her with a narrow pink box opened to reveal a dozen long-stemmed red roses tied with a crisp yellow ribbon.

"I didn't know you cared," said Louise, trying to be nonchalant.

"I don't," said the receptionist, touché. "There's a note."

Louise took the note but left the bouquet.

"Don't you want them?"

"Roses give me hives," said Louise, taking the note and turning her back on the young woman who seemed so keen to share a valentine moment with her.

The note said: *I can explain. Tonight, the usual place. 5:30.*

The rest of the workday went more smoothly. Rather than soothe her, the roses inflamed Louise's anger, so that her feelings came to a boil and frothed over. The clichéd posies were insulting to her; did he have no idea who she was? Roland would never have given roses. The first thing he ever gave her was a fossil he'd found on a tramp through the woods near West Point. A piece of rock with half a jaw in it, three pointed teeth still stuck in their grooves. They'd argued playfully about the jaw's owner. Just a regular ol' tomcat like you, she remembered saying, dismissing his suggestion that it was from a creature no one had ever seen before. He'd chased her across the field behind the gridiron; they had kissed and kissed and rolled around in the grass, barely making it back in time to meet the others for dinner. Mother had been her co-conspirator then, whispering to her about the hay in her hair before the colonel and Bruce came in the room. Father must have known, even then, that she was detaching from him. He kept asking Roland why he didn't play football, or any other sport, for that matter. Horseback riding didn't count.

She allowed herself the little reverie, but then she shrugged it off and shifted her attention to the remixing and pouring and measuring that was her work, the combining of ground fungus and bacteria to see what one would do to the other. By the time she left work, she had convinced herself that she would simply never see Kit again. The last word had been hers, had been the line from the poem, the trick's over. If his little wife remembered any part of the Masefield poem, he might have known, even before he opened the envelope, that Louise was done with him. She stayed until six to add a few better measurements to the log to make up for a wasted morning. It was still light out when she drove out of the lot and toward Shepherd's Glen. She could see the car behind her quite clearly. Kit's black Studebaker could have been anyone's, but she was certain that he was behind the wheel of the car that pinned her so carefully, allowing another to get between it and her green Packard, reappearing after slinking around a corner as if he had somewhere to be other than on her tail.

As she came around final curve of Oxford Street that sloped down toward her driveway, she looked into the rearview to find it empty. But she knew that he was near, tucked just out of sight, waiting for just the right moment to appear. To do what, exactly? To enact his revenge? To walk right up to her door, as she had walked right up to his? To take Roland away again, to stop pretending he was possessed by her husband? Yet she believed it, despite every possible rational argument. She had seen Roland's eyes in his face, had felt Roland's touch coming through his sturdy hands. His strokes lit her, charged her nerves with the erotic thrill of familiar moves transmitted through an alien body. Being with him was like dancing a dance to which she knew all the steps, but with a partner from an unknown country. Yet all of that was no reason to let him squeeze her neck, to let him plunge her head under the water and hold it there. She had let him draw her toward oblivion, just that much. Roland wouldn't have done that any more than he would have given her a dozen goddamned long-stemmed roses. As if all women were these creatures whose feelings could be nullified with sweet fragrances or plugged up with chocolates. She felt that fuel again, that dose of invigorating anger. "I am done with you," she said aloud.

Yet as the gravel crunched under her tires and she saw a tall figure walking toward her front door, her hands shook against the steering wheel. But it was not Kit Blunt stepping up to knock on her door, but a neighbor, Tad Sklar, and Ed was with him. She stepped out of the car. Mother appeared just then, opening the door. Ed was looking at the ground, his face drawn and sullen. Louise could see a spasm in his cheek, a ripple on the surface that reflected a locked jaw beneath, a movement so like the one that had changed Roland's face on the rare occasions when he was angry.

"Hello, Mr. Sklar," said Mother. "I thought Ed was staying for supper?"

"I'm not," said Ed, shifting from one foot to the other. "Can I go inside now?"

"Hullo, Tad," said Louise, walking across her front lawn of dry summer crabgrass. "What brings you by?"

"Louise." He nodded at her gravely and adjusted his thick-framed glasses, which were sliding down his nose. He was a lawyer at a DC firm, someone she knew only to say hello to in the post office or at the pool, but she thought well enough of him. Lately Ed had been spending time with his daughter, taking walks and drawing landscapes.

"Stay there, Ed, while I tell your mother where I found you."

"Say, your tone is rather severe, Tad," said Louise. "Why don't we all go around back and have a glass of something. I've had a long day—"

"My wife found your son and my daughter in our toolshed."

"I don't like what you're implying, Tad," said Louise, repeating his name with what she felt was a weightier intonation.

"I'm not implying anything," said Tad, folding his arms and leaning back on his heels, in a posture of weary authority. "I am saying it flat out. They were stark naked. We've banned Ed from our house until further notice. I've come to ask you to make sure he stays away from Anna."

Mother looked at Ed, but his eyes were fixed on the ground. Louise watched the bloom of blood in Ed's face, the heat of his embarrassment, then the cooling accompanied by a wry smile.

"You go inside now, Ed," said Mother, crossing her arms across her chest in a gesture that mirrored Tad Sklar's. "I'll speak a bit more with Mr. Sklar and then we'll talk."

A burst of bile struck Louise in the gut looking at the two of them, meting out judgment against Ed, who opened the door and stepped inside without another word. Tad Sklar had a pudgy, florid face, but she had never noticed before how very porcine it was.

"Mother, I'll speak with Mr. Sklar," said Louise, in an effort to seize the parental authority she so often ceded. Mother did not move an iota. "So, this is Ed's fault?"

"Yes," said that Tad Sklar in the tone of one used to interpreting the law. "They're only fourteen, after all—"

"Yes, they're both fourteen."

"Your point being?" said Tad, stiffening.

"Louise—" Mother touched her elbow lightly, trying to draw her gaze. Louise refused the invitation, keeping her eyes squarely on the piggish neighbor.

"What, Mother? Last I heard this kind of thing takes two."

"Look, Louise, I think you should have a talk with your son. Give him a sense of responsibility." Tad tightened the clasp of his arms across his chest.

"Louise and I will talk to him," said Mother.

"What do you know about my son's sense of responsibility?"

"Louise, come on now," said Mother, shaking her head as if she expected Louise to just swallow the insults.

"No, Mother. I don't like your tone, Mr. Sklar."

"My tone has nothing to do with the fact that my wife found Ed and Anna together in the toolshed, neither of them wearing a stitch."

"So why is that Ed's fault?"

"Anna is a good kid, but she might be a little bit gullible. She told her mother they were drawing in the shed."

"Maybe they were!" Now Louise folded her arms across her chest too, so they were all three in the same position, as if they were trying to contain themselves, to keep their hands from lashing out.

"Louise, don't make a scene," said Mother. "Tad, perhaps you should go now."

"Look, Louise," said Tad, pointing an index finger at her as if he were nailing his point in front of a jury. "Maybe art or whatever, maybe anything goes at your house; as Anna tells us, that's your business. But you better tell Ed to stay away. Good evening, Martha."

Tad Sklar, the very figure of rectitude, turned his back to them and strode away in lightning-quick righteous steps.

"Oh yes! Case closed!" Louise could not resist the rush of her own loud words. "Tell your slut of a daughter she's not welcome here!"

"Louise! Don't be a fishwife!" Mother hissed, looping her arm through Louise's and attempting to draw her back into the house.

"Yes, that's what I am, a fishwife! That's exactly what I am." She felt dizzy, exhilarated, yelling right out on the front lawn, loud and natural before the rhododendrons nodding in the breeze.

"Have you been drinking?" Mother asked, speaking more softly, changing tactics now, wrapping her arm around Louise's waist, coaxing her up the stoop and into the house.

"No, but I certainly could use one."

"Dinner's going to be late. I've got to put the croquettes in the oven. Or you could do that while I go talk to Ed?"

"What'd Ed do?" It was Helen walking around from the backyard. Her hands were gloved in mud and mud spatters played among the freckles on her face. Louise ignored the question and the filth and spoke to Mother.

"I'll talk to Ed. Helen will get cleaned up and help you in the kitchen."

Mother looked at her doubtfully, cocked her head as if she were about to argue, or to open a line of questioning, a hint that she hadn't forgotten the other bit of business. The Blunt business. But she just narrowed her eyes and shrugged, and told Helen to wash up.

Louise went upstairs, placed two rapid knocks on the door of the boys' room and went in. Ed was lying with his head at the foot of his narrow bed, his legs up, his heels resting on the wall. She sat down near enough to his head to make him uncomfortable. He swung his legs down and sat up.

"Let me see it," she said.

"What?"

"The drawing. I hear that you were drawing her. I'd like to see the drawing."

"I had barely started. There's nothing to see." They sat side by side, glancing at each other in an off-rhythm way, not locking eyes.

"So why were you both naked, if you were drawing her?"

"She wouldn't do it unless we both were."

"Is that so?"

"Why would I lie?"

"Hmm, I could think of a reason." She tried to make her tone light, tried not get lost in admiration for the long slender fingers that curled helplessly in his lap.

"Look, Mother, I know how babies get made if that's what you mean."

"You know by experience?" She was teasing him a little, elbowing him gently in the ribs.

"No. Anyway that's none of your business."

"I beg to differ." They were quiet for a moment. This is the time for me to say what it means to be a man, she thought, but I have no idea what it means.

"Can I have a smoke?" Ed asked, as if to remind her of their trip to the beach that night that seemed so long ago, when he had been her co-pilot.

"No, you may not."

"Am I grounded?"

"Yes. For the rest of the summer."

She wasn't in the habit of refusing Ed anything. Usually she let Mother mete out the punishments, but she wanted to manifest this strength.

"Helluva punishment coming from you."

Stung, she turned to look him in the eye.

"What's that supposed to mean?"

"I'm not deaf. I heard you and Granny talking about your married man."

The slap on his face didn't seem to come from her, but her hand hummed with it. He jumped up, but she grabbed his hand, pulled him toward her, hugged him. "I'm sorry," she breathed into his red-gold hair, inhaled his boy scent. Something so pure and sweet in the smell of him, clean seed. She began to cry and he held her tightly. A great wracking sob came out of her, a deep, quick squall. When it passed, he released her and she held his hands in hers. If I speak of Roland now, the tears will come back, she thought, but she spoke of him anyway.

"Remember what your father wrote, remember how he told you to respect me and Granny and all women?"

"No, I don't think you ever told me about that."

"Didn't I?"

"You never read us his letters."

"I didn't?"

"You just told us that he sent his love from far away."

"What a terrible mother! No wonder you got in a toolshed with a slut." She toyed with his hands, which she still held in hers, swinging them slightly. His lips curled in a half-smile, and he let her keep talking.

"Your father wrote, tell Edward to always listen carefully to what women say and to respect their wishes, for they are the holders of the world."

"Okay." He dropped his eyes. She released one of his hands and held his chin, locked eyes with him.

"Okay what?"

"I'll try."

"Good." Charlotte could be heard calling up the stairs that dinner was ready. Louise released Ed's chin.

"Oh, and, Ed."

"Yeah?"

"I wouldn't tell anyone about drawing Charlotte. Most people don't understand what art requires."

Purple Heart

August 1964

Charlotte sat up and asked Gil again what she'd said.

"I must've been talking in my sleep," Gil answered, pulling Charlotte back down on her. "Or it was my stomach talking. I smell fish. If I weren't so hungry, I'd make that into a dyke joke."

"You called me your pearl," said Charlotte, tracing the long scar below Gil's collarbone, the place where her right breast wasn't. My Amazon, Charlotte called her. Gil would never answer Charlotte's questions about how she got this scar and the others. Maybe you'll tell me one day, she would whisper, her fingers following the oddly smooth purple river that ran the length of Gil's inner left arm. She thought to tell Gil about the letters—what a strange coincidence that Gil had called her what Louise was once called—but she didn't want to bring her mother into their bed.

"I did? I think you of more as a ruby, no, a garnet. But all this talk of gems is making me hungrier."

"I can take a hint." Charlotte pressed herself up again. "We'd have already eaten if—"

"I was even hungrier for you. Starved," said Gil, grabbing Charlotte's hand and interlacing her strong bony fingers with Charlotte's soft milky ones. Charlotte bent to kiss her lover, then reached for the cool pink silk robe she had bought herself in Chinatown to celebrate getting her job at Dunne and Crowne. How long ago that seemed!

"Dinner will be ready in two shakes of a lamb's tail."

"Sometimes you talk like a Southern belle."

"Well, fiddle-dee-dee!" she answered, pulling the robe open to reveal one breast for punctuation.

"Keep that up and I'll eat you alive."

"Didn't you already?" Charlotte grinned and straightened the robe.

"Anyone ever tell you you are a homosexual?"

She went into the kitchen and put the fish back in the oven, then began to reheat the oil for the Jerusalem artichokes. Gil came in and made them gin and tonics just as if they did this all the time. To the tune of fish and butter and better-than-potatoes, Charlotte let herself float in the fantasy that they did. That they could belong to each other, make house. Just then Gil passed behind her, reached her arm around with a drink in it, and kissed her neck.

"I was thinking—" Charlotte started.

"Uh-oh!"

"You never stop joking, do you?"

"Not if I can help it," said Gil, perching on the step stool.

"I had quite a time in Shepherd's Glen."

"With a name like that, it's got to be good," Gil said. She had put her jeans and T-shirt back on and extracted a packet of rolling tobacco and some papers and something else from her pocket. "I have a little grass, if you'd like to smoke some."

"Sure. But I was going to tell you about my time at home."

"I'm all ears. But can I tell you a few things first? Yours sounds like a long story."

"All right." She took down the plates from the shelf over the sink and handed Gil a baguette, a knife, some butter.

"First, there's a job waiting for you at The Strand. I lined it up. You'll work the register."

"Wow, thank you. I guess I didn't know I wanted to work there." She tried to keep the irritation out of her voice, the feeling she couldn't quite name, that she had been demoted. Gil picked it up.

"I know, it's not being an editor at a fancy publishing house, but you're done with that. This'll be perfect for you. You'll bring in more customers just by looking gorgeous through the window. And employees get a discount."

Charlotte turned her back to get the fish out of the oven. Was it the job itself that bothered her, or the way that Gil spoke about it? Wasn't that quality of absolute assurance something she adored?

"Thank you, yes, of course."

"Anyway, anyone bothers you, they'll have to deal with me. I'll be working stock in the back. Though might not be exactly the same shifts."

Charlotte put the fish on the table. The lilacs Gil had brought lay on the counter. They had wilted a bit during the lovemaking. She filled a clean old Chianti bottle with water and stuck them in.

"That's great news, thank you."

"And there's more. I found a bunch of cheap wind-up toys. We can take them apart and attach the little motors to your winged bicycles."

"How about after dinner?"

"Oh, honey, I can't stay. Sorry, thought I told you. Late shift."

"Oh." Charlotte brought the pan with the hot Jerusalem artichoke chips to the table and scraped half the mound of them onto each plate.

"Don't get down in the mouth, sweetie."

"Fish?" Charlotte cut the cod in half and placed the white flesh on each of their plates.

They had just finished eating and were smoking the joint that Gil had rolled when the buzzer buzzed. Gil blew a cloud of smoke toward the ceiling, passed it to Charlotte, and stood up.

"Let's ignore it," said Charlotte, grabbing Gil's tough-padded hand and trying to pull her back to her seat. But the buzzing continued in an insistent, irritating pattern, so that finally Charlotte stood up and went quickly to the intercom before Gil could. It was Ed, of course. French-drunk and hard to get rid of.

"Lottie! *C'est moi!*"

"Ed, I can't talk right now."

"I'da *je te telephonerai* but your phone's still not working—" His words were drowned out by the sound of two cars honking at each other, voices rising. An argument, Charlotte guessed, between two taxi drivers.

"Listen, Ed, I mean it. I can't talk right now."

"*Mais c'est une catastrophe!*" Ed was yelling over the voices.

"I mean it. I'll come by tomorrow."

He kept repeating the word, CA-TA-STROPHE with his horrible French accent, with a hard hit on the second syllable, with the rhythmic obsession of the drunk. Then Gil was there, standing over her.

"Go home, Ed!" she barked.

"Who is that, Lottie? You have company?"

Charlotte elbowed Gil softly in the ribs, trying to get her to move away from the speaker. But she stayed where she was, leaning above, her head looming over Charlotte's shoulder.

"Yeah, she has company." Gil's tone was hard and cross, and in response to Charlotte's elbow, she stood more firmly.

"Let me handle it," Charlotte hissed. "Please."

Finally Gil stepped back.

"Oh, *excusez-moi,* I didn't know you were having your study group."

"Ed, please, I'll come over tomorrow first thing."

"Okay, okay. Go back to reading Sappho. I hear the weather on Lesbos is lovely this time of year."

"Bye, Ed."

"*Au revoir, ma petite chou.*" Ed kept his hand on the button a bit longer, letting the argument happening in the street come in. The yelling was loud enough now that for a moment they could hear it through the window as well as the intercom, a chorus of fuck yous in stereo.

"Your brother could use a kick in the ass."

Charlotte didn't answer. The grass was kicking in and she wanted to enjoy it. She went over to the hi-fi and put on Art Blakey and The Jazz Messengers.

"I love this record, don't you?"

"I'm not familiar," said Gil, sitting down on the love seat and relighting the joint. "I'm not one for jazz."

"Oh, I'll take it off," said Charlotte, feeling that the mood of the evening was permanently ruined. Feeling suddenly very disappointed in her lover, noticing for the first time the way Gil's forehead wrinkled while she sucked on the end of the joint, the way her cheeks hollowed and filled like billowing garbage bags. She stood up but didn't yet move toward the hi-fi.

"You don't have to do that to please me. I'm not your brother."

"What's that supposed to mean?"

"You're going to have to stand up to him sometime," said Gil, letting two streams of smoke pour through her nose. Charlotte took the joint that Gil held out, but she sat in the chair, not next to her. The evening was totally ruined now, the grass was overcoming her, and all she wanted was to lie down and listen to the music.

"I do," was all she could manage to say. Gil seemed to read her mind.

"Sure. Need to walk and clear the head before work." Gil took one more drag and put the joint out, put it on the lip of the stork-shaped ashtray, and stood up.

"Okay," said Charlotte, not moving.

Gil kissed her on the forehead like she was a child.

"Oh, come by The Strand tomorrow, earlier is better, and ask for Nancy."

"All right."

"You're welcome," said Gil.

There was an unmistakable chill in Gil's voice. Charlotte stood up, receiving the message from her grass-addled brain as a stage actress receives the prompter's whisper. She did then what she was supposed to do, leapt up and embraced Gil, kissed her hard on the lips and thanked her for her help. When Gil had gone, she started the record from the beginning, let her mind find the rhythms to follow, let the patterns in their perfection wipe away her feeling of uncertain progress.

THE RETURN

I for you and you for me
Forever after promisingly

I am we, beneath the sea
You are not done with me.

KISS OF DEATH

AUGUST 1948

A day passed without incident, but Louise knew that Kit was near, that he was watching her. She felt his eyes on her, saw herself as through the end of his lens, as projected on the screen with all the subtleties of black and white. He accompanied her, he was with her, magnetized to her. Walking into the Institute, her shadow on the pavement made her start—it seemed barrel-chested and hitched at the hip. But when he did reappear, it wasn't in the location she had expected.

Mother called her at work to tell her that Bruce had been picked up by the police for "roughhousing," as they called it. Apparently he and his friends had been hanging from the bridge over Rock Creek, then pulling each other up just as they were about to fall. Mother had to pick him up at the station, but she didn't want to leave Helen, who had spiked a fever, alone.

Louise agreed to come home, made her arrangements in the lab, and got in her car. Leaving the lab felt to her like the greatest danger; taking off her heavy apron, goggles, and gloves, she felt like a knight removing his armor, preparing himself for a bloody betrayal, a death while sleeping. A line came to her, as if she were a poet, as if it were proof that Kit was planning something: I nest in your shadow. She said it aloud to the inside of her car.

Her feeling of dislocation increased with every turn toward home. It wasn't that Kit was following her, but that though she could see that the road was in front of her and that she was driving along it, she could also see herself from the outside, see the green Packard stopping at the light, taking the turn, rounding the low, smooth hill that led to the easy glide into her loose gravel driveway. But the eyes that she saw herself through were not hers alone. They belonged to Kit, whose own eyes and mouth and tongue were not really his but served Roland. The gaze that followed her came from the man uniquely equipped to judge her.

Mother left soon after she arrived, and though Ed was theoretically grounded, neither he nor Charlotte was anywhere to be found. A mutiny, Mother had said, offering no further explanation. Louise went up to Helen, wiped her head with a cool wet cloth, promised soup that she hoped could be found in the refrigerator. Helen nodded and slipped away into sleep. What a good idea, Louise thought, straightening the covers on Charlotte's bed and lying down on it. Just for a moment, Louise whispered. Her eyelids had only just closed when she heard the sound of tires crunching on the gravel. She leapt up a bit guiltily, straightened her skirt, and headed downstairs.

"That was fast," she was saying as the front door opened. There, with his hat in his hands, was Kit. Louise froze halfway down the stairs.

"The door was open," he said, shrugging and looking at her the way that he did, with a half grin on his face, the expression of surrender that contained in it his victory. There was something soft in his face, his eyes widened and settled into his head. Though his face was so different from Roland's, it seemed to her that his expression was just exactly the one that Roland had worn when he had come home on leave unexpectedly. Roland walking into their filthy kitchen, finding her feeding toddler Ed while jostling the crying baby Charlotte on her hip, dissolving her anger with his soft eyes and open arms. All of the good and hearty spite she nurtured, the stabs of anger that overtook her as she read his letters from camp, from the field, from the training, the letters that reneged on the previous letters' promises of a visit home. All of that disappeared when he walked into the kitchen, radiant and red haired, the fine brows of his forehead crinkled in wonder at the sight of her as if she were still a miracle to him. As if even reeking of sour milk and tired as a wrung dishrag, she was this miraculous creature, the very portal to the only real life. Kit is not Roland, she told herself, shaking her head as if to prevent the next thought from landing, but he nests in Roland's shadow. She gripped the railing and narrowed her eyes, tried to see Kit clearly, to shake off the poetic thought. This man with a hitched-up left hip and a blue tie and a light gray suit was just a man, and she had been a fool. She had been suckered into sympathy by this wounded man, had projected her own light on him and read the shadow it made as Roland's. She had been suckered by the softness of the place where his leg once was. Believed, like a fool, that survival itself merited celebration.

"Get out," she said, holding herself fixed to the banister, gripping her knuckles white.

"The door was open, so I walked in." He smiled and there was something sheepish in it, something apologetic. He held his arms open as if to show he had nothing to hide and meant her no harm.

"Open it again and walk back out."

"Look, I just want to talk with you."

Remain calm, she told herself, smoothing the stray hair that had fallen out of its thick blond bun, but not moving down the stairs.

"I have nothing to say to you."

"But plenty to my wife, apparently."

"I pity the poor fool," she said.

"Please, Louise. Please, just listen to me."

"Why should I?"

"For the truth."

"The truth? That's rich!"

She walked toward him then, he with his hat in his hand, he another hat-in-hander after all. Just like all the rest. She could see it now, that he was like every man, every single one of them, seeing as far as himself and no further. Holding his hat in his hand in some prescribed gesture of contrition. The only thing different about him was that he carried Roland with him—yes, that was real, she believed it in spite of herself. Roland was dead and somehow this man had taken on Roland's spirit like a husk, a dried skin that refused to shed. No, Roland was the more real, even dead. Kit was just a parasite feeding on what Roland had left behind—his disappointment, his abandonment, his eternal sorrow. She took one step down, then another, and then she was upon him. There was no strategy in her attack; she aimed the shin-kick carelessly, forgetting she was barefoot and what his left shin was made of. Her big toe slammed into the metal and the hot-white lightning of pain put power in her arm, propelled the hand that slapped him hard across the face.

Their eyes met and they were just two wills suspended. She took two steps back, but he grabbed her forearm with his meaty hand, pulled her toward him, and slapped her back. Her stinging cheek gathered round her mouth and she aimed and spat, hitting him with a gob in the eye. He released her arm and wiped away the foam. An odd smile came together on his face.

"Louise, Louise." He shook his head, chuckling softly. "You should pick your battles more carefully. What did you think? We were going to play house?"

"Get. Out." She walked to the door and opened it.

"All right, I shouldn't have come here. But you wouldn't meet me. And I want to explain some things."

"Why did you lie?"

"I didn't. You never asked if I was married—"

"About your leg."

"People just assume I lost it in the war. I don't disabuse them—"

"I'm not people," she said, realizing the silliness of the sentence. Through the open door, she caught a glimpse of Dr. Gasparyan, the strange, quiet Armenian neighbor, standing in the middle of the street, looking right at her. I see it now, she thought. I and Dr. Gasparyan and Kit, we are what has been shed, we are not what generates, but what remains. What was true is gone forever. I see us now, trembling in the suburban breeze.

"Look, I never lied to you, Louise. I just told you what you wanted to hear," said Kit, moving toward her. "If you had lost your leg in a stupid way, a way that was entirely your own fault, but people looked at you and said, Oh, what a noble sacrifice, wouldn't you—"

From upstairs Helen called out to her.

"My daughter is sick. Please go now."

"I'll go when you promise to see me, just once more. I have a little fishing cabin on the Indian River inlet." He held out a piece of paper in a trembling hand. "Directions. Meet me there as early as you can on Saturday. Please."

Later she would tell herself that she decided to see him because the hand trembled, the hand that had slapped her, that had pressed her head under the water, it trembled for her. In fear and desire, the big hand with tufts of dark hair near the knuckles shook, this hand that had touched Roland, that had taken from her husband a photograph of her steering a boat on Long Island Sound. He said it again, in a near whisper. "Please, Louise, please."

"Leave now and never come here again. My daughter is trying to sleep."

He nodded, dropped his head to his chest. Placed his hat back on it. He stepped out onto the stoop and then looked back at her.

"Roland isn't done with us, Louise. I need you." His face was soft, his eyes large and dark; they seemed to her like the eyes of a child. He paused, seemed to calculate something, then spoke again. "I want you to know that you saved me. When I lost my leg after a stupid drunken night I fell into a very dark place. The glimmer of light was you, my curiosity about you, why you wouldn't write to him. That's when Roland began to use me."

She let herself look at him then, eye to eye again. Again a pause, the silence between combatants. In the deep hooded sockets of his eyes, she glimpsed the terror of dying men in the moment before they renounced the will to live. In the moment when they might have done anything to keep living.

Dr. Gasparyan was still standing there, in the middle of the street, staring without focusing. He had seen his village in Armenia burned to the ground, it was said. Mother said that Dr. Gasparyan always saw the burning village, the rape and murder of his sisters and mother. She said that the peace of Shepherd's Glen could not cover that, any more than wallpaper can cover blood and char.

Louise closed the door and leaned against it. Then she called up to Helen guiltily that she was bringing soup, went into the kitchen to fix a tray. She was ladling out the vichyssoise Mother had made when she saw Ed coming through the backyard. He was picking his way through the ivy-covered path that skirted the Sklars' yard. He was looking down, deep in thought apparently, but wearing the slightest grin around the edges of his mouth. She tapped the window with the ladle and he looked up, startled. The look in his eyes changed rapidly from pleasure to surprise to fear. He stopped in his tracks. She stepped out on the back porch.

"How's your girlfriend?"

"Did you get fired?" he threw back, standing still in the middle of the yard.

"Come inside now."

"Maybe I shouldn't. Granny might never let me out again," he said. He shifted his weight, cocking his pelvis to the left, putting his hands on his hips as if he were one of the men she worked with standing in a circle of peers parsing the results of a long and multi-layered experiment. He squinted at her as if to ask her to prove that she and he were allies, rebels against a dictatorship of regular meals and rule following.

"She knows you left," said Louise, but she knew that he had won. She knew too that she couldn't keep him from his forbidden love any more than Mother could keep her from hers. "If you go straight back to your room, I'll plead your case with her."

He walked toward her, grinning wildly now. Halfway up the porch he stopped and looked at her carefully.

"What happened to your face?"

"What do you mean?" She felt the hot throb of blood rushing into her face.

"Now you're red on both sides instead of only half," he said, stepping up on to the porch. With his cool fingers he brushed her cheek softly, as if replacing Kit's slap with a caress. Her whole body came alive with his touch and she felt the rush of erotic pleasure and the shame that pursued it, a feeling she had had when she nursed him. When she nursed them all, actually, when any hungry mouth grappled her nipples. The illicit lighting of the nerve paths that no one may ever speak of.

Purple Heart

September 1964

Charlotte hadn't expected to be put to work straightaway at The Strand, a place she'd spent so many hours browsing and seeking. It was a place she loved, but she would never have considered working there if Gil hadn't suggested it. But it wasn't a suggestion, she thought, it was an order. No boy she had dated—well, she didn't date, she thought, she just fucked and hung around for greater or lesser amounts of time—no boy who had ever claimed to be interested in her had given her such a clear directive. In fact, she couldn't think of a time in her life when anyone had told her so exactly what to do. Louise and Granny and teachers had told her what not to do and what she was doing wrong. Her once-favorite professor in college had let her know that she ought not to pursue academia, but instead ought to give her gifts to support his great work, which was, after all, a surer bet. Gil was different from everyone, wasn't she? Gil seemed to her to be this miraculous creature who held in one strong and loving frame the firm hand of a man and the subtlety and warmth of a woman. That she had never met a man or a woman who had exactly those qualities in steady supply didn't enter her mind. Gil would hold her, Gil would keep her, she was certain of it.

Nancy, the woman Gil had said to ask for, was a chain-smoker who dressed like a grandmother. She couldn't have been much older than Charlotte—the skin around her eyes and neck was taut, and her makeup-free face still held a hint of teenaged bloom, that child-light that Charlotte, at the age of twenty-eight, believed she had already lost. Wearing a purplish-gray cardigan despite the heat and a pair of glasses joined at the stems by a silver chain that disappeared provocatively behind her shoulders, Nancy looked up from her desk in the small office at the back of the store, and asked Charlotte if she knew how to work a cash register.

"No," said Charlotte.

"You're hired," said Nancy. She gestured for Charlotte to follow her to the front counter and introduced a skinny young man with two pens tucked in his shirt pocket. He had wild dark curly hair and was in the process of cleaning a pair of very thick-lensed glasses. "This is Stan. He'll show you the ropes. Stan, show Charlotte the ropes."

"Am I on the clock?" asked Charlotte.

"No, this is strictly a volunteer operation," said Nancy, pausing a moment for effect. "I'm yanking your chain! My uncle didn't get jailed by HUAC so that I could employ people for nothing. Stan will show you where to punch in."

"Hi, Charlotte," said Stan, extending his hand.

Charlotte took his hand and gave a firm reciprocal shake.

"Let's get something straight up front," said Stan as Nancy left them. "I've got a girlfriend. I know, I know, I'm a gorgeous redhead with an enchanting smile—oh, wait, that's you!"

Charlotte took him in for a moment—the dark hair and eyes, the skinny body and the dusky undertone of his skin. She decided he was one of those New Yorkers who could tell his life story by triangulating across street numbers and neighborhood names. She liked him so much and so immediately that she almost told him that she was a homosexual, but then thought better of it.

"I'm sure your girl is swell," she said.

"As a Mayberry pie!" he answered. "This is a cash register and that over there is Charles."

Charles was also thin—she probably weighed as much as the two of them together. But he was taller than Stan, a dark-skinned Negro man who looked at once old and young, but in a different way from Nancy. He wore a striped T-shirt and a very serious expression. He looked up from a pile of receipts he was going through and waved.

"He's not much of a talker."

"Stan does enough talking for all of us," said Charles.

"He's right. Except when it comes to Wittgenstein," said Stan. "He reads that crap for fun and won't hesitate to explain it. Let's go for the tour."

"Fun is a construct," said Charles, in a tone that may or may not have had a whiff of humor.

"But are constructs fun?" asked Charlotte, lobbing a salvo that resulted in a snort from Stan and a shrug from Charles.

Stan took Charlotte around the store, indulging her as she slowed by the philosophy section and let her fingers trail across the art books, the glossy compendiums of Klee and Delaunay, the photographs of Eudora Welty—"I didn't know she was a photographer, but I love her stories," she said. They agreed that "Why I Live at the PO" was probably the funniest story ever written.

He took her to the break room and showed her where to punch in. He waited while she wrote her name on the thin cardboard, pulled the lever, and placed the punched card next to the others in the metal bracket on the wall. As she placed it in the slot, Louise's voice came to her mind, speaking of punching the clock in contradictory ways—first as something that Ed-the-artist should never have to do, then as something that Louise herself had done with pride when she worked at Lockheed during the war. Charlotte heard the metal bite through the cardboard and felt an odd twinge of pride at the thought that she was no longer dressing in skirts and pretending she wanted a career at Dunne and Crowne, but that here she would wear pants and have a job.

"We don't eat in here much," said Stan, gesturing to the dingy round table of chipped linoleum with an overflowing ashtray at its center like a dirty daisy losing seeds. "Ya like kasha varnishkes? Bubbe's on Third is the best and they have cold borscht for summer."

Down the hall past the lunchroom was the storeroom, where the books were piled in dusty chaos, in bins and across tables, some with notes and tags sticking out. Charlotte craned her neck to see into the depths. There was someone at the back sorting a disordered pile into two orderly stacks, but that someone was not Gil. Charlotte wasn't sure of her lover's schedule, but the thought of Gil's presence heightened her senses, tuned her ears to seek Gil's voice, which even more than her eyes had made Charlotte love her. That low voice, soothing as the scent of soot that rose from the pavement in the first moment of a summer rain. Charlotte realized that she was carrying Gil with her now, seeing herself through Gil's eyes, imagining Gil watching her make a joke, work the cash register, punch in. Was Gil seeing her now, admiring her soft white neck, the curve of her hip?

As they came back up to the front and Stan set her up at the register, the subject of music came up.

"I peg you as a Dylanite," said Stan.

"Everyone loves Dylan," said Charles, over the head of a clearly irritated customer.

"I don't give a damn about Dylan," said Charlotte, following Stan's instructions to open the register and put in the tray of change he'd given her. "I'm a jazz fan."

"Well, you don't say. Didn't know you had to choose."

"Maybe not," said Charlotte, jamming the drawer into the till, feeling the thrill of a declaration. "But I'm sick of the folkies. I'm after a different sound."

"What do you think about *Out to Lunch?*"

"I thought you weren't going to try to date me?"

"Touché! Naw, Eric Dolphy? C'mon, it's best jazz record of the year."

"Dolphy…maybe I've seen him play at the Pussycat…"

"Not bloody likely."

"They get some good acts there. Not everywhere can be the Vanguard."

"Dolphy's dead."

"Oh."

"Died in Copenhagen," said Stan.

"Berlin," interrupted Charles.

"Pretty sure it was Copenhagen," said Stan.

"I'm telling you it was Berlin."

"Overdose," said Stan, changing the subject.

"No, man, it was insulin shock. He was a teetotaler."

"You sure talk a lot for a guy who doesn't talk much."

"Look, Stan, not every jazz man is a dope fiend."

"Did I say they are?" He turned to Charlotte for confirmation. But Charlotte was looking toward the back of the shop. Down the almost endless corridor of books—books stacked from floor to the high ceiling, picture books on tables, the leather-bound and the paper-backed, volumes thin and fat, purple and brown, red and yellow and white— way at the end of that endless-seeming stack, past the sturdy wheeled stepladders, way down at the end of that long corridor, Charlotte saw Gil. She was maneuvering a wheeled cart stacked with three boxes, and then stopped for a moment to talk to Nancy. None of these books, she thought, not a one, has a character like Gil. She was certain, though she could not possibly know this, that no writer had ever described a body like Gil's, a being like Gil; her story, whatever it was, had not been told. Not exactly, not precisely. The sewn seam where the right breast once was, the diagonal slash across the stomach, the shiny keloid that ran the length of Gil's inner left arm. That one was the strangest—what accident could have led to that, she wondered, the position of the arm was so awkward, it was as if Gil had been caught, had her arm held open and sliced. Gil's body, she thought, was a book of days, the scars as permanent as holy holidays, fixed by believers who had agreed that there are days that time does not change, days that remain fixed in their meaning. There is a day when the angel speaks, a day when the waters rise, an evening when the raven returns empty clawed and is spurned, a morning when the dove brings the olive branch and is celebrated. Gil's body was, Charlotte thought, enchanting herself, Gil's body was a book of miracles, a celebration of continuing in the face of all that would destroy her. Perhaps in all of these shelves, this massive arrangement of confluences and particulars, a mirror for Gil could be found, but Charlotte didn't know what it was called. She was more certain that she was in one of them herself, her sort of body described as a location of desire and potential disaster. She had always thought of herself as Tess of the D'Urbervilles, used and spoiled, sold off to save her family. But seeing Gil there, at the end of the long corridor piled high with volumes of every color, size, and shape, she thought that perhaps she was Catherine and Gil Heathcliff, and that the thing between them was as wild and natural as the moors. Charlotte stared right at her lover, willed her to look back, to send her a sign of her love. The staring gave her a feeling of seeing through binoculars, of moving closer to Gil with her vision, of blurring the swimming stacks of paper bound and held, now to shapes, then to colors, then to nothing at all, so that all she could see was Gil, leaning slightly into the cart, cigarette tucked behind her ear. Finally Gil looked back and sent flying and ricocheting across the wildly high stacks a wink, a grin. Like a frog catching a fly, Charlotte lunged and then snapped back to standing. Come to me now, she tried to telegraph to her lover. I'll kiss you right here in front of everyone! But quickly as Gil had issued the wink, she retracted her glance and turned away without so much as a wave.

"Hey, Charlotte," said Stan, the fingers of his waving hand abruptly entering her vision. "Why don't you take this customer."

For the rest of the afternoon, Charlotte helped customers, smiled, and learned where to find things, but everything she looked at was counterfeit in her eyes. Everything was a prop on the stage set for the only drama she wanted to pursue, but Gil, her co-star, was nowhere to be found. Nancy also seemed to have disappeared, and despite her best efforts, Charlotte began to believe that they were somewhere together. Purple and green bolts of jealousy flickered and struck the soft gray cloud of her love—because she believed it now, she was really in love.

A few hours later, saying, to no one in particular, that she had left her bag in the break room, Charlotte went back into the bowels of the store in order to accidentally pass by the storeroom. But Gil was not there. She punched out and was about to search the cards for Gil's but just then Charles came in, asked her how her first day was, and wished her well. So she stepped away, and with the little money left from what Granny had given her and her employee discount, she bought Eric Dolphy's *Out to Lunch*.

Before she could go home and listen, she went to see Ed. Whatever he wanted to tell her—she suspected it had to do with money—she had something far more important to tell him. Since her return from the house on Oxford Street she'd been planning to tell him what she had learned there. She wanted him to understand that Louise was not some pure being whose approval they needed to live. That their sacred forebears, the colonel in particular, the hero of the First World War and martyr of the Second, had abused his power as a father. That he had used Louise and was not a man of honor after all was clear to her. Or at least he was not honorable in every way, in ways that she knew mattered. To her that knowledge, after the initial shock of it, made her feel a kind of freedom. In her purse sat the letter that she believed was irrefutable proof that they should stop paying homage to the past and make it new. She thought that she was bringing her brother a gift of freedom. Or at least a gift of insight, an understanding of Louise that Louise could not control.

The door to Ed's apartment was propped open with a brick. The scent of frying meat and char wafted out.

"Oh! Lottie, I've burnt the frites," Ed called out from the kitchenette. He quickly formed a patty from a mound of ground beef piled on a plate. "But I've got enough burger for you."

His tiny apartment was in an unusual state of disarray. Every drawer in his dresser was pulled open, and there were several piles of clothes, a stack of issues of *Art in America*, and a bucket of brushes of various sizes on the bed. Cardboard boxes, open or closed, filled or empty, were wedged in every possible corner.

The promised move to Paris appeared to be happening.

"When did you did you do this?" Charlotte said, her eye landing on a small painting that was propped on top of the phone book that rested on top of a basket of what appeared to be clean and folded laundry. It was a portrait of Louise that she had never seen before.

"What? Oh that." Ed turned to look, brandishing a dripping spatula. "Louise doesn't like it."

"I suppose she wouldn't," said Charlotte, though she was surprised to hear him say so. It had never occurred to her that Louise could not like something Ed had done. It was a very small close portrait. The colors were rich and deep, the surface of the painting a lens so clean it could be forgotten. The face wore an expression that was not the sort of forced thoughtfulness that sitters for portraits often wore. Louise's mouth was slightly open and her brow was furrowed, the muscles around her eyes contracted as if she were angry. No, as if she had been wounded and did not understand why. As if she wanted to object or to defend herself but could not fully believe the injury had taken place. The ground behind her was dark green, a wall that Charlotte didn't recognize. Charlotte liked it more than she wanted to admit.

"It's like a snapshot," she said, then quickly qualified the compliment she knew he would hate. "I mean it's so—unguarded."

"Take it if you want it," he said, wrapping a pile of French-fry-shaped charcoal in a newspaper. "No one will buy it anyway. Don't know why I bother, honestly. I should just go out and hunt squirrels, tack their skins on the wall, and invite audiences to have a drink of their blood. *Art in America* might finally take notice. Don't know why Louise thinks the French will be any more interested. No one wants to really look at this world. Or themselves in it. Everyone just wants to be entertained or deluded by grand ideas. Advertised at."

"Maybe your painting will become fashionable because it's so unfashionable. You just have to get the right agent—someone who can sell your work as so old it's new again."

Ed snorted but didn't laugh.

Charlotte felt a sudden stab of empathy for her brother. For the hunch of his shoulders as he put the patties on a plate. For the hours he spent, trying to share his way of seeing, all the while pretending he didn't care what others thought. For continuing to go down the road he had found for himself, the lonely road that made sense to him. For trying to extract nourishment from the bitter bone of being misunderstood. Even for doing the kind of art that Louise celebrated as timeless. Because that was part of it too, pleasing her. If you were a child of hers, you could try to reject that directive, but you couldn't ignore it.

"You could eat the burgers later and I could take you out," she said, wanting to cheer him up. She should have known he wouldn't let her feel kindly for long. "I just worked."

"I knew they'd take you back," said Ed.

"Who?"

"Dunne and Crowne."

"I'm working at The Strand," she said, and then, surprising herself: "I like it."

"That's nice," said Ed, in a tone that contradicted the words. Maybe he can't help it, Charlotte thought, this tone of disdain, the vinegar around his curdled little heart. She opened her purse, almost took out the manila envelope containing the three letters, including the one that she itched to show him. But it wasn't time quite yet. She held out the LP to him, knowing that she was inviting a hotter shot of his bile.

"I'm told this is the best jazz record of the year. Want to listen?"

"I'm sure you heard that from someone of impeccable authority." He gestured for her to join him at the small table that sat directly under the window to the street. It was an attractive but somewhat rickety antique, clearly intended to hold the mail in the entryway to a house of some respectable people, rather than a painter's lunch. Two pairs of milk crates impersonated chairs around the table. She sat on one stack. He put a plate of sliced cucumbers and tomatoes on the table, salt and pepper, hamburgers and toast.

"Brit's come back," he said, setting down two glasses and handing her a bottle of wine and a corkscrew. "She brought this horrible bottle of wine from Italy and a whole suitcase full of prosciutto and mortadella. The customs officials never stood a chance when she showed up in that dress."

"What dress?" said Charlotte, not pressing her case about the record. Playing along, as she always did with Ed. But, no, the feeling remained, some sense she had that her brother was trapped and always had been. That he was always playing the role of who Louise supposed him to be—the last champion of what they supposed was a deeper beauty. An Old Master trapped in a world of abstract expressionism.

"Whatever dress she was wearing. All she has to do is walk into a room and all bets are off. You've almost got her power, Lottie, if you would just learn to use it."

"I'll keep it in mind," said Charlotte, with a drop of vinegar of her own. She assembled the burger, took a bite, swallowed. "What's this catastrophe you were on about?"

"Billy's uncle didn't like the portrait," said Ed between wolfish bites. "He's refusing to pay."

"But you've been working on it for months!"

"Indeed," said Ed. "Said he didn't like the expression. Says it has a sissy look. Seems he's under the impression that I'm buggering his nephew."

"You're joking."

"Apparently not. Thing is, he wants to bugger me himself, but he doesn't want to look like a buggerer. The homosexuals don't have an easy time of it, Lottie. I recommend you stop pretending to be one."

Instead of responding, Charlotte took a big bite of the burger and drank a deep swallow of the Italian wine, which was very good. That was Ed's way, the Galle way, to call something delicious horrible and vice versa. To poison the air, so that nothing could be easy or sweet, but the dream of sweetness and ease would float above, laughing. They ate in silence for what seemed a long moment.

"I had quite a time on Oxford Street," said Charlotte, catching a piece of falling burger and stuffing it quickly in her mouth. "I learned some things about Louise."

"What's there to learn?" Ed brought two fingers toward his lips, the gesture Charlotte understood as a request for a smoke, which she answered by retrieving her purse. She gave him a cigarette, put the pack on the table, and pulled out the manila envelope, extracting one of the smaller envelopes from within it. She thought about telling him what Granny had told her, but she felt a twinge of guilt about betraying Granny's confidence. She told herself that showing him the letter was not the same thing.

"Quite a lot actually," she said, unfolding the letter that was all of a piece with its thin blue victory mail envelope. "Read this."

"Read it to me, will you. I've got a headache."

Charlotte pushed her plate back, wiped her hands on the napkin Ed handed her, took a hearty slug of wine, and read. As she held the letter, her hands shook ever so slightly and the thin paper stuck to her sweaty fingers.

Formosa
February 8, 1943

Dearest Lou,

Will this letter get to you? I sincerely hope it will.
I dreamt of you last night, and the night before, and quite possibly the night before that and on and on, back through the days of my captivity. You came to me, just the way you used to. We were in the boathouse when you found me. You took me in.

I would not have entered you if you had not invited me. You came into the world a child of perfection, and you grew that way. Your body flowered, your breast buds blossomed. You opened your pink mouth and drew me to you.

No one will ever understand us. I knew that all of the world, society, good intentions, rules and regularity, would have you turn to Roland. I gave you up, but it stung. I want you to know that even now, as my body fails me, as our country may be failing, I feel the loss of you. You gave me your innocence, and you took what was clever in me and what was strong. I will not say it was wrong.

I hope that one day, when you are done with this woman-business you've gotten yourself into, you'll go back to learning the secrets of the universe. That is my greatest wish for you, that you free yourself of your brood-duties and become the woman of science you truly are.

Your own and only,
Papa

Ed sat very still for a moment, not saying anything. He looked at her, then reached across and grabbed the letter from her hand, placing it on the table in front of him.

"It's a fake," he said. He stubbed out the cigarette he was smoking and reached for another.

"What do you mean?"

"The censors would never let something like this through." He folded it back into the envelope and peered closely at the postmark. He held it up to the light that came in through the barred window of his basement apartment, as if looking for some watermark or government seal that would remove all shades of doubt. He ran his fingers through his thick red-gold hair.

"Listen to yourself, Ed. Who the hell would fake this?"

"Where did you get it?" Changing the subject was one of his favorite weapons. I ought to use that myself more often, Charlotte thought.

"Louise's room."

"You mean you stole it." He placed the crumpled letter on the table and smoothed it with the hand that held the cigarette, letting the cherry get dangerously close to the paper.

"Borrowed it." Charlotte reached to take the letter back, but he snatched it away, then stood up and held it up above her head. She stood up quite close to him but didn't try to reach for it. She kept trying to look into his eyes, to get him to look directly at her, but he would not. His eyes were roving, like those of an animal in fear.

"So she knows you have it? Let's call her right now." He started walking toward the phone that sat on the narrow linoleum counter in his dim kitchenette.

"For crissake, Ed, that's not the point." She was chasing him now. When he put his hand on the phone, she put her hand on his. In the other hand, he kept the letter aloft. He was not much taller than she, but when he spoke, a soft mist of spit fell down on her face.

"What is the point, Lottie?"

"The point is that Louise and the colonel—"

A slight smile formed on Ed's face. He wriggled his hand from under hers and moved away from the phone. He brought the letter down to his eye level, seemed to read it again, seemed to relax.

"Well, so what. Even if it's true, so what."

"What do you mean, so what? The colonel raped—"

"Raped? How many rapists write their victims love letters?"

"Look, I'm just trying to say—" Charlotte wondered then, what was she trying to say? Hadn't she thought they could be witnesses together? That was it, she wanted him to be on her side, for once. To look with her at the people who had raised them, to see them not as marble statues, not as awards and citations and *Life* magazine photographs, but as soft, fallible, partially rotten human beings.

"Glass houses, Sappho. I wouldn't throw any rocks if I were you."

"Excuse me?" Charlotte stood very still. She felt her eyes narrow and her jaw clench tight.

"Whatever you're doing with that dyke—that's taboo too, isn't it?" He stood by the table again, crushed his cigarette out and picked up the pack. Finding it empty, he crushed it too and tossed it on the floor. "You should be the last person to try to take the moral high ground. Anyway, they were both exceptional people. Maybe their love was real."

Charlotte winced. She had not prepared for this. She had not thought that bringing this letter to him would make Ed attack. She had not thought he would excuse the colonel, that he would not see what he had done as wrong. She had thought he would join her, that they would consider it together, that together they might understand Louise, or even begin to be free of her. There was a point she wanted to make but it seemed to disappear, a buoy in the mist.

"Ed. Come on."

"Come on yourself."

She hadn't thought that he would dismiss it so easily. In desperation, she found herself breaking Granny's trust, as if that would drive home the point that she could not find.

"Granny told me. She said she knew it was happening."

He shook his head.

"And again, so what? That's Granny's problem, isn't it? Just like it's my problem I don't want to see you waste your life on some low-rent dyke."

"You don't know what you're saying."

"Oh, but I do," he said. Then he moved so quickly she almost didn't see him pick up the lighter from the ashtray and light the corner of the letter.

"No!" Charlotte lunged toward him, but he held the burning letter above her as she leapt and tried to grab it. Drops of embers and ash drifted down; one caught in her hair and singed it. The thin dry paper went up quickly and Ed dropped what remained of it in the ashtray. Charlotte picked up the charred bit, the corner that held the words *your own and only, Papa.*

"There," said Ed, sitting down on his milk-crate stack and folding his arms. "Let's talk about something else."

Charlotte was so angry that her body seized up and released itself in a kick to Ed's shin.

"Ooow!" He was mocking her now, the way he used to when they were children, calling out in an exaggerated voice of pain in one of the rare moments when she hit him. He would tackle her, hold her down, let spit gather on his lip only to suck it up just before it could fall in her eye. She knew that when her fury passed she was going to weep and she didn't want to cry in front of him. She smoothed her hair, broke off the charred end, picked up the best jazz record of the year, and turned to go.

"Come on, *cherie*, can't we still be friends?" He was smiling now, almost laughing.

"Why start now?" she answered, not looking back as she opened the door.

"Oh, Lottie, so glad you got a job. I'll be needing some money when I get to Paris."

"Not one red cent, Ed," she said, stepping outside.

"We'll see!" Ed sang after her. "*On va voir!*"

As Charlotte stepped onto the pavement it started to rain. One big, soft, warm drop landed and hung from the tip of her nose.

THE RETURN

We who were once so bold
We who shall never grow old

I am we, beneath the sea
You are not done with me.

KISS OF DEATH

SEPTEMBER 1948

That Saturday morning Louise slipped out before the others woke. She left a note under Mother's door saying that she would be back in a day or two and not to worry. Tuna whined and thumped her tail on the floor as Louise crept through the living room and escaped into the morning light. Every sound was amplified in the theater of her guilt. She knew she should not see Kit again, but she was opening the car door as she argued with herself, and as she decided that she would be good now, would pay more attention at work, would take Mother and the children on a nice vacation next year, that she would become a better gardener, would cook sometimes, she was putting the key in the ignition.

She drove past the different houses—Shepherd's Glen was not like those new developments that were beginning to be hacked into the piney woods. The houses were of different styles, though as she drove by that morning it struck her that there really were only two kinds—the lace-hung, porch-wrapped Victorians and the brick and glass moderns built into hillsides like hers. Surely, she thought, there must be other kinds, must be other ways to live. Not only the show of petticoats or the big panes of glass that showed watching eyes that those inside were living as they should and that from the inside framed the trees and grass without as if they were another thing on order. As if nature were a set to play their drama on, instead of the great mouth that always salivated, always consumed.

She took her time getting to Kit's cabin, meandering through the back roads with her windows open. These days she often listened to the static between the radio stations, seeking the signal she could almost hear in the noise. She didn't worry anymore that she might be mad, that it was madness to know that a message from Roland was trying to come through the sonic slurry. Empiricism was in her nose—she breathed deeply, trying to detect the moment when the air took on the underbelly of the sea, a game she had played for many years. Try as she might, she could never discover the moment of the shift; it always seemed to have already been there when she noticed that first touch of brine.

That she could never find the moment of the shift seemed to her to prove that nothing could be known. That was the secret she held in her heart as she drove toward a man who had deceived her, the thought that sat in her head like a gargoyle. Standing before the columns in the lab, noting the changes in weight so carefully, hour after hour, day after day, year after year, she thought, chasing this approximation of knowing while the bacterium continued consuming and the viruses constructed their sentences, the decree of nature, suffering without meaning. This time the brine was in the air immediately, as soon as she thought of the game. She was startled by the presence of the sea still so far from the shore; the pine trees and their needles seemed to exude it as strongly as if she were driving through a forest of kelp drying in the sun.

As she followed Kit's directions toward the Indian River inlet, she began to feel that she was driving though time as well as space, that what the air and trees and water witnessed was not this day in early September 1948, but all the days at once. Once her life had been the life of cells whirring joyfully, organelles cranking together in rhythmic union. She had loved and been loved, she had won prizes as a girl, had been celebrated and admired. Even Mother had admitted it in those days, that Louise was special, that no one could hold a candle to her. Her superiority was a simple fact, there was nothing wrong with knowing it. And yet while she had won the prizes and the tennis matches, had sailed the boats and spurned the suitors, there was always something cruel in her. Over and under and within the joyful whirring of the organelles that made her a marvelous machine was a dark, devouring arrhythmia. There was always in me, she thought, an invitation to destruction, a desire to destroy that was as strong as the desire to create. As she drove on in what seemed to be in time all at once, she tried to recall the purity of her own heart but could not. I am not kind, she thought, and I never have been. There never was any innocence in me. The trees knew and the river she was driving toward knew and the ocean it led to knew, and halfway around the world, where Roland and Father had given up and left the earth, the land there knew it too. Everything colludes with my cruelty, she thought, taking a turn on the pine forest road that reeked of kelp, seeing the fallen weather vane that Kit had described.

The piney woods opened to reveal a gray cabin with a barnacled dock thrust into the river like the scaley tongue of a dead lizard. The sound from the radio began to organize itself, to form a perceptible shape. To form a sphere, a whole sound, a scream muffled and caught in a bubble released from a drowning man's mouth. As she pulled up, she was overtaken by the feeling that this day in early September 1948 was not after all, every day at once. No, it was laid very thinly over another, truer day. The banks of the Indian River were glutted with cattails and dune grasses grappling their way toward the lowering river waters. But though she saw the grasses and the late summer river, Louise began to see other things more clearly and to smell the acrid smoke of oil fires on Subic Bay. The cabin's gun-metal gray door seemed to open of its own accord, drawing her in to the rank dark inside. The air there was close and reeked in a changing way, first of kelp and brine and then of other, sourer things.

These are objects, she told herself, stumbling over a pair of hip waders, but her hand touched the rubber and felt skin. That is the floor, she said aloud, staring into the dark her eyes were adjusting to. She knew that the floor was not a sea of vomit and shit and yet she smelled it, smelled what Roland had smelled, what Kit had soaked in. Her eyes and mouth and nose sought in vain to extract what part of the air she could use. That is a rocking chair, she thought, falling again over an object that she knew was an object but felt as a man starved so quickly that his skin hung loosely over his brittle bones. The reek of bacterial rampage made her gasp, the evidence of each body's resistance to its end, my God! Every one of the men in the hold of that ship, every one of the cells inside their bodies fought and fought in the dark and rank to live. And I'm mad at last, she thought.

A different door opened. A splint of light struck the dark and disappeared again as the door closed behind him. The smells disappeared, the presence of other bodies. Only his was there now. His presence a change in the air, an electrical charge at once more and less than that generated by someone still in their body. She knew it was him even before he spoke, even before he said the most painful things. Before he surrendered. She would have preferred his anger.

"I left you first, I see that now."

"I meant to write. I started to write. Please." Louise reached into the dark but touched nothing. "Please forgive me."

"But I didn't know you, did I?" His voice was just the same, exactly the same as it had been on the day they met. She had walked into the room he'd shared with her brother Bruce and he had locked eyes with her and said, before Bruce could introduce them, that he was glad to know her, as if they'd been raised side by side like a pair of summer squashes. That was the kind of thing he said, like a pair of summer squashes, like a hummingbird at the lily's lip, that was the way he talked, as if spring had always come and would come again. As if he could not help living at the center of all that was created and so close to its creator.

She reached toward him until her hand struck the door that opened to the brightness of day on the barnacled dock. Yes, there was the dock and, yes, the river, yes, September 1948, on the Indian River in the state of Delaware, but she could see the other day as clearly, the day the Americans torpedoed the ship the *Oryoku Maru* that was full to the brim with young men from Tennessee and Massachusetts and Indiana. The sky full of soot and flame, the churning water of Subic Bay, a man standing at the open edge of a prison ship torn open by an explosion.

Her voice came out of her, not from her mouth, but as if from all of her cells aching for their joy in his name, Roland, Roland! She called louder and louder over the dirge of destruction, the groans of buckling metal and dying men, the explosions that overtook the horizon and made everything too near. She could see him now. Jump! Jump now! But he only looked at her, and with the slightest smile on his face, the slightest shake of his head, as if to say, no, I was just passing through. She could see it just exactly, the moment when his soul departed. The shake of his head, his small renunciate's smile. It is true, she thought. I killed him. I was the invader of the cells of his heart, I took for myself the nourishment I could have given him, the strength to jump and swim to shore. But no. He smiled again. No, this is just how the story is written.

Kit called to her then and she saw that she was on a barnacled dock thrust out from the small gray house like the tongue of a dead lizard sticking out from its desiccated body. They were standing over the Indian River, far, far from Subic Bay, where Roland's bones had turned to coral. There were three strings tied to the railing, and Kit was pulling on one of them, and saying something. And smoothly as in a dream, she stepped into the changed scene.

"So, you came after all."

"You knew I would," she said and stood beside him, placing her forearms on the rail. She let her live leg brush against his aluminum one, which caught the sun's rays and reflected them. The metal calf exposed by his Bermuda shorts was warm against her own bare leg beneath the thin polka-dotted dress she wore.

"This is the lazy man's way to crab," said Kit, pulling slowly and steadily on the string until it came out of the water, attached at the other end to a raw chicken leg, from which dangled a large blue crab. What's the difference, she thought suddenly, between this raw chicken leg used as bait and Kit's own leg, caught in the clamps and wheels of the mill? That was a kind of bait for her, she thought, his missing leg. Perhaps that's what drew me to him, that he should still be at all, that death had come so close to him so often, yet he remained.

He threw the crab into a bucket at her feet and slid the remains of the ragged leg back into the water. There were two crabs in the bucket already, trying to clamp the unyielding metal, touching each other blindly. Foolish animals, she thought, forever trying and failing, trying and failing, to escape.

"Just now I had the strangest feeling. I saw, I smelled—"

"What he never wanted you to see," said Kit. "But what he had to show you."

"I wanted to know how it really was. No one ever tells us. He would never tell me."

"He didn't want you to despair. Didn't want you to suffer the way we suffered. The generals and presidents don't want you to see it either."

"I'm rotten."

"Yes," said Kit. "So am I. So are they, the rulers who make us do the whole miserable business."

"When I told him the war was over, Bruce, my younger boy, was very upset. He kept crying and saying what are we gonna do now?"

Kit laughed.

"He had a point." Kit leaned slightly toward her, so that she could feel the warm weight of him, the smooth skin of his forearm against hers. "Some of the men in my unit want the Japanese to apologize for their treatment of us prisoners."

"But not you?"

"I can't spend time that way, pursuing that. I keep thinking of a time after it was over, when I was in Tokyo just briefly with our troops there. I was walking with another soldier, someone who'd just arrived. It was rubble everywhere, you know, just nothing. Craters on the moon where markets once were. And this old man approached us, unarmed. And this soldier shot him dead, just like that. I asked him why he did it and he said, 'He was a Jap.'"

She looked out at the gently rippling river, the marsh grass and cattails nodding along the shore. In the distance she could just barely make out the blue-gray line of the ocean on the horizon, the water that was not at all different, and yet was so different from what blanketed Roland, the weight of which he would always try and always fail to throw off.

"So, what do we do now?" she asked, feeling strangely at ease.

One of the crab strings tensed and he began pulling it in. "Maybe you'll marry again and maybe you won't. I'll stay married. But we can meet here, if you like. It can be a place where no one will bother us. Where we can be dirty and rotten together. Where we can relieve ourselves of goodness and righteousness."

She smiled then in spite of herself. Because after all she was being given this, this one place for escape. And because, as he led her into the cabin, his eyes had gone hazel again. Because he touched her thigh in just that way and took her in just that way, not the roughness of Kit, not the anger of the men that had poured through Kit, that had placed his hand on her head in the water, that had bruised her neck with their rage at being robbed of their lives. No, this time he touched her with the sweetness of Roland, with the hummingbird's graze of the lily's lip.

He made her again in the image of herself, the lover. Because he did know her. Because she was death too, and death was beyond rot, it was the everlasting line, narrow as a photon, long as the universe. It was the place, at last, where every possibility burned and drowned at once and microbe and metal alike prepared to be again.

Purple Heart

September 1964

With a sudden brass blast the record began. A herald for the walker in the city. Charlotte listened, Charlotte walked with, Charlotte was the protagonist of *Out to Lunch*. The music made patchworks of city people, cut one shape and laid it out against another, where the shined shoe of the doorman at the Astor met the dirty scurry of the running rat. Here was the headline damning the society lady, there was the old man in the newsstand slapping the hand of a would-be chocolate thief. Here was the landlady selling soup dumplings, there the blind man shouting hey as the coins spilled from his cup, here the switchboard operators putting down their headsets, and there the dwarf with the cart selling a sandwich. Another brass blast was the neon sign martini glass flashing, the vibraphone tones were the rhythm of the flashes, the bass in the back was the talk of the mafia men. The drums tripped out like the high-stepping trot of the eager young photographer catching Joe DiMaggio eating a hot dog. These were the directives given: have a Chock full o'Nuts and take the stairs to the train two at a time.

If she left now, she could make it to Schnapzli's in time for a strudel before work, but when the second side was over Charlotte flipped the record and started it again. She lit a smoke and put on another pot of coffee. If I can just listen carefully enough, she thought, I'll understand the magic of this music. How it cuts and collages, how it unifies and makes particular. I'll pick up my wire cutters then, she thought, looking at the collection of dismembered coat hangers piled on the coffee table, feeling a sculptural urge like a spike of the fever to make that had gripped her the night before. But, no, I see it now, I need finer wire. Yards and yards of it!

After arguing with Ed, she had come home and put on the record, her ears perking to it like a dog's cocking to a whistle. As she listened she began to draw, barely seeing what she was drawing, careening through the pages of her sketchbook, sharpening and resharpening her pencil down to the nub. She turned the record over and over, and the lines on the page looped and repeated and varied their themes. The sketchbook had only two previous drawings in it, one a scene from her window on Houston Street, the other the window itself with its sooty curtain half hung out. This was something different.

She didn't usually draw her sculptures first. They were just a bit of foolishness, she always said. Just things made from scraps of other things: broken umbrellas, used brassieres, wind-up toys she glued to other wind-up toys. She bent and wrestled the wire until it became a winged bicycle or fish struggling on a hook or a wheel of fortune that wouldn't spin because it was a square. But that night she sketched and sketched something different, the kind of thing she had never made before. She became so involved, listening and relistening to the record, drawing the orb and what was inside it, what complicated its surface and cut it in two or eight or thirty-two parts that joined and made the whole, she was so involved that it was past midnight when she realized that Gil hadn't come by or called. They hadn't had a plan, exactly, but it was Wednesday, wasn't it? Hadn't Wednesdays become regular for them? Still, she kept working, smoking, drawing, and listening until she heard the three thumps of her downstairs neighbor's broomstick thudding up, making the universal request to quiet down.

The experience, the more-than-dream, had come on almost immediately after she got into bed sometime after three. With a clap she was under the cold magnetic weight of herself, straining to move against her body that felt fixed to the core of the earth. As usual, she felt her eyeballs, the only part of her that could move, rolling in the dark as if in a sea of ink. Then the sliver of light, the door opening, the sound of someone, some thing, crawling toward her across the floor. But there was another sound this time, a kind of rushing whir, a static that was also visual, a vibration in the blackness she was trying to see through. It was not uniform but seemed to be in motion, seemed to be trying to arrange itself as the orb she had been trying to draw. And with it was a smell. For the first time she knew that this creature coming to torment her had come from a particular place and that that place was deep in the depths of the sea. She took in a breath to give herself strength, tried to grab from the fetid air the part of it that she could use. With tremendous effort, she opened her nostrils and took in as much of that sea-sick rank air, the olfactory underbelly of that particular darkness, as she could without gagging. She knew that she needed the air to fuel herself for the great effort of opening her mouth, of forming the words she had needed to form for so long. The magic words, the talisman of her will. With the whole of her body in concentration as fine as a period on a page, she shouted them.

"GO AWAY!"

Clap! She sat up. Light was coming up through her sooty curtained window over Houston Street. She was not alone, but she was not afraid. The figure by the window was someone she had known always, someone whose presence she had always felt more than seen. When she was little, she thought the others could feel him too, that they must know how he breathed in the crawl space at the back of the closet. How he could be with you only if you didn't say his name, if you didn't look at him directly. Yet she could see him standing there; yes, she could make out that long, narrow nose. Finding herself beside him, she could see his hands, too, the elegant fingers. Why had Louise never talked of the beauty of his hands?

He pulled back the curtain with the long fingers that were so like Ed's and they looked out the window together. Walking across the empty street was a Negro man dressed in a loose suit. He walked as he played, he curved his shoulders like a question mark. In the middle of the street, he stopped to blast a note from his shining saxophone.

"That's Eric Dolphy," she said.

"The love of music is the greatest love," said her father. "He's come to us now. An artist. Like you."

"Is that what I am?"

"Serve your gift, my dearest girl."

"Have you been haunting me, Father?"

"Trying to tell you not to waste your hands."

"Will you come back to us now, Father?"

Eric Dolphy blasted his horn and the streetlamp burned with his electricity. She could see her father's face clearly then, his soft renunciate's smile and eyes fathoms deep. The slow, smooth shake of his head. She had fallen into a real sleep afterward, had woken refreshed, had gotten up and put the record on again.

When the buzzer buzzed she started. The light through the window was bright, midday light; she really didn't have time to listen to the record again, to be pulled into her work on the sculpture. She really should get dressed for work. The buzzer buzzed again and then again.

Her first thought was that it was Ed, come to apologize. At the very least, she thought, he'd try to curry favor so he could use her money. No, he'd admit he was wrong this time. That what the colonel had done to Louise was wrong. What would he say when she told him that Father knew that she was an artist? She let herself have the absurd thought that she would tell him this and that he would be interested.

But it was Gil, who'd forgotten her keys. Charlotte buzzed her in, cracked open her door and moved to set more coffee going. Gil was breathless as she entered, as if she had taken the steps two at a time.

"Hi, sweetie," Charlotte said, trying to conjure a smile. Trying to forget the presence of Father and of Eric Dolphy, who seemed far more real to her in that moment than her lover.

"I can't have you following me around," said Gil, as if they had already been in conversation. She ran her fingers through her short-cropped hair and then rubbed her face with both hands.

"Coffee'll be a minute. What?"

"I know the bartender at Dagmar's, okay? I know everyone there. If you want to know something about me, just ask."

"Honey, I'm sorry, I've just been caught up—" She gestured at the pile of wires, then went back to the kitchenette, only then realizing she had not put water in the percolator. "Have a seat, let me get this coffee on."

"I'm talking about last night, at Dagmar's," said Gil, still standing, arms folded, near the door she'd bounded through.

"What's Dagmar's?"

"It's a dyke bar, Charlotte. Where women go to meet women? You know, that kind of place?"

"Would you close the door and sit down?" asked Charlotte, trying to be calm.

"I'm not staying."

Charlotte stepped to the door and closed it herself. She leaned against it and crossed her arms across her chest. She looked Gil in the eye, but Gil would not look back at her; her violet blue eyes wandered first to the floor, next to the window.

Charlotte went to the hi-fi, turned it on, and put the needle back down on *Out to Lunch*.

"Will you turn off that godawful noise?" said Gil.

"You mean the best jazz record of 1964?"

"I told you I don't like jazz."

"Last I heard, this was my place," said Charlotte. "Just wait two minutes. I can't stand being accused of anything before I've had my coffee."

"Okay, okay. Whatever, keep it on. Do what you want, but don't go snooping around behind my back."

"How many times do I have to say I don't know what the hell you're talking about?" She went back by the now-bubbling coffee and pulled two mugs from the narrow shelf by the window to the air shaft where she used to hear Gil and Daisy fighting and fucking.

"The bartender at Dagmar's told me someone was asking about me." Gil was looking at her now. Her brow was furrowed as if she was trying to remember a speech she had memorized. "Wanted to know how often I hang out at the bar, who I go home with."

"Well, it wasn't me," Charlotte said. "I'm guessing you know a few other women."

She poured coffee in the two mugs and opened the refrigerator to get out the milk, which curdled as she added it to the coffee, making sour little strands near the dark surface. She drank it anyway, resisted the urge to spit the mess out in her sink, as if that would have been too much emotion to reveal. Suddenly she felt very powerful, as if the games she'd played for years with Ed and Louise had made her fit to defend her own heart against any invader. She closed her mouth firmly, looked at Gil and thought, You're nothing to me. Nothing at all.

"What's that supposed to mean?" Gil's voice was hard and flat. A battering ram.

"Oh, come on. We've both been around the block." Just go away now, she thought. Let me get back to drawing and listening. Let me have this one moment to make one more sketch before I have to go to work.

"Who I go home with is my business," said Gil, standing with her legs spread slightly apart, her hands on her hips.

"I guess I missed my cue."

"What?" Gil waved away the coffee Charlotte held out to her.

"I was supposed to react earlier to your line about the bartender being asked who you go home with."

"I never said we were exclusive," said Gil, picking up the argument she wanted to have.

"Guess I'll take that ring back to Tiffany's," said Charlotte, relishing the coldness in her voice, feeling thinner, blonder, more scientific, and more Louise-like by the second. Gil started, her expression shifted, softened into confusion.

"Oh, come on, that's not—"

"What, am I off book?"

"Lottie, baby, listen." Gil stepped toward her now, reached out to touch her shoulder. Charlotte stepped aside and opened the door.

"Get the fuck out."

Gil stood still for a moment, let her eyes settle on Charlotte's. She stepped into the hall, then turned back. Over her hard-worn face she now wore a thin wash of humility. When she opened her mouth to say something, Charlotte shut the door firmly. She turned and leaned her forehead against it, listening. She was certain that on the other side Gil was also listening, that at that moment their foreheads pressed against the door like figures on either side of a mirror. After a breath or two, there was a soft knock. Okay, she thought, I'm being hasty. I'm being crazy! She opened the door, there was Gil again, and, yes, she did care for her. There was so much sadness in her violet-blue eyes.

"Look, I'm sorry," said Gil. "I guess I just need to tell you—"

In spite of herself, Charlotte softened.

"Yes?"

"Daisy's come back," said Gil, her face now full of humility. "I'm sorry. It's just—she really needs me."

No, it was pity in her face, and pity was the one thing Charlotte hated more than loneliness. Later, she would be proud that she did not say another word, that she shut the door firmly, but did not slam it.

The needle skipped and dragged toward the center of the record. It was time for her to go to work.

THE RETURN

Without you there is no home
Three thousand steps a day I roam

I am now one point of light
Come to you across the night.

KISS OF DEATH

SEPTEMBER 1948

Louise had thought to stay another day with Kit, to call in sick to work on Monday, or to leave Kit's place early enough in the morning to make it to work on time. But around five on Sunday evening she lifted Kit's sleep-dumb arm off her and pressed herself up from the wet sheets. Kit barely interrupted his snoring as she extricated herself and dressed in the half-dark room, standing on legs wobbly from two days of fucking, eating, drinking, sleeping, and fucking again. With the occasional reading of poems thrown in for ballast.

Picking her way through the wreckage of empty bottles and plates and crab shells, just barely avoiding the overflowing ashtray on the table, she pulled herself through the soup of air that was full of ripe seed and vulva expression. She got to the door and gripped the handle to steady herself as she slipped on her sandals.

Perhaps she had changed. Perhaps she really believed now in unseen things. In things that could not be found with a microscope, or even explained by atomic theory. As she picked up the purse she had dropped on the floor the day before, she recognized that she did believe that Roland's will was being done. That Roland's voice was in Kit's hands and that the change of hands had made them better. The poems that Kit showed her were not all terrible. They seemed to her to have something of Roland in them, yet to be free of something that had burdened him. A need for goodness and righteousness perhaps. A belief that the world would always honor him as it had in his youth. That God and America and he were all of a piece, all points on the righteous line. She felt a great deep wash of pity for him for having lost his compass. For having believed that she was his North.

She looked back at her sleeping lover, knowing that she would see him here again. Then she opened the door and walked out. The air had cooled, and it felt good on her face. As she walked to her car, she felt that she could taste a teaspoon of the sorrow she had worked so hard to avoid. She could take in the smallest bit of it now. It was strangely sweet.

The steering wheel felt alien in her hands, but she started the car and drove slowly away from the little barnacled shack. I am a scientist who believes in a ghost, she thought as she drove past the fallen weather vane. Who has sex with the dead! Well, no one has to know. I also believe that something bad is happening at my home. That I have forgotten something.

Perhaps I've fallen so deep into superstition or madness that I can no longer operate this vehicle. No, I'm driving. But my tongue is a bale of oats in my mouth. She took one look back at the cabin, thought to go back for one drink of water, but she knew he would wake then and give her the sleepy-sweet smile, draw her back to bed before she could argue. No, she'd stop on the way. She had to go now because something was happening at home.

It was early evening, still light, as she drove back out on the dirt road through the piney woods, but she could make out the moon. It seemed to her that she had never before seen it in exactly this orientation; its crescent seemed hooked into the flesh of sky, like a broken harpoon tip in an ever-living leviathan. She rolled down the windows and tried again to notice the exact moment when the air lost its salt. Once again, she missed it. Once again, the scene had changed before she noticed, and as if by magic or with the logic of a dream, she found herself quite suddenly no longer in the inlet marsh and piney woods of the Delaware flats, but in the rolling hills of Shepherd's Glen. Cresting the Oxford Street hill, the green Packard filled with the rot-sick sweet scent of the giant magnolia, whose once-bright white flowers were now dropping bruised and rusted petals onto the road. Ahead was her own house, the mortgage she was paying, the place she had got for her family. She felt the pride she often felt, looking at the pretty little place she had provided, with its screened porch and picture-window living room, its basement and garage dug into the hillside. The grin on her face fell away as she paused on the crest. In place of the lift of pride and satisfaction, she felt a stab of anxiety. There was a car parked in the driveway, one that she recognized as belonging to Dr. Tretheway, who rarely made house calls.

As she pulled up in front of the house, the doctor paused for a moment on the front steps and spoke with Charlotte, whose mouth was drawn into a small, tight line. Louise got out of the car and ran toward them. She had never before seen the look the good doctor gave her then, a narrowing of his eyes and set of his jaw that turned his usually round and kind face into something harder and leaner. He judged her, she could see that, and she knew she had been found wanting.

"Ah, Louise, there you are," he said. "I knew you'd be back, but I'm not sure your family was as confident."

"What's going on?" She ignored the doctor's little jab and reached out to touch Charlotte's arm, a gesture of familiarity that her daughter rejected with a barely perceptible flinch.

"Charlotte is the heroine of this story, so I'll let her tell it. Just know that with rest Martha will be her old self again in no time." The doctor lifted his hat and bowed slightly before walking briskly to his car.

Before Charlotte could answer Louise's question, Ed, Bruce, and Helen all appeared and Tuna barked and wagged her greeting.

"I told you she'd be back," said Helen.

"Shut up, smells," said Bruce, pulling Helen's braid. "Smelly smells!"

"You shut up!" said Helen, punching Bruce in the chest. Bruce grabbed her arm and redirected her thrust at her own face.

"Stop hitting yourself, Helen!"

"Goddamn it, Bruce! Stop it!" Helen could probably be heard by the whole of Oxford Street.

"Helen! Watch your mouth! Bruce, let your sister go!" Louise tried to take a tone they would listen to, but they only changed their rough-housing. Bruce let go of Helen, but then he poked her in the ribs and ran away. She chased him through the kitchen and out into the yard with a slam of the back door. Louise turned to Ed.

"What happened, Ed?"

"Like the doc said, Charlotte's the heroine. She can tell you about Granny's accident," he said, running his long, elegant fingers through his red-gold hair, looking so much like his father just then. He pressed his lips together as if he was holding back from saying something unpleasant. "I'm glad you're home."

"Where else would I be?" said Louise, in a tone that she found unconvincing. Ed looked at her for one beat too long for her comfort, then shrugged and went upstairs. There was no one left for her to talk with but Charlotte, who seemed to her to radiate anemia, but at least did not have Ed's power to make her feel guilty.

"Is your granny in her room? I'll ask her myself," she said. But Charlotte gestured toward the couch.

"Sit down with me first for a moment," said Charlotte. Her daughter seemed to have aged twenty years in two days. In the reflection of the glass that covered the map of Nantucket, the one that had been created by that seasick Galle navigator in the nineteenth century, Louise caught a glimpse of her hair half in, half out of its customary bun. Charlotte sat down in the chair that she knew Louise favored, seeming almost to dare Louise to say something about it. Louise sat on the couch.

"It wasn't an accident," said Charlotte.

"What wasn't? Don't start in the middle, dear, I'm completely confused." Louise leaned into the backrest and held her palms up, as if asking her daughter to place the information in her hands.

"The doctor, the others, Granny herself, they all say it was an accident. But I know it wasn't, Louise." Charlotte trembled slightly then. Louise could see her fear, but she could see the anger in her too. And the anger was winning. She seemed to grow taller, to lengthen her spine as she rested against the back of Louise's favorite chair.

"You're not old enough to call me that," she said, trying to hide how much Charlotte's tone stung. How uncomfortable her daughter's pale face made her feel, how small. It was as if they had traded places and she, Louise, was the very bad child, shrinking into the cushions and awaiting punishment.

"Today I found Granny in the garage, slumped over the wheel of your old car, which she had turned on without opening the door."

"What?" Louise stood up and stepped toward the door of Mother's room.

"She's resting, she's okay. Sit down, Louise." Charlotte emphasized her name, looked her dead in the eye as she said it. Louise did as she was told.

"But that's horrible! And what do you mean, of course it was an accident! Mother wouldn't—"

"Wouldn't she? She said she would. I heard her tell you so."

"What do you mean? When?"

"She told you she would if you didn't stop seeing him. Remember, that day you came home sick from work. Other times too. I may only be twelve, but I have had ears for all my years."

Louise was quiet then. She could not think of the words, the words would not come. She pulled the ivory hairpin from the Philippines out of her hair, remade the chignon, and stuck the pin through the tidier knot.

"Seeing who?" were the words that finally came, childish, meek, and silly.

"I saw him through the window. He slapped you! He pushed you under the water at the pool!" Charlotte's face was changing, losing its mask of calm.

Louise opened her mouth, but the words would not come. She remembered now, Mother's words—try me, she'd said. I'll do it. The sweet spoonful of sorrow she had tasted after losing herself in Kit's hands, after passing through the pinprick of light that turned death into life, that spoonful of sorrow was not so sweet after all. It was part of a bitter meal she was being served now, her comeuppance for too much pleasure. In the tumult of her thoughts, one presented itself clearly: Mother, I need you. Charlotte spoke again.

"Do you know what yesterday was?"

Louise shook her head.

"It was the awarding of the Purple Hearts at the Pentagon."

"Oh." That's what it was, the something she had been forgetting.

"Yeah. You and Ed were nowhere to be found when it was time for the ceremony. Bruce stood up for our family. He received Father's medal."

"Oh." Louise looked down at her lap. Her fingers seemed to twitch of their own accord. Then at last, Charlotte began to soften. Her voice caught and a sob forced its way through her words.

"I don't understand…why you…he slapped you!"

"Oh, honey. Oh, baby, please come here." Louise opened her arms, then patted her lap. She wanted her daughter in her arms, wanted to let her cry for them both, but Charlotte wouldn't come. She stayed in the chair, she covered her face with her hands, then ran the back of her hand against her nose. Louise almost admired her for what she said next. For the first time she believed that her meek and passive and altogether too soft daughter truly had a spine. Had something ferocious in her.

"I won't." Charlotte half smiled as she said it, a trembling half smile, a smile that revealed a touch of fear, a touch of disbelief that she was taking a stand against her mother.

"Charlotte, look, there are things you can't possibly understand."

"I'm looking at you, Louise, and I understand a hell of a lot."

If Charlotte had not said her name like that once more, she might not have gathered her own ammunition and shot back.

"It must be your time of the month, dear," said Louise, straightening up and coming forward on the edge of the couch. She reached toward the lacquer cigarette box on the coffee table, took out a cigarette, and lit it with the accompanying lighter. "I can smell it on you."

"Go away!" Charlotte shouted, jumping up and moving away herself, but stopping at the foot of the stairs to deliver one more blow before running up. "Next time stay away!"

Louise crushed the cigarette out, steeled herself, and entered Mother's room. The half-drawn curtains let in the twilight from the yard, the soft shadows of the leaves from their own magnolia tree. She remembered how its silvery bark had caught her eye when she and Mother first looked at the house, how wise the gnarled branches had seemed to her then. How like a veiny old man's its limbs, yet it produced those glossy leaves, those enormous flowers.

Louise approached the bed and reached her hand toward the still figure curled there, stopping just before her fingers reached Mother's shoulder. Mother stirred, rolled over in the bed, and looked up at her with an expression that seemed quite blank. For a moment it seemed that Mother did not recognize her. Louise looked at that pale, blank face and her guts turned cold. When, she wondered, had her family become these masked people keeping her from knowing them?

"Oh, Louise. It's you." Mother pressed herself up, letting the blue quilted coverlet slide away to reveal the slip she was sleeping in. At sixty-eight, she was still a well-built woman, and she struck Louise as oddly glamorous in that moment, with her bobbed wild white hair in disarray, like some flapper who had been out all night.

Louise propped the pillows against the headboard and Mother pressed herself up and released into them. Louise took hold of Mother's hand and squeezed, and Mother squeezed back with an almost painful ferocity.

"I thought you might not be back," Mother said, her wandering eye rolling away from Louise's gaze.

"Didn't you see my note?"

"I did. You didn't say when to expect you back."

"I suppose I didn't," said Louise, sitting down on the chair by the bed without loosening her grip on Mother's hand. "What happened to you?"

"Well, I suppose I was distracted. Just forgot to open the garage door."

"That seems very unlike you."

"It does, doesn't it?"

"Charlotte thinks you did it on purpose."

Louise expected Mother to deny it, or to change the subject, but she did neither. She looked right in Louise's eyes when she spoke next.

"Well, I told you I would do it." Mother's strong right eye seemed to pin itself to her wandering left one, to will the two eyes into line. "I asked you to stop seeing him." Mother's breath was sour as old milk solids.

"Who?" Louise knew that the game was too far gone for her to attempt to take such a position, but she took it anyway.

"Who do you think I mean, your father?" Mother's eyes aligned then, narrowed for the transmission of spite.

Louise felt as if all of the fluid in her body had suddenly been drained away. When she spoke, her voice was as light as the rustle of dry leaves. "What?"

"You think I didn't know that he preferred you, in every way?"

Louise released her grip on Mother's hand and stood up. She straightened her dress as if pressing away some wrinkles could bring some order to her feelings. A dark wave was rising within her, and she felt that she would be consumed by it if she did not leave the room immediately. Yet she stayed, because the thought came again. Why couldn't she say it? Mother, I need you.

"I warned you. I told you to try me. And you tried me. You with your married men!" Mother's voice got louder then. Louise stepped back to her place by the bed. "You who forgets your family, forgets that her husband was being honored at the Pentagon."

"Please—" she started, but what could she say? She didn't know what words should come next as she stood before the one living person who had the power to judge and condemn her. But for what, she thought. What have I done that is truly wrong? Nothing, nothing! Nothing others haven't done, nothing that really matters, nothing that makes up for what I've lost. But I can't make a case for myself, not with this judge. I can only beg for mercy, mercy. She sat down again and took her mother's hand in hers.

"Mother, I don't know what to say. I want you to forgive me."

Mother was quiet for what seemed a long time, just long enough for the dark to fall outside the half-closed curtain. She turned on the light on the nightstand. Her expression was softer now.

"I think we're both tired, my dear."

"Very," said Louise.

"Yes, very. Will you promise me one thing?"

"Anything."

"That you'll never marry again?"

"Yes, but only if you promise that you won't leave us."

"I won't, dear," said Mother, lifting the hand that had Louise's two hands clasped around it, kissing Louise's knuckle. Louise leaned forward and kissed Mother on the forehead, just as if she was the mother and Martha was the child.

That night when the house was quiet, Louise made her way to the pigeonholed rolltop desk. She unlocked a certain drawer and extracted two tied bundles and one loose stack of paper. The pages were almost all victory mail, pale blue and lightweight, with tabs that could be folded over to make page and envelope one seamless whole. She took the kitchen matches from the sill above the sink.

Outside in the yard she could not find the harpoon moon. It was hidden somewhere behind the trees whose leaves made susurrus in the breeze. The night was clear; the dark ground of the sky still struck her as alive, like the skin of a leviathan. The stars were bright like barnacles on the back of the great creature. She stepped away from the house and found the stump of the old oak they had had to cut down after a storm. She put the coffee can on the stump and untied the first bundle, which was Roland's letters. Next to that bundle she placed the stack of loose pages, which were all unfolded and mostly unused victory mail. Most of the pages had a date and two words written on them, some a few more. Next to that stack she placed and untied the second bundle, which was smaller than the first, but just, she thought, as worthy of burning. These were letters from the colonel.

She had kept them in chronological order, even the ones she had begun to write. The ones that said *Dear Roland*, that floated the greeting on a pale blue sea. She crumpled one of Roland's letters, set it in the can and lit it like kindling, then added her own nearly blank page, her waste of precious victory mail, to the flame. These were the blanks she had hoarded like evidence, whether for the defense or the prosecution she could not say. It had been one of her peculiar wartime habits, to date the blanks, to greet him, but to stop there. To be unable to continue. To waste at a time when wasting was a sin.

She made a rhythm of it: one or two of Roland's letters, then one of her blanks went into the flame. Three of his and the one of hers with the most words: *Dearest Roland, A woman died today at Lockheed. Before the wing dropped, I swear I heard the harness slip, a quiet deadly sound before sound, before the crash that crushed her.* She kept feeding the fire until the blanks were gone and just one of his letters was left. The typed one that had been forwarded to her by the army, the one that included his hackneyed poem. She kept that one and she kept one of the colonel's too. But all of hers, all the pale blue fields where her love should have been performed, all of those she lit and watched drift up as ember and fall away as ash.

Purple Heart

September 1964

Charlotte had been working for hours when Katie buzzed. First drawing the shape that the wires would take, again and again, breaking it down from this angle and that. Then taking out the rolls of wire of three different thicknesses that she had bought and beginning to clip and straighten and assemble, only to realize that she needed yet another kind of wire altogether. And a new pair of needle-nose pliers. And that this piece was but a model for the real thing, which would be made with a material she had not yet found. She played *Out to Lunch* again and again, turning it up and up at first because it was her source, and then in order to hide from her ears the sounds of Gil and Daisy fucking next door. There was something cruel in their choice to leave the window onto the airshaft open and let the sounds go ricocheting around the sooty bricks. If she was sad, she couldn't feel it above the anger that was the dominant tone of her heart. A ferocious feeling, manifesting as actual pain in her chest, her anger was also a fuel. She felt it as a bright light, like the light that entered the room when she was paralyzed in her nightmares. Evidence of a crack in the tomb. Yes, the tomb, she thought, fitting one looped end of wire inside another, then closing the loop.

Katie screamed when she came in and saw the burgeoning mass that nearly covered the coffee table.

"Jesus, Lottie, what is that?"

"It's art, Katie. Nice to see you too."

"Wow—it's…big."

"And getting bigger. Coffee?"

"It's…interesting. Do we have time?"

"Just a quick cup and then we'll go," said Charlotte, stepping into the kitchenette to put on the pot. "Thanks for coming. At the moment I don't know if I could stand a Galle luncheon without you."

"Still on the Dolphy tip, eh?" Katie picked up the record cover, flipped it over, and read the notes. "It is really good."

"Best record of 1964. Bar none," said Charlotte, with a tone of finality intended to avoid an argument with her friend, who had a much higher tolerance than she did for music that was not jazz.

"Anyway," said Katie, perching on the step stool by the kitchen table and lighting smokes for them both. "I don't mind. I actually like Louise."

"*Et tu*, Katie?" Charlotte took the cigarette and blew smoke just above Katie's face.

"C'mon, you know I'm on your side. But Louise has always been all right to me, and she's so sharp and funny sometimes."

"You're not her daughter, so she doesn't feel the need to kick you when you're down. Or up, for that matter."

"At least she's interesting. My mother's edges have all been filed off so she can fit in a suburban cabinet."

"Hey, that's good!" Charlotte put cream and her favorite mugs on the table, the one with the tiki face and the other with a picture of a barefoot and pregnant woman, the words "Maw, git yer coffee" printed on it. She filled them both and gave the tiki mug to Katie.

"Did I tell you about Alex's happening? I'm gonna play clarinet. He's showing one of his films. I think he's got a dancer or two lined up. Tuesday night."

"I have to work, but I'll stop by after."

"It'll go late," said Katie.

Just then the record finished and as if on cue, a guttural moan could be heard emanating from Gil and Daisy's apartment.

"Jiminy crickets!" exclaimed Katie in mock horror. "I guess that's what you were talking about."

"They've been at it for days," said Charlotte, carefully lifting the needle and turning off the hi-fi. "It's beginning to feel like an attack."

"Were you that loud when she—" Katie shifted uncomfortably. "When you?"

"When we fucked? Yes, Katie, it's called that when women do it too."

"Sorry, I guess I can't get used to—I mean what do you do, without a penis?"

"Oh, I have one, didn't I tell you?" Charlotte teased. "But c'mon, Katie, do you really think that a cock is some magic wand that unlocks your pleasure?"

"Well, I mean—" Katie seemed to be preparing to ask for details, but Charlotte didn't feel like providing them.

"Look, however I feel about Gil—" Charlotte sat across the cracked linoleum tabletop from her friend. "And, yeah, I don't feel good about her right now—it was still better than anything I ever had with a man."

"What was better?"

"The fucking, for one thing. She knows just what to do and when. It goes on and on. She lives to serve. But the other thing that she taught me is that we don't need them."

"Not unless you want a baby—"

"That's not an option for me anyway."

"Sorry—"

"I'm not. Hell, who wants to make babies when they could make art? Who wants to make babies when there's a war on?"

"Alexander and I do. And he wants me to keep working after we're married."

Charlotte ignored her friend's comment and went on.

"What's funny is that I have a new kind of fondness for men now that I'm not hoping they'll be my life's purpose. Ya know, they're just people."

"Yeah, people who rule the world," said Katie, crushing her cigarette out and looking at her watch. "We better go if we wanna catch the 11:15."

Charlotte put out her own cigarette and grabbed her purse from the hook on the wall.

"They've done a great job of it, haven't they?"

Katie snorted. "Point taken. Well, someone new waits for you."

"Yeah, maybe I'll find somebody. Gotta get the sculpture done first."

"Oh, is that what you call it?" Katie teased again. "I'm joking. I think it's kinda beautiful, actually. It's big, at any rate. Are you almost done?"

"Not at all. It's going to be twice as big."

"Wow. And four times as intricate?"

"Yeah."

"Speaking of on the prowl, Pussycat look out, or are you going to take Alex up on his offer for you to meet his cousin Phil?"

"No. I'm headed to Dagmar's, my friend."

"What's Dagmar's?"

"A place where women go to meet women. You know, that kind of place."

They got to Mitchell's a little bit late. Louise and Ed were already one martini in. Charlotte could tell by the way Ed waved them over, the exaggerated gesture of his protodrunkenness. Louise too had the early glow about her, the warmth she radiated in Ed's presence not yet obscured by the meanness that sometimes overtook her when she'd had a few. "Katie's here!" said Louise.

"Yes, I told you—"

"Must've slipped my mind," said Louise. "Katie, you look great, like you've been out in the sunshine."

"My boyfriend has a boat," said Katie, sitting down next to Ed in the red vinyl booth. Charlotte squeezed in next to her.

"Have the crab Louie," said Ed to them both. "It's really good."

"I don't like crab," said Charlotte.

"That's right, you prefer oysters," said Ed, winking at Charlotte as if they were in cahoots.

"How long are you in town, Louise?" asked Katie.

"Just a couple of days," she answered, smoothing her hair. She tapped her pointer finger on the rim of her glass and made a swoop with her open palm, a gesture the waiter seemed to know and read as martinis for them all. "Seeing Ed off to Paris."

"Yes, we're all thrilled he's off to live in a garret at last," said Charlotte with an unmistakable tone of sarcasm in her voice.

"I'll have to find another excuse to come to New York," said Louise. She paused for a moment before she added, "Of course, Charlotte'll be here."

"I will, especially since I got a job," said Charlotte, leaning back to let the waiter place a martini in front of her. She drank half the drink in one gulp as if to celebrate the news.

"I was so pleased to hear that Dunne and Crowne took you back," said Louise.

"Whoever told you that?" said Charlotte with an acid tone. Katie elbowed her as if to say, Slow down, take it easy.

"Charlotte's working at The Strand now," said Katie. "I'm thinking of joining her there. Publishing is feeling terribly stuffy these days."

Charlotte swallowed the rest of her drink and gestured toward the waiter, who didn't seem to notice her. She was beginning to have that feeling she always had at a Mitchell's luncheon, the sense of sliding into a grave.

"Yes, Mother, I just assumed they'd taken her back. Who wouldn't want our Lottie?" Ed was grinning at her wildly, as if he'd only just discovered how wonderful his sister was. Trying to cover their recent breach with a thick layer of fudge.

"Oh well, I'm sure Charlotte will make the best of it," said Louise, opening the heavy red leather menu. "Has everyone made their choices?"

The luncheon went on, the waiter came, more martinis were drunk. Katie had them all laughing, as Charlotte had known she would, telling a story of her boyfriend's psychiatrist parents who were too brainy to steer a boat, and had run them aground in Long Island Sound. Charlotte laughed too, but it was as if she were laughing from a distance. The martinis were hitting her, but that wasn't all. She felt the imprint of Dolphy's music on her brain, the blasts of the horns and the quick clips of the drums. She began to see them there, in a busy restaurant in New York City in 1964, and they weren't the people, they were just some people. Katie's arch tone was the tone of someone who believed, as much as Ed believed, that the world was as it should be. Even as she laughed and threw in a word or two, Charlotte felt that whatever this world was that agreed with them, it wasn't the only world. They, drinking their drinks and eating their treats, weren't the only beings, or the important ones. She saw the waiter walking toward them. For the first time she noticed the mole on his chin. She thought, as if for the first time, of the waiter taking off his apron and leaving this place, of the waiter living in the world as a human being. Of his railroad flat, his sick mother, of his standing in line in the grocery store. She looked around the restaurant at the people in silence or in the middle of a laugh, the serious and the melancholy and the joyful people at their tables and booths. As if for the first time, she understood that they all carried their histories with them, and that they were formed by the world and forming it, that they were not separate from it, and neither was she. They were part of this humming thing, this great thriving organism of city life. Ed would go, and she would not miss him. I understand, she thought, I know exactly what I'm supposed to do.

"What's that, dear?" Louise was asking her.

"What?"

"What is it that you're supposed to do?"

They were all looking at her now. Had she interrupted them?

"Just thinking out loud, I suppose."

"But you sounded so definite, Lottie," said Ed.

"Yes, dear, a penny—no, a nickel, for your thoughts," said Louise.

"I'm supposed to make art," said Charlotte, wincing at her self-betrayal. She had sworn she was not going to tell Louise about the sculpture, and now here it was coming out of her mouth.

"Well, dear, I remember you made some nice watercolors once," said Louise, perhaps being kinder than usual because Katie was there.

"You should see what she has going at her place," said Katie. "I think it's really something."

"Oh, do tell," said Ed, with a wink in his voice. "I'm guessing it's avant-garde."

"It's just something I'm building," said Charlotte. "Let's talk about something else."

"Of course, darling," said Louise. "You brought it up, you know."

"Lottie always likes the latest things," said Ed. "Especially if they involve jazz musicians."

"She's making this incredible shape, like the shell of an enormous deep-sea creature," Katie was saying. Under the table, Charlotte pressed her foot against Katie's.

"Did you know Mother is an artist too?" said Ed. "She joined the Shepherd's Glen Players and right away took the lead in *Hedda Gabler*."

"That's rich," said Charlotte, before she could stop herself.

"It's just a lark," said Louise, shifting uncomfortably in her chair. Had she blushed? Charlotte was certain that she had. How strange that Louise's discomfort did not make her feel triumphant. She quickly changed the subject.

"Ed, are you all packed and ready?" Charlotte squeezed the stem of her martini glass. It was hard between her soft fingers.

"Yes, let's talk about me instead," said Ed, in his half-joking way. "I am packed and ready. Nothing stands between me and the third *arrondissement*."

"The apartment will do until we find you a studio to paint in," said Louise. "I'm sure we can find something suitable."

"At least the apartment is free," said Ed. "But I may have to get a job to pay for the studio."

"Nonsense, you're going there to paint!" said Louise, carefully loading a fork with crab Louie. "We'll help you, won't we, Charlotte?"

She could feel Katie's eyes on her. This was exactly why she had wanted her friend with her. Katie elbowed her lightly in the ribs as if to say, Go on, they're just words. Just one word.

"No." Charlotte said it and having said it, raised her empty glass in the direction of the waiter, who this time nodded.

Louise paused with the fork a breath away from her lips, then opened her mouth and placed the food inside. There was another pause as she chewed. In that brief silence sounds from the other tables seemed to get louder—the metallic scrapes of forks on plates, the cheap laughter of women on dates, the assured sounds of men ordering their lunches for them. At the table nearest them, a woman leaned across and said playfully to the man she was with, "Stop. Oh, do stop!"

"We'll talk about this later," said Louise. The waiter who arrived with Charlotte's drink was sent back for three more. "I'm sure that Katie doesn't want to hear a squabble."

"There's nothing to squabble about. I barely make enough money for myself."

"Surely an editor of your skill—" started Louise. She cast a look around the room as if she could find, among the inhabitants at Mitchell's in midtown on a Saturday afternoon, someone to back her up.

"I told you, I work at The Strand now. I sell books, Louise."

The waiter arrived with the three other martinis. Louise picked hers up by the stem and announced a toast.

"To brilliant careers! To Ed's next masterpiece and Charlotte's next... sale!"

Katie and Charlotte exchanged a look. Katie knew, she thought. Katie understood how Louise was. She felt a rush of gratitude for her friend.

"Lottie's more than a bookseller," said Ed. He was grinning at her now, his face flushed over the white broadcloth of his shirt. She looked into his eyes, silently begging him not to mention the letters. Not to mention Gil. Not to suggest that she read *The Well of Loneliness*. It seemed to her that he read her fear and offered up a subtle wink. "She's a keeper of family secrets."

Just then there was the sound of breaking glass and voices in outrage and apology. The woman at the next table leapt up, cursed the waiter who had spilled the drinks and smashed the glasses, and ran to the bathroom. Charlotte watched the woman's round, smooth bottom twitch this way and that beneath the tight fabric of her red dress. It struck her forcefully, as if the red dress were a flashing siren, that she was in a state of emergency. Artistic emergency. She did not have to stay in this restaurant, playing the game she had played so many times with Ed and Louise. That game of who-knows-better, that winking game Louise always played with the invisible audience she seemed to believe followed her everywhere. Charlotte could see it now, the power that her mother and brother had. It was clear to her then that the source of the power was everyone's belief in it. But she, Charlotte, did not believe in it. Her father and Eric Dolphy had told her what to believe in.

"The love of music is the only love," she said, standing up and taking Katie by the arm. "C'mon, Katie, let's go."

"What, dear?" asked Louise, turning back around from watching the drama at the next table.

"We have to go. There's a poetry reading at The Strand. I said I'd help out."

She took Katie's arm rather sharply, threw her purse over her elbow, and began making her way quickly to the door. Louise called after her.

"Don't you want to say goodbye to Ed?"

"Not good-bye! Call it *au revoir*," called Ed. "*Nous nous venons au Paris!*"

Charlotte stopped and turned to look at her brother. It seemed to her that he had appeared many times throughout the history of the world. An emperor in a robe of his mother's making, taking the gifts of all women as his due.

"Goodbye, Ed," she said.

Katie waited until they were outside of Mitchell's to voice her confusion.

"Wow, I don't think I ever realized that poetry could be an excuse," she said, tripping lightly over a raised edge of sidewalk. "Gosh, I'm drunk. The Galles can drink us mortals under the table."

"It isn't an excuse," said Charlotte, suddenly noticing a splash of martini on her blouse. "There is a reading and I agreed to help set up. You don't have to come."

"I should be off to meet Alexander and his mother. She's a shrink, you know."

"So you've said. Very impressive."

"You know what's impressive?" Katie stopped suddenly and put her hand on Charlotte's shoulder. "You are! You held your ground."

"Thank you. I was hoping you'd notice."

"I did. I'm proud of you!"

The words startled Charlotte; they went to the core of her, the raw core that had always wished to hear exactly those words. She hadn't realized those were the words she had always longed for from Louise and even from Granny. Those were the very words that they never said. They did say I love you sometimes, as perfunctorily as a Christmas card. I'm proud of you, she had wanted when she brought home her good grades, when she won the prize for the best essay. When, as a girl, she worked hard with Granny, cooking and cleaning and trying to help. But her offerings were accepted, as girls' offerings most often are, as the world's due, nothing to be celebrated. Loose from the martinis, flush with unexpected joy at her friend's remark, Charlotte said goodbye to Katie and stumbled along the sidewalk, deciding to walk at least part of the way to The Strand.

She walked down the sidewalks, first of midtown, which was nearly empty on a Saturday, feeling the absence of the weekday throng, which she had once been a part of. She and all the others pouring out of the subway stations in nearly predictable flows and ebbs. In the creek that ran through the enemy farm boys' land in Shepherd's Glen there was a chorus of frogs in the summer. It began and stopped by some invisible signal, gathering ribbiters in a frenzy and then dissipating and stopping. Then another began, a first singer, the one the others could not deny. Here in midtown Manhattan, a flock of pigeons flew overhead, following the impulse that arose to left or right. She passed the drugstore with the soda fountain where two sailboat schmucks with their tennis tans once tried to pick her up. She might have gone somewhere with them once. In her first days in the city, she had done an experiment to see what would happen if she said yes to every man who showed her that he had seen her big breasts and knew exactly what to do with them. That, she thought with the assuredness of the drunk, is our greatest confusion, not knowing the difference between what we want from the world and what happens to be in it. Men saw the world they made and believed it was made for them by something divine, wasn't that it? Those smug men wearing their penises in their remarks, in their disdain. The assured movement of Dr. Bedford's hand along her thigh as he took "a little peek inside," as if he had to use such childish language. His tut-tut cluck in the throat as he shook his head over the waste of her "equipment," which was clearly good only for the one thing, but not for its result.

She turned down Broadway, walking briskly through Times Square.

In her mind *Out to Lunch* came back, the sudden blasts of the horn that changed the music's direction, like that decision of one pigeon to do something different that would bring all the others along. The blasts were like the sudden opening of the metal doors in the sidewalk, the sudden presence of a stocky man in an undershirt rising up out of the sidewalk on a loading elevator like some hairy-knuckled Venus on the city's metal clamshell. Then there was the cart vendor selling chestnuts and the man who bought a bag, then smashed the bag against the sidewalk, screaming, "They're all burnt! All of them!" and the bespectacled woman walking with him, patting him absently on the arm. Charlotte was caught in it again, the rhythm of the city, walking through it with Dolphy's music as the soundtrack to the blinking neon martini, to the argument of two pimps, to the pawnshop desperation and the Italian waiter calling out, "Hey, psst," gesturing to the door of his little restaurant. "Hey, lunch!"

In spite of her drunkenness she walked briskly, nearly entering, but always avoiding the dive underground that would bring her more quickly to The Strand, so that by the time she got there the reading had already begun.

Charles was standing at the back of a row of chairs that seemed to be full of older people. The crowd was lightly clapping as Nancy stepped away from the podium, taking her schoolmarmish glasses off and pinching the bridge of her nose.

"Nancy thought the guy was from New Directions." Charles was clearly trying not to laugh. Charlotte was about to join him in the struggle. "She thought he was going to introduce a cool new anthology of experimental poetry—but she misunderstood him. Apparently, the guy's from Georgetown and his press is called, get this, Onionskins! He put out a collection of World War II poets. I probably won't stay. Can you put the chairs away?"

Charlotte nodded and tried not to look at Charles or repeat the word Onionskins because the urge to laugh was very strong indeed.

A man stepped to the microphone with great assurance—the assurance, Charlotte thought, of someone whose mother folded his socks. He wore a broadcloth shirt with the sleeves rolled up, and his tie was loose, as if he had just come to the podium after an all-night editing session. He had dark blond hair and the easy manner of a person who had never been hungry for anything. Standing at the microphone, he picked up a slim volume with green lettering on a cream field: *Great Poems of the Good War*. The man adjusted the thick-rimmed glasses he was wearing, leaned his elbows on the podium as if he had already been talking for a long time, and began to speak.

"Thank you, Nancy, and thanks to everyone at The Strand for inviting me here to share with you a few of the poems from our new anthology." He cleared his throat and rocked back slightly on his heels. Charlotte could just barely hear Charles snort.

"In literary circles, when one speaks of war poets, at least in the tradition in English, one thinks of the Englishmen of World War One, Siegfried Sassoon and Wilfred Owen. One barely hears about Americans at all, either from that war or from the more recent world conflict, the effects of which we continue to feel. What prevents the poets of the Second World War from stepping into the literary consciousness? Perhaps, though nearly twenty years have passed, the wounds from that conflict are still too fresh. Or perhaps the lack of truly great poetry describing the experiences of soldiers struggling across Europe and the Pacific can be ascribed to the presence in our lives of nuclear possibilities. Did Fat Man and Little Boy change us so thoroughly? Perhaps the atomic shockwaves blasted through our literary production and we now wish to start afresh. In our current moment, art of all kinds is becoming unmoored from traditional approaches. In these days of cultural upheaval, we may be reconsidering both the nature of the barbarians and of the gates that keep them out. Perhaps we feel that war poems, or even poetry itself, isn't up to the task of looking straight at what took place during the Second World War. Because in these times of grave uncertainty in Southeast Asia, as the machine of war rolls on, perhaps we don't wish to look too closely at the war that we have decided was, above all else, good. Poets, real poets, don't look away from what is ugly. Do we, as a society, want to look directly at the costs of war, or even the experience of the individual soldier battling malaria and an empty stomach as much as the Japanese? In researching potential selections for this book, I found it particularly difficult to find worthwhile work written by the veterans of the Pacific. I'll begin with one such veteran, a name that I doubt anyone in this room is familiar with. Kirstein Blunt is a modest and reclusive man, a talented poet whose only book, *Bafflewall*, was the first book of poetry published by our small but mighty press, Onionskins. Very little seems to be known about him, and my attempts to interview him have been unsuccessful. What is known is that he survived the Bataan Death March and the sinking of the Japanese warship the *Oryoko Maru* in Subic Bay off the Philippines in 1944, and was ultimately taken to Korea, where he was liberated by American troops the following year. Somewhere along the way, he lost his left leg."

Across Charlotte's face the pores opened. Tiny floods drenched her face. She knew the name, of course. She reached into her purse where she carried them always, the two letters remaining of the three that she had found in Louise's room, taped under a drawer. One, now ash, was from Colonel Daddy and one was from her father. The third, with a return address K. Blunt, contained nothing more than a poem called "Bafflewall" and a note on a scrap of paper that read: L—*will this do? K.* She had read all the letters that night in Shepherd's Glen, while Granny was in the hospital and Louise was asleep. By the white fringed shade of the wedding cake lamp in her girlhood room, she had read her father's letter first, and then she read it twice more, looking for, but never finding in it, herself or the mother she knew. Finding instead a poem that seemed to choke on itself, to be hampered by an idea of what poetry should be. A poem that touched her deeply but only because of who had written it and when. And then in the third envelope she had found the other poem, the one by that man.

But where was her mind? Charlotte wondered. She had been hungry to hear more about this Kirstein Blunt, but had fallen into a reverie, standing there behind the folding chairs. The editor continued.

"In 1950, Blunt's manuscript had been submitted anonymously, and when my colleague called Mr. Blunt, the poet expressed some shock that the manuscript had even been sent to our offices, much less had been chosen for publication. Apparently, he also made an odd claim— that he was not the true author of the poems. He went on to explain that his hands had written the poems at the direction of someone else, a friend and fellow soldier who had died in the sinking of the *Oryoko Maru*. He also refused, quite adamantly, to give any readings or in any way participate in promoting *Bafflewall*. Perhaps as a result, the book was quickly remaindered. It is an uneven collection, but the better poems suggest that Blunt, with some effort, could have developed into a talent to be reckoned with. I have tried, without success, to contact him about this anthology. Among the many questions I would like answered is the identity of the woman to whom he dedicated the book. For my Pearl, the dedication reads, but that is not the name of his wife or of any woman I can discover in connection with him."

People shifted in their folding chairs, and as happens in a creek during frog season, when one made a sound others felt at liberty to join, one croak and then a chorus of croaks, one cough and then a chorus of coughs. The editor cleared his throat and began to read. As he read Charlotte recalled, with the full force of discovery, how she had come across the poet before. How she had seen him at the pool in Shepherd's Glen, how he had driven them home in the rain, how he had slapped Louise, how he had nearly taken her from them, had nearly taken Granny too. How Louise had made promises to Granny after Granny tried to die. She had been home more often after that, but every so often she would go away for what she and Granny called her private time. She thought she understood it now. Louise had continued seeing the one-legged man. No one spoke of him, or asked where she went those days, or why she was gentler than usual when she returned. It struck Charlotte forcefully that her own secret lover had also more than once nearly died. She thought of Gil's scarred body, her missing breast, the way Gil fucked as if her life depended on it, brought every inch of her body to the task of giving pleasure. Charlotte knew then that she would love other women, but that her every kiss would be an act of longing for the first one. The editor read the poem and Charlotte's face was bathed in saltwater.

Bafflewall

We do our best from day to day
to confuse the enemy. We hold him
to his loneliness, starve his skin to slack
him loose, coddle his bones with

Press of sky. The captured one is he
the freer one is I. This is the lie
of our good work, we soldiers who
defied our enemies with fire,

Or crushed them with the sea's
weight against what lived there.
We burned the water black to turn
their bones to oil. To fuel what

Dreams do not spoil, and is worth
the pouring blood and gnashing teeth.
The light that flashed upon the Earth,
our war as good in death as in our birth.

ACKNOWLEDGMENTS

This book changed shape several times over the years it took me to write it. The writers' group I that I relied on for many of those years—David Booth, John Vlahides, Karl (K.M.) Soehnlein, and Catherine Brady—responded artfully to a not so artful early draft. I am grateful for the many wonderful literary conversations (not to mention food and drinks) we shared. I must give an extra shout out to Catherine for her feedback on a late draft. Karl also needs another line, or several—he supported the creation of this book in so many ways. I know I am not the only one who has benefitted from his deep knowledge about the art and business of writing, and from his wisdom about life in general.

Nina Schuyler was an invaluable advisor guiding me through the first truly workable draft, offering practical and philosophical insights that helped me grow as a writer and make this book what it could be. Daniel Cuddy, Merlin Coleman, Elka Deitsch, Bridget Evans, Stefanie Kalem, and Kaya Oakes read early drafts and made me feel like something was there. Later, just when I needed to believe in this project again, Andrew Joron buoyed my spirits, suggested a key edit, and got me back in the saddle.

For their writerly comradery and advice, I thank Marina Lazzara, Monica Regan, Glori Simmons, Malena Watrous, and John Wray. For her musical accompaniment and dedication to expansive modes of creative expression, I thank Sheila Bosco.

I am grateful that my aunt and fellow writer, Sarah Swan, sent me an archive of letters that served as a primary source. In one letter, my grandfather, then a prisoner in Cabanatuan Prison in the Philippines, asked my grandmother why she did not write to him. Decades later, a plot point was born.

I thank my family of voracious readers and opinionated critics, all of whom encouraged me in the writing of this book. My father, David Costello, can always be relied upon to clarify aspects of the Second World War and suggest further reading. When my sister Sarah organized the Costello Family Russian Literature Reading Group during the pandemic, our brother Brooke and our father responded with enthusiasm. We four remain surprised that in our zeal we managed to clear the Zoom room of my brother- and sister-in-law, Chris Dumm and Justine Kalb. They are also deep readers, but apparently, they did not need to hear our opinions about *War and Peace*. To my nephews Nic, Redd, and Greer, thank you, you are rascals and you give me hope.

To my sweetheart Morgan Senkal, thank you for taking me sailing. Jibe ho!